Firebird

Harbingers Book III: Child of Fire

Jane M. Wiseman

Shrike Publications

Albuquerque, New Mexico

Shrike Publications
Albuquerque, New Mexico

Publisher's Note: This is a work of fiction. Names, characters, places, and incidents are a product of the author's imagination. Locales and public names are sometimes used for atmospheric purposes. Any resemblance to actual people, living or dead, or to businesses, companies, events, institutions, or locales is completely coincidental.

Book Layout © 2017 BookDesignTemplates.com

Firebird/ Jane M Wiseman . -- 1st ed.
ISBN 978-1-7328141-5-8

For Will and Wallace

What is a riddle for? A riddle is a test, it's a space for insight, it's a place of power. A riddle is a maze made of words. When the gods give you a riddle, you must walk the labyrinth until you wind into its heart.

The Stormclouds/Harbingers Fantasy Novels

Stormclouds: The Prequel Series

Book I, *A Gyrfalcon for a King*

Book II, *The Call of the Shrike*

Book III, *Stormbird*

The Harbingers Series

Book I, *Blackbird Rising*

Book II, *Halcyon*

Book III, *Firebird*

Book IV, *Ghost Bird*

Betwixt and Between: The Companion Series

Book I, *The Martlet is a Wanderer*

Book II, *The Nightingale Holds Up the Sky*

And now:

Dark Ones Take It, being the origin story of Caedon and his brother Maeldoi, the Dark Rider

All available now on amazon.com in paperback and for Kindle and other e-book devices.

Thanks to the following for their royalty-free work used to create the composite cover art and the graphics elsewhere in this book:

Image by <a href="https://pixabay.com/users/Willgard-4665627/?utm_source=link-attribution&utm_medium=referral&utm_campaign=image&utm_content=4334610">Willgard Krause</a> from <a href="https://pixabay.com/?utm_source=link-attribution&utm_medium=referral&utm_campaign=image&utm_content=4334610">Pixabay</a>

Image by <a href="https://pixabay.com/users/darkmoonart_de-1664300/?utm_source=link-attribution&utm_medium=referral&utm_campaign=image&utm_content=3688040">DarkmoonArt_de</a> from <a href="https://pixabay.com/?utm_source=link-attribution&utm_medium=referral&utm_campaign=image&utm_content=3688040">Pixabay</a>
Image by <a href="https://pixabay.com/users/Clker-Free-Vector-Images-3736/?utm_source=link-attribution&utm_medium=referral&utm_campaign=image&utm_content=311786">Clker-Free-Vector-Images</a> from <a href="https://pixabay.com/?utm_source=link-attribution&utm_medium=referral&utm_campaign=image&utm_content=311786">Pixabay</a>

MAP OF THE KNOWN WORLD

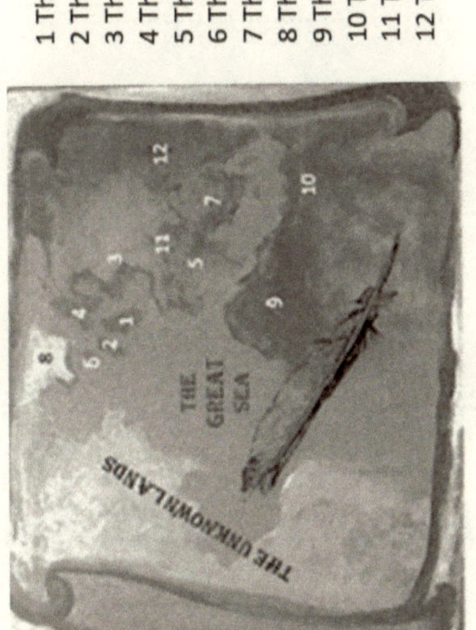

Contents

A Riddle

The ravenous wurm of the mountain
devours the great streets of men.
Battle storm of Hildr, life-harm of the hall,
the hound of the forest with its hot mouth
swallows every house; fell dog
of willow, ash, yew, oak
casts its baleful eye on the yard-gate.
Woe, that red-gaping hound of the wood.

Firebird the True, carry her on your back
to the isle of the thousand suns.

My troubles started with a riddle. Shall I tell you what happened when I, Keera, daughter of his most sacred majesty Walter the First of the Sceptered Isle and his beloved wife, Lady Mirin of the High Sea Cliffs, lost my powers?

I suppose I have no choice. The farwydd of the Fire Child compels me to tell you.

Why you? Who are you, and why are you the one I have to tell? I see I have more questions than answers, and I don't even know you, lady. I can barely make you out. Your outlines are kind of fuzzy, and your voice is wispy. Yes. That's it. If I had to describe you and your voice, I'd say you were kind of wispy.

If it were up to me, I wouldn't be sitting around telling some strange wispy person like you the story of my life, and I certainly don't see how you can offer me any good advice about my predicament, especially now I've lost my powers.

But the farwydd, Dark Ones seize her, has made me take you on as my companion. In fact, she's made this a condition for regaining my powers.

And I must regain them.

I must.

Having no choice in the matter, then, I will make you my Companion, and I will tell you everything you think you need to know. I'll exercise my duty to you faithfully, whether I understand the why of it or not, even though that wicked old crone compels me.

What? I didn't catch that. Speak up.

What? Am I really hearing what I think I'm hearing?

You shut up! You take liberties, my lady Companion. You do. Who are you to scold me? Yes, I really did say that. I'm going to say it again.

Ready?

Dark Ones take that farwydd of mine, she's a wicked old crone.

What a coward you are, Companion. What a fopdoodle, cringing away from me like this. I've a mind to say it over and over again, just to watch you cringe.

Oh. Don't cry.

No, really. I'm starting to understand you a little better.

I apologize.

We're both in her control, that wicked old thing. Our fate is in her hands. That's what I hear you telling me. If we don't behave, she'll punish both of us. It seems to me you're my punishment, Companion, and I'm yours.

Strange that it should be so. I'm a Child of Fire, and so the Fire Child's farwydd is my farwydd, and it makes sense that she'd try to control me. I'm not sure what I did to deserve her punishment, but if someone is going to punish me, it would be she.

You, Companion, or so you tell me, are a Child of Earth. The Earth Child's farwydd should be the one attending to you. So how is it you've come under the Fire Child's control?

No, I agree with you there, Companion. I don't understand it, either.

Well, here we are, then. It doesn't make any sense, but here we are, both of us under the thumb of the Fire Child and her nasty old farwydd. It's just as well we straightened that out, right here at the beginning of our journey.

Now, then. What do you want to know about me, Companion?

Very well. We'll start there.

As I told you, my name is Keera. And as I told you, my father is his most sacred majesty Walter the First, the exiled monarch of the Sceptered Isle, and my mother is the king's beloved wife, Lady Mirin of the High Sea Cliffs.

This is important, Companion, so pay attention. I am my parents' true daughter, and their real daughter, too. I live with them on a rocky island in the middle of the Northern Sea, where they can defend themselves from their enemy, Caedon the Usurper.

My hair is red as fire, and I bear the Fire Child's mark on my shoulder.

Would you like to see it? Here. Look. A little flame, and the firebird rising from it.

I'll tell you about my firebird later, maybe.

You already know about my red hair. After all, you can look at me and see it for yourself. So you may be wondering why I bring it up, and why it's so unusual. My father's hair is as fair as the ripe barley in the field, although now as a sign of his troubles it's streaked with gray. My mother's hair, he tells her, remembering, running his fingers through it, is spun bronze. His protector is the Earth Child; hers is the Sea Child.

Earth Child and Sea Child are not incompatible. But Fire Child? Out of those two? Not the usual thing. If you were to meet my Grandfather Fylkir, though, and my Uncle Stefan, you'd see where my red hair comes from. You'd understand more about the delicate matter of what is true and what is only real. You'd see how it eats at me.

True and real. Remember that, if you please.

As for my difficulties, I thought I told you. They all started with a riddle.

I had traveled so far to reach the lair of the Fire Child's farwydd, and then she would only see me for a moment. I went to her for help, and she didn't give me any, the creature. In fact, as we see, it looks like she's punishing me because I've asked for her help. My very own farwydd, too. When my mother was in trouble, she made an arduous journey to the farwydd of the Child of Sea. That's her Child, the Child of Sea. And her farwydd helped her. I wouldn't be standing here if not for that farwydd's help. I'd be in the clutches of that monster, Caedon.

Aaaaaaa!! What an unearthly shriek out of you, my lady. That hurts my ears! Please stop it. I know that Caedon has a bad reputation. But do you have to screech so loud the brains jump out of my ears? Please stop.

Whew. That's better.

Where was I before your rude interruption? Oh, yes. The insulting behavior of my farwydd. She ejected me from her cave, and sent out her servant—just a servant, can you believe it?— who handed me a scroll. It was inscribed with very pretty script. I did appreciate that part. I unrolled the parchment, sure I'd get the instructions for a wonderful solution to both of my problems. Instead, I read on the scroll this riddle:

The ravenous wurm of the mountain
devours the great streets of men.
Battle storm of Hildr, life-harm of the hall,
the hound of the forest with its hot mouth
swallows every house; fell dog
of willow, ash, yew, oak
casts its baleful eye on the yard-gate.
Woe, that red-gaping hound of the wood.

Firebird the True, carry her on your back
to the isle of the thousand suns.

And at the bottom, neatly lettered, that farwydd—my own farwydd!— had penned these insulting words: *Don't come back until you answer this riddle.*

A riddle.

Of course I didn't know what any of it was supposed to mean, except for maybe the firebird part. I'm not a mind-reader. They say I am, but they're wrong. Some say I'm a witch.

I'm no witch. Sometimes I get a feeling, and then it's as though I can read my mother's mind. So yes, that's true. But she gets the same feelings. You may get feelings like that, too, Companion. I think maybe everyone does, and calls it intuition, or maybe imagination. My mother's dear father (her true father, not Grandfather Fylkir, who was only her real father) told her she had a "second sense." Sometimes she can trust these feelings, but only sometimes. I have the same kinds of feelings. Mine are stronger and more definite. That's the only difference.

Fine, Companion.

I'll admit it to you. Lean over here so I can whisper it in your ear.

I'm always right. When I look into my mother's mind, or anyone's mind, I always see what's in there. You don't have to be rude about it. I'm not ashamed. Some people's thoughts march right into mine, as if they think they're entitled to be there.

I can read my mother's mind, my father's mind, other people's minds. Just not all the time.

Or I could.

And now I can't.

Instead of helping me with her own powers, as I prayed that she do, that farwydd of mine removed my powers altogether. How insulting! She has cast me out to find my way by myself.

The Children help those who help themselves. That's the only other communication I got from her. No, not in the same way as before, from a servant bearing a scroll with all of it nicely written down. I got this message when she spoke it into my mind.

And that's the last time it happened, someone speaking into my mind.

No more mind-reading.

I was on my own.

What's that you're asking? Regular reading? The kind you do in books? Of course I can read.

Oh, very well. I see I must have patience with you, my lady. You're right. Most girls can't read, so I shouldn't take offense at your amazement.

Most boys can't read, either. Only a few who are allowed to go to school can read. And beyond that, only a very few chosen to attend the Lady Goddess's schools to study for Her priesthood can read the language of the Old Ones.

Or children of rich people, like my father, whose families could afford to send them to school using their own coin. Most rich people don't bother, since reading is not a practical skill for a warrior. So it's still kind of a mystery how my father learned to read.

I'm guessing all of the sons of King Ranulf learned to read, because the crown prince Artur (the poor murdered crown prince, yes, he, the very one) was a noted scholar, and then all of his brothers learned too. Just a guess. I'll have to ask my father sometime if I'm right.

You see there? See what that wicked farwydd has done to me? Before, I could have just popped into my father's head to find out. Now I can't. I have to ask, like everyone else.

My mother knows how to read in spite of growing up in poverty. Her mother taught her. How my grandmother Elsebet learned to read, now that indeed is a puzzle. I wonder if her husband, my true grandfather Drustan, taught her. He was something of a scholar, my father tells me.

I may be royalty, but I didn't grow up knowing I was. Mind reader or not, that was one tidbit of information kept hidden from me for quite some time. When I was a small child, I lived a life of privilege, if you can call being around that horrible old man, my Grandfather Fylkir (only the real one, not the true one), a privilege. But that didn't last long. My mother got me away from Grandfather Fylkir, and then I grew up poor the way my mother did.

During my entire childhood, my mother and I were on the run. We thought my father was dead. I didn't know whether he was dead or alive. Even when I had my powers, I didn't know, although I did see him in a vision once. So as you see, I didn't know everything. As I say, sometimes the Fire Child would let me see things other people couldn't know, and sometimes She didn't.

Now I know nothing. That makes me angry, Companion.

So. Back to my story. You're sure you want to hear this? It's not pretty. My mother had to rescue me from the clutches of Grandfather Fylkir (her real father, but not the true one), because he was going to sell me as a concubine to the king. Not my father King Walter, you ninny. To the false king, Caedon.

Please don't get so upset, Companion.

Oh, there you go again, with the screeching. Please stop. So much screeching. I didn't mean to upset you so. Forgive me? I know stories like mine can be hard to hear.

You mustn't worry yourself on my behalf. I wasn't scared. That's one of the things the Fire Child did let me know, even though I was very young, only five years old. I knew beyond doubt that my mother would come for me. Then, exactly as I had foreseen, she came. So you see, even though I was in real danger from that nasty man, I knew he wouldn't be able to act on his evil wishes.

Feel better now? Good, Companion. Here's my handkerchief. Try blowing your nose.

You see? We can be friends. I'll always have a handkerchief for you, when you get upset. Just no more screeching, if you please.

Anyhow, the day my mother rescued me was the first time we went on the run, but not the last.

On the run. For a long time, that was our whole life. She and I had to live catch as catch can. Once, we lived in a barn. Once, over a tavern in a tiny attic room.

Let me backtrack, because you're probably pretty confused. We'll start with the basics. My father is the true king. But his kingdom was stolen by the man you probably think of as king. King Caedon, the man everyone thinks is king.

No. No. No. Stop, Companion. Easy, there. No screeching, remember? Good.

To resume. Caedon stealing the realm. I suppose that makes Caedon the real king, just not the true king. This Caedon fellow is the same man who wanted to buy me. At only five years old.

Here, Companion. Keep the handkerchief.

But pay attention. True king. Real king. Do you get it?

What awful faces you're making. I know it's shocking, King Caedon wanting to buy himself a five year old girl. That's just the kind of despicable person King Caedon is, and that's how despicable my grandfather is, because he was ready and willing to sell me. I don't think of him as my grandfather, even though he's my real grandfather.

My true grandfather is my mother Mirin's true father, Drustan, Earl of the High Sea Cliffs. My grandmother Elsebet fled with my mother when she was only a baby to get away from Grandfather Fylkir, who was Grandmother Elsebet's real husband. Grandfather Drustan became her true husband then. So even though I never knew my true grandfather Drustan, I know he would not have stood for anyone selling me.

Drustan adopted Mirin, my mother, and loved her as his own. She grew up thinking he was the only father she had and loving him back with every part of her being.

What a shock, to discover a horrid man like Fylkir was her father. Only her real father. Still, quite a shock. But it does explain my red hair.

True father. Real father. True husband. Real husband. True king. Real king.

Put your mind to it, Companion. Do you see the difference? The true ones run deep into the very roots of existence. The real ones are only what the world holds, and the world is often wrong.

I hope you see, because if you don't understand the difference, we're going to have a hard time of it, you and I.

You might say I have a complicated background.

Then, to make it more complicated, may the Dark Ones take her, my own farwydd , the farwydd of the Fire Child, took away my powers.

You're telling me that's blasphemy, Companion? I suppose I've committed it. But I do. I do want the Dark Ones to take her, nasty woman.

Now what do I do? Now what? Those were the thoughts that roiled around in my mind once I realized what she had done to me.

I was stuck here on the Fire Isle with no way back and no clear way to accomplish my tasks.

I have set myself two tasks.

I suppose you want to know what they are.

Here are my tasks.

The first one is hard. I want to cure my father of blindness. I know I can't replace his arm. Caedon had his men chop it off.

Nor do I think I can replace my father's missing eye. Caedon may have gouged my father's eye out himself. I'm not sure. My parents won't talk about it to me, and for some reason, I could never see deep enough into either one of them to find out.

But my father's other eye—I think that can be cured and made to see again.

He can sort of see out of it. He told me sometimes he sees flashing lights, sometimes even misty shapes.

In spite of his blindness, he gets around the fort just fine. He told me if that's all I wanted to do, make him see again, I shouldn't bother.

"I have everything I need," he told me. "You, and your mother, people who believe in me, and safety for my family. Those are riches beyond any expectations. I'd be greedy to ask the Children for more. I only had one true malady, grief. Your mother cured that when she came back to me, and I knew she was alive, and I knew you were not just a vision. People can have strange visions, you know, when they're in extreme pain. But here you are. You exist." Then he'd reached out and tousled my hair.

True maladies, real maladies.

Now wait, Companion. I have to tell you something before we go on. People like to tousle it, my hair. Please don't touch it.

Maybe when we get to know each other better. Maybe if you ask politely.

Oh. You're right, Companion. I haven't told you about the second goal.

The first one, restoring my father's eyesight, might be pretty hard to accomplish, especially hard now I've lost my powers.

The second one is simple.

I want to kill Caedon.

CHAPTER TWO

Companion

Today, when I woke up on the Fire Isle, I almost didn't remember where I was. I thought I was in my bed at home, in our fort carved into the rock on our own small outcropping in the middle of the Northern Sea. Then I looked around at the bleak landscape out the window of this little cottage, and I knew where I was.

I just didn't know what I was. A girl with powers—that's what I used to be.

What am I now?

It's depressing when you wake up and realize you can't read people's minds any longer, or get any messages from the beyond. The flat gray landscape, gloomy under a steady drizzle, mirrored my inner weather. But beyond the stark land stood mountains, and after a long time I came to understand how beautiful this island is in its own strange way.

I was depressed about something else, though. I started to brood about how much harder my first goal was going to be than I'd originally thought. Curing my father of blindness. I was relying on my powers to help me with that one. Now I'll have to rely on myself alone.

Killing Caedon, that's just an ordinary task.

No help for it. I'd better get started, I told myself.

You. You hush about it, Companion. I don't want your advice.

I pulled my kirtle over my head and fastened the apron the way women wear them in these parts. One panel of the apron falls down the front of me. The other panel falls down the back. The two parts are held together by straps over my shoulders, and these straps are fastened with two round brooches. Mine aren't very fancy, just carved wood. You should see the beautiful gold and gem-encrusted ones the high-born ladies wear around here.

Oh. I see you know that already, Companion.

No one around here knows I'm a high-born lady. Only the Lady Jehanne knows, and now you do. But Lady Jehanne and I agreed I'd keep mum about it for my own safety. We agreed I'd dress like a simple village maiden, and she brought me the proper clothes. I hope you'll keep my secret.

Huh. That's interesting, Companion. You know the Lady Jehanne too. I wonder where you could have met her.

Not talking about it? Well, you have your secrets and I have mine. We'll leave it at that.

Not too long ago, Lady Jehanne came to us on my parents' rocky outpost. She introduced herself as King Haakon Hardaxe's emissary. King Haakon is one of the most powerful men in the world, the monarch of the Ice-realm. I suppose we should have been flattered to receive his emissary, but my parents were mostly just suspicious. We are tiny. He is powerful. But Lady Jehanne seemed on the up and up, and she spent a lot of time with my mother.

Lady Jehanne wanted to know about my mother's sister, my Aunt Jillian. But my mother really couldn't tell her much. My mother hasn't seen her sister for years and years, except for this one bad time, and then only for a few moments. I don't want to go into it right now. Maybe someday I'll tell you about it.

You've certainly gone quiet, Companion.

At least let me explain how the Lady Jehanne brought me here, and how that's connected to her questions about my aunt. After she had quizzed my mother about my Aunt Jillian, and after she had finished her diplomatic mission from her king, she got ready to go back to him empty handed. My mother and father wouldn't make alliance with him against Caedon. It's not that they were on Caedon's side. Exactly the opposite. They hate Caedon. He has tried his best to kill my father, and he actually believes he owns my mother, the creature. And me. He thinks he owns me too.

But I was listening when my parents talked it over between themselves. They thought I was just strolling around the garden, but I was listening. What I didn't overhear, my powers filled in for me later.

"No revenge," said my father. He said it in his firm voice, the voice he uses when he really means something.

After what Caedon did to him, you'd think he'd want revenge.

"Right now," he told my mother, "we have to think strategically. We need to think with our brains, not just our gut. Of course I'd like to stick a knife in that man's heart. And someday, somehow, I hope to do it. He's hurt me, and he's hurt the ones I love. You. Your parents and sister." He began ticking them off on his fingers, all the ones he loved, hurt by Caedon. "John. Avery and Conal. Aedan. My mother. Diera. And he tried to hurt Keera. Praise the Children he failed with her, at least. Thanks to you, my darling."

Let me explain what he was talking about. John and Avery and Aedan were his brothers. My grandfather Drustan might just as well have been his brother. Caedon killed them all. Oh, you knew that, Companion? I knew you knew about Diera.

I kept listening, that day in the garden. My father went on. "But alliance with Haakon is not the way. He wants to use us. I'll not be used."

"I may stick a knife in Caedon's heart before you get to him," my mother said to him. "But I understand what you mean. I stand by you in this. As in everything," she added, and then they—well, you don't really need to know what they did after that, but it was very sweet, I thought.

Here's what came to my mind as they talked Lady Jehanne's mission over between themselves.

They weren't going to take revenge on Caedon, and they weren't going to become tools of King Haakon.

I sat in the garden long after they'd left, and I took it in. I sat there, just thinking. I'm good at that, Companion, sitting and thinking. My thoughts naturally led me to a conclusion. My parents have had enough of violence and killing and fighting. They'll not take revenge, I thought, and I understood that.

But, l thought, revenge must be taken.

So then, very naturally, I thought, *Why not me?* I don't care about Haakon Hardaxe one way or the other. I'll be the one to stick the knife in Caedon's heart.

Me.

I decided to talk it over with Lady Jehanne. She kind of laughed at me. I think she thought I was a silly young child.

She underestimated me. I can't stand that. As I say, Companion, I knew some things. Here's one thing I knew. I knew Lady Jehanne, on her way back to Haakon's court, was going to make a detour to the Fire Isle. Her next mission was to try to convince my Grandfather Fylkir to reconcile with my mother and father. *Good luck to her with that*, I thought to myself. That task was going to be even harder than her failed first mission. My parents loathe Grandfather Fylkir.

But Haakon wanted alliance with my parents, and he wanted alliance with Fylkir. He wanted both, you see. He thought both would be assets when he went after Caedon. They would make him stronger when he faced Caedon. So the Lady Jehanne, on King Haakon's orders, was going to my grandfather next.

I sat and thought some more until these reflections about Lady Jehanne's mission led me to an important insight into my two tasks and how I could accomplish them.

Restoring my father's eyesight was going to be hard. But if I had the support of my farwydd, I reasoned, I'd be able to accomplish the hard task, and I'd be able to speed up the easy one. So I needed to get to the Fire Isle myself. I knew that was the place I'd find the portal of the Child of Fire. That's where I had to go in order to talk things over with my farwydd.

I realized that when Lady Jehanne's knarr sailed in that direction, I had to be on it.

First I tried to convince my parents to let me go along with her. Of course I didn't tell them about my two tasks. If they thought I had even an inkling of doing either of those two things, they would have locked me up until the top of the sail of Lady Jehanne's knarr had disappeared over the horizon.

The first because it was too crazy. The second because it was too dangerous.

Companion, shut it. I didn't ask you.

And, well, they wouldn't have locked me up. That wasn't their way. But they would have made me promise not to take them on, my two tasks, and then I would have had to lie to them.

So you see my dilemma.

Instead of the real reasons, I used Lady Jehanne's mission to Grandfather Fylkir as an excuse to beg to go along with her.

"If I could talk to Grandfather Fylkir," I told my parents, "maybe he'd see how wrong he has been, and how much he has wronged you, Mother. And me," I added. "Lady Jehanne says King Haakon has an alliance with Fylkir, but the king wants an alliance with us, too, and he's worried it won't work, since we are at odds with Grandfather Fylkir."

"But we've already told the Lady Jehanne that we won't have any part in this alliance," said my father. I loved him then. He didn't treat me like a silly child. He explained things to me as if I were a person on a diplomatic mission too.

"And besides," said my mother with a sour look, "I'm not putting you in reach of that old man." She meant Grandfather Fylkir. "Never again," she said. Her tone did imply I was a silly little child.

"That too," my father said. He put a conciliatory hand on my shoulder.

So my ruse backfired, but I couldn't be angry with my parents. I loved them both too much. Besides, I was—

No, that's not it, Companion. You're wrong, and it's mean of you to say so.

I wasn't lying.

I was shading the truth.

A bit.

Besides. As I was about to say. What I really wanted to do is get sent to the Fire Isle to see my farwydd. I didn't want to put myself in reach of that old man, either.

So? You think so, Companion? You think it would have gone better if I had just told my parents I needed to see my farwydd? You think honesty is the best policy, huh? But then, you see, I would have had to tell them about my real mission—accomplishing my two tasks. They wouldn't have approved of those. So I couldn't. Telling them the other thing was worth a try.

Next, I tried persuading Lady Jehanne to sneak me on board. I told her the same story about Grandfather Fylkir, and I could see she was tempted. In the end, she denied me.

"Your parents would never forgive me, Keera," she told me. "It would just make things worse."

I suppose I could see her point.

So how did I do it, you ask? Get aboard her ship?

Easy. I stowed away in a barrel.

I know a lot about how to stow away in a barrel. I'd done it before, you see.

No, I'm not going to explain that right now. It's too complicated. I'll explain later, maybe.

Lady Jehanne was pretty upset when her mariners pulled me out of that barrel. She screamed. She sent me off to her bondservant to be bathed and fed and brushed. She wanted to send me back, of course. But by then, we were too far out to sea, too close to the Fire Isle, and we couldn't turn around.

When we landed, it was Lady Jehanne who set us up here in this house. Well, me—she didn't know about you, of course. But here we are with this nice goodwife who has been feeding us the eggs and porridge, and giving us her excellent goats' milk to drink. Don't you just love her, Companion? I'll be sorry to leave her.

Lady Jehanne made me promise to wear these clothes I have on now. She disguised me as a simple village maiden so no one would realize who I was, especially not Grandfather Fylkir, and she booked passage home for me on a knarr that agreed to drop me off on our own little island during its next voyage.

"Stay here with the goodwife, Keera. Don't even think of trying to get to your grandfather," she told me. "I have to go on, as soon as I've talked to him, and my ship can't sail back to your parents. King Hakkon needs me. I'll get word to your parents, though, so they won't worry. I'll let them know you're heading to them on the very next ship." Then she had put her hands on my shoulders and made me look at her. "Promise. Promise not to go to your grandfather."

I did.

No, that wasn't a lie, not at all, Companion. That's not what I planned to do, remember? I planned to seek my farwydd, and I didn't promise not to go seeking her. Lady Jehanne didn't even know about that part. So everything was fine, and I didn't have to lie to her. I like her a lot. I see you do too, Companion. I'd hate to have to lie to her.

"Promise me you'll go straight down to the port and board the knarr back to your parents," Lady Jehanne said to me.

I didn't lie to her then, either. I told her yes, I would. No, it was not a lie, Companion. I believed it when I told her yes. I thought I'd zip over to my farwydd, get her advice, and get back to the port in time to sail on the knarr. How was I to know my circumstances were about to change so drastically?

Now Lady Jehanne has gone away, back to the court of King Haakon 'Hardaxe, and I'm still here, and the knarr that was to carry me home has sailed without me.

I have to think about something else now, really fast. So wait. Wait just a second, and don't talk to me. No. Stop right there. No talking, Companion. You're always talking and talking, and right now I need a moment.

All right. I'm fine now. I just—well, every so often I think about my parents, and how worried they probably are because they don't know where I am, and then I have to think of something else before I start to feel terrible about it.

Very well. Where were we? Lady Jehanne.

Don't say such mean things about her, the poor lady. She wasn't irresponsible. I stowed away, remember?

Very well, I admit it. My idea of going to my farwydd turned out to be a pretty bad idea. You're right, I feel pretty terrible about that and terrible about what I'm putting my poor parents through.

In fact, I'm devastated. If I hadn't gone to my farwydd, I'd still have my powers, and then I'd still have a more than even chance of accomplishing my tasks. As it is now, I am totally flummoxed. I'm done for. I am a failure. I feel an utter fopdoodle. A complete addlepate.

Proud of yourself? Satisfied? You made me cry, Companion.

I thought the farwydd attached you to me to help me, not make me feel terrible about myself. Why don't you go away now? I'd be better off without help like yours. If I'm going to succeed, especially now I've lost my powers, I need every shred of confidence I can summon up, and you're making me doubt myself.

Oh. You poor thing. Crying again.

Here's my handkerchief. I'm just angry. Not your fault that the farwydd took away my powers.

Let's agree to be kinder to each other. There. Friends?

We were speaking of Lady Jehanne. She has gone now, back to the Ice-realm, and I'll have to decide what to do with myself, now that I'm on my own. I don't think I can stay here in this cottage much longer. Lady Jehanne gave the goodwife here something for my keep, and as I say, she has paid for my passage back, but her ladyship had no idea I might need to stay here longer.

I'm not a deceitful girl at heart. Not really. But sometimes, what people don't know won't hurt them, and you have to make sure it stays that way.

As for me, I had believed my two tasks were going to be quick, and now I know they won't be.

I may be in for a long stay here on the Fire Isle. I can't get on that ship and go home. That ship has sailed, Companion. I'll have to stay here and see what I can work out. That means, as I see it, I'll have to earn my keep somehow. Or give up and try to earn my passage home.

Quite a dilemma, you say? No, Companion. No dilemma at all. My choice is pretty simple. I won't give up.

Don't try it, Companion. Nothing you have to say is going to change my mind. I came with two goals. I'll leave once I've seen my way to them.

Oh, I understand what you're asking now. Why I have to stay here on the Fire Isle to accomplish my goals. Well, you're right. I came here to get advice from my farwydd, I didn't get any, and now why don't I head home. I can see why you'd think that. You just don't know what I know.

I should tell you a thing or two about my grandfather. Then you'll understand.

Grandfather Fylkir is allied with King Haakon because the king helped Grandfather regain his lands here in the Fire Isle. Otherwise, he'd still be sulking at his estate on the Western Isle, where he'd gone in exile when his brothers had driven him away. In return for King Haakon's help, Grandfather Fylkir is pledged to him against Caedon.

And that's why Lady Jehanne is here, or was. She was here to cement the alliance between Grandfather Fylkir and her king, and maybe try to talk Grandfather Fylkir into reaching out to my father. King Haakon was torn about this alliance with my grandfather, because he knows my grandfather and my father are enemies.

You see how it is, don't you? If Haakon can get my father on his side, many people will rise up, because even though our parents' outpost in the sea is tiny, my father is beloved, and people will flock to support him. If he's seen as allied to Haakon, those people will support Haakon, and any weaklings and vacillators and cowards among them will not support Caedon, whom everyone hates.

But Haakon, allied with Grandfather Fylkir, won't be able to get everyone's support unless my father and grandfather stop being enemies. People hate Grandfather Fylkir almost as much as they hate Caedon.

Actually, it's my mother who has the say-so about that, and she'll never trust her father (the real one, not the true). My mother, Fylkir's own daughter. She knows him too well. My mother hasn't agreed to any such alliance. She told Lady Jehanne as much. And she spoke for her husband (who is both real and true and the only one she says she'll ever have, in this life and the next through all eternity), my father, Walter the First.

She wouldn't have disallowed the alliance with Fylkir without talking it over with my father. They are together always. I think if my father is out of her sight for very long, my mother starts to fret that they'll somehow be parted again. And he thinks the same, except of course for having no sight. They were apart for so long, and they each thought the other was dead, so they expected they'd be parted forever. In this life, at least. It makes them anxious now, when they can't touch each other.

Nine Spheres, they're always touching each other.

I don't expect I'll ever marry. Not because I find it disgusting or anything, all that touching. I just don't think I'll ever find anyone to feel that way about, not the way my mother feels about my father. Not the way he feels about her. I just don't think it's likely. I look around me, and I don't see any other two people who feel that strongly about each other. There's always an imbalance. But not between those two. They are soul-mates.

My father even calls her by a name that means soul-mate, a name he learned when he and Mother sought refuge on the Western Isle from Caedon and from my father's evil half-brother Audemar.

The name my father calls my mother is anamcara. That means "soul-mate" in their language over there on the Western Isle.

Most people aren't like my parents. They may feel affection, but not like that.

Then there are people like Caedon. You know how people have their animal spirits? You don't? Well, they do. Mine is a bird made of fire. A firebird.

Go right ahead and say it, Companion. Say it. Go ahead. You don't believe in firebirds. I don't care. They exist. Mine does. I carry her mark on my body.

But as I was trying to explain. When I think of Caedon's animal spirit, I figure it's probably some poisonous snake. I don't think poisonous snakes have soul-mates. My mother says he makes her think of a wolf or some kind of twisted wolfish creature like Man-Dog Rough-Gray. Do you know that story? I thought so. Everyone does.

I'm figuring Caedon couldn't possibly have a soul-mate. Maybe he doesn't have a soul, or maybe it's so warped and twisted that it's of no use to him, so it just coils up like a dark, wefty thing somewhere inside him. His stomach, maybe. Wonder what made him that way. Or who.

I saw him once. At Grandfather Fylkir's. I was only five years old, but I remember him. Don't scoff. It's perfectly possible to remember something from your fifth year. Yes, even in that much detail. It was the time he came to Grandfather with his bags of gold, to buy me.

I think I saw Caedon when I was even littler, too. I think I remember seeing him then. I was two years old. Maybe not even that.

But when I was five, I know I met him, because I remember Grandfather Fylkir bringing him into my room to see me. Caedon told Grandfather Fylkir he wanted to examine me before he bought me. The idea was, he'd buy me for a bride. But when I stood there before the fire and he reached down to . . .

Nine Spheres, to tousle my hair, satisfied?

. . .I looked into his eyes and saw he had no such intention. He wasn't going to marry me. He was going to do something worse.

I saw this in him just as I was becoming aware of my powers.

I thought Grandfather Fylkir would see that, too, and wouldn't sell me to him. But Grandfather Fylkir was going to sell me anyhow, bride or no bride. Caedon added a whole bag of gold to my price, and Fylkir loves gold, so he accepted, even though that would bring shame on the family, Caedon taking me for a concubine.

My Uncle Stefan didn't like that. Uncle Stefan isn't a nice man, but maybe underneath—oh, I don't know. Maybe there's something under there. Uncle Stefan had heard what Caedon does to little children. He didn't want to sell me.

Don't cry, lady. My story has a happy ending.

My mother got me out of there, so nobody sold anyone to anyone.

Although Caedon did hand over the gold, Fylkir did take it, and now Caedon has the ridiculous idea I belong to him.

I do not. Fylkir didn't have the right to sell me. He just thought he did.

But I remember Caedon's eyes. They're very light. Too light, and strangely golden. I could see right into his head through them. His face is very thin. His lips are thin. His hair is very dark. And his eyes and skin are pale. Pale.

He's a good bit older than my father, but no hint of gray streaks that black hair, not to this day, or so Lady Jehanne tells me. Then again, no one has gone around torturing him. He's the one who has done all the torturing. Maybe it keeps him young.

Lady Jehanne. That's what would have happened to me, if Mother hadn't come for me in time. Lady Jehanne was one of Caedon's concubines.

You know this already, Companion? I didn't realize that.

Then you probably know Caedon traded her to King Haakon. I believe King Haakon may love her.

Love. I don't know much about that, except the love between my parents, of course. And the love they have for me.

I suppose I do know about love, then. You're right, Companion. See, I can admit it when I'm wrong.

My father's mother was beloved of King Ranulf the Fourth, maybe in the same way Lady Jehanne is beloved of Haakon. That makes King Ranulf, that long-dead king, my other grandfather. Strange, I never think of him that way. I think of him as some figure in the history books.

Of course I've read the history books. I told you I can read. You need to listen!

Where was I? Oh. Complicated feelings about my other grandfather. I suppose I feel this way about King Ranulf because my father says he barely knew him, despite being his son. His bastard son. My father's mother was a concubine, not a bondservant, but her family still felt she was disgraced and refused to have anything to do with my father and his brothers. King Ranulf had bondservants he got children on, too.

Listen, now. King Ranulf had his three legitimate children by his real wife. Artur, the oldest, was supposed to be king after him. Audemar, the middle son, treacherously killed his older brother and tried to be king himself. Avery, the youngest, led the Rising against Audemar.

If this were a story, everything would have ended happily right there. The valiant Prince Avery would have defeated the treacherous Audemar, and now Avery would be our king. Although if Avery had really had his way, he would have seen his brother Artur's older son crowned king. Audemar treacherously killed that boy before he could inherit his father's crown, and then Audemar killed that boy's even younger brother. I doubt Audemar did the killing himself. Everyone says Caedon does Audemar's dirty work for him.

With no son in Artur's line to inherit the throne, Avery did become king. My father told me that this man, my Uncle Avery, was king for not even a day before he too was killed. My father says my Uncle Avery—King Avery— knew he would be.

That sounds very sad to me, knowing you'd be king and then be killed. A short time after Uncle Avery inherited the throne, he was killed. So he was right. He was killed by Caedon. I wonder if Uncle Avery had powers that told him so, or if it was just common sense.

He went out on a dangerous mission the very day he became king, and then he was killed. In the brief hours before he died, though, Avery made sure the law was changed to allow Artur's last surviving child to become monarch after him. She was a woman, and at that time it was against the law for a woman to become queen. In spite of Avery's dying wish, no one supported his niece Diera.

Now Caedon has made himself king and has killed Queen Diera. As an excuse to move against her, he reinstated the rule about no women monarchs.

Poor Queen Diera. May the Dark Ones turn on those who turned on her.

I see you're upset, Companion. Don't cry. It was very sad. I honor your tears, I do. I'll wait quietly until you're better. Would you like my handkerchief again? There. Just keep it. But really, my lady, my story upsets you so much that I'm not sure I should be telling you any of it.

I have to.

The farwydd is making me.

Forgive me, lady. If I don't tell you my story, I won't be able to regain my powers and then my tasks will be left undone. My father has to see again, lady. He has to.

Oh, as for killing Caedon, I can do that with or without the powers. It would speed things up if I had them, though.

I see you don't believe me, lady. Well, you have your opinion and I have mine.

I'll go on with my two tasks. I must.

I hope you understand now that the last surviving member of the royal family, my father, has become our rightful king, no matter what Caedon goes around telling people.

You're right. Some would disagree. My father was bastard-born and some would argue that takes him out of the royal line. Even when his half-brother King Avery adopted him as son, he did so out of the line of succession. But that was to make sure there'd be no question Diera should be queen. No legal question. My father supported that matter fully. He did everything in his power to bring Queen Diera to the throne and keep her there, and he nearly got killed doing it.

Other people would argue that the middle brother, Audemar, being next in the line of succession after Artur and his sons, is the rightful king. I guess he's still out there in the world somewhere. Caedon defeated him in the civil war, and now no one knows where Audemar is. But my parents believe—and I agree with them—that Audemar lost his right to the throne through his treachery and fratricide.

Really? You amaze me, Companion. You really don't know what fratricide is? It means he's a brother-killer.

Whether Audemar has a claim to the throne or not, he's gone now. Good riddance, I'd say, except that when he fled, we got Caedon for king. I don't know if Caedon has any brothers, or if he ever did, whether he would have killed them. If they'd gotten in his way, I suspect he would have.

My father had two brothers, two full brothers besides his royal half-brothers. I may have mentioned them. They were killed. You guessed it. Caedon.

Caedon keeps trying to kill my father, but as my mother always tells him, "Wat, you're hard to kill."

As you see, I have a bloody history.

All the blood and violence. That's what makes Lady Jehanne's task really hard, trying to persuade my parents to ally themselves with Caedon's enemy, Haakon Hardaxe. You wouldn't think it would be that hard. You'd think my father would do anything for revenge.

Actually, he wants nothing to do with all this feuding over who is king. He says he has gained perspective as he has grown older. He says people can think of him as king, or not, just as they please. He says it will be fine with him if Haakon defeats Caedon, and it will be fine with him if that means Haakon is the one who takes over the Sceptered Isle and declares himself king. But my father says he won't help.

Just the same, he doesn't want Caedon to be king, because Caedon is an evil man.

That puts my poor father in a difficult position, wouldn't you say? He longs for peace, but his conscience pricks him.

Here's another thing about Lady Jehanne. I'll bet you don't know this. Her best friend was my Aunt Jillian. Jillian the queen, the one who died so tragically. I never met her, though. She and my mother were separated when Jillian was a very young girl, and although they were reunited, their time together didn't last long. Jillian went off to live in some other court over in the Eastern Baronies, and then, somehow, she ended up Caedon's bride. That's strange, isn't it?

One of the last times I looked into my mother's mind, I saw how strange. My mother was filled with grief. Why would her sister marry such a monster? That's what my mother asked herself, over and over, and couldn't let it go. And then, when she found out her sister had died, her grief was redoubled.

Oh, stop snuffling about, Companion. You keep dissolving into tears. If you don't watch out, you'll turn into a puddle. Sometimes I look at you and I don't know who you think you are.

Pull yourself together. Or don't. But if you're coming with me, you'd better. And quick.

I need to bestir myself. I'll tell the goodwife of the cottage thanks for her hospitality, and then I'll make my way down the road to the big town on the sea. They tell me it's called Mist Cove. It is, isn't it? It's a beautiful misty harbor.

I need to get started on my tasks, but to do that, I'll have to figure out how to live, somehow.

Don't worry. I'm used to it. Before we found my father again, that was our whole existence, Mother's and mine. Figuring out how we could live from one day to the next. I'm pretty resourceful that way. I'll bet not many princesses are.

What? What? Always interrupting.

Oh, I see.

That's actually a very reasonable question, my lady.

I think I started to tell you, before I got sidetracked.

Why I need to stay here on the Fire Isle to accomplish my two tasks. You're right. I only came here to consult with my farwydd.

Why not go home now. That's what you're asking. Why not, indeed?

I'm going to stay here because of something I learned in the goodwife's house. I didn't need any powers to learn it. I just needed to keep my ears open.

Haakon wants the Fire Isle for his own. He says he wants to make alliance with Grandfather Fylkir, and maybe he does. But in the end, he wants to take possession of the Fire Isle for himself. Everyone on the Fire Isle knows it, maybe everyone except Grandfather Fylkir.

That's odd, isn't it? Grandfather Fylkir prides himself on being a canny man, a political genius. But he can't see the most obvious thing in the world, right under his nose. Is he especially self-deluded, or are all of us like that?

Let me finish. I know, that doesn't answer your question. But this will.

Grandfather Fylkir doesn't see it, but Caedon does. Caedon probably really is some kind of political genius.

I see you agree with me about that. I'm amazed, lady. We're not in agreement about much, we two.

Everyone on the Fire Isle except Grandfather Fylkir sees and dreads another thing. If King Haakon wants the Fire Isle, Caedon wants it more. Someday, probably someday soon, Caedon will swoop in and take the Fire Isle before Haakon can manipulate the Fire Isle into his own hands. Haakon is moving slowly and carefully. Caedon will move fast.

When that happens, Caedon will come here. All I have to do is wait.

I don't know about my first task. But my second task? The best place in the world to be, if I'm to accomplish my second task, is right here on the Fire Isle.

So now I need to figure out how to earn my keep here until Caedon shows up and I can kill him.

I have a few ideas about how to do that, earn my keep. I only have two practical skills. Three, if you count one that's forbidden me.

Do you want to know what they are?

Then get a grip on yourself, and sit still, and listen. No, I mean it. Stop crying, silly Companion.

Here's the first of my practical skills. I can keep a tavern. I helped out old Teasag the tavern-wife back where we used to live, and she told me I was as good at it as she was. She was kind of like a grandmother to me. I miss her. Someday I'll try to find her. Won't she be surprised to find out I'm a princess.

Here's another thing I know how to do. My mother is a fine healer, one of the best. I was her apprentice. I learned from her, and she learned, she says, from the best of all, back on the mainland, a woman named Old Cwen. Later, my mother added midwifery to her skills. I can do all those things.

I don't particularly like them, though. Once, I thought to myself, *let's just get on with it*, and I used my powers to heal a woman. That didn't work out so well. The woman thought I was a witch. Of course, now I wouldn't be able to take a shortcut like that, so I might probably do very well. But as I say. I don't really like it. Especially all the blood. Once, I was trapped in a barrel while my mother cut off a man's leg. That was unpleasant.

Oh, no—she wasn't trying to hurt the man. He had been in a sea-battle. His leg had been crushed. She had to amputate.

Why was I in the barrel? That might take too long to explain. Some other time.

What I do love is hunting herbs in the woods and mixing potions. It's part of the healing profession, you know, the one part I like. That's what I think I'll do. We'll head out toward the city, you and I. On the way, I'll search for useful herbs, and when I get there, I'll find the market square and sell them. Mother and I used to do such things. I know how it's done.

There's something else I like. I like thinking things through. That's part of healing too. Did you know that? I'll bet you didn't. It is, though. It's a very important part. My mother and I once stopped a dread dis-ease in its tracks, just by thinking. You don't have to believe that. No one's making you. It's true just the same.

Oh, the third thing I know how to do? That's the forbidden thing I mentioned before. Please promise not to tell. You already know what it is. I can read and figure, and girls are not allowed.

So now, it's high time for us to stop all this chatter. It's high time for me to head out to the city.

I don't care if you don't want to go to the city. I'm going.

Really, I don't know why you keep tagging along, Companion. Haven't I told you enough? I suppose I'm stuck with you, though, thanks to that accursed farwydd of mine. Come on, then, if you insist on following me around. There's no time to waste. Caedon could show up any day now. I have to be ready.

Liar

I'm not going to talk to you any more, Companion. You lied to me.

Liar! Liar!

There we were, setting up in the market square with all the herbs we gathered. Not that you helped much. Not at all, come to think of it. But there I was, doing well. I had a little pile of coin beside me already, and it was growing nicely.

A goodwife came by to haggle with me.

"Mistress, what hold ye this bunch of thyme? Or what is it worth, the whole of this basket of bilberries?"

"Goodwife," I replied to her. "You shall have it good and cheap. Four groats the basket, and for the thyme--"

"For that much I could buy an entire tun of berries," said she, scowling. I knew she was just trying to get me to drop the price.

"I shall give it to you for my own price. I'll abate nothing," I said, making myself sound outraged and insulted. "The basket of bilberries is worth four groats, and that's what you'll pay if you want them, goodwife." I matched her scowl for scowl.

I sold it to her for three groats, and threw in the bunch of thyme as a goodwill gesture. She left smiling. And so the day went. I was very pleased.

Still and all, a person might have to visit the necessary shed. And you'd think that in such a matter, a person's friend would offer to take over for a short time. But no. I turned around to ask you, and you were gone. What did you do, wander off somewhere? See the sights?

So then I had to pack all the unsold bunches of herbs up, and the baskets of berries, and fold them into my cloth, and tie my coins into the pouch at my waist, and lose my place in the square while I went off looking for the necessary shed.

By the time I got back, someone else had taken over my spot.

Oh, so you think that's not so very awful, do you? It meant I had to go to the outer edge of the square by the alleys to set up, and as we both know, that's where the nasty people lurk. Some urchin ran past, grabbed my money-pouch, ripped it from my belt, and made off with it.

"Thief! Thief!" I screamed to the beadle. I pointed out the culprit. "That boy, I want him pilloried!" I shrieked. But that sly boy ducked between a building and a dung-heap. While I shrieked and stamped my foot, the beadle seized him by the back of the tunic. That filthy urchin wriggled out of the beadle's grasp, leaped over an overturned cart, and disappeared down a maze of muddy lanes. I was left with nothing.

Now here you came again, with an innocent look in your eye, just as if nothing bad had happened.

What do you have to say for yourself, Companion?

We'll go without supper tonight. Don't come complaining to me when your belly begins to growl.

But I see I've gotten side-tracked. We're talking about how you lied.

Fie, Companion, *not really a lie*. It was just as good as a lie. You misrepresented yourself.

I set up again, and you saw how angry I was, so you got busy putting on a big show about how helpful you are.

You're really not. Nine Spheres, what you did to me. There we were, finally all set up again after having to move and after being thieved of all our coin, and then, just when I thought no customer would ever come over to our tiny corner of the market square, that man stepped up, that bent-over long-bearded fellow, and I could see he was really interested in my wares. You could see it too. Don't try to weasel out of it and pretend otherwise. You saw it too.

And he said, *How much for the whole lot of your herbs, my child?* The whole lot! After having all my coin thieved off me, here comes an old fellow ready to buy my entire stock. We were going to make out well after all. We were. Don't try to deny it.

"And the berries, good sir?"

He said he'd take the berries too. The berries too! Then he reached out to pay me, and then. . .

And then. . .

I'm so angry.

His eyes got really wide, because he spotted you, Companion.

I reached toward him for the coin, but he stepped back. He waved his arm. He waved it right through you.

Don't deny it.

Right through you.

And then he turned and walked away.

I'm leaving now, Companion. Don't follow me around any more.

I said, don't follow me. I don't care what that dratted farwydd told me.

Nine Spheres! Get away from me! What are you, anyway? What kind of creature, misrepresenting yourself as an ordinary woman?

"My child."

I whirled around. It was that man. That same old fellow who had wanted to buy me out.

"I didn't mean to startle you so, back there," he said, falling in with the two of us as I strode down the lane toward the outskirts of the city, moving fast in hopes of shedding myself of you, Companion. You were still following me. I was hoping to find a spot to sleep, out in the countryside, and figure out how to rid myself of your odious company. Yes. Odious. That's the word I'm using, and I mean it.

But I pulled myself together, because here was my customer, back again in spite of everything. In spite of you, Companion. I still might make a sale in spite of everything.

"Do you still want my herbs?" I asked the man.

"Yes, I do. Why don't you come to my house. It's just at the end of this lane here. I'll have my woman find you something to eat. You look hungry."

"I am," I said, giving him a hard stare. Could I trust this man?

Oh, shut up, Companion. I didn't ask you.

"I was taken aback, my child, by your—"

"Oh, her? She keeps following me around."

"So," he said carefully. "You see her too."

"Yes. I do. Maybe you and I are the only two who do see her, because no one else has mentioned her, not even the nice woman we stayed with these few days past."

"And don't you find that strange? That you see her and no one else does?"

I shrugged. "Many things are strange, good sir," I told him.

"I wonder why you see her," he continued. "I know why I do."

"Why do you?" I was really curious now.

"Let me introduce myself. I'm not from this land, the Fire Isle. I come from far away. My name is John. People call me Old Dee."

I noticed he hadn't answered my question, but I said only, "I had an uncle named John."

"That's unusual."

"I know. His mother, my grandmother, was from the very eastern edge of the mainland. Most of it belongs to the Sceptered

Isle, but that one little part belongs to the Eastern Baronies. The name is common there."

"The Sceptered Isle. I'm assuming you mean Caedon's realm, not this one."

"If you regard Caedon the Monstrous as our king," I retorted.

"So you're from this monstrous king's realm, are you?" he said.

"I am, but my grandfather is from right here on the Fire Isle."

"And this is the reason for—"

I stepped back quickly before he could tousle it. "Yes. For my red hair."

Now I glanced back at you. Are you taking this all in, Companion? What are you making of this fellow, this Old Dee? I'm a bit intrigued by him, myself.

He looked to be an old man. That didn't mean he wasn't dangerous, I reminded myself. Grandfather Fylkir is old, and he's very dangerous.

"How would you like to become my apprentice and live in my house?" he asked, stopping abruptly in the middle of the lane.

"Apprentice? What is your profession."

"Sorcerer," he said. At my blank look, he added, "Around here, they'd call me a galdrmaster."

"Like our seanchai at home?"

"Oh, you're from that part of the world, are you? Yes, something like that."

"Since I've lost my own powers, and need new ones if I'm to accomplish my tasks, yes, I accept," I said.

And you. You be quiet. You have nothing to say about this, Companion. You've foregone any trust I might have had in you. If you insist on coming along, at least keep quiet.

I must confess, I do feel a bit uneasy. The farwydd won't approve of this man and his sorcery, I'm sure of it.

But she's the one who dispossessed me.

Now I have to make my own way. And here a means of earning my keep has just dropped into my lap, thank the Child.

This, then, is how you and I came to take up residence in Old Dee the Galdrmaster's home, Companion.

His home is the place where he taught me all he knew from the grimoires scattered around his cottage. And he himself was writing the Arch-Grimoire that would overtop all others. "This book will contain all the wisdom I've accumulated over the ages, every spell," he told me, tapping a tall pile of parchment on his desk in his study, a special room in his cottage that he had filled with books and papers. "Every procedure. All my research notes. Reams of data. I need to hurry. I may not have much time. Then, deeper than any of these sailors can drop their plummets, I'll drown my book. But I'll mark where to find it again in after times."

When he saw I could read, even in the language of the Old Ones, he was ecstatic. "What a find you are, dear child!" he exclaimed to me as I circled my arms protectively over a big bowl of stew his woman servant ladled out for me that first night.

His woman's name was Gudrun. She looked to be older, if possible, than he.

As for you, Companion, I noticed then you ate nothing. Gudrun didn't seem to notice you, and you hung back in the corner and didn't intrude.

Here's what I think. You stay in your corner of Old Dee's house, and I'll stay in mine. For now, let's keep it like that. You're determined to stick with me, I see. But I think I'll practice ignoring you. It will be better for both of us that way, and we'll just forget the farwydd's little command that I tell you everything. I've told you enough, and all you've done is blubber and cry about it. A fat lot of help you've turned out to be. I thought that's why the farwydd insisted I take you with me, so you could help me. That must not be the reason. I see I'm stuck with you. Let's try to make your companion status as painless as possible, shall we?

I'm turning my attention to Old Dee now. It's my duty as his apprentice, so you hush up and don't bother me.

It's clear, isn't it, that one of the reasons Old Dee wanted to make me his apprentice was my knowledge of herbs. He didn't want them for healing; he wanted them for spells. He made these spells sort of the same way my mother and I used to compound our potions, but instead of a small bowl and pestle, he used a big kettle and a stout stick to stir his concoctions with.

He'd swing the kettle on its tripod over the fire and stir it until it bubbled. Sometimes he'd send me out for more ingredients.

"You know," he said to me this one day, "I need a frog. And I need a newt."

"Why?" I asked him. I was suspicious. I had watched him make his last batch and had noticed certain objects floating around in the bubbling liquid. Maybe body parts of animals. There was this eye .. . .I shuddered. And a toe.

"Please go out to the pond down the lane. You'll find them there."

"No," I said.

"No? But I'm your master and you're my apprentice."

"I know what you're going to do to them, those poor frogs and newts. I won't be any part of it."

I thought maybe he'd beat me. That's what masters do with disobedient apprentices.

He didn't. He just sighed. "Very well. We'll do it the hard way, then."

After that, Old Dee spent the better part of the morning puttering around his library, seizing this grimoire off the shelf, and that bestiary, and then a few of the herbals. Then he sat with his chin in his hand and thought.

You know, I approve of that, Companion. I do. When my mother and I were trying to figure out what was causing the disease at the viceroy's manor on the Northmost Isle, the place where we lived for quite a good bit of my childhood, that's what we did, too. We sat and thought until we came up with an answer.

Late in the day, Old Dee must have discovered his answer, because he was back at his kettle. This time, he was muttering words and spells. "There's rosemary," he said, sprinkling some in from my herb pouch. He looked up at me. "That's for remembrance. Pansies. . .hmm. We'll add some of those. That's for thoughts," he instructed me. "Cobweb. . .and some peasblossom, I think. A little mustard-seed. Moth. Is moth fine with you, Mistress Keera? Will moth violate your precious scruples about the ethical treatment of animals?"

Before I could open my mouth to protest, he'd dropped a few moth wings in, scraped up from off the window sill along with the cobweb. I closed my mouth again. *Oh, well,* I thought to myself. Those moths were already dead.

"Oh, yes," he said, reaching for the fresh material I had just found for him the day before and laid out to dry on his shelf. "A few of these midnight mushrooms. That will do, I think."

They're just regular mushrooms, I thought to myself, but I didn't tell him that. I felt a pang of guilt. I was misrepresenting regular mushrooms as this midnight variety he seemed to need. I knew I should speak up, but I didn't. Maybe he wouldn't know the difference.

Grimalkin, Goodwife Gudrun's old cat, kept wreathing about Old Dee's legs during this entire part of the procedure, but Old Dee didn't seem to mind. He bent down to scratch her ears.

Now he muttered more words over the kettle. I knew these were spells of great power.

"Murmur…Morax…Pursan…Aym," he said. I tried to follow along.

"Rex .. Pax… Nax," he chanted, then "Erex… Arex … Rymex …"

The drone of his voice was making me sleepy. Maybe his spells were sending me to sleep so I wouldn't be able to recite them myself before he thought I was ready.

"Up, bottom, down, top. Through the sharp hawthorn blows the cold wind," Old Dee intoned. "Go to thy cold bed and warm thee." Then, in a whisper, "Strange … charmed."

My head felt heavier and heavier. Gudrun helped me up. She threw Old Dee a disapproving look. "This girl's plain wore out."

To me she said, "Bed, girl. Let's get you to bed now."

As we left the room and headed to the alcove where I slept, I heard Old Dee behind me: "Bless thee from whirlwinds, star-blasting, and taking . . ." Gudrun tucked me in and leaned over to kiss my forehead.

My heavy eyelids closed and I fell into a sound sleep while Old Dee was chanting more words of power: "Diranx . . . celmagis . . ."

I slept until dawn. I do think I roused in the night. Beyond me, I could see Old Dee hunched over his fire and his kettle. He seemed to be making warding gestures. The words he was saying were different. "Gilles, I adjure thee," he said, following it with a rapid string of language, hard to make out: "puton, purpuron, metton, ardon, lardon, asson, catulon." Something like that.

I drew in my breath. I was suddenly frightened. Old Dee was heading over to the alcove where I slept, but there was someone else, some menacing shadowy presence. I squeezed my eyes tight shut. I could tell Old Dee was standing just above me. I could hear his breath, and I could smell the herbs he'd just been burning in the kettle. "Gilles," I heard him say softly. "I adjure thee. Do not touch this child." And then I could sleep easier.

When next I opened my eyes, it was full morning. Maybe what I'd seen and heard was all a dream.

Old Dee was cheerful, nothing like a man who had stood over a sleeping girl to murmur words of power and protection. With his fingers he combed through his long pointy white beard and hummed as he circled his kettle. "Things went well last night, apprentice. I made excellent progress. Decant this concoction into the bottles and range them on my shelves, if you please."

I spent the entire morning doing that, and the dream from the night before, as dreams will, fell into shreds and receded from my mind. Only much later did I recall it.

All morning, Old Dee scribbled notes for his Arch-Grimoire. "One of the results was, hmm . . . a bit unexpected," he told me, pausing and scratching his ear with the quill. "On the whole, a success, I think."

I felt a fresh guilt-pang over the wrong kind of mushroom. *Maybe I should have said something*, I thought. I bent quickly over the kettle to hide any telltale blush. *I really should have said something.*

Then I sprang back. The contents of the kettle were foul. But the moment passed without incident.

After we ate a midday meal of bread and cheese, I dusted Old Dee's artifacts—his black mirror, his big glowing ball in its protective silk pouch, his various seals with magic runes inscribed on them. The mirror was his favorite. He called it his black stone although actually, you know, it was a mirror.

The mirror or stone or whatever it was, that wasn't my favorite. It scared me a little. It was not of the Earth Child. Not of the Sea Child. Certainly not of the Fire Child. That left only . . . but that made no sense. Old Dee couldn't have gone out there, to the lands far west, the Sky Child's unknown territories. So I wasn't sure what to make of it, and unless he directed me to, I never touched it.

Now where were you, all this time, Companion? I know you were in the corner when I went to bed. What did you do all night? I'm just wondering.

There you are again. I'm thinking you've taken up residence in that corner. It's your corner now.

Two Tasks

I've just realized something troubling. Some of Old Dee's noisome liquid is still pooled in the bottom of the kettle, an evil green. I need to get more of the empty bottles and scoop up the last of it. Ugh.

I'm tired, though, Companion. Why don't we have a chat, you and I. That will give me a bit of a break.

Let me tell you something about us, you and I. It's the real reason why I don't drive you off. It's because I promised.

Now, pay attention.

When I first reached the Fire Isle and found the farwydd of the Fire Child in the molten basin of the great mountain over to the west of us, and when I found the entrance to her lair and went in, and when I presented my two tasks to her, she said one thing to me.

She said, "Child, I'm sending you a companion. I want you to tell her everything."

I promised her.

Then the next thing I knew, her imps were escorting me out of her lair none too gently, and depositing me, bruised and angry, at the bottom of her mountain. Then came the messenger with the riddle. Then came the farwydd herself, sliding into my mind as if she were entitled to walk in there any time she pleased. *The Children help those who help themselves.* Then nothing. Powers gone, poof, like that.

That's when you showed up, Companion.

See, this is what I thought. The only part of the riddle I understood was the part about my firebird. The farwydd said she was sending me a companion, and I thought my firebird was the companion she meant. Not you.

You can believe or disbelieve in my firebird as much as you like. I don't even think you believe in animal spirits. You're the companion the farwydd meant for me, though.

But let me tell you something. My firebird is real, and more important, she is true. The riddle mentions that.

I just don't see my firebird very often. The first time I saw her—I don't want to tell you about this, because I know you'll scoff. The farwydd told me to tell you everything, and I promised, so . . .

The first time I saw her was the moment I opened my eyes on this world.

She was perched on my mother's shoulder, looking down into my face when the midwife handed me to my mother for the very first time. She was small then, and so was I.

They took me away to swaddle me, these kindly women tending my mother, and by the time they brought me back to her, my firebird was gone.

I remembered her, though, and she left behind a small mark of remembrance on my right shoulder. I think I mentioned it to you once. Do you want to see it? Let me pull my kirtle down a bit so you can have a look. See there? It's a little flame.

Fine. Call it a birthmark if you want to, Companion. It's a flame, and my firebird left it there.

The second time I saw her was in my vision, when my mother and father were with me in a beautiful garden. This time, she was enormous. She blazed up into the garden's pear tree. She became so tall and spread so wide that she was the pear tree.

The third time I saw her was that bad time, in the barrel, when I thought I was going to die. The barrel? That's a complicated story. I'll tell you later.

I haven't seen my firebird since that awful day. I was really hoping she was the companion the Fire Child's farwydd meant, but she meant you.

Forgive me if I find that a little disappointing.

Oh, there you go, Companion. I didn't mean to hurt your feelings. Please don't cry.

Compose yourself, please. Old Dee needs me. I must go to him, but I promise you, as soon as I have a free moment, I'll come back, and we'll talk. We'll have a nice chat, just the two of us.

I went to Old Dee. He sat me down before him at our table. "Now then, child," he said. "You're a good apprentice. I've observed you closely these last few weeks, and I'm very pleased with your work. I wanted to tell you that."

Uh oh, I thought. *This is the kind of thing people say when they're ready to blast you with some misdeed or fault or shortcoming. They say the nice thing first. Then they say But. Then they let you have it.*

"But," said Old Dee.

Here it comes, I thought. *The mushrooms. I brought him the wrong kind of mushrooms.*

That wasn't it. He wasn't going to scold me. He said something truly astounding.

"But you have two tasks that need doing, and we haven't made any progress on those," Old Dee said.

I nodded, giddy with relief. When we first met him on the road, I told him I had two tasks, and he had remembered.

"Tell me what these tasks are. Maybe we can get started on one of them," he said.

"First," I said, "I need to find a cure for my father's blindness."

Old Dee blew out his cheeks. "That will be difficult," he said at last. At my crestfallen look, he added, "But not impossible." He covered my hand with his and smiled at me.

I smiled back.

"And the second?"

"Kill King Caedon."

He snatched his hand back. "Oh, child!" he cried.

I stared at him, nonplussed.

"That's dark magic you're talking about, dear child. No, no, no. That's not the magic I practice."

"I wasn't thinking of magic," I said hastily. "No, I would never ask that of you."

"What were you thinking of?" His voice had gotten a little testy. "Were you just going to walk up to him, and—"

"—and kill him," I finished.

He sat looking at me silently. Finally, he said, "You have your reasons, I suppose?"

I nodded vigorously. "First, he was going to buy me from my grandfather when I was only five years old, and make me his concubine." I squinched up my eyes, counting them up, all the reasons, all my grievances. I ticked them off on my fingers. "Second, he was going to do something terrible to my mother, and still will, if he can find her. Third, he killed almost everyone in my family. Fourth, he tried to torture my father to death." I stopped and looked at Old Dee sitting with his mouth agape. I nodded reassuringly. "He failed. My father is hard to kill." I resumed. "But he'll try to kill my father again."

"That's why your father is blind, from this torture?" guessed Old Dee.

"Yes," I said. "And fifth, Caedon is a very bad, cruel man who oppresses the people."

"Funny," said Old Dee. "Many of the folk around the Sceptered Isle—and I've traveled your realm, you know—seem to like him just fine."

"They're wrong," I told him. "He's sneaky about it. They don't realize."

"I see," said Old Dee. "And I agree with you. Any knowledgeable person hates Caedon. What else?"

"That's it," I said. "Oh, wait. There's another thing."

"What's that?" said Old Dee.

"He also either pushed my Aunt Jillian into the sea or made her so sad that she jumped into the sea herself." There was a pause. "And died."

Before Old Dee could react, an ominous rumbling began to shake the house. The rumbling grew. The house shook harder.

I looked around wildly for you, Companion. I knew you'd be scared. There you were, in your corner, but you didn't look scared. I swear to you, Companion, you looked angry. Your eyes had turned into two glowing rings. Your arms were spread out on either side of you, pressing hard against the walls of the house.

The house rattled and then it shook and then— this part is hard to describe— it kind of undulated as if it weren't quite solid. And at that point, Old Dee's kettle burst into flames. Then it exploded into metal shards that zinged in crazy ricochets all over the cottage kitchen. Old Dee seized me and we cowered under the table. There was an enormous clanging sound that startled me so badly I crawled into Old Dee's arms and lay quaking there.

Then a second explosion. Then a third, and then a series of diminishing pops.

It was quiet.

"Nine Spheres, what was that?" said Old Dee. I extricated myself from Old Dee's arms. We were both shaking.

"Old Dee, Old Dee," I cried, casting myself abjectly down before him. "Forgive me, master. I did it. The mushrooms!"

"The mushrooms?" Old Dee tried to stand up but bumped his head on the underside of the table and sat back down with a *plumf*, his robes puddling about him.

Before I could finish my confession, Gudrun was in the room exclaiming and tut-tutting. She pulled us each out from under the table and brushed us off.

"My, my," she said. "Look at the mess you've made."

"I'm sorry, dear Gudrun," Old Dee said, patting her awkwardly.

"You just about scared Grimalkin into the next world," she scolded. Old Dee and I looked at our toes, shamefaced.

"Smelly potions. All that muttering." She was breathing hard. "And then the big messes. And I'm the one has to clean them up."

"Oh no, Gudrun. I'll do it," I rushed to tell her.

"See that you do," she said, and turned on her heel, and went out into the yard, where we could hear her pacing back and forth and talking to herself.

"It was my fault," I told Old Dee. "I brought you the wrong kind of mushrooms, and then, when you put them into the kettle, I didn't say anything."

"You did?"

"No. I didn't." At his look of confusion, I clarified. "Say any-thing. But I should have spoken up."

"You brought me the wrong kind of mushrooms," he re-peated.

I started to worry that one of the shards of kettle might have clipped him on the head.

"Yes," I said.

"Oh," he said, and wandered out of the kitchen. I heard him clumping up the stairs to his study. But before he went, he did a strange thing. He walked over to where you hovered in the cor-ner, Companion, and he fixed you with a long look.

I got the broom and began sweeping up pieces of kettle. I was just hauling a bucket of water from the well to wash down the floor when he came back into the kitchen.

"The wrong kind of mushroom," he said.

"Yes, remember? You said, *we'll add some midnight mushrooms,* and you took my mushrooms from the shelf, and you threw them in. But mine weren't midnight mushrooms. They were the regu-lar kind. Slippery jack, I believe."

"But Keera. Midnight mushrooms . . . that's just a poetical trope, my child. A poetical flourish. A poetical arabesque, as it were."

I stared at him.

"A mere bauble." He looked perturbed. "Slippery jack was just fine."

"Then—"

"I don't know. These things, sometimes they just happen. Something goes wrong, and you never figure out what. You might try holding everything the same and changing just one variable, seeing what happens, trying again but changing a different variable, seeing what happens. . .and so on and so on. And remember this, Keera. When you do this, keep really good records. Data. That's what's needed." He stopped and thought for a moment. "But really, we may never know. So this wasn't your fault, and you mustn't blame yourself." He gave me a dazzling smile and headed back to his study.

I sloshed the bucket over the floor and went down on my hands and knees, scrubbing and rubbing. By then, I was sweaty and greasy. Then I got down the second-best kettle, and I keeled that pot until my hands came out raw and red. Even my nose was raw, I expect from the fumes.

And you. You just fluttered in the corner and watched the whole thing, and you laughed. Didn't you, Companion. Admit it.

No?

Wait—what's wrong? I'm sorry! I didn't mean to upset you. No, wait—

CHAPTER FIVE

The Shifty and the Gullible

Old Dee and I decided it would be best to work on the blindness cure first. The killing of Caedon could come later.

We were sitting at the table in the kitchen, and he had one of the grimoires open, and one of the herbals, and a thick messy sheaf of his notes.

"Now, child. Tell me how your father lost his eyesight. Tell me everything you can remember."

"I wasn't there. I only heard what he said about it."

"Tell me that, then."

I thought. What he did say wasn't much. It was what he didn't say that was the worst part of it. "I really only know that Caedon gouged out one of his eyes. I don't know what happened to the other one."

"And chopped off his arm."

"Yes."

"Well," said Old Dee. "There's nothing to be done about the missing eye and arm. But as for the other eye. You say he can see a little out of it?"

"He says flashes of light sometimes, and sometimes misty shapes."

"So, actually, he has some eyesight left."

"I suppose so," I said.

"Let's start with that," said Old Dee. He leafed through his books and papers in silence. Finally he looked up at me. "I think," he said, "that it might be possible to make a magic hat for your father, and that this hat might restore his eyesight."

"A magic hat?" I said. I tried to keep the doubt from my voice.

"Let's think about it," said Old Dee. "Now this King Caedon took something, let's say a knife, and he stabbed your father in the eye, and he destroyed that eye, true? The eye that will never see?"

I nodded. "I suppose that's how he must have done it."

"Meanwhile, his men are hacking off your father's arm with a sword, and I'm imagining your father is throwing himself around, and I'm imagining people are hitting him."

"I suppose," I said.

"Looks like it," said Old Dee.

"How do you know that?"

"Well, your father's other eye wasn't stabbed out, was it? What does it look like?"

"It looks like any other eye. It's blue." Now I couldn't help myself. I teared up.

"Dear child," said Old Dee, and placed a sympathetic hand on mine. "Now listen to me. I'm thinking your father's other eye was not damaged at all. I'm thinking something inside his head was damaged. You know, there are lots of—" he looked at me anxiously. "Have you ever seen a calf butchered, perhaps, and its head split open?"

"Yes," I said.

"And what's in there?"

"It's—I don't like to think about it."

"There's something in there, in the head, right? Something grayish with a lot of strange folds and lines."

I nodded, feeling a bit sick. I never liked watching our pigs and cows getting butchered, even later, when old Teasag's husband the tavern owner did it out back before cutting them up for tasty stews and haunches. I'd usually go somewhere else until it was over.

"Those folds and lines are miraculous, my child."

I looked at Old Dee, puzzled.

"Those enclose the pathways down which we get signals to think and to see and to taste and—well, most of the things we do. Breathe. Move. So if there's damage inside the head, it can damage some of the pathways, and then we won't be able to do those things."

"How do you know these things? Magic?"

Old Dee tapped one of his books. I looked at it more closely. It wasn't like the others. I have a hard time describing to you what it was like, Companion. You might want to flutter over here sometime and take a look yourself. The pages weren't parchment. They were smoother and slicker. The cover wasn't leather or wood. It was—I don't know what it was. There were words on its pages, but I couldn't read them. They looked strange, though. They were very even. Whoever copied them down had the steadiest hand I've ever seen. There were pictures inside, but they weren't like any pictures I had ever looked at. Old John opened the book to one of these pictures. It showed what he was talking about, the inside of someone's head.

I gulped.

"This may be a bit much for you, Keera. Would you like Gudrun to brew you a nice hot posset?" Gudrun had been hovering around anxiously, and now she bustled off to do that. She brought me the cup, and I inhaled the fragrance. I sipped it and felt a little better.

"What I think is this. I think head trauma did this to your father."

"Head what?"

"Never mind. He was hit hard in the head, and that's what did it, because it messed up the pathways in these folds and lines that help him see."

I stared at him, and I knew my eyes were big. "You really are a sorcerer," I said.

"Around here, some might call me that," he said.

"What about where you come from?"

"A neurologist," he said.

That was a strange word. I rolled it around on my tongue. "Neurologist."

"Oh, I'm not a really important neurologist." He gave a modest laugh. "My practice is softball players with concussions, people with MS, things like that. I've just had occasion over the cent—over the years to—well, learn things I might not have otherwise—" He paused, stymied.

"Your studies taught you about the magic hat? What's softball?"

"Yes, there are studies that show this magic hat can help your father. There are studies that show how wearing the hat will help those folds and lines inside his head, and then he'll see again. It will be hard to make such a hat, though, under these, uh, conditions."

"Can you do it?" I wanted to know this, and Old Dee wanted to tell me, but I still wanted to know about softball, too. We never did get around to that one.

"I can try."

"Can I help you?"

"Surely," he said. "First thing we do, we build a generator."

"A generator."

"Yes. That's going to be hard. I have some books I'll need to look at. Let's get started." Then he stopped and took my hands in his. "Keera, this may not work. And even if it does, your father's eyesight will probably never be the perfect thing it once was. Especially not after all these years of living with his condition."

"But he'll see better?"

"I think so. If it works."

"Will he be able to see me?"

"Yes."

"Will he be able to see my mother's face?"

"Yes."

"Let's do it," I said.

We worked hard. We visited the blacksmith in the village just beyond Old Dee's cottage, and we gave him a picture Old Dee had drawn of some of the things we needed. A metal band. And a lot of long thin metal things that looked like the fibers of the ropes my mother and I had woven, when we worked long ago with some salt-makers.

The blacksmith was used to Old Dee.

"I can do'ee, sir," he said, pulling his forelock. "I'll send down to the bloomery today, and then we'll make'ee." He showed how he'd draw out the metal into long strands from the forged steel. "We turn them into rings for the mail, sir, but no reason we can't leave them long for 'ee."

"Good man," said Old Dee, clapping him on the shoulder.

All didn't go smoothly, all of the time. Some of the long steel fibers broke and had to be re-done. There were other problems.

"I wish we had some rubber," Old Dee fretted one time. "Or nylon."

"What are those?" I asked him.

He didn't answer, just sat thinking. "Silk will have to do," he said at last. He sent his factor into the city with a whole bag of gold to buy enough silk for the magic hat. I don't know where he got all that gold.

My job was the easy part. He explained to me how to build a small wooden box. Then he sent me to the smith for an especially long nail. We drove the nail across the mouth of the box and a little way down from the top.

"You know what we need?" he said another time.

"What?"

"These steel wires may work for the hat, but to generate the electricity, I think we'll need copper wires."

"What's electricity?" I said.

"You know when there's lightning in the sky? That's electricity," he said. "Or when it's cold, and you stroke Grimalkin, and then you put your hand on someone else, and there's a spark. That's electricity."

I nodded. I couldn't imagine what it had to do with the magic hat. But I did know about copper.

"On the cliffs near where my grandfather had his estate, there are copper mines," I told Old Dee. "They've been there since the days of the Old Ones."

"Really?" he said. "I didn't know there was ever any copper mining on the Fire Isle."

I looked at him as if he'd gone soft in the head. Then I realized. "No, Old Dee, on the Sceptered Isle. I see what you thought. You thought I was speaking of my Grandfather Fylkir. My real grandfather. He's the one who lives on the Fire Isle. But I'm talking about my true grandfather, Drustan. He lived on the Sceptered Isle, and that's where the copper mines are." It took me a while to get Old Dee to see the difference between real and true. You saw it right away, Companion, when I explained it to you. Didn't you?

"Hmm," he said. The next morning, he told us he was going on a journey to the port city, and he'd be back in a few days. We waved to him from the door of the cottage.

"Isn't Old Dee too old to go off walking to the city like that?" I asked Gudrun.

"He's very old, that he is. But sturdy. I wouldn't worry about him, mistress," said Gudrun. "He's been around a long time."

When Old Dee returned, he carried coiled up strands of metal fibers, but they were copper, not iron.

"Jewelers work with these," I told him.

"That they do. We'll use them for a different purpose." He had me wind the strands around and around the wooden box I'd made.

"Looks good," he said when we'd done that. We had set the copper-wound box on the table in the kitchen and were sitting there admiring it. Every so often, Gudrun would sidle in, shake her head at us, and sidle back out.

"We need something important now," he said. "I have the things I need in my box of magical treasures."

He went to his study and came back with two rocks. "These are lodestones. Magnets. Nobody knows about them here, but I do." He showed me how they worked. How iron filings flew to them and stuck to them. He showed me a needle made of this metal and how, if we floated it in one of Gudrun's wooden bowls filled with water, it would always point north.

First, we chipped at the lodestones until we had made two rough-looking bars. Now we placed them inside the copper-wrapped box and fastened them to the nail with a glue Old Dee had gotten from the knacker down the road.

"If you turn the nail really fast," he told me when we were done, "we'll get a current."

"A sea current?" I was confused.

"A current of electricity."

We tried it. Nothing much happened. The wires got warm. That's about it.

"Damn," said Old Dee. He said that sometimes. I think it means something like *Dark Ones take it.* I thought at first he must have come from the sliver of land belonging to the Eastern Baronies, where my father's mother came from, simply because his name is John. Now, though, because of his strange way of speaking, I'm thinking he must come from some place I don't know about. Some very strange land, maybe very far away from here.

"We need to insulate this wire, and I don't know how we're going to do it," he said.

For a long time after that, he looked down-hearted, and I felt my own heart sink. "We can't do this, can we?" I said.

"No insulation. The magnets are too weak. And . . . and other things. But you know—" He suddenly brightened. "—we can use scraps of silk from the hat to make little silk sleeves for the copper wire. That will insulate them nicely. How are you at needlework?"

"Bad," I told him.

"Gudrun can help you." I looked up to find Gudrun scowling in at us from the doorway.

"Not very good-quality steel, though," he told me, looking down-hearted again. He sat for a moment silently. "I don't think we should hold our breath."

I experimented with holding my breath.

He did make the magic hat. It looked very strange. It was made of silk, made to fit close around my father's head, like a leathern helmet. There was a steel band stretching across the top of the opening for my father's face, and a lot of the steel wires stuck out all over.

I couldn't help it. I laughed when I saw it.

Old Dee laughed too. But then he stopped. "We need a more reliable power source," he said. "We don't need a very strong current," he mused to himself. "But we do need one."

"I had powers once. But the farwydd took them away from me."

"Oh? And what powers were those?"

"I could read people's minds."

"And now you can't."

I shook my head no. "The farwydd said to me, *The Children help those who help themselves*," I told him. I couldn't keep the bitterness out of my voice. Then after a minute I said, "Old Dee, you'll think of a way. I'm sure of it."

Old Dee sat looking down at our box and running his hands through his pointed beard. "Why are you sure of that?" he asked in a subdued voice. "I myself think I'm a failure."

In the past, I would have known for a certainty whether we'd ever succeed. But now, I was just trying to make him—and myself—feel better, and both of us knew it.

"Here, child," he said, and he dropped the magic needle, the little sliver of metal that always points north, in my palm. "At least keep that as a memento of our very good effort."

"Maybe it's time I get started on my other project," I told him, trying to put a good light on it.

"Killing Caedon."

"Yes."

"Keera, listen to me. You say you'll just walk up to this king and kill him, right?"

Old Dee did have a strange way of talking.

"Yes," I said.

"Think about that for a moment, please. Everyone hates Caedon. Everyone who has any sense. He's heavily guarded. You think you'll walk right up to him and what? Stab him?"

"Yes. I have a knife. It was my mother's. She kept it in a leather sheath strapped to her leg, hidden under her skirts."

"I see," he said. "Does she know you have it?"

I gave a guilty start. "By now, I suppose she does."

"You suppose right. And how do you think she's feeling about that, just now? These violent people," he said. He muttered that last thing under his breath, but I heard it.

"She's feeling bad."

"Damn right she's feeling bad. That's because she probably knows what you're up to, and she probably knows what will happen to you if you try this out on Caedon."

As I say, Old Dee had a strange way of speaking. Most of the time, he sounded like everyone else.

But in moments of agitation, like this moment, he sounded really strange. I don't know how to describe it.

"Okay. Again. Caedon. Heavily guarded. You walk up to him with your knife. How close to him do you think you'll get?"

I began to cry. If I were my mother, I could stand at a distance and throw that knife at him, and hit him, and kill him. But I wasn't my mother, and I knew I didn't have the skill. Also, Old Dee was getting stranger and stranger. That disturbed me. What did he mean, *Oh Kay*. Who was Kay?

"I'm Keera. Not Kay."

Old Dee started to laugh, and then he couldn't stop. I didn't think it was funny.

"Need to leave this place. Need to move on," he said, when he could breathe again. "First things first, Keera. Let's go back to my question. Really. How do you plan to get close enough to Caedon to kill him?"

"I can sneak close enough."

"How."

"My father could do it. He's a trained assassin."

"Let me get this straight. Your father the trained assassin got caught by this Caedon, and tortured and nearly killed, and now he's missing an arm and an eye, and the technology in this damn place is so primitive I can't think how we're going to restore his vision even though I know perfectly well if I could just get him to the experimental ophthalmology clinic back in St. Louis, and—"

"You're scaring me, Old Dee!" I cried.

"Get a grip, John. You need to help these people," he said. He was speaking to himself. "Indirect trauma to the optic nerve," he told me. "Transcranial magnetic stimulation."

I screamed and ran out of the room.

Much later he coaxed me back down. "Let's begin our conversation again. I apologize. My magic is powerful, and sometimes it gets the better of me."

"It did, Old Dee."

"I'm sorry. Friends?"

I took his proffered hand, and he squeezed it and smiled at me.

"It's just because I'm so worried about you, and so sorry I'm having trouble figuring out how to help your father. Under these damn primitive conditions—" but he caught himself and stopped talking like that. "I think if I knew your father, I'd be even more upset. He sounds like a fine man. Your mother sounds like a fine person, too. And I'm worried about you partly because I know how worried they probably are about you. It makes me think of my own family, see. And I know how worried they are."

"You have a family?"

"A wife and two children. Boy's at SLUH. Girl's at Mary I."

I shook my head to clear it. "But you're really old."

"Yes, I am," he said. "Now let's think about your situation again. You're planning, you say now, not to walk up to Caedon and kill him, but to sneak up on Caedon and kill him."

"Yes," I said.

"Sneaking will get you close enough to kill him."

"Yes," I said.

"Let's think that one through together, shall we. Let's say you do that. Let's say you succeed. Unlikely, but let's say you do. What do you think will happen to you then?"

I looked down and wouldn't answer him.

"We both know what will happen. Caedon's men will then kill you. And what do you think that will do to your parents?"

"But suppose I sneak in while he's sleeping, and then sneak away before they realize."

"How will you figure out how to do that, if it's even possible?"

I knew he was right. Before, I would have just used my powers. Now I didn't have them.

"I can use myself as bait," I said.

"What do you mean, bait?"

"Caedon thinks he owns me. He thinks I'm his stolen property. So if I let him take me, then I can get close to him. And then, one day—"

"But do you know what kind of life—"

Before Old Dee could finish, his mug of ale began walking by itself across the planks of the table. We both watched, fascinated.

I could see you in your corner, Companion, watching too. Your eyes had become those glowing rings again.

"I love this place," said Old Dee. "It's on the rift between two tectonic plates. It's got more seismic activity per square mile than just about any other place on the planet. Why, just the other day, I was reading—"

"You're starting to do that thing again, Old Dee," I said, feeling my voice get quavery.

"I just mean, oh look, we're having an earthquake. And here on the Fire Isle, they are very frequent."

I understood now. I sat back with relief. His magic books have given him some strange magic words, and I just have to realize, he's so used to reading them all day that he starts speaking in them without meaning to.

"A very small earthquake. You may have noticed, they happen all the time out here," he went on. He really did look very happy about the earthquake.

"I've noticed."

"And there are volcanoes." At my look, he added, "Mountains of fire."

"Yes, my farwydd's portal is inside one of those."

"It is, is it."

"I've been there."

He looked skeptical.

"I have."

"Okay."

There was that exhortation to Kay again. "Keera," I reminded him.

"Sorry. Keera."

"I can't see why you keep forgetting my name like this. I've been in your house for an entire season."

"You don't understand. Okay. That's just an expression. It's not about anyone named Kay. It means all right. Sure. Yeppers."

"Oh," I said. Now I understood. "Okay!" I said.

We beamed at each other. "Very well, then. We were speaking about your using yourself as bait, and what that would likely mean Caedon will do to you, when he has you in his grip. I've heard some things about the man. They aren't pretty."

A general rumble filled the room, and the table and benches started to slide around. Coals from the fire leapt out beyond the hearthstones onto the floor. Gudrun rushed in to sweep them up before they could burn down the house.

When the rumbling and shaking subsided, Old Dee smiled at me reassuringly. "Big one," he said.

He threw you a keen look, Companion, over in your corner. Before I could wonder why, he was talking again. "Not as big as the one last year. That one heaved up the high road toward the city and broke it in pieces. The authorities had to send out a team of laborers with picks and mauls to repair it. That earthquake was apparently associated with a violent eruption of the nearest volcano, the one you can see from the gate-yard. I mean by that," he explained, seeing my blank look, "the mountain spouted fire and caused the earth to shake. Violently. And that tore up the road."

I was struck with a sudden thought. *"The ravenous wurm of the mountain devours the great streets of men,"* I recited.

"Huh?" said Old Dee.

"It's my riddle." I was excited now. "I thought the ravenous wurm might be some dragon that lived on the mountaintop. But now I see. It's a fire-breathing wurm. A dragon spouting fire. The mountain spouting fire. That's what the first part of my riddle means."

"Good job," said Old Dee.

He'd heard of my riddle by now. I'd quizzed him endlessly about it, thinking surely a man of his learning could explain it to me. "I get it now," he said. "It's a metaphor." Before I could respond to that, "Listen," said Old Dee. "We're at an impasse here.

I don't know how to help you with your first task, and I think it's clear to both of us you need a better plan for the second one."

I nodded, feeling a great weight settle about my heart.

"We're not giving up, though. We'll find a way."

"Do you really think so?"

"About the first problem, yes."

"You don't want me to find a solution for the second." I glared at him.

"I have to confess, you're right about that. I think you should stay far away from Caedon, and I think your parents would agree with me. Do agree with me. I think if they knew what you were thinking about doing, they'd die of fright. I think if you tried to do it and something happened to you, they'd die of grief. I'm saying to you, *if*. But I'm thinking to myself, *when*. Just being honest here, kiddo. Do you really want to do that to them? After all they've been through?"

I shook my head no. And I went into my alcove, lay down in the furs, and stared at the walls for a long time.

The next morning I dragged myself out into the kitchen. Gudrun silently handed me a bowl of warm gruel.

Old Dee descended from his study. He sat down at the table across from me. "I have to go on a journey," he said. "It may be a long one."

"Where do you have to go?"

"I serve a great queen. Her name is Elizabeth."

"That's my grandmother's name. Elsebet."

"Yes, the same name," he agreed.

"And this lady of yours is a queen? That's not allowed. Poor Queen Diera the First. My uncle Avery tried to change the law so she could be queen, but no one supported her in the end. Caedon killed her."

"Diera the First was ahead of her time. My queen is almost ahead of hers, but she is so bold and so brave that she's making it work anyway. I'm very proud of her."

"Where is her realm?"

"In a way, very close. In a way, very far from here."

"Everyone always speaks in riddles around me," I said, scowling. But I was interested. "How will you serve this queen of yours?"

"She thinks she needs the horn of a unicorn, and she thinks I can bring her one."

"I'd like to see that horn," I said.

"The problem with that horn, there aren't any unicorns."

"Of course there are. How can you be a magician and a sorcerer and think such a thing?"

"Funny. That's the exact same thing she said to me. So I have to produce one."

"They're hard to catch."

"The captain of a fishing fleet says he can get me one, so I'm heading to the port to see it and buy it from him. Then I'll have to go on to London."

"London? Do you mean Lunds-fort? But that's not far. It's on the edge of the Sceptered Isle mainland, the part that belongs to the Eastern Baronies. True, it's a bit far, but you make it sound like it will take you years to get there and back. Why is this queen of yours in Lunds-fort?"

"That's her capital—uhh. She's there on a visit."

"When will you be back?"

"I'm not sure," he said.

"You're just leaving me, aren't you? My tasks are too hard, and you're giving up."

"You know how I feel about the second task, but I promise I'm not giving up on the first. Here's what I want you to do. I want you to go back to your parents and wait for me there. Will you do that?"

I looked down at my toes and then back up at him. Going home. Going home with my tasks undone. That was a hard one for me to think about.

He waited.

I heaved a great sigh. "Yes, Old Dee, I promise."

"Good. Gudrun has a bag of gold for you so you can buy your passage."

"You've been thinking all along you were going to just send me home," I accused.

"You know, Keera. Going home. It's the right thing to do, isn't it? Think hard and answer me."

I thought hard. And you, Companion, just stay out of this. I'm perfectly capable of thinking this through on my own.

"Yes, I agree. It's the right thing to do, and I'll do it, Old Dee," I said, getting teary. "But you promise you'll come back? You promise you'll find me and help my father?"

"I promise," said Old Dee. "I'd like to meet your father. I'd like to examine him. I'll bring the magic hat, just in case. And in London. . .er, Lunds-fort, I may be able to find better materials." Then he said, as if to himself, "How far along will we be, by then? Anything's better than this, I suppose."

He stopped and stared at his hands for a moment. "I guess things could be worse," he said to himself after a while. "I could have gone back to the Neolithic."

I tried to ignore this, more of his disturbing muttering cant. "Promise that's what you're doing? And not just leaving me?"

"I'd never leave you. You're the best apprentice I've ever had. The things I can teach you. . ."

"Very well. I believe you. I'll do this. And you'll come as soon as your queen releases you. As soon as you've found the unicorn horn and have brought it to her?"

"I promise," he said. He stood up and reached for the cloak Gudrun was already holding out to him. "I want you to promise me something in return."

"Yes, master. Anything."

"Promise me to think about this. Ready?"

"Yes, master." I stood up and faced him.

He fixed me with his intense eye. "There is a small kind of whale. It's called the narwhal. Repeat that."

"Narwhal."

"It has a long protuberance at the end of its snout, a horny protuberance."

"What's a protuberance?"

"Just say it. Horny protuberance."

"Horny protuberance."

"People take this protuberance, which looks a lot like a horn but is really just a long helical tooth or tusk, and they sell it. They pretend it is a unicorn's horn."

"They do not!"

"They do. The world is full of shifty people, Keera," he told me. "The shifty and the gullible. The shifty prey on the gullible and somehow, don't ask me how or why, the gullible need the shifty. Don't be either one."

He whisked out the door before I could cry after him.

I went to the door to look. It's as if he stepped through some magic portal. He was gone.

Bait

Once I had bid Gudrun good bye and had received from her the small bag of gold Old Dee had left for me, I began the long tedious walk to the port city myself to buy my passage home. I had a funny feeling I wouldn't come across Old Dee on the road. I had a funny feeling his magic powers had allowed him to speed ahead to buy his unicorn horn—his narwhal tooth, I corrected myself—and then on to Lunds-fort.

I was alone again.

Oh. Right. Not alone. You're always there, Companion. But you've gone so quiet I barely notice you. All this time, you've crouched in your corner.

We've talked about you from time to time, Old Dee and I. I expect you've overheard us. Old Dee is very interested in what type of creature you might be, but I don't know why we can't just call you a woman. You look like a woman, talk like a woman, act like a woman. You have only this one strange characteristic of being invisible to everyone but me and Old Dee. I wonder about Gudrun sometimes, though. She might actually be able to see you but not want to say so. And Grimalkin definitely knows you're there.

Old Dee thinks maybe you live on a different plane from the rest of us, and for some reason, he and I can peer through the thinned veil between the planes and see you. By that reasoning, I can understand why Old Dee can see you. He's a powerful galdrmaster, sorcerer, and neurologist. He knows all the most efficacious spells. Even purson. Even metton. Even transcranial electromagnetic stimulation. Even erex. Arex. Rymex.

I'm very proud of myself for getting those spells right. They're difficult on the tongue, but I have been practicing.

And I suppose I do know why I see you. The farwydd assigned you to me as companion. Otherwise, I'm sure I wouldn't be able to.

As we walk along, I find myself humming and then singing.

Come all you mothers, listen well to me!
Come to catch your elf child, elf child, elf child,
Chase your naughty elf child

underneath the sea.

Elf child. . .elf child. . . .

What comes after that? I don't remember.

What? What?

You're right, Companion. I admit it. I grew up singing, because my mother was always singing, but I'm no singer. Not like her. Not even like a sort of good singer. In fact, I'm a downright bad singer, like my father. No need to rub it in. It's her power, not mine. But sometimes my mother's songs rise up in me, and I sing them anyway.

Well, here we are on the last hill before the city. I'm ready to go home. I feel bad that I didn't get my two tasks done. I feel ashamed of what I've put my parents through. I know if I just wait here long enough, Caedon will come within my reach. But I've promised Old Dee not to try to get to him, so there goes my second task. I've made peace with that. Sort of. And I do have hope for my first task. I believe Old Dee. I really believe he'll come back to help my father. I believe he'll at least try.

I stopped and shaded my eyes. I had come to a fork in the road. Two lanes lay before me, both wending down the hill, both equally crooked. I tried to think back to the day we'd come up the hill to head for the market town. Which lane had brought us up from the port city?

I see you don't remember, either, Companion. Fat lot of good you are.

In the past, my powers would have let me know which lane to take.

Oh, sure. Go ahead and gloat. It's all very well for you to see this as a lesson to me not to use my powers as a crutch. That doesn't help us right now, though, does it?

Chase your naughty elf child, elf child, elf child...

As I stood hesitating between the lane on the right and the lane on the left, I heard a clanking of harness behind us.

underneath the sea...

Good. I'd ask directions.

It was a contingent of the beadle's men of the town. Even better. They were sure to know the right way to the port.

I waited at the roadside as the marching men and their creaking wagon drew abreast of me. Then I stepped out into the road.

Chase your little elf-child, underneath the sea...

"Sir! Good sir!" I called up to the man on the wagon seat driving their ox.

The man on the wagon seat glanced down at me. His eyes widened and he made a whoaing noise to his ox. "Cap'n," he called to the man marching at the head of the contingent.

The man, their captain, swiveled his head around.

"This the one, cap'n?" The man on the wagon box indicated me with a jut of his jaw.

"By the Lady Goddess!" said this captain. His face lit up in a glad smile.

I stared back at him, puzzled.

"Take her, lads," he told his men.

Two of them grabbed me under the armpits and began dragging me, squawking with indignation, toward the wagon. A third swung the door of it open. The two who had me then heaved me inside its dark, smelly interior and slammed the door. I heard the sound of a bar rammed home.

I had been too startled to think of running until now, when it was too late.

From the inside I heard the man on the wagon seat cluck to his ox, and we went lurching down the hill. I was tossed from wall to wall inside the wagon. I yelled and hammered with my fists on its interior, but of course that did no good. I even heaved myself against the door. It held tight.

"Damn," I said, conjuring up one of Old Dee's strongest, strangest oaths. Then I tried out one of his others, probably the strangest of all. "Jesus, Mary, and Joseph," I shouted. These appeared to be words of great power. Nothing happened. The door of the wagon did not fly open to release me. I may have been saying it with the emphasis on the wrong syllables.

So I sank down on the floor of the wagon and tried to brace myself against the walls.

Look at you, Companion. What are you doing up there on the ceiling of the wagon? *Holy moly* (actually, I already know that moly is an herb of great power, although I've never seen it), *you make me so angry I could chew nails.*

Chewing nails. I knew what a nail was, of course. I'd never thought about chewing them before I met Old Dee. But Old Dee was right. It's a very satisfying thing to think, when you're extremely angry.

I tried again. *Holy guacamole.*

Nothing. I slumped back down into the bottom of the wagon and let it jolt me every time it hit a rock, and I beat my fist against the floor of it.

At the bottom of the hill, the rude men who had grabbed me opened the door to the wagon and disgorged me, blinking, into bright sunlight. They hustled me inside a building, the beadle's hall, I suppose, and threw me into a cell and locked the door. At least this new dark, smelly place wasn't moving. Just the same, I went over to the corner and vomited up my breakfast.

Then I sank back into the fetid straw to wait for whatever it is these people wanted to do to me, and to find out why.

Later in the day, I heard footsteps. I moved to a corner of the cell (not the corner with the puddle of vomit) and assumed a defensive posture.

The door creaked open.

Oh, man. (One of Old Dee's milder oaths.) It was Uncle Stefan.

He looked older, thinner, and meaner than the last time I'd seen him, but I knew right away it was he.

"Thank you, captain," he said over his shoulder. He crooked a finger at me. "Come out of there, Keera. You're going with me."

I followed him disconsolately out of the beadle's hall. I could see no point in trying to run.

At least Uncle Stefan's wagon was open to the sun and air, and he let me sit up on the wagon seat with him.

"You smell very bad," he told me as we rode along.

I didn't reply.

When we got to Grandfather Fylkir's Fire Isle estate, an imposing turf building much larger and grander than his manor in the Western Isle, he handed me off to Mistress Berit.

She looked older, fatter, and meaner than the last time I'd seen her, but I knew right away it was she.

She exclaimed over me in disgust and led me to the *badstu*, where the delicious steam and heat scoured me clean.

Neither Uncle Stefan nor Mistress Berit remarked on you, Companion. I suppose that must mean that they, like everyone else, can't see you. Almost everyone else.

Did you enjoy the badstu? It was good, wasn't it?

Now Mistress Berit came into my room and set to work on me. She combed me and brushed me. She didn't tousle. Mistress Berit is not a tousler, I'll give her that much. She pulled a new and beautiful linen underdress over my head, and then a kirtle with rich tabard-woven bindings about the neck and wrists. She settled a short veil over my hair and held it in place with a circlet of beaten gold.

"Like a queen," I said.

She just grunted. Then she said, "Master thinks he's a king. That way." She nodded in the direction of the door. At least she wasn't going to lead me by the hand into the presence of Grandfather Fylkir, as if I were a little girl.

The door led to a room, which led to another room, which led to the great hall of Grandfather Fylkir's estate. I went in.

At the other end, seated in an enormous carved wooden chair that dwarfed him, his chin bent down almost to his chest, crouched my grandfather. He had shrunk. He looked extremely old and frail.

When I got closer, though, I saw his eyes were as mean and shrewd as ever. And his voice.

"Granddaughter. Home at last."

Old Dee's phrase *make a quick buck* came to mind.

"As you see, Grandfather," I said. "Planning to sell me for a few bags of gold?"

"A disobedient woman like you, maybe you're not worth it," he said.

That was a new thought. I hadn't regarded myself as a woman. Just a girl. But I supposed I was nearly a woman, at that.

"Granddaughter, I have great influence now, and I expect you to behave in a way that will bring credit to me, not shame."

"Yet you're the one, I believe, who intended to sell me to Caedon as a concubine. Not a wife. A concubine." I felt my blood rising. "At age five."

"That's as may be," he said, making a dismissive gesture with his hand. "It's a new day now."

"I want to go home to my parents."

"What are you doing in my realm, then?"

"Your realm," I said. "King Haakon Hardaxe wants to grab it, you know."

"Change drives the world, Granddaughter. He does now, but what about tomorrow?"

"I thought you and King Haakon were allies. He sent an emissary to my parents. He wanted them to join his alliance, too. He wanted you and my parents to make peace with one another."

Grandfather Fylkir cackled at this. "Looks like your parents didn't fall into that trap."

"It was a trap?" I was amazed by this. I knew why my parents wanted nothing to do with it, but they had believed Haakon to be an honorable man.

"Not that king's trap," said Grandfather Fylkir.

Your trap, I filled in silently.

"But we're not here to talk about your parents, or politics. We're here to talk about your duty," he continued.

"I have a duty to my mother and father, not to you," I said.

"You do have a duty to me. You must produce an heir to reign after me."

I overlooked the word "reign." I saw I could talk until I was blue in the face about his unrealistic ideas about himself, but he'd pay me no heed.

"Why can't Uncle Stefan do that?" I felt that was a reasonable question to ask. I also remembered some scheme they had had, Grandfather and Uncle Stefan, to get Grandfather another wife. That scheme must have fallen through.

"Ask him," said Grandfather Fylkir, shooting his son a grumpy look. Uncle Stefan had come into the room and was standing silently by the hearthstones, watching us.

"And besides," I went on. "If I produce an heir for you, that means you'll have to marry me off to someone. And if you do, that will come to the attention of Caedon the Monstrous. And if it does, won't he demand his property back? You never returned his gold to him, did you, Grandfather. The gold from the sale of me. Caedon thinks of me as his property, not yours."

"Ah, even better," said Fylkir. "You'll be the bait. We'll draw him out. He'll come after you. Then we'll crush him."

I shivered. Where had I heard those words before? *You'll be the bait. I'll be the bait.* They'd come out of my own mouth. But I said, "Why should he bother?"

"It hurts his pride. And now that his bride is dead . . ."

"He didn't buy me to marry me," I argued.

Please stop tugging at my sleeve, Companion. I'm trying to pay attention to Grandfather here, to see what he's up to. I'll pay attention to you later.

"Things are different now."

"How?"

"You're only a silly child. A girl. You don't need to know how. I'm just warning you. I expect a certain standard of behavior from you. I'll have no more sulky girls driving their suitors away."

He means Mother, I realized.

I went over to sit down at the hearth ring by Uncle Stefan. "Can't you give him an heir, Uncle?"

"Three wives. All their babies dead. All of the wives dead," he said, poking a stick into the fire and stirring it around. "The Children don't want it. They kill every babe I sire, and then they kill the mothers."

It's back to the Children now, is it? I thought. Last time I was here, Grandfather was making everyone worship the Lady Goddess. I gave Uncle Stefan a sidelong glance. He looked tired. Sad. I felt a bit sorry for him. I felt sorrier for those poor wives, though.

"And what about Grandfather's own plans to marry again?"

Uncle Stefan looked startled. "You remember that?"

"Of course I do. I remember everything about this household."

"We felt Father didn't need to. We felt I'd be giving him many heirs. And now it's probably too late for Father."

"I'll bet you talked him out of it. Other wives, other sons. You might have had to divide your inheritance."

"You're certainly a saucy girl," said Uncle Stefan. Two red spots appeared on his cheeks. "I agree with Father. You need a husband to teach you some manners."

"What are you talking about over there," Grandfather Fylkir called to us irritably.

"Just the need for Keera to mind her manners and become an obedient granddaughter," Stefan said. He got up and stalked out of the room.

"Go back to Mistress Berit, now," Grandfather told me. "You tire me."

I do have that effect on people, don't I? You don't need to answer that, Companion.

I dropped Grandfather a curtsey and went off to my own room then. But I was already scheming about how I'd get away.

I certainly didn't plan to sit there passively and let him sell me off, the. . . . the. . . . a phrase Old Dee had used once came to mind. *. . . the old coot.*

As I walked the grounds of the estate, I mentally evaluated all the many ways I could slip away. I mentally reviewed all the times in my childhood when Mother and I went on the run. No use putting it off. I'd do it that very night.

For one thing, I had promised Old Dee to return to my parents. For another, I needed to let someone know—the Lady Jehanne, for example—about Grandfather's double-dealing.

But then my steps began to slow, and I began to think. Task two. Kill Caedon. *And how do you plan to do that, child?* The words of Old Dee. *I'll make myself the bait.*

Here the means to make myself the bait had dropped, as it were, right into my lap. All I'd have to do is marry someone, and I wouldn't even have to go out hunting for this someone. Grandfather would find him. That would turn me into the bait. Then all I'd have to do after that is wait for Caedon to snap it up.

Quit plucking at me like that, Companion. I've told you how much I hate it. So much plucking.

I rushed back to my room, planning to turn myself into the perfect, perfectly obedient granddaughter.

Then a big distraction destroyed me completely.

You, Companion. You are not to laugh. You are not to snigger.

I was removing my garments, getting ready for bed, when I let out a shriek.

Mistress Berit came running.

"I'm dying!" I cried to her.

She stopped and stared.

"See, blood! I'm bleeding! I'm bleeding to death!"

Mistress Berit threw her apron over her head and began to shake.

I thought it was out of fear for me. Then I saw she was laughing.

I shrieked again.

"Child. Child. Lady Keera. Forgive me. I am so happy. You are a woman. Lord Fylkir will be overjoyed, that he will," said Mistress Berit. She ran from the room, leaving me outraged and still frightened and beginning to feel silly, all at the same time.

In a short while she came back into the room and helped me clean myself up. Then she sat me down and explained some things to me.

"Why didn't my mother tell me about this?" I said. I knew my voice was sullen.

"Didn't you run away, Lady Keera? Maybe she was planning to and never got the chance."

I started to cry then. I felt a perfect fopdoodle. Over the next few days I felt, variously, cheerful, fearful, weepy, angry, stupid, and resentful. Mistress Berit told me every woman went through such feelings at such times.

I didn't like that.

Mistress Berit was really very kind to me just then. Still, I couldn't help remembering the moment, when I was a tiny child, that she had snatched me from my mother's arms. I'll never forgive her for that.

No, really, Companion. I do remember things from my early childhood. The farwydd may have removed my powers, but at least she didn't remove my memories. I expect if she had thought about doing so, she'd have had to remove one of my three memories of my firebird. She doesn't want that. She wants me to connect with my firebird. I know, because that's almost the only part of her riddle I've deciphered. Oh, yes. Right. The first lines, too. Thanks for reminding me.

Grandfather Fylkir was now wreathed in smiles whenever he glanced my way at the big table during the evening meal. I was required to be at board every evening. Even Uncle Stefan looked a little more kindly on me. A little wistful, even.

In fact, everyone on the estate appeared to be rejoicing. *They all know my private business*, I fumed to myself. *And they also know what a sillyhead I am.* That didn't set well with me. It didn't seem to sink me in their estimation, though. The bondservants passed me in the hall with smiles. The carls and their wives called out jocular, friendly remarks to me. If we happened to meet on the paths in the pleached garden, they'd reach out and, if I didn't step back quickly enough, they'd tousle. They would.

After that, the placing of me on the marriage market proceeded apace.

I endured dinner after banquet after dinner during which men of all types looked me over like a prize cow in the market square.

Grandfather Fylkir was not going to settle for just any old mate for me. The lucky man had to be strategically important to Grandfather's interests. What is it with all these old grouchy men seeking a crown?

But you know, Companion, I was thinking hard about what had happened to my parents. Not just the horrors they had endured recently. What they'd been through in their youth, and why it had happened to them. All the bloody doings when King Ranulf died. I imagined the day when Grandfather Fylkir died. He only looked like he'd live forever. One day, he'd die. I imagined myself with a husband and baby. I imagined Stefan, realizing he'd been passed over for the throne, or the estate, or the manor, or the farm, or whatever it happened to be he'd be passed over for. I imagined what would come of that.

Part of me urgently wanted to communicate something to my grandfather like, *Better find me a strong man, Grandfather. He and I are going to need to fight for that baby's rights.*

But then I'd shake myself, and I'd think, *Keera, you're moving right into Grandfather's fantasies. That's not what will happen at all. Bait, remember? There will be no strong husband. There will be no baby. Only Caedon, lured into action. Caedon, nearer the point of my knife.*

I'd shake myself, and I'd smile, and I'd think, *That's fine, then. I don't need any strong husband. I just need myself.*

You. What are you looking at? Oh, it's a man's world? Oh, a lone woman doesn't stand a chance? Oh, remember what happened to Diera the First? I can take care of myself, Companion. Just watch me.

CHAPTER SEVEN

Moneybags

Grandfather Fylkir had narrowed my suitors down to three.

There was a rich old man in the Ice-realm, richer than King Haakon. He'd make an excellent ally and moneybags, once Grandfather had Haakon where he wanted him.

I know, Companion. I know. This was Grandfather's fantasy, not mine. He was acting just as short-sighted as ever. But anyway, that was suitor number one.

There was a stout warrior lord from the Eastern Baronies, suitor number two. With him by his side, Grandfather Fylkir thought he could catch Caedon between the pincers of two iron weapons of war, himself and this warrior lord, and crush him.

There was his own vassal here in the Fire Isle, for third. This man, too, was very wealthy, and while Grandfather wouldn't realize the same strategic advantages from alliance with him as he might if he chose one of the other two for me, Grandfather did know he could trust the man. That was worth a lot.

Each of these three men had sent me rich gifts. Each was packed into a beautifully carved, beautifully decorated chest. Grandfather Fylkir had them on display in the great hall of the estate, and a stout guard by each.

From time to time, I'd wander into the great hall and lift the lids of these coffers to gaze inside. Today was one of those times.

The guards smiled at me when I entered. No one else was about. It was the dead time between the noon meal and the evening meal.

I went up to the chest of the rich man from the Ice-realm and lifted the lid. It was filled to the top with gold. I closed the lid and moved to the chest from the lord of the Eastern Baronies. I lifted that lid. This man's chest was filled with beautifully chased swords, beautifully painted shields depicting marvelous beasts, and many other weapons of war. It was the biggest of the three chests, because its contents were so bulky. Now I went to the third chest and lifted that lid. The Fire Isle ally's chest was filled to bursting with rich fabrics—clothing, tapestries, woven bindings, silk, embroidery, and to sweeten the deal, a nicely-plump bag of gold on top.

I wandered back out of the hall. I enjoyed looking into each chest and rummaging around. I felt like a child playing with her toys.

None of these gifts would be accepted, I knew that, because by now, surely Caedon had heard about my return to Grandfather Fylkir's control, and by now I was sure he was going to do something drastic about it.

Once Caedon had seized me away from Grandfather, poor Grandfather would have to send all these rich gifts back.

I imagined all the ways this would happen. It occupied most of the long days of waiting.

I know. I know. You don't have to keep reminding me, Companion. *It's a dangerous game you're playing, foolish Keera. You don't know. You don't realize.*

How many times have you whispered this in my ear? If this is why the farwydd made you my companion, I can't imagine what she hoped I'd get from the arrangement.

I don't want to hear any more of your doleful warnings. Stop.

And yes, I'm leaving one thing out. But it's useless to think about, so why would I? It's not part of the plan.

There were other suitors, but one in particular, and he was persistent. Grandfather kept sending him away, and he kept reappearing at our table. A young man. I don't think he had much to offer Grandfather. Just the assurance that he'd love me and take care of me forever.

Privately Grandfather said *pish*, and *tush*. To his face, Grandfather was polite. He might need all the allies he could get, if Caedon invaded, or Haakon, and this man was from the Fire Isle. He lived on a modest piece of land to the west, on an island a short distance out to sea.

"Nothing out there but a lot of birds," said Grandfather to Stefan. They both laughed. "But the lad has a strong arm, he can muster his men if I call, and even though he's young, he does command a fleet of longboats, so I'll not drive him from my board."

They laughed at this young man behind his back, but when the young man and I spoke at table, I laughed not at but with him. He set himself to amuse and charm me. He did succeed.

He was pleasant to look at as well.

His hair, held back by a beautifully worked sea-green leather thong, was dark and combed just to his shoulders, which were very broad. He had a twinkle in his gray eyes that never failed to capture me. He was always maneuvering to sit beside me at table. Usually, Grandfather Fylkir could send a bondservant to tactfully forestall him, but not always.

Careful, Keera, I told myself. This man was not part of Grandfather's plan, and I didn't care about that. But he wasn't part of my plan, either, and that's what mattered.

During the latest dinner, this charming young man had managed to sit to my left. Now he told me a bit about himself. He told me his name was Gwyl. He said he had been born in the Eastern Baronies, although now he lived on an island in the territories belonging to the Fire Isle. He told me he'd spent a few years living in the Sceptered Isle. His mother was from there, he said.

"My parents came from there," I told him.

"And do your parents still live there?" he asked me, taking the mead jug from the manservant and politely pouring some into my cup.

"No, they left long ago. I wasn't born there. I was born on the Western Isle."

"How interesting. You must have been born during the height of the civil war between Audemar and Caedon."

"Yes, that's true," I told him.

"A dangerous time. The Western Isle is quite a voyage from here," he said. "You must miss your parents sorely."

"They live closer than that now," I said, taking a bite of meat from my trencher to hide my sadness. "But still too far away. I do miss them."

"Perhaps they'll visit soon."

"I doubt that," I said. Then I glanced over at him. He was giving me a shrewd look I couldn't quite fathom. How much did he know about my parents, I wondered.

Keep out of this, Companion. You don't know either.

Oh, you have your suspicions? Well, la-di-da.

Grandfather Fylkir didn't like it when I paid too much attention to this friendly fellow, and just now I needed to keep on Grandfather's good side. So then I turned to my neighbor on my right at table and talked to him instead.

This man was another of my most persistent suitors, even though he, too, had no chance. He was ancient, hollow eyed. Woebegone. His name was Oisin.

As we were rising to go, though, the young man, the one to my left, leaned over to me and said in my ear, very quietly, "Lady

Keera, if you ever need a friend, you can call on me, and I will come." His name, and the few pieces of information he'd revealed about himself, were really all I knew about him.

I looked up at him, startled, and he flashed me a roguish smile that lit up his whole face. "I've met you before, you know."

Now my hand flew to my mouth.

"Some fellows and I were pulling you out of a barrel."

Then the crowds of guests parted us, leaving me astounded in the middle of the hall.

I made my way to my room and sat down on the bedstead, staring into nothing. My mind flew back to that terrible sea-voyage, four days stowed away in a barrel.

No, Companion. Not the time I stowed away in a barrel on the Lady Jehanne's ship. That was easy. By then, I knew what I was doing. I was an old hand by then at stowing away in a barrel.

No, I mean the other time. The dangerous time. By the end of that voyage, I wasn't sure if I were alive or dead. But I'd had to do it. Otherwise, my mother and father might never have been reunited.

How is it this man, this Gwyl, was there? I asked myself. Although I hadn't known it at the time, I'd stowed away on my father's ship, and this man, Gwyl, must have been one of the mariners.

And why is he here now? I asked myself. Only one explanation made sense. Now the tears poured down my cheeks. My parents knew where I was, and they were protecting me. *Call on me if you need a friend,* he'd said. Calling on Gwyl for help, though. How in the Nine Spheres was I supposed to do that? Yet his kindness, however impractical, touched me deeply.

The next morning I was breaking my fast underneath a birch tree in the pleached garden. Servants had brought me bread and cheese. That's all I wanted. I had cried for homesickness all night, and I was pale and tired.

Grandfather Fylkir and Stefan were walking in the garden, too. They stopped by me, where I sat on a little bench.

"Granddaughter, even your suitors with the hopeless cases are sending you gifts. One arrived this morning from that young fellow who keeps intruding himself on you," said Fylkir.

I gave a guilty start.

Grandfather didn't appear to notice. "It's in the mews, if you care to take a look. No harm in it. The man sent over his bond-servant as well." Grandfather exchanged a smile with Stefan. "The poor besotted fool," he said to Stefan. They laughed and walked on.

As soon as they'd gone, curiosity got the better of me. I headed for the mews behind the stables at the edge of the estate.

Grandfather Fylkir's falconer nodded to me as I stepped into the long, shadowy building. Grandfather's falcons and hawks were all chained to their perches along one wall. I felt sorry for the birds. Grandfather hardly ever went out hawking now, and Stefan didn't care for the sport. Those birds must be getting bored and restless.

"Lady Keera, this boy has been sent to you as a gift," said the falconer, nodding in the direction of a half-grown boy standing by one of the perches.

The boy stepped forward and pulled his forelock. "I'm yours now, my lady," he said.

"What are you called, boy?" I asked him.

"Aevarr, if you please, lady," he replied.

"And who sent you to me, and why?"

"Sir Gwyl sent me," said Aevarr, confirming what I thought Grandfather Fylkir must have meant by *the poor besotted fool.* "And," Aevarr continued, "he sent me to care for she." With his thumb, he stabbed over his shoulder at the perch behind him.

I stepped around him to look.

A falcon sat on the perch. A merlin, suitable for ladies. "This is a fine gift," I told him.

"Aye, lady, and she is a lovely bird."

The merlin sat turning her head from side to side, but she was hooded in richly embroidered red leather and couldn't see me. A pang of grief pierced straight through me. *My father sits in his island aery, a noble falcon, hooded, his powers useless to him now.*

The falconer gave me a friendly wave and wandered off down the row of perches to fuss with one of the big peregrines belonging to Fylkir.

Aevarr extended his finger to my merlin's perch, and she stepped daintily onto it. He brought her down so I could see. The copper bells tied to her jesses made a musical jingling.

"Smyrill," he said. "That's what we call them, this kind of bird, over on our island."

"And what is her name?"

"Hildr, Mistress," said the boy.

The hairs on the back of my neck stood up. *Battle storm of Hildr.* That was in my riddle.

I reached out my hand to stroke her, and she blindly struck at me.

"Careful, lady. She doesn't know you yet."

"I've never been hawking," I said. I never had a chance to learn such things, as a child. Mother and I were poor folk.

"Sir Gwyl says, *Teach her*, he says to me."

"Teach me now," I demanded.

"My lady, this teaching takes time. You must learn to hawk, but you must also learn your bird. Hildr loves the ones she loves."

"Will she come to love me?" I asked.

"Yes, my lady."

"Then let's get started."

Grandfather Fylkir approved. He said every high-born lady should know falconry. He said it was a disgrace that I did not. He said, "What was your neglectful mother thinking, that she didn't teach you this skill?"

I overlooked his spiteful words. Otherwise, I might have kicked him.

But Aevarr and I got started that very day. Hildr did come to love me, and I came to love her back.

The days were dreary, waiting as Grandfather Fylkir dithered amongst my three main suitors, and as I waited for Caedon to make his move. Surely he would, wouldn't he?

I'm not asking you, Companion. Geez Louise. That was a rhetorical question. You know, the kind that doesn't need an answer. Only annoying people try to answer other people's rhetorical questions.

Privately, not for the first time, I wondered who Louise was. The next time I saw Old Dee, I made a note to myself to ask him.

But I did worry about Caedon. Suppose Caedon didn't rise to the bait? Suppose he didn't actually care? Suppose I was made to go off on the arm of some nasty old man with long hairs sprouting from his ears?

There was one thing that reassured me, though. During the first days when Aevarr trained me to fly Hildr, and trained Hildr to love me, he told me a secret.

"Mistress, I must tell you a thing."

"What is it, Aevarr?"

"Sir Gwyl told me to show you this." He reached into the pouch at his belt and pulled out a narrow strip of parchment.

I read it. "Lady Keera, Aevarr is your friend, as am I. Hildr is your friend, too. If you are ever in need or distress, write a message on the back of this and tie it to Hildr's jesses. Release her. Tell her, *Home, Hildr.* She'll bring it back to me, and then I'll come to your aid."

I was filled with relief. I'd had so many vague fears, and now I knew I had an ally. I didn't have any illusions how much help Gwyl would be able to give me, but it was a comfort knowing someone understood my predicament and cared about what happened to me.

I'd realized from his revelation at dinner, the last time he saw me, that he knew all about me. My parents must have sent him to me. At least they knew I was alive.

Now I found out more about this Gwyl from reading his message. He could write, and in a neat, flowing hand, too. And he wrote in the language of the Old Ones. He was highly educated.

I was pretty sure he and I were the only two people for leagues and leagues around who could read his message, priests of the Lady Goddess excepting. How had he learned? Who was he, really? How did he know I could read, too? He knew a lot about me, and I knew almost nothing about him.

But I doubted his plan would work.

"Try it, lady," said Aevarr, peering at the paper over my shoulder.

"You can read this?" I looked at him, startled.

"Nay, lady," he said, and grinned ear to ear. "But I know what'ee says. Master told me."

So, later on, I took quill and ink and wrote a reply. I felt oddly shaken. *The poor besotted fool*, Grandfather Fylker had said. I thought about Gwyl's gray eyes, and his smile, and his broad shoulders, and got a strange kind of shivery feeling. I thrust this feeling away. I dipped my quill in the ink and wrote out, on a thin strip of parchment similar to the one he'd sent to me, "You are so kind, Master Gwyl. I will send for you if I need you, and you have my thanks."

I stared at my work, and then I tore it up. I got a new piece of parchment and wrote out the same message, except in place of "Master Gwyl," I wrote "Sir Gwyl." After all, he was a landowner, according to Grandfather Fylkir, a landowner who commanded armsmen and a fleet of ships.

But when I squinted hard and tried to bring my mind back to that awful day when I was pulled out of a barrel, all I could remember about the men who'd hauled me out was that they were rough sailors. Could it really be true that this interesting Gwyl was both gentle lord and rough seaman? He was an enigma for certain.

I took my little slip of parchment to the mews, where Aevarr tied it to Hildr's jesses. We brought her out into the field behind the mews. A fresh breeze was blowing in off the sea, not so far away from Grandfather Fylkir's lands. Of course, no place in the Fire Isle is very far away from the sea. I gazed around me. The mountain looming behind us, the boulder-strewn thin forest on both sides, riven by deep gullies, framed Grandfather Fylkir's manor nestled in the hollow beneath. And then, before us, broad meadowlands reaching all the way to the sea.

I raised Hildr up on my gauntleted hand.

"Tell her," Aevarr said to me. "Hildr should get used to her command from your lips, lady."

I lifted the little merlin high. "Home, Hildr," I said to her. I released her jesses.

Hildr spiraled up. Turning and turning in a widening gyre, she could no longer hear me. She was a mere dot. Then she was gone.

"You think she'll really return?" I tried to keep my tone light-hearted, but suddenly I felt bereft. I turned away, pulling the padded leather gauntlet off my hand, trying to hide my expression from Aevarr. I knew tears were springing into my eyes. Suppose she didn't return. Suppose something happened to her.

A bleakness far beyond my own situation descended on me. Sometimes it seemed mere chaos had been released upon the world.

"Oh, aye, Mistress. She'll be back, Hildr will. You wait and see."

So then I shook off this strange despairing mood of mine and tried to get on with the business of the day, which meant getting myself ready for one more of Grandfather Fylkir's boring dinners. Especially boring because I knew Gwyl wouldn't be there.

Careful, Keera, I said to myself.

Two days later, when I went into the mews, I gave a glad cry and ran to Hildr's perch. She was sitting on it, consuming a mouse Aevarr had allowed her to catch for reward.

I tried not to look at the struggling poor mouse. Hildr has to eat, doesn't she?

"Here, my lady," said Aevarr, and he handed me the bit of parchment I'd sent.

I'll be ready, Gwyl had written on the back of it. That was all. I tucked the little parchment into the pouch at my waist. I tried hard not to think of Gwyl. I tried hard not to think about his gauntleted hand reaching up for Hildr, and Hildr landing on it, and Gwyl extracting the little piece of parchment with my words written on it. I tried hard not to imagine Gwyl bent over the parchment in the firelight, with his quill in his hand, reading it and turning it over and writing his words on the back of mine.

I'm a ninny, aren't I, Companion? You don't even have to say it. I know I am.

The moon waxed and waned, turned and turned again. Grandfather Fylkir's dinners grew more and more unbearable. Gwyl stayed away. Flying Hildr was the only thing that kept me from going (as Old Dee would put it) bonkers. *It's a medical term*, he'd explained to me once.

I'd raise my gauntlet to the sky and release Hildr's jesses. She'd ring up, then plummet down in her stoop, and woe to the small bird or animal she'd spotted. Or she'd move to some high perch, like a limb or a stump. One time, she even perched on the back of a sheep. That made us laugh, me and Aevarr. The sheep didn't seem to notice. It just kept munching grass.

But if Hildr hunted from a perch, she'd take off horizontally, speeding low over the ground, looking out for prey. She'd drive a flock of pipits before her, herd them, select a choice one out of the terrified cohort, tail-chase it, pounce with her talons extended, deal it a death blow with her beak, and bring it back, triumphant.

We'd reward her from her catch, just not every time. She needed to know she worked for us, not for herself. And she did understand.

I had to learn not to be so tender-hearted toward her prey. One day, though, when she caught a kingfisher, I had to go to my room in the manor house and lie down in my bedstead under the furs. I couldn't explain this very well to Aevarr.

I knew why. The kingfisher is the halcyon bird, harbinger of the Sea Child. My mother's Child. I cried for my mother all that day, almost leading Grandfather Fylkir to summon the priestess of the Fire Child to see about a cure.

"No, I'm fine, Grandfather," I said, getting out of my bed at last.

"One of her woman moods," he muttered aside to Uncle Stefan.

I ignored this. Life resumed.

But the dread day came at last, the day my marriage was decided. Grandfather Fylkir made his choice, the rich man from Haakon's Ice-realm. A chestful of gold was too much for Grandfather. Every time Grandfather lifted the lid of that particular chest, he started to drool. He actually did, and actually had to wipe it off his chin with the back of his hand.

Stefan spent a day or two trying to force him to consider the arguments of the other two suitors. I think Uncle Stefan was leaning toward our own rich vassal from the Fire Isle. I keep forgetting the man's name. That's how memorable he was. You know the man I mean, Companion. The one whose chest was filled with beautiful clothing.

In the end, Uncle Stefan threw up his hands. Grandfather's mind was made up.

Grandfather Fylkir set the day. I recall hearing my mother describe her own forced marriage, a quick, wretched exchange of vows in the dooryard. Mine would be nothing like hers. Where my wedding was concerned, Grandfather Fylkir was determined to put on a show.

He shamelessly plucked some of the fine clothing from his vassal the third suitor's chest for me to wear. That poor suitor would never see his chest of goods again, and he'd hardly be able to complain, since his allegiance was sworn to my grandfather, and Grandfather's protection was most of the reason he was so rich and successful.

When I mentioned this to Mistress Berit, she just shrugged. "It's on him," she pointed out. "You must dance with them that brung you." How does she know? "The Lady Goddess tells me so," she said. She was a Lady-liker, not that Grandfather cared a whit.

I did think it would be unnecessarily hurtful for the poor man to watch from the sidelines as I was wed in his fancy clothes to another man.

Grandfather Fylkir didn't see it that way. He dismissed my worries as womanish and silly.

Where is Caedon? I kept thinking nervously. *Why doesn't he act?*

No, I don't agree, Companion, so you may as well save your breath. Yes, he's a cruel and despicable man, but he needs to grab me. He has to. It's part of my plan. I wish you'd just cower in your corner and leave me to think this through.

And yes, I know I promised Old Dee to abandon my second task. But the fates had thrown it right in my lap, hadn't they? Old Dee and I had agreed I should take this second task off my list. Now it was on again.

Finally, the day of the wedding came. Mistress Berit dressed me in my finery and led me to the gaily painted wagon in the courtyard. The bondservants had woven flowers in and out of its wheel spokes. The day was sunny and mild, but I couldn't enjoy it.

My husband-to-be was waiting to hoist me into the wagon. I barely remembered him, because once he'd sent us his chest stuffed with gold, he hadn't thought it necessary to pay further court to me.

He smiled at me. I tried to smile back. Tufts of hairs sprouted from his ears.

We rode together to the ring of sacred stones where the Fire Child's priestess would marry us. She did. The ceremony went by in a haze. I was dumbstruck with fright. I could barely force out my responses.

Afterward, we all had a big party. I wafted through it as if I were a ghost. As if I were you, come to think of it, Companion. As if I could see everyone, but they couldn't see me. As if they and I were separated from each other by some thick, invisible barrier.

People talked to me, and their mouths moved, but their words never reached my ears. Yet I sensed I was responding, so I must have heard them, mustn't I?

Mistress Berit walked me back to my room, where I put on my traveling things. Into the pouch at my waist, I secreted a few things most precious to me. Laugh if you like, Companion. Jeer, even. Yes, I tucked in Gwyl's parchment.

Now the time came for me to sail away with my new husband to his home in the Ice-realm. There, I'd know wealth and ease and luxury. I'd see King Haakon's court, reputed to be among the most magnificent in the Twelve Realms. I tried to feel excited, but I couldn't. *At least*, I told myself, trying to comfort myself, *I'll see Fiona's sister Sorcha there. At least I'll have a friend at court. And maybe I'll be reunited with Fiona. Maybe someday she'll make the journey across the Northern Sea to visit her sister.*

You've heard me speak of Fiona, haven't you, Companion? She is my best friend in the wide world, and I miss her dreadfully.

In the gaily decorated wedding wagon, I passed the trip to the port in the same kind of daze that had afflicted me all morning long. At the docks, my new husband helped me up the planks onto the sturdy knarr that would carry us to his home.

I stood at the topmost strake of the ship, looking out to sea. I was determined not to look back toward land. I wasn't sure what I'd do if I did. Maybe throw myself into the sea and try to swim back.

Oh, hush, Companion. No more squeaking and gibbering. I can swim. My mother taught me. It's not that dangerous, and what do you know about it, anyway?

My husband stood at the upper strake beside me and squeezed my hand. "My wife, I am sure you are a frightened modest maid. You have no reason for fear, I assure you. I promise to take care of you and see that you want for nothing. I promise to cherish you and set you up in a place of honor and comfort, and get upon you many stout sons."

I tried to smile at him. He meant well. He actually did seem to be a kindly older man. The getting upon me of many stout sons did make me cringe, though. Not just the act of the getting. Also the idea it had to be stout sons. What about stout daughters? But I kept this thought to myself.

Still, it looked like my plan had failed. When I thought about my life as it stretched before me into the future, I could only see those sprouts of hair, those liver-spotted hands, those. . .that. . . whatever else he had hiding underneath his rich furs.

Don't mistake me, Companion. I'd attended many sickbeds with my mother, and many times we'd had to wash and lay out a body. I knew about men. But a man with me? That was a daunting thought. In fact, I had to go discreetly to the high curved stern and lean out beside it and throw up my breakfast, taking care not to do it into the wind.

The voyage would not take very long, my husband reassured me. He probably thought I was seasick. We'd departed at noon. Now, late in the day, we were skimming along. We'd left the land behind.

"Don't worry in the least," my husband told me. "These mariners are very skilled. They can look at the sun, at the moon and stars, and they know exactly where they are."

I looked up skeptically into the sky. It had fast clouded over, and now I saw we were sailing into a bank of mist.

"They can even tell their way by scent and sound. They know the sounds the waves make when the knarr is approaching a rock. They can smell the smells of the land."

Behind us, the kendtman, the man aboard who knew how to guide our way, called out, "Release the ravens." Another seaman stood up beside him with a cage and opened it. Three ravens came flapping out, soared up, and then away.

"You see, my wife? Those ravens know the way to land, and we'll follow them," said this old husband of mine.

I smiled up at him uncertainly. Then I looked around to make sure the cage with Hildr in it was close by. It was. My husband gave me a reassuring smile back. But then something caught his attention. He strained to see, and I strained with him.

Something in the banks of mist. Something coming out of the banks of mist. Four dark shapes.

"Longships," he whispered to himself. Then he was shouting. "Master kendtman—"

He hustled me into the very bottom of the ship, where the cargo was stowed, and appointed one of the sailors to guard me.

"Don't worry, my wife. We'll outrun them, whoever they are," he said, as he made his way to the place where the captain was vigorously gesturing.

"Good sir, please step over there with your wife," the captain was saying. Then he was bawling directions at the top of his lungs to his crew.

I huddled in the bottom of the knarr, remembering the sea fight on the voyage my mother and I had taken to the rocky island fortress of my father.

During that entire fight, I had been inside a barrel.

Yes, Companion, it was terrifying. The barrel? I'll explain later.

Anyhow, I didn't see much, then. Now I saw plenty. I cringed back while men from the longships jumped across the gap between their ships and ours, and fastened the two ships together, and fought it out with our sailors back and forth along the uneven footing of the deck and the plank attaching the two ships.

One of these pirates ran at my husband and grabbed him by the furs. I gasped. In a twinkling, two of them bundled my poor husband overboard. I rushed out of my protected spot to the ship's upper strake and gaped down at him as his furs pulled him under.

I didn't have time to scream. Someone grabbed me up under his arm and hustled me over to . . . well. To a barrel. And thrust me in.

Why is it, I thought, *that I spend every sea fight of my life in a barrel?*

There was a terrifying clatter and clamor, screaming and horrifying squishing and swatting and thwacking noises.

I expect you saw it all, Companion.

I saw almost nothing.

It's not fair.

An eerie quiet descended. I tried to climb out of the barrel then, but someone stuck his hand on the top of my head and pushed me back down.

Then I felt the swaying when a couple of them, pirates I supposed, hoisted up my barrel with me inside. I felt a sick lurching. Then a thunk, and I knew my barrel had been set back down on something solid. Some deck.

During the whole thing, I couldn't help hoping these were my father's pirates.

They weren't.

They weren't even pirates.

They were Caedon's men.

Caedon, it seems, had taken the bait after all.

Snapped Up

There's something I haven't mentioned, and you're right, I should.

It's Hildr.

Since Aevarr and Hildr were my property, of course, I had brought them along on the knarr as we sailed away from the Fire Isle. During the attack at sea, I lost track of both of them.

As the longships sped away, one of them carrying me, I could only hope Aevarr was safe on one of the others. I didn't know, though. I tried not to think about Hildr at all, especially when, as I was stuffed into my barrel, I glimpsed her cage, broken and trampled. It was too painful imagining how, tangled in her jesses, she might have been trodden underfoot, or some other horrible thing might have happened to her.

Sad, isn't it, that I mourned and fretted far more about my bird than I did over that poor old drowned husband.

The sailors let me out of the barrel once the ships were underway. Behind us, I watched the smoking knarr slowly sink.

I wrapped myself in my cloak and tried not to think too hard about what was happening to me.

I was sorry for my husband, but glad I hadn't had to live with him and have his stout sons gotten upon me. My mixed feelings about his sad demise troubled me, I must confess.

You were there for me to talk to, of course, Companion, so I wasn't terribly lonely.

The sailors didn't say much at all to me, but I realized who they were. I recognized Caedon's insignia, a golden wolf's head, on the square black sail towering above me.

Beyond feeding me, they mostly ignored me. Where could I go? I wasn't a threat.

I should be feeling triumphant. My plan had worked. Caedon had taken the bait, and now I was about to come face to face with him, something that hadn't happened to me since I was five years old. I was about to realize my opportunity to avenge my family.

Instead, a sick dread overcame me. Maybe it's your fault. Yes, you, Companion. You've planted all these bad feelings in me about my plan. You and Old Dee.

Maybe you and Old Dee have been, all along, to use one of his exotic phrases, *in cahoots.*

No, you're right. That's unfair. Old Dee is my friend.

Very well. *Okay.* I'll say it. You're my friend, Companion.

I brooded about these things for a day and more. I could tell our journey was going to take some time. The sailors rowed vigorously, but a longship isn't a knarr. It's built for quick strikes, not long-haul voyages over the open sea.

The ships stayed in convoy. I admired how the sailors accomplished that, especially in the dirty weather we'd encountered during that first day, soaking us all to the skin. Always I could see at least one of the other three ships keeping pace beside us. Once, when the weather cleared, I could see all three.

In the bad weather, our boat plunged and reared like a horse gone mad, and all I could do was cling to the kerling and hope for the best.

You were the lucky one, Companion. I saw you sitting cross-legged high on the sail's stretching pole, staring out to sea and humming to yourself. How I envied you.

Late on the second day, a small shape came flashing from the sky. I squinted up at it. Then I squealed with delight. Hildr! She plummeted in for a landing on my shoulder, and her talons bit into my skin, but I didn't even mind. She put her beak against my cheek. Her hunting jesses were trailing from her ankles.

"What's this, then?" a passing sailor said, getting a look at us.

"Just my merlin," I told him.

The man came over and reached out to grab Hildr. Instead, she flew up at his face with her talons, sending him stumbling backward.

"I'll kill that bird," he muttered, reaching for the knife at his belt.

"No!" I cried.

"We'll see what the captain has to say about it," said the man, stalking off.

I knew then I might not have much time. If only I could attach a piece of parchment to Hildr's jesses and send her winging to Gwyl. If only I could put down my plea for help with quill and ink. But I had none.

I was beginning to panic. Somehow, my plan for revenge had been driven from my mind. I started getting frightened. Then I remembered.

I felt in the pouch at my belt where I had secreted my few small treasures: the magic needle Old Dee had given me, and both parchments, the first one Gwyl had sent to me, and also the second one, the one on which I'd written my thanks, and on the back he'd written his reply.

No, hush, Companion, I hadn't kept them as love tokens. I'd kept them because. . . I don't know why I'd kept them.

I took that second one out now and looked at it. *You are so kind, Master Gwyl*, I had written. *I will send for you if I need you, and you have my thanks.*

Now quickly I tore the little parchment. I tore off the part that read, *I need you*, and I attached that to one of Hildr's jesses. I put the other bits back in my pouch.

The sailor and several other ill-looking fellows were advancing down the planks, stepping around the men sitting on their sea chests straining at their oars. I extended my hand and Hildr stepped out upon it. "Home, Hildr," I told her.

As she ringed upward, one of Caedon's men drew a bow and shot at her, but his arrow fell far short. I knew it would. Hildr was fast.

"Mistress," said the most imposing of this group of men, the captain, I supposed. "If that bird comes back, I'll wring its neck and spit it and have it for my supper."

"She won't," I told him, and settled back against the wall of the boat. I deliberately pulled up my hood and turned a disdainful shoulder away from them. After a moment, I heard their footsteps going away.

It probably won't matter, I told myself. *We're probably too far away by now for Gwyl to do anything to help me.* He probably couldn't anyway. It was just a game we were playing, to while away the time. A futile courtship where he took the role of the gallant suitor and I took the role of the lady who needed his protection. Neither of those things happened to be true. Gwyl was actually not a suitor at all, but a spy sent by my family. And I didn't need his protection. I was on the mission I'd set myself almost two full years ago. I had to remind myself of this, and drive the fear away.

But I felt much better. Hildr was alive. That was a huge relief. And now I'd released her back to Gwyl, where she'd be safe.

That captain was glad when he got me off his ship. On the third day, the miserable weather turned killer. A storm howled out of the north and just about swamped us. The captain, making his way past my usual spot, sneered at me. "Frightened, Mistress?"

"Not at all," I replied calmly. "Are you?"

"The seas won't kill me. I'm protected by this." He held up a long thin object strung about his neck on a leather thong. "It's the horn of the unicorn. No seas will get me."

"Foolish man," I said. "That's not a unicorn's horn. It's the long helical tooth or tusk of the narwhal."

His eyes widened. When he resumed his way, by grabbing onto the stays attached to the mast so he wouldn't be swept overboard, I had the satisfaction of watching him tremble.

As for you, Companion, you didn't leave your perch above the sail. Your long hair streamed out behind you. You looked almost transparent, as if you were made of water yourself. I saw more than a few of the sailors glance up to where you sat, and heard them call upon the Sea Child or the Lady Goddess, whichever they worshipped, and turn pale, and tremble as the captain had trembled.

Maybe at certain dire times ordinary people can see you, at least in glimpses.

On the fifth day the weather cleared and we could all spot a smudge of land on the horizon. As we neared it, I began to realize where I was. The Northmost Isle where the viceroy had his residence, the same isle where my mother and I had lived so comfortably in the tavern by the docks for so long.

Pretty soon, with a burst of speed, the longship's rowers brought us up into the harbor, and two of the sailors were taking my arms and hoisting me off the ship, over the shallow water at the shore and onto land. Another of the ships had come in before us. What a relief to see Aevarr on the pier. He ran to me.

"Mistress!" he called out. But the sailors thrust him aside.

"Go to the tavern called the Sun-Stone," I cried over my shoulder to him as they hustled me off. "Ask for Teasag. Tell her you know me." I hoped Teasag and her husband, the tavern owners, were still there. They had become like second grandparents to me.

But that's when I was twelve, I realized. And now I am sixteen, a woman grown. A widow, even. A widow before I was ever really made into a wife.

My captors marched me through the streets and then up the winding road to the viceroy's manor on the hill. Hope rushed into me then, just as the sunshine came flooding down on us past the storm clouds as they rolled away. The viceroy was my friend. And my best friend of all was his daughter, Fiona. They'd surely help me.

I smiled to myself. I'd been thinking perhaps I'd see Sorcha, once I got to the Ice-realm, and perhaps persuade her to send for her sister. And now here I was, against all odds, at the home of that very sister. My friend. My dearest friend in the world, Fiona. The Children do work in mysterious ways their wonders to perform.

At the manor, my captors handed me off to a guard, who took me away and locked me in a room. It wasn't a cell. Just a room with high slits of windows too small to climb out. There was a bench. I sat on it, drumming my heels with boredom.

Later on a serving woman came in with a tub so I could wash myself. After the bath, she handed me rich clothing to wear.

"Please tell the Lady Fiona that her friend Keera has come to her manor," I told the serving woman. She looked uneasily away from me and did not reply.

When I had put on the clothes she brought me, she told me to follow her, and I did. We crossed the courtyard of the manor. I looked fondly over at its well. My mother and I had had that well dug and installed, and far, far beyond it, I could make out the manor jakes.

What, Companion? You think these sites too homely for me to mention. You don't know, do you? They are very important structures, and both are dedicated to the Children. If not for them, most of the people in this place would be dead. How? I'll tell you later, sometime.

Now we made our way into the main hall of the manor. I looked around hopefully for the viceroy. He wouldn't let anyone mistreat me here.

But I didn't see him. Only one other person was in the room, a man standing before the hearthstones, leafing through a pile of parchments on a small table at his side. He looked up. I could tell by his paleness, and his eyes. It was Caedon.

The bondswoman curtseyed and backed out of the room.

Caedon and I stood staring at each other.

Now he began to smile. It was terrible to watch. His pale lips stretched wider and wider, and one side of his mouth quirked up in a cynical curl. But his eyes were fierce. "Lady Keera, how like you are to your mother in some ways. How unlike in others."

I dropped him a curtsey.

"Come closer so I can get a good look at you."

I stepped a little closer, but not very close. I looked at him warily.

"So here you are," he said to me. "Your plan worked. Now what? Are you going to kill me?"

"You know I have no knife, no weapon of any kind," I told him. "Otherwise I would." I pushed away the thought, *How does he know what my plan is?*

"Instead," he said to me, "I might kill you."

Shh, Companion. I don't think he will. Don't get so agitated. He's just trying to frighten me.

If he does, though.

Then, look away.

"And will you do that, kill me, do you think?" I asked him.

"Not yet," he said. He crossed the room to me and took me by the hand. "It's good to have my property back. I don't like that, losing what's mine. Your husband thought you were his property. Sadly, his heirs cannot charge me with breach of covenant in this matter of his contract with your grandfather, since you already have an owner. I believe the law is on my side."

"The poor man is dead," I said, ignoring his legal mysshe-masche. All his drif-draf. Or as Old Dee would put it, his mumbo jumbo.

"My sailors can be rough and unruly. A pity," said Caedon. "But you don't look to me to have gone into deep mourning for the fellow."

"I barely knew him. He seemed kindly."

"He was too old for you, my dear."

"You're old," I told him, looking up into his face, into his strange amber eyes.

"Oh, do you think so? We old men, we tend to be self-deluded. I could swear I'm as strong now as I was in my younger days, but you're probably right. I'm probably weak and doddering, and just haven't admitted it to myself yet. Do you think that's it?"

He came close to me now and seized my wrist and started bending it back.

I gasped in pain.

With his other hand, he grabbed me by the hair and twisted and pushed down, forcing me to my knees, forcing my head back.

"Do you know, I think I could break your neck with a quick jerk. Pretty easily, too."

The weather outside had picked up. The shutters of the windows in the room began to bang as if some invisible hand were madly, angrily beating at them.

Caedon ignored this, just kept forcing my head back further.

I think I whimpered. I have to tell you, I think I did.

"But instead of breaking your neck, maybe I'll—"

He didn't finish the thought.

There was a knock at the door.

He stepped back. I scrambled to my feet. The two of us stood staring at each other, breathing hard.

Then he went to the door and opened it.

"Lady Fiona," I heard him say politely. He stood aside to let her enter.

With a glad cry, I shoved past him and into the arms of my friend.

"Keera! I thought we'd never see each other again," she said. We were both crying a little.

Caedon stood frowning at us.

I turned to him with a curtsey. "This is my good friend the Lady Fiona," I told him. "We haven't seen each other in some time."

He made a silent bow to the two of us and turned on his heel.

Fiona and I listened to his footsteps ringing down the corridor away from us.

"I dislike that man," she said after it was clear he was gone.

"I hate him," I said.

"Yet he rescued you from that forced marriage. That was gallant of him."

"That's what he has told everyone?" I said.

Fiona looked hard at me.

"Oh, Fiona. He has grabbed me for himself," I said, and I began to cry.

"You loved your dead husband?" she said, her eyes wide.

"No, I didn't," I said. "It's complicated." I cried harder.

She took me by the hand and sat me down on a bench and comforted me. After I got a grip on myself, we had a long talk. I told her about my life since I'd seen her last, but there had to be so many holes in my story, so many mysteries, that I'm not sure I made much sense. She was my friend, my dearest friend. Even though she didn't understand everything, she understood I was in trouble and had been snatched away from my family. She'd never met my father, but my mother had saved her life. So she was outraged on my behalf.

After we had cried and hugged and talked, Fiona said, "It's coming on time to get ready for the evening's meal. Follow me to my room. I see they've brought you something to wear, but we'll find other things for you."

We didn't have to say it to each other. It looked like I'd be there in her family's manor for a long time.

Everything I owned had been lost at sea. Maybe even—and here I teared up a bit—Hildr. Lost to me, anyhow. At least Avarr was safe.

Fiona took me down a long winding corridor to her own room. I exclaimed in delight. I remembered it well. We had shared it as girls, when I was brought here to live as her companion.

Yes, Companion. Just like you. Well. Not exactly like. But close.

Fiona and I talked more while she and her bondsmaid dug deep into her big chest for something that would fit me. Fiona is taller than I am, although otherwise we are the same slender type. I saw she had grown up since I had seen her last, and she was probably thinking the same about me.

"Here, these should do," she said at last. She handed three or four kirtles over to the bondsmaid, who took them off to hem them up so I wouldn't trip on them.

"It's the dinner hour. Come with me, and I'll say to everyone, My friend will sit by me. That way, the awful Lord Caedon can't make you sit by him," Fiona told me. "Ugh," she corrected herself. "King Caedon."

By then, I'd explained all about how Caedon thought he owned me, and why. All about the bags of gold he'd paid for me when I was only five. All about how he had seized me at sea. All about how he'd maybe just tried to kill me.

Fiona was horror-struck and silent when I had told her these things. They are hard to hear, aren't they, Companion?

"I've been lucky," she said quietly. "I've lived in a family where there is nothing but love."

I remembered her poor dead brother, though, and how she and her sister nearly died of the same dis-ease that had taken him off to the Land of the Dead. That's how she and I had met, Companion. When I helped my mother nurse her back to health, that's when she and I had become close. So her life had not been all ease and serenity.

"Besides, you need to sit near me," said Fiona, dimpling up. "Ahead of me, in fact. You're a princess, and I'm only the daughter of a viceroy." We had to giggle when we thought of the old days when Fiona believed I was just some tavern singer's daughter. True, a heroic tavern singer who had saved the town from dis-ease. And I had helped. But still. She'd thought I was a poor woman's child.

"This explains a lot about you, Keera," she said, holding me out at arm's length from her and marveling at me. "How you talk. How you can read."

"That happened in spite of me being a princess, not because of it."

"But you knew all along."

I nodded. "Mother and I were on the run from Caedon. We couldn't tell a soul, not even you. We were living incognito," I said, giving her a hug. I didn't explain to her that I knew who I was because I had had a vision, and because I could read people's minds. That I kept secret. Even though she's my dearest friend, I doubted she'd understand.

I see you agree with me, Companion. Well, it matters little now. That nasty woman, my own farwydd, has robbed me of my powers. Very well, I'll stop referring to her in that way, since I see how much it upsets you, Companion.

And Companion . . . I hesitate to bring this up. I don't want to distress you further. Does it bother you that I call Fiona my dearest friend, and not you? Because, Companion, you have become strangely dear to me.

No? Good! That relieves my mind. It surely does.

I had a hard time keeping my mouth shut when we were changing from our everyday clothing to the kirtles we'd wear for dinner.

"Oh!" exclaimed Fiona. "Look at that! I've never noticed that before. You have a little birthmark on your shoulder, and it looks like—"

"That's my firebird," I said, looking around at it as I pulled the kirtle on.

"It does look like a bird perching there. And I see what you mean. The bird looks like it is leaping out of the flames."

I smiled at her, but I didn't explain. She probably thought it was just a birthmark, the way you do, Companion. Both of you are wrong, however.

At dinner, Caedon scowled down the board at me, but there was nothing he could do about it, not without causing a big scene. Fiona had seated me beside herself, and he couldn't gainsay her without looking high-handed and rude. Companion, remember this. There's a lot to be said for good manners. They can protect you when other means fail.

Because he was king, Caedon had seated himself at the head of the board, with the viceroy at his right and the viceroy's wife at his left. Then Fiona. Then, a comfortable distance away from Caedon, me. I persuaded Fiona not to make a big fuss out of my status as princess. That would just rile Caedon up. It might even get the viceroy in trouble, and Fiona in trouble with her father. Caedon claimed my father and mother were rebels. But Fiona had persuaded the viceroy to treat me as an honored guest, not some captured rebel spawn. The viceroy had agreed (*had gone out on a limb for me*, to use one of Old Dee's colorful expressions) because he credited me, just as much as Mother, with saving his daughters from death.

He and I had had a joyful reunion. He had rushed to me and hugged me to him, exclaiming over how big I had grown, and what a lovely young lady I was now. I think he took quite a risk, doing this. I saw Caedon hovering just past his shoulder, a black look on his long, lean, wolfish face.

"I hear Sorcha lives in the Ice-realm now," I whispered to Fiona as the servingmen came in to ladle heapings of meat onto our trenchers.

"Married, can you believe it?" Fiona whispered back. "Her husband is at King Haakon's court, and he took her off with him to live there."

I made some appropriate comment or other, although I didn't explain that I knew this already. But I gave Fiona a quick sidelong glance. Fiona looked perfectly cheerful. Most daughters of powerful men would be *all bent out of shape* (another of Old Dee's expressions) if their younger sisters were allowed to marry before their fathers found husbands for them first.

Fiona must have realized how unusual her situation might seem. "I didn't mind it," she whispered. "Please pass the muddled pears," she said aloud. Under cover of a loud political discussion, she explained further. "A young lord from the Ice-realm spotted Sorcha on a diplomatic visit here, and he wanted her desperately. I think she wanted him back. I think they secretly met a number of times out in the garden."

We giggled. Fiona's mother cast a disapproving eye at us, so we looked demurely down at our trenchers. But Fiona's mother also had to hide a smile. She too was overjoyed that her daughter at last had her best friend back. She, like her husband, had kind words for me later, and gave me a special message of thanks and regard to send to my mother when I saw her next. If only that would happen, Companion. I have to be realistic. It may not.

"But you know how it is," Fiona was continuing, at dinner, as she described Sorcha's courtship. "Her young man couldn't ask for her hand as long as I remained unwed. So he got another member of his diplomatic mission to ask Father for my hand."

"That sounds very romantic," I said.

"No, it was not, as you should know better than anyone."

"Old? Hairs sprouting from his ears?"

Fiona nodded.

"So then Father was stymied. He won't make me do anything I don't want to do." She cast a loving look at him.

He, looking back over the board at her, smiled at her.

I saw how it was. I had seen it before. When she as good as came back from the dead, all those years ago, her father could deny her nothing. And Fiona was smart. When I went to the manor to be Fiona's companion, she and I had persuaded her father to allow us to study together, just as if we were boys. He, twined about her little finger (Old Dee's phrase), agreed and gave us the best tutors in the city. Fiona wasn't what you might call the usual high-born maiden.

But Sorcha. I smiled to myself, thinking of her fresh loveliness. Even then, when she was still a young girl, everyone could tell she'd grow up to be a beauty.

Sorcha confided in her sister. "She was besotted with this man," Fiona told me, smiling fondly. Fiona explained she'd persuaded her father, then, to allow Sorcha to marry first. As she murmured to me how they achieved this feat, I lost track of what she was telling me. I think her parents made up some silly story about how Fiona had made some silly vow to the Lady Goddess. Fiona, of course, doesn't believe in the Lady Goddess. I suppose she believes in the Children, but really, I'm not sure what she believes in. No one in her family believes in the Lady Goddess. Her father is a firm believer in the Sea Child. But they all have to pretend otherwise.

"I never want to marry," Fiona whispered to me.

"Me neither," I whispered back, oblivious to the fact that I'd already done it. My marriage hardly seemed to count, though. But I was distracted.

I lost track of what Fiona was telling me, I say, because of the intense look Caedon was aiming at me. His eyes had been on the viceroy during the political discussion they were having. Now he turned them on me.

I knew he was biding his time, and the gleam in his vulpine amber eyes told me he knew I knew it, the look of a predator sizing up its prey.

You're right, Companion. Once he gets me where he wants me, then he'll do something awful to me. And no, I don't underestimate the danger I'm in. See, my hands are trembling. I'm glad you're with me, Companion. You're the only one who really understands.

Damsels In Distress

After the dinner was over and the board removed from its trestles and we had all taken our rushlights with us to our sleeping rooms, I started actively worrying. What if Caedon sneaked up on me while I slept?

I thought of begging the waiting woman to stay with me. She was helping me undress and get into my sleeping garment. It was thin and gauzy. Summer was nearly here, and the nights were warm. I was too embarrassed to ask her, though. How would I explain that I feared the king? She'd think I was a timid, timorous creature afraid of her own shadow.

So when she left with the rushlight and I was alone in the dark, and when I heard a noise behind me in the room, I couldn't help it. I shrieked.

The serving maid was back with her light in a trice. But by the time she got back, she frowned in irritation. She saw only two giddy girls doubled over laughing, and she went away again.

"You scared me into the next world, I swear you did," I told Fiona.

"I didn't mean to startle you," she said between fits of giggles. "I was waiting here for you, and I stepped to the window, and then there you were with the maid, and I didn't want to show myself. So I just waiting in the shadows."

I looked at her, puzzled.

"Don't hate my parents," said Fiona. "They love you, both of them. You know that. But they've warned me to keep my distance from you. Then, at dinner, I suddenly grew afraid for you."

"Funny. That's exactly what I thought, too. I was afraid, and I thought of trying to make the servant stay with me, her and her light, but I was sure she would think I was just a silly young girl."

We stopped giggling then and sat together on my bed, our knees drawn up under our thin nightdresses.

"But I am afraid," I said, and at almost the same time, Fiona was saying, "But I really am afraid for you."

"Caedon," I whispered.

"Caedon," she whispered too.

And you, hovering above us. I felt sure you were thinking the same, Companion.

"He gave you the most vicious look," said Fiona. "It chilled me to the bone."

"I thought I might be imagining things."

"You didn't imagine that look," she said.

Then, with a sinking heart, I said, "Your parents think I'm too dangerous for you to associate with."

"You don't understand," Fiona said. Her voice was careful.

"What—" I started to say.

Then we both froze. Outside in the corridor, we heard a noise.

I stole my hand into Fiona's and we sat on my bed, tense and listening.

"Probably nothing," I whispered after a moment.

Then we heard it again, a stealthy padding of feet outside the room.

"Probably just one of the servants, checking things out before going to bed," Fiona said quietly.

"I'm going to make sure," I said. Companion, settle down up there. It's perfectly fine. Fiona is with me, and a whole manor house-full of servants just outside my room.

I recalled then that I was staying on the opposite end of the manor house from the viceroy's sleeping quarters. The great hall stood between me and the viceroy's family, muffling any sounds of alarm that might come from my room.

I'm letting my imagination run wild, I scolded myself, and not for the first time, I beamed angry, aggrieved thoughts in the direction of my farwydd.

"I'm going to check," I said again. To Fiona, I said, very low, "Hang back over there in the corner with my Companion. Then, when I open the door, whoever might be there won't see that you're here."

"Your . . . Companion?" Fiona faltered.

"Oh. That's just a silly way I have of speaking," I said, cursing myself. Of course Fiona can't see you, Companion, and she'll think I'm addled in the head and have made up the whole story about Caedon and his evil intentions.

Bless her for a good friend. I saw she believed me and feared for me in spite of my crazy talk.

"But anyway, stand over there," I whispered to her. "Don't you think that's the best idea?"

In the darkness I felt rather than saw her nod at me, and I felt her ease off the bed.

Very quietly, I made my way to the door and stood listening at it. I could swear I heard someone breathing, just outside. I yanked the door open, then fell back, dazzled by the rushlight torch the person outside my room was holding high. For indeed a person stood just outside.

The dark shape that was that person shouldered into the room, shoving me backward with a hand.

I knew then it was Caedon.

"No!" Fiona leaped out of her corner and came toward us. Her eyes blazed in the rushlight.

Caedon had me around the neck by now, holding me to his body and shoving me ahead of him into the room. He kicked the door closed behind him. "Nine Spheres," he said. His voice was low. Then, in normal tones, "Lady Fiona."

He maneuvered me with him to the wall and shoved the rush torch into the holder there, never taking his eyes off Fiona.

"Unhand my friend," she said to him.

With his free hand, his right, he drew the sword from his scabbard and pointed it at her.

She gave a little scream.

"Silence, lady. Sit there on the bed." He advanced on her. I tried to kick away from him, but he held me too close for me to get any kind of momentum. I think I did pretty severely kick his shins, though. If I gave him any pain, he ignored it.

He gave me a violent shove, and I stumbled to the bed.

"Sit there, mistress," he directed me. I did.

He stood over us, the point of his sword wavering from one of us to the other.

An amused smile touched his pale lips. "Two of you. What a dilemma."

"My father will not take this kindly, sir."

"You'll address me as Your Majesty," he said to Fiona. "And you've put your father in danger with this act of yours. Grave danger."

Beside me, I could feel that Fiona was shaking.

"Your Majesty," said Fiona. Scorn dripped from her voice. I admired her courage, but now I was afraid for her. "Why have you done this discourteous thing, invaded the room of our guest?" she said to him. Her voice was formal, icy.

"I don't have to explain myself to you, Lady Fiona, but I will. This guest of yours is my stolen property. I'll take that property back." He stood back from us a little, looking from one of us to the other. "But now you've presented me with a difficult choice.

When I take what's mine, what in the Nine will I do with you, Lady? Perhaps some unfortunate accident is about to befall you."

I had been so stunned that I hadn't been able to choke out a word. Now I raged at him. "You are one of the Dark Ones, Sir Caedon."

"'One of the Dark Ones, Your Majesty,'" Caedon corrected. "How interesting you should say so. Your mother has said much the same to me." Still keeping his sword trained on us, he stepped to the window just past us and elbowed the shutters open. He looked down and quickly back to us.

"There's a long drop to the ground, Lady Fiona," he said softly.

"Not such a long drop," she scoffed.

"Perhaps not, but people have been known to fall wrong, and, well—" His smile widened. "Accidents happen."

In spite of her brave words, I felt her trembling beside me.

Now I leaped up and rushed at him.

I don't know what would have happened to either of us then, but I was pushed back and away from him by a powerful gust of air from the windows. The wind came up with a roar and blew the shutters open and banged them against the wall.

Caedon's eyes widened. I glanced behind me and screamed.

Two men came bursting through the window.

Caedon whirled to face them, thrusting me down hard onto the floor.

The two intruders, dressed all in black, were completely silent. I picked myself up, grabbed Fiona by the hand, and huddled us both away from all of them into the corner. From where we crouched, I saw these other men were armed with wicked swords.

Caedon had his own sword up in a defensive posture I later heard someone describe as *Sixte*. The combatants were circling each other.

My hand flew to my mouth. One of the intruders was Gwyl.

"Pierrick, get them out of here," he said to the other man, nodding to the corner.

Then he ignored us. He was totally concentrated on Caedon.

The two men closed. I heard the clash of their blades; they were otherwise silent. As they fought back and forth across the room, I couldn't tell which of them was winning. I knew my parents had always said Caedon was the finest swordsman of his generation. My mother used to tease my father about the time, years back, he'd actually taken Caedon on. "Why are you not dead, Wat?" That's usually when she'd say that.

The man with Gwyl, the man he'd called Pierrick, was trying to maneuver around the combatants to get to us, but every time he did, Caedon managed to fend him away from us while still holding his own with Gwyl. Part of me had to admire Caedon's skill.

I tried to keep the two of us out of the combatants' way. By now, Gwyl had positioned himself between Caedon and the door to the room. Without taking his eyes off Caedon he spoke to me. "Get the two of you to the window and stay there, Keera," he said.

Then he resumed his attack, parry, attack, approach, retreat, parry, attack.

I saw something then. Both men were breathing heavily, but Caedon was becoming winded.

Caedon was old.

The man named Pierrick was coming up behind him from his blind spot.

"No," Gwyl shouted at him, always without taking his eyes off Caedon. "No time. Get them out of here."

Pierrick saw his chance and moved to our corner. While Gwyl kept Caedon busy, Pierrick hustled the two of us to the window.

From deep inside the fort, we all heard noises. *Someone's coming*, I thought.

Caedon whirled, went on a ferocious attack that backed Gwyl away from the door, and then he flung himself out of it down the hallway, shouting for the guards.

Gwyl didn't follow. He was with us at the window in two steps. He took me up with him onto the sill, and we tumbled out together. Pierrick and Fiona followed. I lay on the ground beneath, winded. Gwyl hauled me to my feet.

Fiona and I stared at each other in the moonlight, breathing hard.

"Not such a long drop," she said.

We began to laugh. I think it was the shock.

"No time for that," Gwyl told us roughly. He shoved us along the wall of the manor to a place where a man stood holding three horses.

I heard the man named Pierrick say, his voice tense, "We didn't expect two of them, Gwyl."

"You've ridden before?" Gwyl turned to me, sudden doubt in his eyes.

"No," I admitted.

"We'll do it this way, then," he said, pulling me up after him onto one of the horses.

He looked down at Fiona. "You, my lady?"

"I can ride," she said. An edge of scorn came back into her voice.

I realized she had no idea who these rescuers were. For all she knew, they were ruffians too. So I forgave her.

She and Pierrick mounted the other two horses.

"Let's go," he told them. "Not fast. Easy." The three of them trotted their horses calmly to the manor gates.

Gwyl's companion saluted; the guard at the gate saluted back. "Children go with you," the guard called after us softly.

As we rode downhill away from the fort, we could hear a clamorous outcry behind us.

"We'll need to ride fast now," Gwyl called across to Fiona. "Can you do it?"

"Of course," she said. Her voice had changed. Her whole manner toward him had changed. I saw she knew something.

"Now," said Gwyl, and the three of them spurred their horses to a gallop. I clung like a limpet to Gwyl. We went careening downhill, then in a lunging, sliding flight through the crooked streets of the town. A few townspeople coming late out of taverns made a panicked scramble out of our way. Soon we were out into the countryside. We pulled up then on the verge of a dark country lane.

Gwyl swung off his horse and helped me trembling down. Out of the corner of my eye, I saw Fiona and Pierrick dismounting, too. "We'll leave the horses here," Gwyl said quietly.

He took me by the arm, motioned to the other two, and we slipped off the road into the underbrush. "I'll explain later," he told me. "But now I must talk things over a bit with your friend."

To Fiona he said, making a little bow, "My lady, may I assume you are one of the viceroy's daughters, or attached to his household in some way?"

"I am Lady Fiona of the Northmost Isle," she told him. Her voice had turned cold again. I realized she must be assailed with doubts and conflicting ideas about the men who had grabbed us. For all she knew, they'd rescued us from Caedon just to menace us themselves.

"Sir Gwyl of the Baronies, at your service, my lady," said Gwyl, bowing low. "And this man is my brother Pierrick."

I stared at Pierrick. Gwyl had a brother. One more thing to know about him. Even in the light from a dim moon rising now, I saw the two of them didn't look like brothers. Gwyl was slender and dark. Pierrick was brawny and fair-haired.

"I know our intrusion must seem strange, your ladyship," said Gwyl to Fiona.

"I believe you've saved my life, Sir Gwyl," said Fiona, her voice turning gracious. "That man Caedon threatened me. And he was about to kidnap my friend and do who knows what with her."

Gwyl smiled at her, his teeth flashing in the moonlight. "That man Caedon is your king, lady."

"He's no king of mine," said Fiona. "He proved that to me this night, if I'd ever had any doubts before."

"And he's no king of mine," said Gwyl, with another bow to her. "As a matter of fact," he told her, "I am liege-man to His Majesty Walter the First, the true king of the Sceptered Isle in exile, and this lady's father." He nodded at me.

"Ah," said Fiona. "Now I understand. The guard at the gate. Everything."

"Indeed," Gwyl said to her. "I'm sorry there was no time to explain, back there." Now he turned to me. "Your highness," he said, bowing even lower to me than he had bowed to Fiona. "I'm to bring you back to your family. And now we must leave this island, because Caedon will send men in pursuit if he hasn't already." He paused. "But Lady Fiona, what will you do? I must advise you to come with us. I fear you won't be safe here."

Fiona looked frightened then. "My father—" she began.

"He'll be in danger, lady, but you're in worse danger. Tell me this. Was Caedon expecting to see you in that room when he came to seize Keera? That is," and he grinned at me now, "Her highness the Princess Keera?"

"No," said Fiona.

"Then you were indeed in danger. You were a witness, and he needed to rid himself of you. But in a way, this may protect you, lady, and protect your family. I don't know what story Caedon will tell your father about what happened in Keera's room tonight and why she's no longer there. I'm thinking he'll make up some story about Keera being abducted, and how he just missed rescuing her. How else explain why he was shouting in the hallway outside her room, his sword drawn and Keera disappeared? Unless he simply tells the truth and reveals himself to be the vile creature he is."

Gwyl paused, considering. "I doubt he'll do that," he went on. "But how will he explain your disappearance too, your ladyship?" We all stood silently thinking this over.

"Suppose he doesn't explain it at all. Suppose he says he has no idea why my parents can't find me," said Fiona.

"Hmm," said Gwyl. "The abductors came for you, too, maybe?"

"That's a lot of abduction, brother," said Pierrick.

"It doesn't seem too likely, does it?" said Gwyl.

"Get word to my father," Fiona said then. "Tell my father to say I'm sick and can't come out of my room."

"Caedon will know that's a lie," I said.

"Yes, but will he want to admit it?" said Fiona. "If he does, he'll have to reveal the truth, and he won't want to. Later, my father can claim he has sent me off to the Ice-realm to be with my sister. He can say my sister has found me a husband there."

"That's a good plan, lady," said Gwyl. "But your father will still be in danger. Caedon will know your father knows about him and his evil ways. That will put your father in a dangerous position."

"He's already in a dangerous position," said Fiona. She and Gwyl exchanged a long look.

Then I realized. I realized what Fiona had been talking about, when she told me her parents had advised her to stay away from me. Fiona's father must be conspiring against Caedon, a dangerous game, and not just for him. He must be sick with fear for his family. He must be on our side, not Caedon's.

"Anyway, lady, there's no help for it. You can't go back there. You've seen what Caedon is, and he'll not let you live. I'll get word to your father. To save face, Caedon might not do anything to your father, at least not right away. That will give us time to strategize. We may have to take action here on the Northmost Isle a little sooner than we'd planned."

I could tell from the tense lines of her face that Fiona was terrified for the safety of her family. But Gwyl was right. There was nothing to do now but warn her father.

"He'll have to save face," Gwyl said again. "Caedon is losing his touch. He knows it, too. That's going to make him angry, and that in itself is dangerous. This way."

As we climbed down a stony embankment to a shingle where a small boat was drawn up, I thought about his words and his fight with Caedon. I thought about how, if Gwyl hadn't had us to rescue, me and Fiona, he might very probably have won that fight, especially with his brother at his side.

And I thought something else, too. I thought with deep shame about my own role. I hadn't gone back to my parents, as I had promised Old Dee. I had turned myself into bait for Caedon, and he had snapped up that bait. But in foolishly rushing into my second task, I had put Gwyl in danger, and I had endangered my friend.

Fiona and I stood by while Gwyl and his brother put the boat to rights.

"Funny," said Gwyl. In the faint gleam from the moon on the sea, I could see him looking around. "The wind had picked up something fierce back there, when we were at the manor, and now—"

"Completely quiet now." Pierrick's voice came to us in the dark.

As Gwyl helped me and then Fiona into the boat, I was grateful the darkness hid the deep blush of guilt and humiliation that I knew was staining my cheeks.

After a long hard pull past the breakers, Gwyl and Pierrick eased up on their oars. A dark shape slid up to us, and soon the brothers were helping me and Fiona up and over into a fast ship, the kind called a skeid, that took us running before the wind

toward the rocky isle of my parents. Pierrick found us both
cloaks in some of the sailors' sea chests, and we wrapped them
around ourselves against the night air.

In the night, as I sat propped sleepily up against the wall of
the ship, I saw Gwyl conferring with his mariners. Gwyl called
back to the man at the rudder, and then to the man at the tack
spar. I could tell by the stars, the ship turned more northerly. My
mother had taught me how to tell north by the stars.

Bundled in my cloak beside Fiona, I tried to sleep, but I
couldn't. Fiona was having the same problem. We didn't talk. I
don't think I could have. Too much had happened too fast, and
too violently. But she and I clasped hands, and finally, towards
dawn, both of us did sleep.

In the morning, I woke to see that we were riding at anchor
in a sheltered cove.

Fiona was standing, supporting herself against the upper
strake of Gwyl's skeid and gathering her very few things together.

She smiled at me when she saw me awake. "I'm leaving now,
Keera," she said. She nodded across the water toward the shore.
"Your gallant friend Sir Gwyl is setting me ashore on this island,
which belongs to the Ice-realm. As soon as I can send word to
her, my sister will get me there."

I struggled out of my cloak to my feet, and she and I embraced.

"My dear friend," she murmured. "I was so happy to see you
again, and now look what has happened to us.'

"I've put you in danger," I said.

"Oh, no, Keera. You know that my father confides in me, just as if I were a son, don't you? Something like this was going to happen, especially with Caedon in our hall. And we knew how strange it was, when he showed up with you. We just didn't expect it would happen so suddenly, with so much drama." She laughed.

I held her out from me, amazed. "You are brave, Fiona. I'm glad you're going to your sister. But will you be safe here on your own?" I looked doubtfully toward the island.

"She'll have an escort, Your Highness," said a voice. I turned. Gwyl's brother Pierrick had come up to us. "If the lady will accept me, I'm going to row her to the island and stay with her there until her sister arranges passage to the Ice-realm's mainland."

In the sunshine, I saw that Pierrick was a strapping and handsome young man, fair of hair and blue of eye. And I saw something even more interesting than that. Out of the corner of my eye, I saw the demure look that Fiona cast upon him as she curtsied, accepting him as her escort. *She's actually blushing*, I told myself, amazed. I'd never seen Fiona like this around a man. Ever.

To fill the moment, I began babbling on. "Why, Sir Pierrick, what a courteous offer," I said. *Shut up, Keera*, an inner voice told me, and yes, so did you, Companion, but I bumbled on. "You look nothing like your brother."

I know, Companion. That was a rude thing to say.

Pierrick only laughed. "We have different fathers," he told us. "Gwyl's father died before he was even born. Then our mother married again, and shortly afterward—" He spread his hands. "As you see. So Gwyl and I are very close in age. But he looks like his father, or so our mother has always told us, and I look like mine."

Shortly afterward, the mariners lowered our small boat. Pierrick helped Fiona down into it. I stood and waved to her as long as I could see her, my eyes blurred with tears. Then the boat rounded a headland, and they were gone.

Gwyl had come to stand beside me. "That was a near thing," Gwyl said after a while. "Caedon snatching you like that. We thought for a while he wasn't going to. Then where would you be?"

It was a rhetorical question, Companion. Geez Louise.

"I don't understand," I told him, surreptitiously wiping my eyes. "How did Hildr get to you so fast? And then how did you get to me so fast?"

"You sent Hildr? Good girl," he said.

"I'm not a girl. I'm a woman," I told him.

"Oh, forgive me, Your Highness. I forgot," he said. He flashed his infuriating irrepressible grin.

"Will you please stop calling me that?"

"What shall I call you?" he asked.

"How about Keera? It's my name, after all."

He bowed to me, and it was an ironic bow. "Lady Keera," he said.

"Keera. Just Keera."

"Keera," he said. And this time there was no irony about the man. His voice and his eyes were soft.

I looked uneasily away. "Well? How did you do it?"

"If I'd waited to hear from Hildr, well then, Caedon would have—whatever he was planning to do in there, he would have done it."

"But you got there in the nick of time. Just like in the stories," I said.

"It wasn't like that. Nothing like that. We knew he'd bring you to the viceroy's manor. Then we just waited for him to do it. And then, when he did, that was my cue to jump in there and get you out. I didn't expect poor Lady Fiona to get caught up in it, though."

"But how did you know that's where Caedon would take me? Or even that he'd take me?"

"Listen, you were the bait. But he hadn't bitten. So I'm thinking to myself, Why? What's he going to do, show up and abduct you at your own wedding? No, he wouldn't do that. Then it was a simple matter of figuring out that of course he'd grab you at sea. And of course he'd bring you to the Northmost Isle."

"Why of course." He sounded so cocksure. It was making me irritable.

"The viceroy's manor has been Caedon's headquarters for close on a year now. He has been biding his time. He's about to attack Haakon."

"Poor Grandfather. All his schemes have come to nothing," I said. "But meanwhile, looks like you're in league with Fiona's father."

"Yes, we are. We have people all over his island. Everywhere. We know everything Caedon is doing. Everything he's planning to do."

"Who is this *we*?"

"Silly girl, your father."

For a long time, we sat side by side in silence.

"I failed." I finally got enough of a grip on myself to say it.

"You failed?"

"I wanted Caedon to catch me. Then I was going to kill him."

"And you think back there you were about to do that?"

"You remind me of someone else who said almost those same words to me," I said resentfully.

"Listen, Keera. There are a lot of people who want to kill that man."

"No one with a better claim than mine."

"Oh, really," he said. "What about my claim?"

"Your claim?"

"He just about killed your father. He did kill mine."

I put my hand on his arm. "I didn't know," I whispered.

"It happened before I was born. But it ruined my mother. Maybe it did." He looked out over the sea to the horizon, his eyes thoughtful. "Still, who knows? If my father had lived, that might have ruined her too. Apparently he loved some other woman, not her. When he died, she re-married. She and my stepfather have lived together for a long time. He's a strange man, my step-father. He takes care of her in all material things, and she—she takes care of him through his strange moods. He put a roof over my head. He did do that. And he loves Pierrick beyond life itself. If he knew Pierrick was here with me, doing what we're doing, serving your father, there'd be the Dark Ones to pay."

"Your father doesn't like mine?" I felt a little outraged.

"My step-father, and no, he doesn't."

"Hmph," I said.

"Don't worry. Apparently my step-father likes Caedon even less." Gwyl gave himself a little shake, seeming to come back to the here and now. "What am I doing, telling you all of this boring family stuff," he said, looking down at me with a wry smile.

I was still intrigued, though. "But if your step-father doesn't know my father, and he doesn't know Caedon, what does he have against them?"

Gwyl shrugged. "I don't know, not really. I've never been able to figure him out. But none of that matters, what he thinks. As I say, he's an odd man. When I was a younger man, I didn't even know why or how Caedon killed my father, just that he had. My mother and step-father were agreed on that but for my entire childhood, never would say anything more to me about it. I didn't know the how and the why of it, not really, until I met your father. The important thing, at least for me, is that I've been practicing to take revenge on Caedon my entire life."

"I'd say you have. In your fight with him at the viceroy's house, I'd say you were winning. Yet everyone says Caedon is supposed to be—"

"I know. The finest swordsman of his generation. I've heard that since I was a boy. So there I was in the Baronies, plenty of instructors over there, and I spent my life from about age eight practicing to get better than Caedon. That little demonstration in there yesterday. I'd say I have a good shot at it. Not that he's no longer great. It's just that the poor man is slowing down, and there were two of us against the one of him."

"And don't forget me and Fiona," I told him.

He looked over at me with amusement.

"I was planning to hit him over the head with a flower pot, if he got close enough."

"Oh, aye?" said Gwyl.

I rushed on, because I was worried Gwyl was laughing at me now, and I worried about wanting to hit him, too, with a flower pot if he did. "How did Caedon kill your father?"

Gwyl didn't answer. He handed me a hard, irregular object.

I held it up. A ray from the weak sunlight hiding behind the clouds illuminated it and made it glint. It was a gold brooch. "The Six Proud Walkers," I breathed. "My father has one of these."

"They all do. Your grandfather made one for each of them, you know. Each of the men who organized the Rising."

"My true grandfather, Drustan."

"My father was one of them, too. His name was Rafe. I went to your father, because I realized enlisting myself in his service might give me my best chance to kill Caedon. Then one day I saw the brooch holding your father's cloak to his shoulder. And I knew. Your father told me everything, what my father was like. How his death had happened."

Gwyl stopped, considering. "Maybe not everything. There's a mystery, hovering about my father, and I believe your father knows what it is. But I don't care. If it's my father's secret, and yours carries it to his grave, I have what I need to know."

We sat together on the deck. The wind was cold, but I felt warm.

"If not for your father, maybe someday I would have made my move against Caedon," said Gwyl in a voice barely above a whisper. "Maybe I would have launched some quick violent strike against him. Maybe I would have succeeded. Maybe not. But I wouldn't have known, not really. I was lost, lost in my own confusion and dark thinking. The Children brought me to your father. He was there when I needed him."

I put my hand in Gwyl's and squeezed it. "Thank you for being there when I needed you. You said you would come. And you did."

Then I hastily drew my hand away.

He laughed. "Hildr was a signal to you that we were there, that we knew where you were, and that we were about to get you out."

"I love Hildr."

"She's a great little bird. I hope she thinks she saved you." Then he jolted halfway to his feet. "Nine Spheres. Aavarr."

"Aavarr is fine. I sent him to the tavern where my mother and I hid out during practically my entire childhood, down by the harbor. The Sun-Stone."

"Thank the Children. I'm responsible for that boy. In the morning, I'll send someone back to find him."

"Whoever you send should ask for Teasag. But tell him to be polite, or she'll clip him one on the ear with her crock."

"I'll make sure to do that." Then he looked sidelong at me. "They killed your poor old husband, I hear."

"Tossed him overboard. I think he may have meant well."

"He was a foolish old man, throwing in his lot with your grandfather like that. He wouldn't have lived long around Haakon or Caedon, either one of them, if he'd made it to shore."

"I suppose he was foolish. He was rich. That's all that mattered to Grandfather. I think I barely said six words to him."

"What we men to do women. Buy them. Sell them. Ravish them. My mother was a serving woman to Diera the First. My father rode out to protect his queen, got himself killed, and left my mother pregnant with me."

"No man is ever touching me again," I told Gwyl.

He just smiled his infuriating smile and inched his hand closer to mine.

"Oh, all right. But only because you rescued me from certain death or defilement or something."

I took his hand, planning, I swear, just to press it warmly again. But then he pulled me close to him, and put his face down to mine, and then we kissed.

You, Companion. What are you looking at?

CHAPTER TEN

Magic Needle

We didn't make it to my parents' refuge. We were maybe halfway there when we were overtaken.

Gwyl, shading his eyes, called out, "Slow rowing, there. It's one of ours."

Our rowers backed oars, and the other longship pulled up to us. A man leaped across into our ship. Breathing hard, he went up to Gwyl and handed him a parchment. Gwyl clapped him on the shoulder.

Gwyl read the parchment.

"Change course to the Fire Isle," he called out. "Head to the cove near my house on the small isle just before. You know the place?"

The master mariner of the big skeid nodded acknowledgement, and we changed course. The other ship kept pace beside us.

Gwyl moved briskly up and down the length of the vessel, speaking to various sailors sitting on their sea-chests pulling on their oars, adjusting equipment, re-reading the parchment. He stood at the upper strake of the skeid a little way off from me, staring out to sea, the wind blowing his hair back off his face. The day had turned hazy. He took out a small crystal and began manipulating it, trying to catch the light in the overcast sky. He was his own kendtman, I saw. He had a lot of skills.

I moved up to him. He was busy. I gave his sleeve a hesitant tug.

"Hmm?" He looked around. When he saw me, he smiled. Then his expression clouded, like the sky. "We're having to change our plans, Lady Keera. I'm sorry to tell you this. I wanted to take you straight to your parents, but this news changes everything for us."

"What news, then?"

"Caedon's forces are moving to attack your grandfather. We think Caedon has decided to eliminate that threat first, before confronting Haakon. It may be he realizes his time feinting with Haakon is over."

"What about the viceroy? What about Fiona?" I was struck with a sudden fear.

"I don't know," said Gwyl. "But the viceroy is a canny man. We've spent long hours together, discussing this strategy or that. He knows the risks. But his people love him. I think he'll be safe. And as for Fiona." He smiled at me. "Pierrick will see she's safely conveyed to the Ice-realm."

"I like your brother," I said.

"I think he likes your friend Fiona," said Gwyl, giving me a wink.

Then he turned serious. "Haakon had the very bad idea he'd connect with your grandfather through this wedding between you and his rich vassal. Now those plans of Haakon's are overturned. So Caedon had better move fast against your grandfather, and I think that will protect Fiona's father. Caedon's forces will leave the Northmost Isle. He won't have time to think what punishment to inflict on his viceroy."

We both knew that was wishful thinking. I feared for Fiona's poor father.

"Anyhow," Gwyl went on. "If Caedon can get rid of your grandfather, he won't need to assign a rear-guard to protect his men when he unfurls his grand plan to go after Haakon. Your grandfather in league with Haakon would be a gnat-bite only, but Caedon doesn't want to have to fend off any gnat-bites. He'll turn on your grandfather first and take the Fire Isle. Then he can use it as a base from which to attack Haakon. And what that means--" He reached out a hand toward me but then dropped it back to his side. "That means, if your father is wise, and we know he is, he'll need to defeat your weak grandfather now and take the Fire Isle before Caedon gets entrenched there. Caedon could use it as a base from which to attack your parents, too, you know."

"My father and mother vowed they'd fight no more wars."

"And now they see they have to." Gwyl moodily flipped his crystal, which I knew from my tavern days and my childhood down at the harbor, was called a sunstone, over and over in his hand. "People want peace. Then they see they can't have it."

"So we're heading to the Fire Isle to defeat Grandfather?"

"Aye. I'm not sure your grandfather will put up much of a defense, though. He's in over his head. Once Haakon sees how things are, he won't waste his resources protecting your grandfather. Especially now that his vassal is dead."

"My poor dead husband."

Suddenly Gwyl seized my wrists. His face and voice turned hard. "That old man didn't put his filthy hands on you, did he?"

Gwyl frightened me. "No," I quavered. "He didn't have time to."

"Thank the Children." Gwyl stepped back from me. His eyes glittered. Then he dropped his gaze. "Lady. Your Highness. Forgive me," he said. "I—I didn't mean to alarm you. I shouldn't have asked you that. It's just. . .we're going after your grandfather because he did this to you. There are all those many high-sounding strategic reasons I've told you about. But there's this other thing, too. It's that one thing sends me into a fury.

"I think I thought about doing something I had no right to do, because it's not my decision. I think I thought about personally strangling your grandfather. With these hands." He held them up to me. "But if I knew that stupid husband hadn't hurt you, or—" he stopped. "—or touched you," he continued, "I might go easier on your grandfather. Might." He swallowed hard. "Because this is your grandfather, Keera. I don't guarantee he'll be alive, at the end of this. No matter what he's done, his death may grieve you. Very probably it will be a violent death."

I pulled my cloak closer around me.

"Please say you forgive me," he said to me in a low voice.

I surprised myself then. Some blood thirst rose in me. "Don't stay your hand on my account. He's not my true grandfather. Just, the Dark Ones take him, my real one."

I doubted Gwyl would understand. True grandfather, real grandfather.

Somehow, he did.

You know, I think Gwyl and I, growing up, might have had a lot of the same kinds of experiences.

What do you think of that, Companion? And what do you think of my bloody-mindedness, I who can't hurt a mouse or a moth or a newt.

Wait—where are you? I can't see you up there perched above the sail any longer, but I do hear you. I think that's you, that high, clear, keening sound of triumph.

"Wind's picking up," Gwyl remarked, looking up at the sail. "Hear it?"

I nodded, but I knew better.

He looked up at the sky again and smiled a little. "I'm a stupid, stupid man," he said.

"No!" I put my hand on his arm.

"The last thing I want to do is frighten you. I had no right to kiss you, either."

But I wanted you to kiss me. That's what I was thinking. I said only, "I didn't mean to interrupt you in the middle of these war preparations. I see you have much to do, and I thank you for stopping to explain everything. I know it's because you don't want to worry me, and you're kind, so you've paused in your duties to explain."

"Kind? You think it's kindness I feel toward you?"

"Kindness is a most important emotion," I said to him. I was perfectly serious about that, Companion. Old Dee had taught me about the word *kind*.

Gwyl gave me a rueful smile.

"I just wanted to give you something," I told him.

"What's that?"

I pulled the needle out of the pouch at my belt. It was the needle Old Dee had given me. "This is a magic needle," I told him.

"Oh, aye?" he gave me an amused glance.

"No, it is. Do you have a noggin of water?"

"Of course, my lady." He turned to the middle part of the ship, where a butt of water stood, and dipped me up a noggin-full. "Here."

"Hold it for me, please." I held the noggin out to him and dropped the small splinter of metal delicately onto the surface of the water. "Watch," I told him.

We both peered down into the noggin. The splinter lazily spun around and then stopped.

"See where it's pointing?" I told Gwyl.

"Aye."

"That's north. That's always north, where the magic needle points."

Gwyl looked skeptical. Then he picked up his sunstone again and sighted along it. He looked back down at me. "Nine Spheres, girl. You're right." He looked back down at the needle. "Like the fleas," he whispered.

"I know," I said, ignoring the part about the fleas. "So here. This is a gift for you. Thank you for saving me, and thank you for giving me Hildr."

Then I moved away from him, out of the bustle of the ship to a private place, and sat in a quiet corner, pulling my knees up and covering myself with my cloak and wondering what fleas had to do with anything, beyond being the annoyances they always are.

Thanks for coming down to sit here beside me, by the way, Companion. I know you prefer your perch on the sail's stretching pole. There are a lot of strange feelings swirling around me right now, and I don't know what to make of them. I'm glad I have a friend by me.

The rest of the voyage, Gwyl and I stayed out of one another's way. I don't think either of us knew what to make of that kiss we had shared. But our voyage to the Fire Isle was a short one. As he helped me over the skeid's upper strake and into a small boat that brought us to the sands in the little cove of his island, he murmured in my ear, "Fastest time I've ever made that run. It was that needle of yours."

I just smiled at him.

"And don't smile at me like that, my lady."

"Why not, Sir Gwyl?"

"Because then—" and his mouth was just by my ear, "—I'll want to take you in my arms and kiss you again."

I blushed scarlet. That's one of the big difficulties of being a red-head. We blush, and when we do, it's—holy guacamole—all too obvious. He handed me off to one of the sailors.

"This way, lady," said the man, offering his arm over the rough stones of the shingle. I stared around as he led me up the steep hill from the cove to the very top, where a turf farmhouse raked by the winds waited to welcome me. And on the roofline were birds. Many birds, most of them flat-faced, strange-looking birds with large beaks. The sailor pointed them out to me. "Lundi," he said.

He ushered me into the farmhouse out of the wind, where a brisk fire welcomed me to the hearthstones. A kindly-looking, bustling woman drew a tot of spirits for the sailor and a mug of ale for me. Later she served me a bowl of stew. She spoke a language I couldn't understand. I'd heard Grandfather Fylkir's servants speak to each other like that, although Grandfather and Stefan used the language of the Sceptered Isle, and so did the nobles, if they weren't speaking in the language of the Ice-realm.

The door banged open again and a lad came in, pulling the door closed behind him. He spotted me. "Mistress!" he cried.

"Aevarr!" I jumped to my feet and grabbed him and hugged him. "Did you go to old Teasag, as I told you?"

"Aye, and then Sir Gwyl's men found me and put me on the ship back to here."

The kindly woman came into the room from some errand she'd had to do elsewhere in the house. She made a glad exclamation, and Aevarr went running to her. He looked back over his shoulder at me. "This is me mam," he said.

Aevarr's mother and I smiled at each other, and at Aevarr. Then he went skipping back out of the house. Aevarr's mother said something to me that sounded fond and proud. I nodded.

Now Gwyl ducked under the lintel of the low entryway into the snug house. "Welcome to my home, lady," he said to me, coming to the fire and holding out his hands. "It's very windy here. Even in good weather, you can become chilled."

"Have you lived here long?" I tried to seem friendly and open; actually I felt very shy.

"Only a few years. Your father sent me here as soon as we realized what your grandfather was up to."

"Gwyl—" I hesitated.

"What is it? You look troubled."

"How do I give Aevarr back?"

"Give him back? Oh, I understand. Aevarr isn't really a bondservant. That was just a ruse to make sure your grandfather let him stay. We needed him there. He could spy for us, keep an eye on you, go along with you on your wedding trip, all sorts of things, and nobody would suspect."

I laughed. "That's a relief. I don't want anyone owning me, and I don't want to own anyone." Then I felt a pang. "I was worried about him, during the battle."

"He's been through battles. He knows how to protect himself."

"He's so young."

"In these times, people grow up fast," said Gwyl.

They do, I acknowledged to myself. I'd had to, and so had my parents.

I'm looking around for you now, Companion, but I'm not seeing you. Lately, I've been anxious about you. Silly, I know. Oh, there you are, over by the window past the fire. You were kind of blending in with the smoke.

How about you? Did you have to grow up fast, too? You did? I see we have something in common, then.

"You must be tired," Gwyl said to me. "Let me show you where you're to sleep." He led me to a back room. There was a big bedstead piled with furs. "I'll be sleeping out on the skeid." That was the big ship we'd come in on, his main longship. The others, fleet little snake-ships, could move right up onto the beach, their drafts were so shallow. "If you need me, send Aevarr to get me," he said, and strode away out of the house again.

I fell into the nest of furs and slept for hours. When I woke, it was full dark. I went back to sleep again. Finally I roused. The sun was shining through the chinks in the thatch. I threw off the furs and saw a warmer dress laid out on the bench beside the bedstead, and a warmer cloak. I put these on and went out into the main part of the house by the fire.

Soon Aevarr came in. "Sir Gwyl sent me to ask, do you need anything, lady?" he said.

"One thing."

"I will get this thing for you."

"You'll have to take me to her instead."

Aevarr's face lit up. We grinned at each other. "Hildr!" he said.

So off we went, our bodies slanting into the wind, to a small outbuilding down a path. There a few horses were stabled. And on her perch sat Hildr.

I went to her, pulled on the gauntlet Aevarr handed me, and held out a finger to her. She came onto my hand and I carefully removed her hood. It was a loving reunion. She put her beak against my cheek and made her tender chuckling purring sound. She only makes that sound for me.

"Hildr," I murmured to her. "You went for help. Thank you." To Aevarr I said, "Can I take her out and hunt her?"

"Better to wait, mistress. She'll chase down the lundi and try to eat them all."

I left her, promising that she and I would hunt soon.

Now I thought I'd be content, but I wasn't. On my way back to the house, I could see the activity down at the cove. Men working on the longships. Men mending sails spread out on the beach; men in knots conferring with each other; men inspecting weapons and racking them on the shore.

I knew I was witnessing the preparations for an attack on my own grandfather. I felt a little sorry for Grandfather and for Uncle Stefan, but not very.

I also felt left out, shoved to the margins. "I'm the enemy of Caedon," I wanted to shout. "I'm the one. I was wronged by my grandfather and uncle. That's right. Me." All I could do, though, was stay out of everyone's way.

And where Gwyl was concerned, I felt a flustered sense of confusion. Did he mean the things he said, about kissing me? I thought about our kiss on the boat. It was my first. He, I felt sure, had kissed many women. And then I thought about his fury when he imagined my old husband had put his hands on me. I suppose, since he was my husband, the old man thought he would be entitled to do that. I suppose, since I'd allowed myself to be married to him, that I'd be required to let him. I was as thankful to the Children as I'd ever been that I hadn't had to endure it.

But it made me think about how many brides were forced into the beds of husbands they hadn't chosen and didn't like. I thought of that sad episode in my own mother's history. I knew I could have escaped the same treatment, if I hadn't been thinking so hard about getting to Caedon. What was I thinking, deliberately inviting such a fate? I felt I was to blame.

Then, too, my mind kept circling back to that kiss. How Gwyl's lips had felt against mine. The dim moon shining down on us, the nearness of him, the warm male scent of him. How much I wanted to kiss him more, and touch him.

Oh, you needn't weigh in, Companion. I know where you stand already. You've told me often enough. You think I was wrong to do what I did. I suppose you're right.

Ah. I did say that, didn't I? About the touching? I had forgotten that. All the touching. My parents, always touching. How I didn't want anyone to touch me. Now, though, I want someone to touch me. I want Gwyl to do it.

Yet I had risked Gwyl's life, hadn't I, by letting my pursuit of Caedon get completely out of hand.

He'd held his own nicely, though, I reminded myself. I was always reminding myself of that, because the next thoughts came at me whether I wanted them to or not.

Suppose something untoward had happened, and he had been killed. In my imagination, I saw the scene again and again. There had been a big table in my room at the viceroy's manor, with a wooden bowl on it. The bowl was piled high with apples. I revisited them in my mind. Red and luscious. There was a lot of crashing around during that fight. A lot of overturning of furniture. Suppose—and here in my mind's eye I saw the apples spilling out of their bowl, rolling around on the floor. I saw one rolling underneath Gwyl's feet, tripping him up. I saw Caedon driving with the point of his sword right at—

And here I would always stop myself. I wouldn't be able to think further than that, but I'd know I was the one responsible for Gwyl's death. This thought made me turn pale and twisted my stomach into knots.

Was there really a bowl of apples? Or had I just thought them up? They were all too real to me whenever I imagined the scene.

I wondered if my parents were angry and disappointed with me over my lack of good sense. They must be.

Gwyl himself entered the house now, and a cold wind followed him in. I turned aside to hide a blush. Luckily, he isn't like me, able to overhear the things inside people's heads, I thought.

Or used to be able.

"Lady Keera! Your Highness." He bowed to me.

Was this a show he was putting on for Aevarr's mother's benefit, or was he trying to re-establish some distance between us? I tried to drive the anxiety out of me.

"Aevarr tells me you've been to visit Hildr."

"Yes, I have. I was glad to see her, so glad."

"I'm sure she felt the same." He stood warming his hands by the fire. Then he turned to me. "I've come to tell you goodbye for a while," he told me. "We're about to head out in the ships."

"Please be careful," I said. Then I appalled myself by bursting into tears.

"How's this, Keera?" He came to sit beside me. Aavarr's mother tactfully busied herself elsewhere.

"I put you in danger because I wanted to get to Caedon," I said. I was ashamed. "Everyone was in danger because of me. I should never have allowed Grandfather to marry me off and be taken away on my poor dead husband's knarr."

"How would you have avoided doing that?" asked Gwyl, his voice gentle.

"I know I could have gotten away from Grandfather," I said.

"No, you could not have done that."

"Yes, I could." I heard my voice turn stubborn.

"They were watching you every moment. You probably weren't aware of how closely. Your grandfather had men standing ready to prevent you, from one sunrise to the next."

"I didn't know that," I said in a small voice. "But anyway, I didn't know that." I made myself keep going. "So I'm just as guilty as if he'd left me free to act. And then there were all those apples—"

"Apples? What are you talking about? But Keera, you're not guilty of anything. Lucky. Brave. That's what I'd say."

"You're very kind to me. They assigned you to pretend to court me, and I enjoyed it. Then you risked your life, and I let you do it. I do feel guilty. You could have tripped on one of those apples. And died." I was nearly whispering now. I didn't want to say these things, but I had to.

"Nine Spheres, girl. I'm not just very kind to you, as you put it. I'm in love with you."

I looked up into his face, startled. "You didn't even know me, before all this got started."

"Now I do. And what's all this about apples?"

He put his arm around me and pulled me closer to him. With his other hand, he smoothed my hair off my face. He didn't tousle it. He smoothed it. He tipped my face up to his with a finger, and he kissed me again. Longer. I wanted it longer still.

But he pulled away. "I have to go," he whispered.

"I'm afraid," I said.

"Don't be. I know what I'm doing."

"I know you do, I watched you fight Caedon, but war is chancy. Maybe that's the only thing I've learned. I've been so foolish in so many other ways."

"Shh. Wait here for me, lovely Keera. Promise me. Look," he said, pulling it out of his belt pouch and holding it up for me to see. "I have your magic needle. I'll be fine. Promise me."

"I promise," I said.

And just like that, he was gone. We never did talk about the apples. After that, though, my imagination let me get some rest, and the apples disappeared from it, disappeared for good.

The Woman in the Clouds

Wait here for me, lovely Keera. I kept turning Gwyl's words over and over in my mind. Sometimes, when I thought of them, I felt a warm thrill rising from deep inside me. But just as often, I felt suffused with fury. Why did I have to wait here for anyone? While I waited, idle and useless, this man Gwyl, the man I realized I loved, was over on the mainland of the Fire Isle, taking action.

Why wasn't I the one taking action?

It made me angry.

My own circling thoughts made me angry, too, as if I were Hildr spiraling higher and higher away from any tether. *The man I realized I loved.* What did I know about that? I was probably acting very foolish and silly reacting this way to the sugared words of a fellow I barely knew. Even though he had saved my life and my honor. Even though he had risked his own life doing it. And then—my fantasies would catch me up again, and that warm thrill would spread through me again, and—

Yes, there I agree with you, Companion. What do we know, really, about love when we're this young, and know it, and know—at least deep down—we don't know a thing about it? I see you've entertained those doubts yourself.

And that warm thrill rises from deep inside all the way out to the tips of my fingers and the tips of my toes and tingles there, just like that magic Old Dee described to me, electricity.

"Jesus, Mary, and Joseph," I muttered, but the thoughts kept circling.

I realized I was engaged in that same circling not only inside my mind but outside it, in the actions of my own body. Every day, I found myself wandering out of the house; making a circuit of the hilltop; next, heading down the steep path to the cove to shade my eyes and stare out over the narrow strait toward the Fire Isle mainland. Then back again. Each time, when I returned, I huddled closer to the fire, wrapped myself tighter into my cloak, felt a little more despondent. I caught Aevarr's mother looking at me with a crease of concern between her brows, when she thought I wasn't noticing.

One day I wandered further afield than usual. I found myself standing on a slope that led down to the coast. But not the coast where the ships drew up. Not the coast of the small strait I could look across and see the Fire Isle. This was the far coast of the tiny island, the coast overlooking the gray and sullen Northern Sea. I walked down to the very edge of the water. The coast curved in here, creating a large protected bay. The waves were not very high.

I walked along the water's edge. The tide was out, and the shingle was dotted with tide pools. They reminded me of the time Mother and I worked with the salt-makers when I was just a small child.

I smiled a little at the memory. The gray clouds hung low, almost touching the gray of the sea. There was a kind of dull reflected light from the hidden sun, a suffused glow

I sat down in the sedges of the salt marsh at the edge of the shingle. The day was unseasonably warm. I grew drowsy and lay back, staring up at the clouds. As I stared, they assumed strange shapes, as clouds will. In particular, one big swollen gray cloud formation resembled a woman's face. In my fancy, I saw her as a grieving woman. I lay gazing at her and the surrounding formations. One was very like a whale. One was like a camel, or at least it was backed like a camel. I'd seen a camel in a book once. These cloud formations merged and created themselves into new fanciful animals, but not the woman's face. The woman's face was there in the sky, and it continued to stare down at me while the other clouds formed and re-formed and re-formed again into their fanciful shapes.

I may have slept a little.

When I woke, I was stiff. I pulled myself to my feet and resumed walking beside the tide pools. I think I thought then the woman's face in the clouds was just some dream I'd had while I slept. I was startled, as I gazed into one of the pools, to see the woman's face staring back at me. I darted a look toward the clouds and then laughed at myself. There was no woman's face. It had just been my fancy.

But when I looked back to the surface of the pool, the face was there, and the eyes spoke to me. *I have something to tell you. Hear me.* I felt drawn closer. And closer. Soon I was standing right at the pool's edge, gazing deep within it. The water reflected the cloud formations. And then, somehow, it didn't. It reflected something else.

I saw a woman. Not the cloud woman, but another, a real woman within the depths of the pool. She was frightened and looking over her shoulder. A man came and guided her away from a pile of rocks. No, a castle. The water rippled. The vision, or whatever it was, devolved into mere shallow wavelets on the surface of the pond. I shook myself. Was I dreaming?

And a new vision now replaced the first. The same woman, holding a bundle. I looked closer. The woman drew back the corner of a blanket from her bundle. I saw then that what she held was a baby.

Again, the surface of the pool rippled. Again, the woman reappeared, this time with a man beside her. He looked weary. And there was some other expression on his face, something else, something I couldn't quite make out. She held him and comforted him, but then he angrily shook her hand off him. She called him by a name. She called him Maro. Her voice was pleading. Two small children played at their feet. Two little boys.

The surface rippled. Two older boys, one dark, one fair. They were running and leaping. Their laughter rang out through the green shade of a woods in springtime.

The surface rippled. Only one of the boys this time, the dark boy, his face serious and intent. He was practicing swordplay by himself in a long white bare room.

The surface rippled. The boy, older now, confronting the man and woman, who angrily accused him. The dark boy, striding to the door of their house and out of it, banging the door behind him. Waiting for him down the path, the fair boy. The two of them, hastening off into the wide world together.

I waited. When the surface of the pond rippled again, I saw the woman's face, looking back at me. The first woman, not the mother of the two boys.

My breath caught in my chest. What else would she reveal? She looked to be on the point of saying something. But then something seemed to happen to stop her. Her eyes moved uneasily to look at something beside her. She looked frightened. It was some dark, malevolent shape. I suddenly recalled something I had completely forgotten. A dream I had had in Old Dee's house. A shape like this one, moving ever closer to me, and Old Dee fending it off. "Gilles, I adjure thee." The woman in the pond's terror grew, and so did my own. When it reached the point I didn't believe I could stand it and would have to run off screaming, the pond went dark. When I stepped to it to peer into its depths, it only reflected back the louring gray sky.

A deep thrum that might have been coming from the air around me, or maybe from inside me, it was hard to know which, began gathering in intensity. I started to tremble. A gong-like sound emerged from the thrumming. "Gilles. Gilles." The gong-like sound thrummed deep into the landscape. And then, abruptly, the thrumming was gone.

As if I were coming out of a dream or a trance, I got slowly to my feet. I began to feel like myself again, but the feeling of the visions didn't entirely leave me. When I could think sensibly again, I sent up a brief prayer of thanks. Indeed, I thanked that old farwydd, and through her, my Child. I realized that while she hadn't restored my farseeing abilities, she had vouchsafed me these brief visions, and I was grateful.

As I made my way back to Aevarr's house on the hill, I realized something else. The woman in the clouds. It was you, Companion. I looked around for you, but I didn't see you. When I got back inside, though, there you were again, hovering in your corner.

Now, how did I know the woman in the clouds was you, Companion? Do you know, I've never seen your face? I've sort of seen it, but never directly. I wouldn't have been able to tell anyone what you looked like, not really, even though I have been aware of your presence for years.

But now I have seen you. I'd recognize you if I saw you again. You know, in an ordinary way. Not the way you are now.

You must have taken a big risk, to show yourself to me in this way. Your eyes were sad. They looked as though they could see down a thousand years. They looked as though they had seen more than one woman, one person, ever ought to see. Really terrible things, Companion. Your cheeks were pale.

And then you looked completely terrified, as if that vile presence would take you and force you to do its bidding.

You and the farwydd together, you must have sent me these visions. I wonder, Companion, if you persuaded the farwydd to let me see them, in spite of her deep misgivings about me and the confidence I used to have in my powers. I see it now. The arrogance I used to have. I see now why she may have thought she needed to remove my powers from me. I see now how she may have been thinking she was acting for my own good.

But you, Companion. Every minute I am more sure of it. You saw I needed to know some things about Gwyl. And you persuaded my farwydd to let me see them.

The two boys of the vision. They were Gwyl, as a boy, and his brother.

When you showed me that, Companion, you put yourself at terrible risk. I'm not sure how or why, but the voice calling "Gilles" and the dark presence tell me you did.

I realized the visions told the story of Gwyl's life to me, the outlines of it, at least. And the menacing figure showed me in some veiled way the price you might have to pay for doing so.

Thank you, Companion. I love you for what you did. You gave me a great gift and, I fear, at tremendous cost.

Ravenous Wurm

During all the many excursions I made around the island, I never had any sort of vision again. I went back to the tide pools several times. Nothing. I appealed to you, Companion. Nothing.

I shouldn't have begged you. That was wrong. I am not blaming you, dear Companion. What you gave me was generous and fine. How do I know what it cost you to give that gift to me? It may well be you went against my farwydd's wishes in doing so. I had the deep conviction you went against someone else's wishes, too. Someone sinister. Who is this Gilles?

No. Don't answer. I see how it distresses you. Just know I am grateful to you for what you gave me. And now I see you better. I know you better.

But my restlessness was growing. I suppose that should have been a warning to me. On one of these excursions—it proved to be the last—when I reached the top of the steep decline from the hilltop to the cove where the ships would be pulled up, I saw a figure at the bottom of the path, thin shoulders hunched. As I got closer, I realized it was Aevarr.

I moved up beside him. He looked over at me, then resumed his long watchful gazing over the strait.

"You do this, too," I said to him.

"Aye, lady."

"I feel useless. I want to be over there."

"Aye, lady."

"Aevarr. . ." I hesitated. Then I sped on. Yes, I know. I'm reckless, and I don't think things through to their consequences on other people or the impact on their poor parents. "Do you know how to row a boat?"

"Aye, lady."

"So do I," I said. I looked pointedly over to the scraggly bushes at the side of the sandy strand, where a small boat had been pulled up and overturned.

As if impelled by the same thought, we strolled over to the boat. Aevarr prodded it with his toe. Together, we bent to turn it rightside up.

Together, we waded it out into the surf and clambered in. Together, we unshipped its oars and began to row for the farther shore. No words had passed between us. We just knew, together, what we longed to do. Now we were doing it.

Aevarr knew the coastline well. Clearly, he was a child of the Child of Sea, although he lived in the lands of the Fire Child. He easily took us in to a protected landing, and we hauled ourselves out onto the stony ground of the Fire Isle mainland.

"I don't know the way to Grandfather's estate from here," I said, stopping in the middle of the path leading away from the shore.

"But I do, lady," said Aevarr. We smiled at each other, a delighted smile of complicity.

Then I stopped stock-still. I had heard something. I held up my hand. We both stood in the path, listening.

A high-pitched, rapid ki-ki-ki kee. A small figure plummeting from the very zenith of the sky with wing-beats almost too fast for the eye.

"Hildr!" Aevarr cried, whipping off his cloak and wrapping it about his hand. He lifted it, and Hildr came in for her landing, as thrilled with herself as the two of us were thrilled with ourselves.

"How did you get out, Hildr?" I scolded. But of course I didn't mean it. We stood smiling at her, and I swear to you she smiled back. So the three of us moved along the path then, and two of us were trying our best but failing to keep warm. Aevarr was using his cloak to protect his hand from Hildr's sharp talons, and I was soaked through by my wet, flapping skirts, which impeded me with every step.

We came to a little rise. A farmhouse stood by the road. "Wait here, Mistress," said Aevarr. He went to the door of the cottage and knocked. Pretty soon, he came back with the farmwife. They talked rapidly together in their language as I stood by.

"I told her, this lady would like to buy your laundry,'" he explained to me.

She looked from one to the other of us, and from us to Hildr, and her eyes narrowed with suspicion. But when I took my pouch from my belt and began counting out coins into my palm, she began to smile.

She ran back to her cottage and returned with a pile of laundry. I pawed through it. Trousers. A cloak. A few other things.

I then counted the coins out into her own palm, and she pulled at her forelock and backed into her cottage, beaming and curtseying all the way.

I turned behind the wall of turfs between her pig-stye and her fields and pulled the trousers on underneath my sodden skirts. Then I struggled out of my kirtle and belted the trousers close around me. I plucked a tunic from the bundle of laundry and pulled that on. "That's better," I told Aevarr, coming from behind the wall. I tossed the cloak to him. I kept out a small kerchief to wrap about my own hand for a Hildr perch, and left the rest of it behind the wall, including my stout woolen kirtle, fine quality cloth I was figuring Aevarr's own mother had woven. May she someday forgive me. There's a good chance she may not, ever.

I hope the farmwife found that pile of clothing behind her wall the next day, at least, and felt herself doubly-recompensed.

As we walked along, my mind fastened on my riddle, the one the Fire Child's farwydd had given me. I often thought about it, puzzling out this bit or that to while away the time. I'd long since given up the notion I would ever solve it. I had only figured out tantalizing bits and pieces. The firebird—certainly that was my firebird, and I knew what the riddle meant by *Firebird the True.* But what did it mean, *carry her on your back to the isle of the thousand suns.* What isle? Who was this *her?* Was that me?

Then, long ago in Old John's house, I had figured out for sure the first two lines: *The ravenous wurm of the mountain devours the great streets of men.* It meant the mighty earthquake and the destruction it wreaks on the things we puny human beings build, the way a mighty dragon might shake the earth with its rage.

As for the rest, I had no idea. *Hildr* was Hildr, of course. Or was it? But what *battle storm of Hildr* meant, who knows?

On an impulse, I turned to Aavarr. "What does Hildr's name mean?"

"Oh? Oh, yes. Hildr is one of the old gods. Even before the Children. The goddess of thunder and war. She's a battle maiden, Mistress."

"That fits her well," I said, reaching out a finger to stroke her feathers. She made her purring sound, like a cat's.

Battle storm of Hildr, I whispered to myself. Maybe that's thunder, I speculated.

"And Mistress," Aavarr continued. "The people in the before-times thought that the thunder and lightning were the arrows from Hildr's battle-bow."

Bingo, I said to myself, borrowing one of the most magical of all Old Dee's words. A big storm could be the *life-harm of the hall* just as surely as an earthquake. Death and destruction to the petty doings of trifling humans. The riddle was beginning to make sense.

The rest, though. . . . I shook my head. I was still mystified.

Aavarr and I spent the night in a comfortable cottage where the goodwife there, for more of my coin, allowed me a room and Aavarr a place rolled up in his cloak by the hearth. She hadn't wanted to, at first.

"Dark dealings upon us, Mistress," she said to me, serving us both a bowl of hot stew, conceding us that much. This woman, unlike the first, could speak the language of the Sceptered Isle. "Soldiers marching through here, trampling the crops, taking our animals. Then in a day or two, here come another group of them doing the same."

"Who are they, do you think?" I asked her.

She rolled her eyes to the heavens and shrugged. "The Children know, Mistress. Some of them's from that mean old man's estate, I think."

"Fylkir?" I said.

"That's him, Dark Ones take him. In Olaf Redbeard's time, there'd never be such doings, or even in his brother Sigismund's day. But this old Fylkir, the youngest of those brothers, he's the one has the estate now. He seized my man a few years back, took him off somewhere, and never did I see him again. As for the others, those marchers—" she shrugged again. "Fire Child help me if I know where that lot come from. And then there's them that come by sea." At that, she gave us a dark look, staring pointedly at my trousers. "And you two, are you connected with them in any way? If it be, then get out of my house."

"We're no soldiers," I hastened to assure her.

The absurdity of that statement made us all smile, and then she was friendly again.

I was just being honest with the woman. Pretty much.

We did have to explain ourselves then, though. "We're searching, ourselves, for a man we've lost," I told her. That seemed good enough for her. It was a situation she'd been in herself, maybe many of her neighbors, too. "I got soaked through in the surf, and had to put these on," I told her, gesturing at my odd clothes. She offered to sell me a kirtle, but I hastily waved her off. "We'll be traveling rough for some days, Goodwife, and these are warm," I told her. I don't know. Am I a natural liar and can't help it? I couldn't resist embroidering the truth a bit. "As soon as I reach my aunt's house near Mist Cove, then I'll have decent things to wear," I told her.

You. What are you doing, Companion, gibbering up there on the rafters? That's just rude. Stop it.

The goodwife quizzed me a little longer about my aunt and where she lived. I borrowed details of the house where the Lady Jehanne had stashed me, years ago. *With a promise to go straight home.* I drove the guilt away from me, that old guilt that kept coming back.

I know, Companion. You can save your breath. Yes, indeed. The guilt that never produces any useful results, since I never seem to be able to stop myself from taking rash action.

But my story and the real details I wove into it seemed to convince the goodwife nicely.

Oh, very well, Companion. I am naturally deceitful. Let's leave it at that, shall we? But you can't fool me any longer. You may disapprove of me, but I know you love me. And here's a surprise. I love you back.

After my story, the goodwife consented to take my coin and give us a place to sleep, and she allowed me to keep Hildr in the barn behind her house with the other animals.

We left this woman's cottage the next morning. She waved us on our way with many admonitions to be careful and watch out for soldiers.

The night after that, it was clear we had reached the lines of battle, or close to. The land was burned over. Dead cows lay feet up in the fields. Carrion birds settled on contorted piles of I'm not sure what. Bodies, probably. I had to look away, and we both had to calm Hildr down. She was making unsettled and unsettling shrieking noises, fluttering up on her jesses and rebuffing our hands.

We slept that night burrowed into a haystack. We didn't dare approach any houses. Hildr nestled in with us. I thought of saying, *Home, Hildr*, to her, but for some reason I couldn't be parted from her. The next morning, I did let her hunt, and keep her kill, too, a redpoll. That settled her down.

We sent her up again, and she came back with a very small rabbit. Luckily Aevarr had flint and steel. I realized not for the first time how unprepared he and I were to do what we were doing. We'd left Gwyl's island on a whim, and now we were suffering the consequences. He unhooked a small oiled pouch from his belt and brought out his fire-starting implements. At least he had those. First he opened his tinder box and took out some of the char-cloth inside. Over it, he struck his striking stone against his fire-steel until a spark fell into the char-cloth. Then he blew upon it and we fed the flame with small sticks until we had a fire. We spitted and cooked our rabbit until it was nicely browned, and then we savored the rabbit meat as if it were a king's feast. Interesting how fast a person can overcome her scruples and squeamishness when she's ravenously hungry. Aevarr and I had had nothing to eat except some field berries since our night at the goodwife's cottage.

We had just finished eating when we heard voices and stamping feet. Aevarr and I jumped up and kicked out our fire. We ran for it, finding safety of a kind behind the high stone wall of a ruined, caved-in barn. Hildr swooped in after us just as the first of the marching men came into view.

They hadn't seen us. If any of them noticed a still-smoldering pile of turves off the road, they were too intent on their mission to stop to investigate.

Aevarr and I stared at each other with enormous eyes. He looked scared, and I know I did too.

Where were you all this time, Companion?

I looked overhead. There you were, up on the wall, sitting swinging your legs and watching after them as the men marched by.

I tried to angle to get a look at them. Were they ours, or Caedon's, or my grandfather's? And if they were ours, were they my father's, or Gwyl's little band of mariners?

It was too confusing.

"Caedon's men, I think," I whispered to Aevarr. "But I can't be sure."

Once they were past and we were safe, I reached down and grabbed up clouts of muddy soil with both hands. I smeared the dirt on my face and pulled up my hood. When he saw me doing that, Aevarr did likewise. Our cloaks were dull, our faces were smudged, our hoods were pulled well up. Anyone looking at us would, I hope, see two poor dirty peasants.

Of course, poor dirty peasants don't walk about with hawks on their arms. I only hoped we'd get enough warning to send Hildr flying, if anyone approached us.

"They were marching that way," I told Aevarr, keeping my voice low and pointing. "If we go that way, too, I'm thinking we'll reach the battle lines." And then do what? I asked myself. Aevarr would want to join Gwyl's men. He had a few cousins in that little squad of mariners. What would Gwyl do when he realized I hadn't in fact waited for his return, but had instead intruded here where I wasn't wanted? "When we find Gwyl," I said to Aevarr, "you join them. Don't mention me. I'll stay hidden. I'll be fine."

"No, lady," said Aevarr. "I won't leave you alone."

I didn't argue with him, but I hoped to persuade him when the time came.

What was I doing here? Just what in the name of the Nine Spheres did I think I was doing here?

I knew you were about to ask that, Companion, so I have asked it first, before you can say anything and act superior, the way you always do.

Saying that was churlish of me. I apologize.

Oh.

Now you've surprised me.

You want to be here? You're glad I brought you? That, my strange Companion, is very, very surprising to me. And let me say it again. I'm sorry I was sharp with you. Forgive me. You've done me kindly service, dear Companion, and I shouldn't forget that.

"Who are you talking to, my lady?" said Aevarr. He looked a bit alarmed.

"No one. Myself. Sometimes when I'm trying to think things through, I have a little conversation with myself. Don't you do that, too?"

"No, lady," said Aevarr.

"Well, I do," I replied.

But now we heard the tramp of more feet coming up from behind us.

I scanned the road on either side. At this point, it ran along a ridge. To our right, the forested hill rose steeply beside us. To the left, the land sloped down, first in a rugged landscape of stones and gouges of ravines, then gently to a little river valley.

I nudged Aevarr and pointed. We headed into the thin tree cover and clambered up the embankment. Boulders studded the hillside. We hid behind one to wait for this new contingent of men to march past.

These, I saw from our hiding place, were definitely Caedon's men. I could tell from the golden wolf insignia on their black clothing. Caedon's army was apparently gathering and pulling up into position. I thought I knew where we were now. I thought we were pretty close to Grandfather Fylkir's estate, situated in a valley between the high road to the south and lower hills to the north, rolling down north and westward to the sea.

"What do you think?" I whispered to Aaevarr. "Looks like they're surrounding Grandfather's land. Then they'll attack."

"Aye, I'm thinking the same, my lady," he whispered back.

As this new group of men went past our hiding place, we crept along the ridge to keep them in sight.

I was right. The two groups that had passed us were formed up along the roadside just behind my grandfather's imposing stone house, the house that used to be his dead brother's. It was surrounded by a protecting wall and gate. Only the pleached garden lay between Caedon's men and my grandfather's household.

Aevarr and I lay on our bellies just above the massing men to watch. A new stream of men joined the first. And then another group came down the road to join those.

"Look," Aevarr whispered, and nudged me. He nodded with his head, indicating the land north of Grandfather's house, where the mews and stables were. Just past was a wooded area, and when I squinted I could see it was swarming with men.

"Those are ours, lady," Aevarr murmured. "I can tell by that banner." Past them fluttered a pennant. I recognized it, too. It was Gwyl's. It was a bold black and white, three interconnected spirals, each ending in the head of a fierce bird of prey. I asked him about it once, what this triple spiral meant. He'd just shrugged and muttered something about the old gods, but I knew his banner well. He'd flown it on his big skeid during our voyage in order to keep the skeid and the five snake-ships together on the ocean.

It looked like Caedon's men were about to fight a battle with my father's, led by Gwyl. And the battleground was my grandfather's house and land.

I felt a sick thudding in the pit of my stomach. A terrible thought made its way into my mind.

"Do they know Caedon's men are here? I don't think Gwyl does know. Is there a way to warn them? Can you sneak around and let them know? Please, Aevarr. I'll be fine." When he hesitated, I said, low, "It's all very well to protect me. But Caedon's men are lying in wait. See, look how quiet they've gone. They're going to let Gwyl attack Grandfather and defeat him, and then those men down there are going to sweep out from hiding and slaughter ours, once ours are tired out from battle. Gwyl and his friends are in terrible danger down there. We have to warn them."

Aevarr looked up at me uncertainly, then back down at the massing men. He saw what I saw. Gwyl and my father's men were intent on overwhelming my grandfather in a surprise attack. But they clearly didn't know that Caedon's men would be waiting to pounce on them from the rear. Aevarr nodded and pressed my hand. He crawled on belly and elbows backward off the ridge and stole quietly away.

I put my head down and sobbed from fear, but I made sure to keep very quiet.

Below me, I could see the commanders of Caedon's men going down their lines and cautioning everyone to stay quiet and lay low.

Now, far below me, I could make out a figure, a man walking out of my grandfather's gates. He headed for the stables. Then he hesitated; stopped; ran back through the gates into the courtyard with a shout. Gwyl's forces had been spotted.

Men came boiling out of Grandfather's walled courtyard around his house. Grandfather must have been expecting some kind of attack. His men were armed and ready.

I nearly stood up and screamed. I balled my hands into fists and tried to keep a grip on myself. It was clear to me. Aevarr couldn't possibly have had enough time to warn Gwyl. But Gwyl's men did see what was happening at the gates of the courtyard, and they came screaming down from the north upon my grandfather's house.

As I had feared, Caedon's commanders raised warning hands to their own men, who stood waiting and ready. Caedon's archers began stringing their big bows.

Meanwhile, Gwyl's men and my grandfather's men were engaged in front of the gates. The sound of clashing arms came distantly to me where I watched. I could see men going down, men slashing and charging. There was no way to tell who was winning and who was losing.

And then there was. The much larger force from the north was overwhelming those at the gates. I could see men surrendering. Very quickly, it was over down there. One man strode to the gates and blew a blast on a horn. He shouted so loudly even I could hear.

"Come out, Fylkir." It had to be Gwyl.

It had to be his voice that floated up to me from far below.

Two figures appeared at the gates. One, tall, supporting another who seemed small and infirm. My uncle Stefan supporting my grandfather.

Meanwhile, directly below me on the southern road, the tension was palpable. Caedon's commanders were making fierce gestures to their groups of men, who were all inching forward. In only moments, I knew, the commanders would release their men on the exhausted victors below. And cut them to pieces.

I looked on in sick horror.

"Ready," I heard the quiet command. And "ready." "ready." "ready." down the line.

The men on the road below me rose up and surged forward shouting, bearing down upon the men at the gates.

Gwyl—I supposed that was he—saw them at last and blew a blast on his horn, and his men, vastly outnumbered, grouped around him and began slowly retreating. Too late, it looked like.

Yelling, savagely cheering, Caedon's men descended on them. And then.

How can I explain what happened then? I'm not sure it's possible to explain.

Something rose up.

Something small that had been crouching right beside me rose up and became immense. Something let out a shrill and eerie cry that echoed across the valley. The earth began to shake, first a bit, then hard, then it was as if the entire world was shaken to pieces. A thunderclap louder than any I'd ever heard burst over the valley, and bolts of lightning so bright I squeezed my eyes shut and hid my head for terror. There was a sizzling and crackling. The entire sky caught on fire.

The cone of the mountain at the head of the valley just beyond Grandfather Fylkir's estate began to glow red. Gouts of flame issued forth from it, and a river of flame began to pour down into the valley. Beyond the oncoming, flaming river, trees caught fire. The fire roared down in a flaming conflagration upon Caedon's men, as Gwyl led his own men back up onto the safety of the northern ridge.

It was as if the flames and the flaming liquid just behind had turned into a pack of yelping, voracious hounds devouring everything in its path. The flaming river reached my grandfather's estate and overwhelmed it. It roared after the panicked men of Caedon and devoured them. And then it swept down the valley, destroying everything in its path, ash and yew and oak and willow, their sorrowful branches outlined in flame.

By then, I was standing, silently watching, not quite believing the nightmare vision below me.

In minutes, it was all over.

I spoke this softly to myself:

> *The ravenous wurm of the mountain*
> *devours the great streets of men.*
> *Battle storm of Hildr, life-harm of the hall,*
> *the hound of the forest with its hot mouth*
> *swallows every house; fell dog*
> *of willow, ash, yew, oak*
> *casts its baleful eye on the yard-gate.*
> *Woe, that red-gaping hound of the wood.*

I picked my way off the ridge into the valley. Beyond, I could see Gwyl's men coming back down, too, in somber groups of twos and threes. The ground I trod upon was so hot it burned my feet through my boots. I stopped in front of the smoldering pile that used to be my grandfather's estate. The wooden gates were burned to stubs. The stone and turf walls stood blackened and destroyed, thrown off their foundations by the earthquake.

Stands of trees surrounding the estate still flamed like torches. All around me rose the nauseating smell of cooked flesh. Blackened piles, I saw, were bodies. Bodies of Caedon's men, and bodies of Grandfather Fylkir's men lying dead among them. I knew my grandfather's body and my uncle's were there, too, but there was no way to tell one twisted charred corpse from another.

I stood weeping in the smoke and carnage.

Gwyl was beside me now, his arms around me. He led me out of there, and we walked the few miles, with his men, back to the tents of my father near the shore.

Where were you, Companion, as this rising up of the Fire Child's wrath took place? Tell me that.

Why do I know it was you in the thick of it? You at the head of it, channeling the destroyer flames down the valley to overwhelm your enemies? Who are you, my Companion? Who are you, really?

CHAPTER THIRTEEN

If this were a story

I was a subdued daughter as I made ready to face my parents. While Gwyl stood guard outside his tent so I wouldn't be disturbed, I washed the grime and soot from myself. By then Gwyl had found Aevarr unhurt, praise the Children. He sent the boy into the neighboring village to find me some clothes.

Meanwhile, I paced back and forth in Gwyl's tent. How were my parents ever going to understand, I wondered. How would they forgive me. I'd put them through so much worry.

I hadn't seen them for three years.

I'd set out to perform two tasks, and I had accomplished neither.

I hadn't even solved the farwydd's riddle and gotten my powers back. True, now I knew I'd solved the major part of it. But two lines remained. I knew they were about my firebird, but that's all I knew.

In the beginning, those two lines had seemed to be the easiest part of the riddle to solve. As it turns out, they were the hardest.

Through all of my troubles, I hadn't even seen my firebird. I was expecting I would. Nothing was happening the way I expected it to.

And I'd broken every promise I'd made to the people I loved. Old Dee had said, *Go to your parents and wait for me there.* I had promised. I hadn't done what I said I would. Gwyl had said, *Wait for me until I return.* I had promised. I hadn't done what I said I would. As for the promise to my parents, the unspoken promise to behave with honor and bring credit upon them, I'd failed there too.

"Keera?" Gwyl's voice, from outside the tent. "Aevarr has returned with the clothes."

"Thanks," I called out to him. I wrapped myself in Gwyl's big cloak and parted the flaps of the tent. Gwyl handed the clothes to me. I looked at him uneasily. He was watching me, a little intent line marking his brow. Was he angry with me? He looked more worried than angry.

I took the clothes silently and retreated back into the tent to pull them on—a plain kirtle and the usual kind of apron that fastened by straps over the shoulders. Then I came out.

"Ready?" Gwyl said to me.

I nodded, but I didn't trust myself to speak. He took my arm and led me down the row of tents to the big one where my father had his headquarters.

At the tent opening, I hung back.

Gwyl looked down at me. "Scared?"

I nodded.

"Don't be scared," he whispered. "I'm more scared than you are."

I looked at him dumbly, not knowing what he could mean.

He ushered me in.

No sooner had I stepped into the tent than my mother rushed to me, folding me into her arms and crying and laughing with joy. She led me to my father, who did the same.

I was crying, too. Tears of shame.

"I'm sorry," I whispered to them.

"Daughter, we're together now, and you're not hurt. That's the only thing that matters," said my mother. My father said almost the same thing at almost the same time, and they laughed at each other and laughed down at me.

Gwyl stood to one side, a wistful look in his eyes. I wondered then about his own family. I knew he must be missing his brother. In the aftermath of our escape from Caedon, and on the boat, I'd seen how close they were. But what about his parents, I thought. Maybe they were as worried about him as my parents had been about me. Maybe they were missing him as much. I decided to ask him about them when I got the chance.

"You're so big!" my mother exclaimed, squeezing me so tight I thought I might not be able to breathe.

"I'm a woman," I said. Then I added, "I think."

My father just pulled me to him and sat me beside him and couldn't stop tousling and fooling with my hair. I let him. My mother was drinking me in with her eyes, but I knew my father couldn't. He saw by touch.

Meanwhile Gwyl had gone quietly away.

My parents both looked older. They both looked as though they'd been through many troubles together, and I knew I was the cause of them—or many of them.

"I wanted to help. It was my dearest wish, Mother. But I couldn't. And Mother, I've lost my powers."

"It doesn't matter, Keera. There were so many bad things that could have befallen you, and in the end, none of them did."

"The Fire Child was looking out for you," said my father.

"Or luck," my mother quickly added. She always does.

"No, the Fire Child was looking out for us, all of us," I said. "I didn't think so at first. At first I was really angry with Her. But now I know She did."

"Daughter," said my father, and his voice was gentle. "Can you promise me not to go looking for revenge any more?"

"Yes, Father. I promise," I said, and I meant it.

"Hate just builds on hate. That's what I've found out. But now, war has come to us anyway. We must try not to make it any worse than it already is."

"But Father! I wanted to—" I stopped, not knowing how to explain. "There was something else I wanted to do. I wanted to help you see again. And I couldn't do that, either."

The tears poured down my cheeks.

My father just smiled. "I doubt anyone can accomplish that."

"With my powers, I could have," I said. I looked to my mother for confirmation, and she looked back at me, troubled. I saw she remembered the time I cured the woman, and the bad things that resulted.

"But now I don't have them. My powers are gone. Dried up. I'm useless."

"That's not true, Daughter," said my father. "We might think that, and then we find out we have other powers buried inside ourselves that we hadn't even known were there."

I took my father's hand and stroked it. I thought about everything my father had had to give up, and everything he'd gained.

"But still," I whispered. "I met a man, a powerful sorcerer and neurologist, and he thought he might help you to see again. But then he had to leave, because he serves a jealous queen."

My mother and father smiled at each other over my head. They thought I didn't see, but I did. Don't ask me how my father knew my mother was smiling at him. He just did. They were spooky that way.

"What's a neurologist?" asked my mother. I could tell she was trying not to laugh. In the past, that would have made me mad, but now I was just glad to be home.

"It's a very powerful magician."

"I see," said my mother.

But she really didn't.

Actually, as I thought it through, neither did I.

We spent a quiet week together in that tent as Father's men went on a mopping up expedition that took them throughout the Fire Isle. Gwyl was with them, leading them. I tried not to think about him. It was too disturbing, what I was imagining about him. *You're being silly*, I told myself. *Stop it!* But I couldn't.

At the end of that time, I was helping my mother with some of the potions she was putting together for the wounded when a horn sounded.

"They're back," my father called over to us. We ran to him and all of us stood waiting.

The tent flap was thrust aside, and Gwyl entered. I tried to control the way my heart infuriatingly started beating faster, and I know I was blushing.

My mother glanced at me, then looked harder. She looked toward Gwyl. Back to me. She smiled.

That was infuriating, too.

Where are you, my Companion? You'd know why this little scene troubled me so much. You've left me, though. I saw you grow huge at the battle, and then I didn't see you any longer. Maybe it's for the best. I have too many questions to ask you, and I doubt you'd answer them. But I miss you, Companion. If the farwydd sent you to me for this one task, defeating Grandfather Fylkir and Caedon's army in one fiery blow, then she may have taken you back to herself now. That will make me sad, if it's so.

In spite of these troubled and troubling thoughts, my eyes had been on Gwyl from the instant he had come into my parents' tent. Now he knelt before my father. "My prince," he said.

"Is he kneeling?" my father said to my mother. "Get up, Gwyl. Don't kneel to me. Too much kneeling," he muttered to himself.

Gwyl grinned at my mother. He stood up. "Your Highness, good news. We've driven Caedon from this land."

"Was Caedon himself here?" asked my father. In spite of his words about wanting peace and not wanting revenge, I saw his mouth tighten into a grim little line.

"He was. I'm sorry to say, we didn't capture him. We were closing in on him, but he slipped away. He has left on his ships with the remnants of his army and has sailed, we think, back to his post on the Northmost Isle."

"Good," said my father. "Let Caedon and Haakon fight it out together, then. We'll send Haakon some of our men, as a friendly gesture from an ally, but we'll not declare ourselves his vassal."

"Will you go back to the isle fortress, Your Highness?"

"That's a possibility." My father rose, shaking off my mother's arm as she rose too, to steady him. Not unkindly, though. Gently. "Thank you, my darling, but that's not necessary." He began pacing. Then he turned back to Gwyl. "My wife, the Lady Mirin, inherits the traitor Fylkir's lands after him. Her brother, who was older, is also dead, and there are no other heirs."

I thought of the many sons my poor dead old husband had promised to get on me. Not for the first time, I thanked the Fire Child he hadn't. How that would have muddied the succession, not to mention how it would have distressed me.

"That means," continued my father, "that the Lady Mirin, by the laws enacted by Avery the First, our rightful king before the succession passed to Diera, is the queen and monarch of this isle." He put out a hand to my mother, and she took it, smiling at him fondly.

"I doubt the laws of Avery apply to the Fire Isle, my dearest man," she said.

But he ignored her. He went down on one knee before her. "Hail, Queen Mirin," he said. Gwyl did the same. After an astounded second, so did I. "I pledge my allegiance to this queen, our rightful monarch. I pledge to defend her with my body and my spirit all the days of my life."

My mother passed a hand over her face. "No," she said.

"Yes," said my father.

"If, in winning this battle, the Sceptered Isle has taken the Fire Isle, you're its rightful monarch," she said, and her voice broke.

"If I'm the monarch of anything, it's not this realm," said my father. "Audemar is still alive. Caedon has the power. But that's over there—" he gestured vaguely south, in the direction of the Sceptered Isle. "We are here."

"And Haakon thinks he is the monarch of this isle," she went on, oblivious.

"Haakon is wrong about that if he thinks so. I believe Haakon will see reason, though. I believe Haakon, in his drive to oust Caedon, will welcome us as an allied although much smaller power."

Gwyl stood up now. "And I believe both Haakon and Caedon will have a big surprise coming," he said.

"What's that?" asked my father, getting to his feet too. "The east?"

"Aye. The Baronies are waiting to see who picks off the other, Haakon or Caedon. Then they'll come in to claim the winnings from the victor."

"And they think they can succeed? I know you grew up there, lad. You know more about it than any of us."

"Indeed," said Gwyl. "They have the power, and they have the grounds. The grounds are, first, that they are the heirs of Diera, cheated of her throne."

"The hypocrites," said my father. "But that's never stopped them. Go on."

"And we recovered dispatches Caedon's generals left behind in their rout. These tell us something interesting. Audemar is with the eastern lords."

"They'll set up Audemar as their puppet."

"That's what we think, yes, Your Highness," said Gwyl. "We've always thought of the barons as fractious, squabbling among themselves. They're not any longer. They're united under a single leader now."

"Gilles de Rais," said my father. I stood astounded. That name again. Gilles. Something in my father's voice, low and vicious, troubled me in ways I have a hard time describing.

"Gwyl. My boy. How much do you know about Baron Gilles?"

"Not much, my prince."

"You should know about him. About him and—" My father stopped with a look I don't think I've ever seen come upon him before. Or since. "About him and your father."

My mother put out her hand to him.

He took it and held onto it fiercely, as if he needed to do this or explode in rage and horror.

"My boy," he said, quietly now. "We'll talk of that someday. There are things you need to know, about Gilles de Rais."

I looked over at Gwyl. Gwyl stood white-faced, staring at my father.

"I know Caedon murdered my father," he said.

"Caedon murdered him," my own father said. "But there was another who stood behind Caedon." My father passed a hand across his eyes.

"Wat," said my mother, her voice full of concern.

"Terrible memories," he whispered. Then, it was as if he shook his mood off. "Gwyl, this is a discussion for another time, when we have some quiet. I promise you, we'll have that discussion. For now, though, I have a piece of good news for you. For you and Keera both. At least, I think you'll both be pleased."

Gwyl stepped to my side and took my hand. He squeezed it.

"In these current dispatches, my people tell me, there's news your brother Pierrick and Keera's friend Fiona were wed in the Ice-realm," my father told us.

Gwyl and I exchanged a delighted smile. "I knew it," I whispered to him. "I've never seen Fiona look at a man the way she looked at your brother."

"Good news indeed, my prince," said Gwyl to my father.

"But now we must turn from happy news to troubling. Let us hear about this threat you've seen from the east."

"We believe the eastern barons are preparing to set up Audemar as monarch of the Sceptered Isle," said Gwyl. I saw him wrench himself back to the details of war and diplomacy.

"Tell that to her, not to me," said my father, hugging my mother to him.

"My lady—my queen. What we've seen makes me think Gilles de Rais will set Audemar up as his puppet, keeping tight control of him. We believe the barons' goal is eventually to rule, themselves, probably through setting up a succession in favor of one of their own. Audemar is weak and ill. He has been living in obscurity, none knew where, but the barons have found him. They're counting on keeping him alive long enough to enact this scheme. Then, when he dies—who knows by what means?—they'll take the Sceptered Isle over for themselves," Gwyl told my mother.

"It's a puzzle," said my father. "Gilles and Caedon have always acted together. But now, it seems, Gilles may be setting up Audemar in opposition to Caedon. Backing Audemar. But always, controlling Caedon. I'm not sure I understand it. Not quite."

"Why is it we can never have peace?" said my mother.

My father seemed to shake off the horror that had overtaken him. "Let us have peace right here, in this isle," he said.

"As long as we can keep it," said Gwyl.

"Wat and I will rely on you, Gwyl, to be our strong arm," said my mother.

"Thank you, Your Highness," said Gwyl. He too seemed determined to shake off the shadow that had come over him at the mention of Audemar and his actual father Rafe. He tried to smile. "I value your regard," he said to my father. "Both of you." Now he looked to my mother. "You'll never know how much. Only there's one matter that may change your minds about that."

"What's this, lad?" said my father, but my mother's eyes were starting to sparkle. She had this advantage over my father, she could see a blush and he could not.

"I would like your permission to court your daughter, but since she is now so highly placed, maybe you won't want that," he said, with a grin at me.

"Hmm," said my father. "It seems to me you've already been courting her, with her grandfather's permission."

"Poor Father," said my mother, and heaved a sigh. "He was a bad man. It feels strange even to refer to him as 'Father.' That's not how I think of him."

Gwyl gave my mother a strange look of sympathy then. I was intrigued. I didn't have time to think about it, though, because Gwyl was replying to her. "Your father didn't give me much encouragement," said Gwyl. "He had other ideas for Keera."

Then I said, "Why are all of you talking about me as if I'm not even here? Has anyone asked . . . you know . . . me?"

"Daughter, you are the first person I'll ask, before I even think to answer this worthy man," my father told me. "And what is it, your answer?"

"It's yes," I said, and then—holy guacamole—blushed to the roots of my hair.

Now, if this were a story, everything would be over. I, the blushing maiden, would become the bride of my handsome and stalwart protector, and I would ride off with him and then he would . . . I don't know . . . get upon me stout sons? Instead, many complications lay ahead of us. So this is not the end of some story at all.

Oh, man. It's you. My Companion. You're back. I don't know what you mean by that, *This is not even the end of the chapter*. I love you. You know that. I've come to love you. But sometimes, your smugness makes me so angry. I wished you were back. Right now I wish you were gone again.

Dark Ones take it. Yes, you're right. There are many undone tasks. I haven't solved my riddle. I haven't restored my father's eyesight. I haven't revenged myself on Caedon. I haven't regained my powers.

But you. You have a lot of explaining to do, so don't try to divert my attention.

White Rocks and Black

The next weeks were among the happiest of my life. Gwyl and I were together, becoming closer every day. I was with my parents again. My father was helping my mother learn how to rule a realm, both of them were as much in love as they always had been, and they both had me to pet and tousle to their hearts' content. Even though I was now a woman grown, I let them. It would have been cruel to deny them that, don't you think, Companion?

And now I was able to see the deep respect Gwyl held for both of them. Affection, even.

"Hmph," I told him, as we paced out the field where my parents were trying to decide where to build my mother's palace. "Do you want to marry me? Maybe you just want to acquire my parents for yourself." My tone was teasing, but then I stopped, because I saw my words had hurt him.

"Keera, I love your parents."

"I see that," I told him. "I'm glad you do. And I can see they love you. If they had had a son, Nine Spheres, they would have wanted him to be exactly like you. Besides, you're a child of Sea, like my mother, always wanting to be near the water."

Gwyl laughed and turned away to point out some feature of the landscape to my mother, but before he did, I swear I saw his eyes fill with tears. It made me love him more, Companion.

As my parents rebuilt, they chose a spot overlooking the sea, and I know it was because my mother loved looking at it so much. Certainly they would never have considered building on the unhappy ruins of Grandfather Fylkir's estate. Bad spirits flitted about the place. That was one thing. But more practically, we all saw that building a big estate in the path of the lava flow from an active volcano (Old Dee's words, not mine) was a bad idea.

The day we moved into the new palace was a happy one.

"I refuse to call it a palace, though," said my mother. "We're acting as though I am a monarch here. That's probably not true. No one has ever ruled this place, not as king. There has always been a strong man. My uncle Olaf, then my uncle Sigismund, and then my father. And that's just recently. In the past, it was much the same. But throughout the ages, there's never been a king here."

I noticed how she always hesitated when she said that word, *father*. I know it's because she doesn't regard Fylkir as her father, her true father, and never will.

During too much of this otherwise happy time, I was lonely for Gwyl. He was taken up more and more with an important project, so we saw less of each other. Gwyl was traveling the Fire Isle, summoning all heads of household to a meeting at a big field just east of the port city. While Fylkir had styled himself king, and while Fylkir was indeed the largest landholder and most powerful man in the isle, a man with his own army, my mother was right. He'd never officially been named king. As the most powerful of all the chieftains of the isle, Fylkir's father had acted as a kind of unofficial king, and then, after his father's death, Fylkir's older brother Olaf Redbeard had continued the tradition. Everyone had looked to Fylkir's father for leadership, and after him, to Olaf.

Grandfather Fylkir was right. The next-oldest brother Sigismund was weak. That probably helped Grandfather when he grabbed control after Sigismund's death. People hadn't been thinking much about leadership, just about muddling through on their own the best way they could. Then Fylkir had swept in, with Haakon's help, and had taken over everything, grabbed everything for himself. Grandfather's regime, if you could call it that, gave a sad knock to everyone's sense of well-being. Old Dee, I know, would name it a wake-up call.

That's a great expression, isn't it, Companion. Wake up! This is what tyranny looks like!

To think of my mother simply assuming Fylkir's position was troublesome to many people. Fylkir was widely hated. And although my mother was his heir, she was not his male heir. My mother had decided she didn't want to be monarch if the people objected, and my father realized she was right. He supported her. So the big gathering would ask the people their wishes, and the field was chosen as the spot to do it because it was the only open space close to the palace that was big enough to accommodate so many people.

"Let's stop calling it the palace," I heard my mother murmur to my father again. "I'm not queen unless these people want me to be queen. Let's call it the manor, or the estate, or—"

My father had forestalled her with a kiss. "Let's wait and see," he told her. "Let's just ask them."

The day of the assembly finally arrived. It was like Fair Day—people had come from all over the isle to set up booths of turf around the perimeter of the field. We had erected our tent at the head of it. Neighbor visited with neighbor. Cousins who lived all the way across the isle from each other met for the first time in many turnings of the moon or even years to exchange happy news of babies born and marriages celebrated, sad news of old fathers and mothers and grandfathers and grandmothers who'd gone across the border to the Land of the Dead. Vendors hawked their wares, the usual ribbons and pans and sweetmeats.

Skalds strolled the grounds, singing their stirring songs, telling their tales of heroes and the weapons they wielded: magic swords, magic spells. One skald, my favorite, dressed all in

motley, a twinkle in his eye, a lilt to his voice, sang of an en-
chanted chain. To make this chain, the hero had to travel the
world to find the most unlikely things: the sound of a cat's footsteps, a woman's beard, the breath of a fish, the spittle of a bird,
the roots of a mountain. Only then could the hero weave the powerful magic he needed to defeat a demon and confine him with
the chain. Other heroes wrestled with fantastic beasts like mon-
sters and trolls. Attempted to outwit ill-intentioned gods.
Quested after dragons crouching on hordes of elven gold.

I didn't want this rich stew of sights and sounds and tales of
the marvelous ever to come to an end. I moved from booth to
booth, skald to skald, from one end of the grounds to the other,
taking it all in. I wanted it to go on forever, especially because,
hovering on the edges of all this wonder, I felt a deep anxiety
about what was soon to come. I think I was more jittery than my
parents were.

My parents send Gwyl out to find me, and he led me back to
their tent. It was time. "It will be fine," he whispered to me.
"You'll see. I feel like I've talked to everyone in this whole land.
They all love your parents."

At noon, my parents and their retinue, which included me
and Gwyl, walked to the center of the field, where we climbed up
on a big flat rock so everyone could see us. I was shaking. Gwyl's
hand was warm on my arm, though, and that steadied me. My
father and mother stepped to the front of the rock to speak. My
mother guided my father so he wouldn't fall off the edge, and
then she stepped back.

My father drew his sword and raised it high. All the people came flocking to the rock and stood around us, looking up at my father.

"Good people," said my father in a loud, commanding voice I don't think I'd ever heard him use before. It resonated across the field. I caught my mother repressing a smile. Later she explained that was Father's "Kenning the Juggler" voice, but I can't say that I ever really understood what that meant to her and why it made her almost laugh.

My father didn't get any further than that. People started to cheer. They yelled and yelled, cheered and cheered. It moved my father so. Finally he raised his sword again, and the cheering subsided.

"My thanks to you all. We have been through a bad time, all of us. The Traitor Fylkir tried to corrupt this isle. The army of the Usurper Caedon tried to take it by force. With the Children's help, we drove them back."

The cheering resumed, so long I really wondered if my father would have to give up and try again sometime later. But again he raised his sword, and again the crowd quieted.

"Now we have a decision to make. We were weak enough that Caedon thought he could invade us. Why was that? Because the Traitor Fylkir kept us divided against ourselves. Fylkir called himself our king. He was no king. His father made claim to be king, and his older brother, and you trusted them both, but Fylkir gave your trust away with both hands. He did not deserve to be king, and the Fire Child saw it and destroyed him for his presumption."

More cheering.

When they quieted again, my father resumed. "I am saying *we* and *us* as if I were one of you. I am not."

Many in the crowd called out loudly, "No, you are ours!"

"I am yours in spirit." My father's voice rang out. "In that way, I'll always be yours. In my youth, I came under the oppression of two usurpers, Audemar and Caedon. In my youth, I joined my brother and my half-brother King Avery the First, and after Avery's untimely and brutal death at the hands of Caedon, I served my niece Queen Diera the First, defending her claim with other brave resistors of tyranny. We all joined together to rise up and fight back. Even when we were broken and scattered, we never lost hope. Even when Caedon had that brave young queen killed, we did not give up.

"Among the bravest of the members of the Rising was a young woman, the Lady Mirin of the High Sea Cliffs." Here he urged my mother forward, and she came to stand beside him. "I loved her and made her my wife." To tremendous cheering, he reached for her and kissed her soundly. "I love her still," he said when the cheering stopped. "And I know who she is, bold and strong. Although she was born on this isle, she was taken as a small child to my realm, the Sceptered Isle. Only later did she realize this was the land of her birth.

"Her father was Fylkir. He died with his son Stefan, both overcome by the Fire Child's fury. The Lady Mirin is Fylkir's heir. My half-brother and adoptive father Avery the First changed the law in the Sceptered Isle so that a woman could become monarch, and his niece Diera did become queen. Then she was treacherously betrayed. I ask you all, honor Avery's principle here in the Fire Isle. Honor Fylkir's daughter and heir by naming her your queen. I don't ask this lightly. I ask that you listen to Mirin herself and then make up your minds."

Gwyl guided my father back, leaving my mother to face the crowd alone. I know if I had been Mother, I wouldn't have been able to do it. Looking out over that sea of faces would have frightened me so much that I think only a squeak would have come from my lips.

But you have to understand something about my mother. Yes, you. I'm talking to you, Companion. I see where you are, scattering yourself in little wisps among the crowd.

My mother is a performer. In front of a crowd, something takes her and makes her into someone bigger, more intense, more compelling than you can know. Watch, now.

"My friends and neighbors." My mother's voice, like Father's, echoed over the field. "I am Fylkir's daughter by birth, but not Fylkir's daughter in spirit. My mother Elsebet was one of you, born to a farmer. Many of you here knew her family. Elsebet fled with me when I was only a baby so that I would not have to grow up tainted by Fylkir's cruelty and greed.

"If you think a woman can inherit the monarchy, then I have inherited it, because Fylkir and his brother and father before him claimed it. They did so because they had the riches and power to do it. But I believe the Children have given us wits and will. I believe the Children do not look down kindly on those who use force and greed to assert their authority over others. If I become your monarch, I will only do so if you affirm it.

"Some think we'd do well without a monarch at all. That may be. I believe, though, that King Haakon will soon make us his vassals if he sees we are without leadership. King Haakon of the Ice-realm is an honorable man, and my husband Walter and I do honor him. If I become your monarch, I will assure him we are his allies against Caedon or anyone else who means ill. But we will not be his vassals.

"We are a free people on this Isle. If you ask me to, I will lead you, and I'll have the help of my husband Walter in that endeavor. I will see to it that all are treated fairly. I will see to it that the poor do not suffer from want. I will see to it that the prosperous have a fair chance to profit by their industry, but not if it means abusing others as my father did. I will see that the sick have succor. I will see that your sons and your daughters grow up in health and safety and wisdom. I will honor the Children in all that I do.

"I ask you this. Think hard. Then step to the foot of this rock. In the trough below me, you will find rocks, black ones and white. If you decide I should not be your queen, pick up a black rock. Conceal it in your hand. It's no one's business but yours if you choose that rock. Then drop it into the hole in the barrel below the trough and step aside. But if you decide I should be your queen, pick up a white rock. Again, conceal it and drop it secretly into the barrel.

"No neighbor should turn against neighbor for this choice. No one but you and the Children should know which rock you choose. Then confer among yourselves and pick three whom you trust. Let these three count the rocks, black and white. If there are more white rocks than black, I will be your queen. If there are more black rocks than white, I will not. The Children bless every one of you for the choice you are about to make. My husband and I will abide by your decision."

She bowed.

They responded, again, with a tremendous cheer. I knew they cheered her gallantry. I did not know whether that meant they would choose her for their queen.

At the end of that day, I did know. They chose her Queen Mirin the First of the Fire Isle, and they cheered themselves hoarse when the three counters announced the decision. They also insisted on naming my father Prince Consort. He grinned at my mother when they announced that. "I'm consorting with a queen," I overheard him whisper to her. "I like that just fine."

So we went away from that field in a joyous mood. The next day, reality hit. My mother was inundated with work. Every day, from the moment she breakfasted to the moment she went to bed, she saw well-wishers and petitioners, pored over official parchments, and met with my father and his other advisors, Gwyl among them, to discuss strategy and diplomacy.

"Why did we think it would be a good idea for me to be queen? Tell me again what we were thinking," I overheard her say to Father one day.

He bent down and kissed the top of her head. Then he slid in next to her on the bench where she sat and quietly got her to read aloud from some document or explain some decision troubling her. He was always there to guide her if she needed it. He never intruded if it was clear she did not. He supported her when she was tired and frustrated, and he worked as hard and as long as she did.

"There's a good model for our marriage," said Gwyl, nudging me when he saw me watching them.

I leaned up to him and kissed him. "So much touching," I whispered.

"As I say, a very good model," he whispered back.

But then he led me outside the big stone building to the little walled garden beside it, and sat me down beside him on one of the benches, and put his arm around me to pull me close. "I have something to tell you."

"What is it?" I didn't like his tone. *Something bad is coming*, I said to myself.

"I'm going away on a diplomatic mission," he said.

"Where? How long?"

"To Lunds-fort. I hope I will not be gone long."

"To Lunds-fort," I repeated blankly.

"Aye."

"Why there? That's far."

"It's not so far. As you know, I grew up in the Eastern Baronies just across the Narrows from there."

I nodded.

"Lunds-fort is in contested territory. The Baronies own it, but the Sceptered Isle abuts it, and Caedon, as the Isles' monarch, wants it," said Gwyl.

"So they're sending you there to make sure he doesn't get it," I said.

"Aye," Gwyl replied. "It's a touchy matter, Keera. Who's to get that strip of land, Caedon or the ones who sold Diera out? Which is better?"

"And what is your role?"

"I'm to go as if on a diplomatic mission, to present your mother's compliments to the barons as one monarch to another.

The barons are not monarchs, exactly, but they may as well be. And then there's the one most troubling of all."

"Gilles de Rais," I whispered.

"Yes. The barons are as powerful as any and richer than most," he said. "And Gilles is the most powerful among them."

I shivered. I thought of my vision in the clouds and the pool. I thought of my strange dream, if that's what it was, in the house of Old Dee. Gilles. He was more than some powerful baron. But I didn't know what he was.

"Has my father talked to you about Gilles?" I asked.

"A little. It's troubling, Keera. He did some things to my father that I have a hard time understanding. And his hold over Caedon—" Now I saw Gwyl shiver too. "But anyway. I'm needed there, Keera, in Lunds-fort. I need to gather information there."

"You say you're going *as if* you're on a diplomatic mission. Why are you really going?"

"To consider how things are there. To assess how weak the barons' hold is. They have many other concerns over in the Baronies that may distract them from protecting that strip of land. How easy will it be for Caedon to gain control of Lunds-fort and its surroundings? That's what I'm to find out."

"You're going there to spy," I said.

Gwyl managed to give me his roguish smile, the one that always undid me completely. "Since you put it that way—"

"I don't like it," I burst out. "It's dangerous. Tell my parents to send someone else." Caedon was dangerous. And now there was this dark force, too.

"Who would they send? Who knows that part of the world better than I do?"

"No one," I said in a small voice. I'm ashamed to say I cried on him then.

He soothed me and kissed me. "I'll be back," he told me. "I'll be back before spring."

"You have to be. Otherwise, I'll—"

"Now, Keera. I told you to wait for me before, remember? And then you didn't? You put yourself in danger coming to look for me. Promise me in the name of your Child you won't try anything like that again."

"I promise," I said meekly. I really meant it this time, too.

No. I really did, Companion. Don't give me that look.

"When I return, we'll plan our wedding," he said.

I tried to smile back at him. I had a hard time doing that.

"You know my ships are the fastest in the Northern Sea. I'll get there fast, I'll collect the information your parents need, and then I'll be back before you even miss me," he said.

"You know that's a lie," I said.

"Not about my ships. They're fast."

They were, too.

"And with the magic needle you gave me, I'm even faster than before," he said.

I thought now of Old Dee. He too had gone to Lunds-fort. But he hadn't come back. I know, because I checked with Gudrun when everything settled down after the people cast their lots at the moot for Mother to be their queen.

I had found my way to that little turf cottage and had knocked on the door.

After a moment, Gudrun had peeked out. She gave a glad cry and hugged me. "Mistress Keera! What a sight you are! You're a woman grown," she exclaimed. Then she and I had sat in her kitchen while Grimalkin jumped into my lap and settled down to purr.

"Nay, mistress, Old Dee's not been back since you were here," Gudrun had said.

"Doesn't that worry you? He has been gone for a long time."

"Old Dee sees time different from the rest of us," Gudrun had told me. "He'll be back, as he said he would. But he'll do it in his own time."

During our conversation, Gudrun kept glancing nervously over her shoulder. Finally she stopped doing that. By the time I left, she didn't seem nervous at all.

You know what I think? I think she was looking for you, Companion, and when she didn't see you, she got a little scared. But she must have forgotten the corner you like most in that house. As soon as we'd entered, you had made for your corner. Finally, I think Gudrun must have spotted you there, and then she could relax.

What do you think of that idea, Companion? Yes, I know. She doesn't appear to see you. But somehow, I think she knows. Maybe she senses you in the same way Grimalkin does. It was good to see that old cat again, wasn't it?

In spite of Gudrun's reassurances, I was worried about Old Dee.

I almost described him to Gwyl so that Gwyl could look for him, but then I couldn't really think how to do that. A nondescript old man with a pointed white beard. That could be anyone.

Oh, well, I thought to myself. At least Gwyl has Old Dee's magic needle to guide him to Lunds-fort and back as fast as ever he can fly in that big skeid of his.

He certainly was proud of his ship, clinker-built from riven oak—oak in honor, he said, of the thunder-god.

He smiled wryly when he told me this.

These old gods weren't his. He had been reared in the Eastern Baronies. But he'd adopted the old gods and the old ways when he'd first come west, even though nominally, it seemed, he worshiped the Sea Child. Once, he admitted to me that his mother had worshipped the Lady Goddess.

"You pick and choose whichever god suits you," I told him.

"I suppose I do," he said, bringing me close and kissing me.

"So really, you don't worship any of them."

"Maybe not," he admitted. "Maybe I worship only luck."

I shivered. My mother said that, too. *Luck go with you now. The gods go with you now, whoever They may be,* I said to him in my mind.

"You must not worry so, my Keera," he told me, a line of concern creasing between his own brows.

"But I do," I whispered. "Would to the Child I could go with you."

He just kissed me again.

Before he left on his voyage, he took me down to the port so I could admire how he'd hired woodcrafters to carve the high prow of the skeid. He'd had them carve it into the shape of a fire-breathing dragon in honor of the Fire Child's famous victory against Fylkir and Caedon, and the big square wool-woven sail had the black and white pattern of his banners, with the three interconnected spirals, each spiral ending in a fierce bird-head that reminded me of Hildr.

All of us went down to the docks to see him off. His men loaded his ship, the Dragon Wind, with the things they'd need.

Gwyl boarded last.

He knelt to my mother and asked her blessing. He saluted my father with his sword. I saw my mother whispering in my father's ear, describing this salute.

Then my parents stepped aside so Gwyl and I could have a private moment together.

He kissed away my tears and showed me where he had tucked Old Dee's magic needle into its own special pouch at his belt. "I'll be back as soon as I can, Keera. I love you."

"I love you," I whispered back.

We all waved as he boarded the skeid with its proud dragon prow, and we waved him out to sea until he rounded the headland outside the harbor and was gone from sight.

Then we all went back to the palace. My mother held my hand and looked into my eyes. "I understand too well, my daughter," she said.

I felt frozen, though. I felt fear, dread, loss. I could hardly eat. The days dragged, and I worried about how I'd ever keep my promise and not go running after Gwyl.

Of course that was a silly thought. Trying to do such a thing would be too difficult.

And yet, a small voice inside me kept insisting, *your mother did. You and your mother roamed the world, when you were a small child. Difficult, but not impossible.*

Still, the sensible grown-up side of me proclaimed, just silly to think about at all. I'm proud of myself for my mature thinking. I can see you're proud of me too, Companion.

CHAPTER FIFTEEN

Blind

I think my parents grew so worried when they saw I wasn't eating or sleeping that they considered something they might not have otherwise.

The Lady Jehanne, our old friend from long ago, came to visit us from the Ice-realm, bringing King Haakon's good wishes. It was good to see her again. She wasn't so much older than I. It was clear, too, that she was very much in love with King Haakon, and that he loved her back and respected her, too, entrusting her with important duties on his behalf. I wondered how it would be, though, to be the mistress only of a great king, and not his wife. That didn't seem to bother Jehanne. Then again, most of her life, she'd known only the pain of being Caedon's concubine. Her life now must seem beautiful and fulfilling by comparison. Perhaps by anyone's measure.

Not long into her visit, she asked my mother to send a trusted confidante back with her when she returned to Haakon's court. "Haakon would like nothing more than to come here himself to honor you, but his difficulties with the Usurper Caedon prevent that. He'd like to have an extended conversation about strategies against Caedon. He wonders if you might send an emissary back with me. That person can communicate Haakon's thoughts to you, and of course yours to him," Jehanne told Mother. "And, Your Majesty, King Haakon would be honored if you'd send your daughter." Here she smiled at me. "A fast friend of hers made me promise to add her own request for this."

"The Lady Fiona!" I exclaimed.

"Indeed, Lady Keera. She sends her dearest love."

"Walter and I will think about this request," Mother said.

That night, as the three of us had our evening meal, Mother told Father about this conversation with Jehanne.

"Whoever we send should closely reflect our own wishes. Someone we trust completely," Father said.

"It's a very sensitive matter," Mother agreed.

"Yet Gwyl is still in Lunds-fort. He'd be the obvious choice," said Father.

Mother turned to me and took my hand. "The Lady Jehanne has asked that we send Keera. And why not?"

I could tell Mother's impulsive comment shocked Father. "But she's so young," he said after a moment.

"No younger than you and I when we brought Diera to her throne," said Mother. "And Keera has proven she can take care of herself."

I glowed deep inside to hear my mother express the confidence she had in me. I still harbored the shaky feeling that I had let her down.

"Also," my mother went on, "Who better than Keera to help Haakon understand Caedon and what he really is? Everyone hates him. Nevertheless, many are deceived by the façade he throws up. He is an educated man, a competent, highly intelligent man. That's no façade at all. It's simply true. And yet, underneath, something has damaged Caedon so deeply that he is not like anyone else. He is broken inside."

"I'd use the word evil," said my father.

"That would be one word for it," my mother agreed. "People who haven't experienced this first hand, as you and I have, may think they are dealing with a man whose better nature can be appealed to. But he doesn't have one. Even when people realize this, they still think that mere practicality will lead Caedon to do the right thing. Nothing can. We two know it. We've both watched Caedon dupe and outwit person after person who has made the mistake of trusting him at least to do what is practical. The only person I can think of who knows Caedon's true nature as well as we do is our own daughter. I'm sure there are others, but among those we trust? No one but Keera."

"Suppose he somehow gets Keera in his grasp?" said my father. "He tried several times and succeeded once. If not for Gwyl—" My father's whole face changed then. I suppose that was the first moment I questioned his admonition to me not to seek revenge. I saw that if my father had the chance, he'd take revenge, and it would be a terrible moment for Caedon when he did.

"Haakon is too powerful to allow that," said my mother.

"Can we really trust Haakon? He wants an emissary. If we send our own daughter, might we not be sending him a hostage instead?"

That idea hadn't entered my head, and I could see it hadn't entered my mother's.

"Do you really think he's that underhanded?" my mother asked him.

"Power does strange things to people," said my father. "Well," he said at last. "We need to send him an emissary. We need that strong connection, if our alliance is to hold. I see no one has thought to ask the person this decision affects most. Keera, what are your thoughts?"

"I want to do it, Father," I said. "I like the Lady Jehanne, and I trust her. I don't think she'd lead me into a trap."

"Not knowingly," he said. "I agree with you there. But Haakon. How far can we trust him?"

"And besides—" I burst out.

"It's her friend, the Lady Fiona," my mother explained to Father.

"The daughter of our ally the viceroy?"

"Yes, poor man," said my mother. My parents sat silently thinking this over. They were grieved. I grieved with them. Caedon had taken a terrible revenge on Fiona's father when he realized the viceroy had defected to my parents. I knew how much this must weigh on Fiona. I thought back to the horrifying day we found ourselves in Caedon's power, and how worried she had been when she made her escape. I thought of the hopeful words Gwyl had said then, about how perhaps Caedon would be too busy with other matters to take revenge on the viceroy when he realized the viceroy was on Father's side and not his. But we had been wrong. Caedon had had the poor viceroy executed. At least Fiona and her sister were out of his grasp, safe in the Ice-realm. And Fiona and Pierrick were happily married. That filled me with joy, Companion.

In the end, my parents decided to send me to Haakon. "After all," my father said. "If I'd had a son, I'd be sending him without a qualm. It's a task his elders would give a young prince on his way to manhood and an understanding of his role as future monarch."

I gulped. I was a future monarch.

"You're a young woman, but no less brave and capable. I learned this about your mother, and I know it about you, my daughter," he said. "You headed out at a very young age on a quest of your own." It's as if he could sense my downhearted look. He took me by the hand. "Were you rash? Yes. Were you unsuccessful? I know you believe you were, but that's not true. You were the channel through which the Fire Child worked. You were the one She chose. And you learned from it." He was quiet a moment. "Believe me, my daughter. I know very well what it's like, to head out as a young person on an important mission and to feel that you've failed. Just trust this, daughter. Each failure makes you stronger, as long as you refuse to let it beat you down. I learned that from my brothers. I learned it from Gwyl's father."

"Send me, Father."

And so he and my mother did.

I could see they were regretting their decision when they saw me off at the docks with my entourage of a few trusted servants, even though we agreed I'd stay only a short time at King Haakon's court. I promised myself I'd use good sense, and not be rash. I promised myself I'd make my parents proud of me.

The breezes favored us. I could see you were enjoying the journey, Companion. You took up your favorite spot on the stretching pole above the sail of the ship that carried us north. Our voyage reached the half-way point quickly. That was the Northmost Isle, crossroads of that sea, the isle where Caedon had executed Fiona's father the viceroy. Now it was in Haakon's hands. Caedon's men had been ousted from the hill fort, and Haakon's men had been installed.

In spite of my pride in my parents' trust, in spite of my eagerness to be on my way to see Fiona, and Pierrick, too, I was stricken to see the Northmost Isle again.

But there were good things waiting there for me alongside the dark memories. I arranged a happy reunion with Teasag, the tavern keeper's wife who had loved me and helped me during the years when Mother and I had lived in a tiny room above the tavern.

"Your mother is a queen," Teasag exclaimed, folding me into her big sweaty arms. "Well, I never."

I tried to get her to promise to come back with me to the Fire Isle, when I made the return voyage.

"Nay, Keera, I thank you, but I'll not. There's the tavern to run." In the time since I'd seen her last, the tavern owner her husband had died, but Teasag was perfectly capable of running it herself, and she was doing that.

"And besides," she told me, beaming. "My oldest grandson has taken a liking to the work. He's here beside me every day, learning the business. When I'm old and just want to sit in peace under a tree, he'll run the Sun-Stone after me."

I had a hard time thinking of Teasag sitting peacefully under a tree. By now, she had ten or so grandchildren, with another on the way, and they came swarming all over her whenever their mothers brought them for a visit.

I spent a wonderful day with Teasag. At first she was over-awed, to think I was a great lady now; to think I was actually a princess and not the low-born girl she thought she knew. By the end of our visit, though, we were both easy and laughing. She hugged me goodbye when Jehanne's man came to get me to escort me to the hill fort.

I had another comfort on my voyage. I'd been able to bring Hildr along. I had sadly neglected her. But Jehanne had given me enthusiastic reports of the great hawking to be had on the Northmost Isle, and also at court in the Ice-realm. Of course, when Mother and I had lived on the Northmost Isle, I didn't know anything about hawking and besides, we were poor folk. If we'd owned a hawk or falcon, people would have regarded us with deep suspicion.

So in spite of the bad memories the isle held for me now, I glad to disembark for a few days. Hildr and I would get some welcome exercise, and of course I yearned to see Teasag.

I must admit—and I think I speak for you as well, Companion—riding through those gates into the viceroy's manor again made my flesh crawl. But the whole place was very different. The rooms were not the dark gloomy places they'd been when Caedon had trapped me there. They were whitewashed and sunny.

Just as I remembered her, Jehanne was good company. She and I laughed and chattered away, resuming our friendship as if it hadn't had an almost four-year interruption. I think you may have been a little hurt, Companion. Did you feel left out? I apologize if you did. I've come to value your company and even your advice. Yes, I admit it.

And I know you better now. You're the one who rose up and smote Caedon down. You're the one who called down on his men the Fire Child's ire. You might seem like a dithery young woman (even if odd and mostly invisible), but now I have seen your face in the clouds, and now I have seen your power. You are the Fire Child's servant, a mighty force. I honor you, Companion, and I thank the Fire Child for lending you to me. It can't have been easy. I know that now.

And Nine Spheres, do I need your counsel, Companion.

Our third day on the isle dawned with beautiful mild weather, a perfect day for hawking. Jehanne had it all arranged. The two of us, and our retainers, rode out with our merlins on our arms. Of course I had brought Hildr along. She showed up Jehanne's fancy falcon right enough. *No one is better than you, Hildr, I* thought fondly.

At midday, we stopped in a beautiful high meadow for bread, cheese, and ale. Our retainers spread a cloth for us to sit on. From our high vantage point, we could look out over the sea.

Jehanne pointed. "The Ice-realm," she said. "On a clear day like this, you can see the southernmost isles of the realm. Although now," she continued, looking around us, "This has become one of them, one of King Haakon's southernmost isles. Soon he'll march on the mainland."

"My father will be glad of it," I told her.

"He's given up his own claim?"

"I'm not sure my father ever really believed he had much of a claim. Audemar is the rightful heir, even though some would say he has forfeited the privilege through his treachery."

"Many would say that. But many would call your father their rightful king."

"You know my father is bastard-born. He's never considered himself in the succession."

"Yet King Avery named him adoptive son."

"Yes, but remember, Avery himself declared my father's adoption outside the line of succession."

"Many would say," Jehanne began, considering me carefully, "that a person in your father's situation would disregard that, now that Diera is dead. Many in your father's situation would boldly assume they did have a rightful claim to the throne. Many others would support such a claim."

"Those people don't know my father," I said firmly. "He feels he has no such claim."

"But your father might also think Haakon has no legitimate claim."

"If Haakon defeats Caedon or even Audemar for the throne, my father will accept that," I told her. "My father will consider the line of Ranulf defunct. If Haakon assumes the throne, my father will consider Haakon has established his own new line."

"What if Audemar achieves the throne?"

"My father will never accept him."

"What if Audemar achieves the throne backed by Diera's relatives, the barons of the east, and by Gilles de Rais, their leader?"

"My father regards Audemar as a traitor. He'll never accept him," I repeated. I thought uneasily of Gilles de Rais, and I did not mention him.

"And Caedon?" said Jehanne, breaking into my thoughts.

Here I laughed. "If Audemar is a traitor, it's only because Caedon enabled him to become one. Caedon is worst of all, and my father's sworn enemy. My mother's sworn enemy." I stared into her eyes. "My own sworn enemy."

"And mine," she said softly. "But what if Baron Gilles takes over without naming Audemar king?"

"That would be different," I admitted. "Yet my father blames the barons, too, for treachery. My father blames them for the death of Diera. And—" I paused, not knowing how to put this, because I was too unsure of the reasons for my father's deep abhorrence of Gilles de Rais and what it meant. "He blames Baron Gilles especially. The barons wouldn't have his support."

"But Haakon would?"

"Yes. My father would support him as an ally, not a vassal."

"Your mother is queen."

"This is her wish as well," I said. "We were speaking of my father only because, as you say, some might regard him as rightful king of the Sceptered Isle, but if we're discussing the Fire Isle, it's my mother you must consult."

Jehanne was about to continue her questioning, but then she shaded her eyes and half rose to her feet. Her retainers ran down the hill to greet a man on a horse. They returned with him, leading him to us.

"An honor!" Jehanne breathed.

As the man rode up, I saw that he was young, even broader in the shoulder than Gwyl, as slim in the waist, taller. He vaulted off his horse and came to us. "Lady Jehanne!" he said with an open smile that lit up his craggy features and blue eyes.

"My lord," she said, making a deep obeisance. Then she stood. "Your Highness, may I present the Princess Keera of the Fire Isle?" Turning to me, she said, "This is His Highness Prince Ansgar, heir to Haakon of the Ice-Realm."

I made him a pretty curtsey.

"I have longed to meet you, Your Highness," he said to me, making his own bow. "My father has told me much about you and your family, and Lady Jehanne has sung your praises. As has your friend, the Lady Fiona. Indeed, my lady," he said, turning to Jehanne, "This princess is as lovely as you described."

I felt myself blushing. I knew Haakon had sons, but I'd never heard much about them.

"We're hawking, Your Highness," Jehanne told him. "Please join us."

So this handsome young prince did. He hadn't brought his own bird into the field, but he applauded while we flew ours, with special praise for Hildr. And for me. The way he looked at me left me feeling flustered. His courtly ways and attentions were a bit overwhelming.

I see you smiling at me, Companion. I know, in many ways I'm just a simple untutored girl, not a fine lady at all. I didn't know what to say to this polished young man. Now that I see you in this setting, my Companion, I have the strange feeling you'd know exactly what to say. I have the strange feeling you've been at court and know courtly manners. Maybe you can give me lessons. Suddenly I'm behaving like an awkward country girl.

We had three more days on the island. I found myself, in spite of my misgivings, looking forward to spending my days and evenings in the company of this exciting young man. Do you think I'm being disloyal to Gwyl in saying so, even secretly to myself? When I say *secretly, to myself*, of course that means to you, too. I can keep no secrets from you, Companion.

Jehanne brought me beautiful things to wear. During the mild blue days, we all went hawking. In the evening, we gathered for a sumptuous meal hosted by the new viceroy, Haakon's man. Then we lingered while Haakon's skalds sang us heroic songs of the north and its mighty deeds. A brave bold man who saved the land by wrestling a monster with his bare hands. Later, he dove underneath the sea to the lair of the monster's hideous mother and slew her too. As an old man, now a king, this hero fought a dragon to the death—the dragon's and his own. One last mighty battle. These tales were thrilling, and the words woven by the skalds were the most thrilling of all, each word a bright jewel.

"Your eyes are shining, my lady," Ansgar leaned over to whisper to me during one of these sessions. I didn't know what to say to him.

I found myself hoping the three days would never come to an end. But at the same time, I found myself counting the hours when I could be free of their spell. The first wish came true—at least, true enough. As we made preparations on our last night to resume our journey the next morning, there came a knock at the door of the room where Jehanne and I slept.

Jehanne answered it. She opened the door wide, and Ansgar stepped into the room.

"Do you hear?" he said to us, gesturing.

I hadn't been paying attention. I hadn't heard. Now, as the three of us listened, we realized the wind had risen, and was rising still.

"A storm is blowing in out of the east," he told us. "There will be no sailing tomorrow. It's too dangerous crossing the strait. The tide race will be ferocious." He smiled at me, a winning smile that lit up the blue of his eyes in a charming manner. "Don't look so sad, my lady. This means I'll have more time to woo you." He stepped back out of our room.

I turned to Jehanne, troubled. "Ansgar is joking, isn't he? He knows I'm betrothed, surely."

Jehanne smiled and shrugged. "Ansgar is a determined young man. He's hard to discourage."

"But he's joking!" I exclaimed. "Surely he is."

Jehanne took me by the hand and sat me down on one of the benches against the wall of our room. "I don't think Ansgar jokes. Not about a thing like that."

"Jehanne. I'm betrothed to Sir Gwyl, one of my parents' chief officers and counselors. I'm going to marry him as soon as he is back from his diplomatic mission to Lunds-fort."

"But you're not married yet," said Jehanne. "You know, marriage to Ansgar wouldn't be a bad thing. It would cement your parents' alliance with Haakon."

I stared at her, appalled. "You knew this was in his mind."

"Well, yes. I did."

"And you didn't tell me."

"No, I was worried you wouldn't give him a fair hearing," Jehanne admitted.

"But Jehanne. I'm promised to another man. The man my father trusts most in this world." As I said these words, all of the charm Prince Ansgar had exerted on me fell away from me. Yes, he was smooth and handsome and exciting. No, I was not in love with him. I loved only Gwyl.

"I'm sure marriage to this Sir Gwyl will be advantageous," Jehanne said. "But not as advantageous as marriage to Ansgar. He'll be a king."

"Gwyl will be a king. My consort, anyway, as my father is Mother's consort. I'll be queen of the Fire Isle someday." I was beginning to worry now. I had trusted Jehanne. What was she up to, really?

"And if you marry Ansgar, you'll be queen of the Fire Isle as well as Queen-Consort of the Ice-realm. Your power will be much, much larger."

"The Ice-realm will swallow up the Fire Isle, in that case," I told her. "If Ansgar marries me, he'll acquire the Fire Isle for himself."

"Oh, no. You'll be its queen."

"Tell me, Jehanne. In the Ice-realm, may a woman become monarch?"

Now Jehanne stopped her bantering tone and looked at me seriously. "No, by law she may not."

"So, then," I said.

"Listen to me carefully, dear friend," said Jehanne. "Haakon is an honorable king. When he says he'll accept your mother as his ally, he means it truly. But anything can happen in this world of ours, and the Fire Isle is small and weak. Wouldn't it be better for the Fire Isle if you cemented a strong relationship with the Ice-realm? Then no one could touch you. I'm sure if you told your parents this was your wish, they'd release you from your betrothal. And if it is their wish, and your wish, Sir Gwyl will step aside. I have met him. He's loyal to your parents. He'd never go against them."

"But I love Gwyl!" I burst out.

Jehanne started to speak again, then stopped herself. "Dear friend," she said. "Let's not argue. It's only a thought. You've come here for diplomacy. I'm telling you one wise diplomatic move you could easily make. The choice is of course entirely yours—and your parents'."

"Yes, let's not argue," I told her. "Let's not talk of it again."

We made ready for bed silently. Lying beside her in the furs, I stared up at the ceiling in the dark. I couldn't sleep. What Jehanne had said to me frightened me to the core. I'd come willingly with her, and I was committed to traveling to King Haakon's court. My parents and I had trusted her. But what if my parents' worst fears were in fact true? What if I were positioning myself so that Haakon could snap me up and keep me hostage?

I knew I had to hide these thoughts from Jehanne. That made me sad. I knew then I couldn't trust her. Not completely.

I tried not to think badly of her. What a life she must have led. What do you think, my Companion? She must have had it hard, sold to Caedon at such a young age.

But you weren't by my side any more. I blinked into the darkness. Usually, even if I couldn't see you, I could sense you near. And now I couldn't.

The keening of the wind outside rose higher. Underneath, did I hear a more human cry of grief?

I returned to my thoughts about Jehanne. I knew my fate would have been all too like hers, if my mother hadn't snatched me away from Caedon in time. Jehanne, too, had been sold when she was only five or six years old. I wasn't sure of her background, but I believe she was gently born. What would have led her parents to sell her, and to Caedon? Even then, many knew of his evil ways, especially where young children were concerned. Maybe Jehanne had been an orphan with no one to take her part. I decided I'd find a good time to ask her. I wanted to know.

So then, during her formative years, what must it have been like, to have been owned by such a man? I shuddered away from the worst of my thoughts. If nothing else, she must have grown from girlhood to womanhood bent on protecting herself at all costs, never considering personal preference, but only safety and security. Once I came to that conclusion, I stopped thinking so badly of Jehanne. She wasn't trying to betray me in colluding with Ansgar in his apparent project of wooing me. She was trying to protect me in the way she knew best.

What resourcefulness she must have exhibited, to draw the attention and then the love of King Haakon. When Haakon bought her and freed her, he gave her more than simple security.

He gave her dignity, maybe even love. I wondered if she loved him back. She must at least be grateful to him, owe him a debt she'd never be able to repay.

Finally I could sleep. In the morning, I'd carefully keep myself out of Ansgar's way, and if that wasn't possible, I'd make it clear to him I bore him friendship only, not love. He'd see that and place his flattering attentions elsewhere. And I'd make sure to tell Jehanne to let him know.

The next several days were difficult to get through. At least you, my Companion, had reappeared. I wish I knew where you had gone, during the storm's height. Although the storm had lessened, it didn't abate enough to allow us to sail, so we were all trapped indoors together.

Prince Ansgar continued his attentions to me, but now I was wary of him. He saw that, and treated me carefully and respect-fully. But he didn't stop his compliments and his attempts to entertain and charm me. "You're so beautiful, my lady," he said to me at dinner one night. "Has no one told you so? Everyone should tell you this. Your hair!" he marveled. "How it catches the firelight!"

I just smiled at him. I had the cynical feeling that he would have said the same if I had been lame, bald, and cross-eyed, with a suppurating wen on the side of my nose.

I see you agree with me, Companion. Now that I can't really trust Jehanne—or, anyway, trust her only in certain ways—I am gladder than ever to have you by my side. As much as I hate that old coot, my farwydd, I have to give her credit for lending you to me. When I see her next, I'll have to swallow my pride and thank her. I hope you take that compliment in the spirit I make it, dear Companion.

Finally a day dawned that promised better weather in the offing. Ansgar gathered us to tell us we'd sail early the next morning. Jehanne hurried away to get packing. I moved to follow her, but Ansgar put out his hand and grabbed hold of my arm.

Startled, I turned to him.

"Your ladyship, may I beg you to take a turn with me in the pleached garden?" he said.

I couldn't think of an excuse fast enough, so I nodded.

My heart pounded as I followed him out of doors and into the garden. The skies were still leaden, but the rain had stopped and the wind had died to a whisper. Under the gray skies, the green of the garden looked almost radiant. Above me, some of the clouds were edged in gold.

I had hoped Ansgar and I wouldn't have to come to an outright confrontation, but now I saw it was unavoidable.

May as well get it over with, I thought fatalistically.

Ansgar led me away into an arbor secluded from the viceroy's grand house. He drew me to him and bent close over me. I tried to step away, but he pulled me closer. "My lady—my shy bird. You must know by now how dearly I love you. Jehanne has told me of your misgivings. But lady, I beg you to listen to my suit. Otherwise, the dagger of your disdain will thrill through my heart forever. Why, lady, you will kill me with your killing looks."

I think I might have laughed, in other circumstances. I wasn't laughing now. To insult the son of King Haakon was not good policy. Not only that, but—I must tell you this, Companion. I was afraid. There was something in the way he grasped at me that frightened me. Something behind the charming mask that I found chilling.

"Oh, my prince, surely not!" I told him, trying for a light-hearted tone. "You have all the women in four realms vying for your attention. You merely flatter me because I am so young and naïve."

"Say you won't reject me, cruel maiden!" he exclaimed, clutching dramatically at his heart. "Say you'll be my bride." He gave me one of his practiced, most charming smiles.

I put my hand on his and looked up into his face with the utmost seriousness. "Prince Ansgar, you do me much honor. I honor you. But I cannot be your bride. I'm betrothed to another."

"That's a trifle," he said, and the brusqueness of his tone took me aback. The mask had slipped.

"Not to me, Your Highness," I said, and dropped him a deep curtsey. "And now I must go help Jehanne pack. Forgive me." I turned and walked away, hoping he wasn't following.

He didn't.

When I returned to our room, I looked around in dismay. Jehanne and her things were gone. A serving maid leaned into the room. When she saw me she came in and curtsied.

"My princess, I'm to tell you the Lady Jehanne has sailed on ahead of you," she said, then vanished down the hall before I could question her.

I was in a bit of a panic then. I got my things together as quickly as I could and ran into the main hall of the house, where I hoped to find Haakon's viceroy. A wave of relief washed over me. No Ansgar, and the viceroy was conferring with some of his

men at one end of the hall. I came to him and waited to be noticed.

When he saw me, he looked startled, probably at my anxious
look. Then he motioned his men away. "My princess, how may I
help you?" he said.

"The Lady Jehanne has already sailed, I hear."

"Yes," said the viceroy. "I thought Prince Ansgar had informed
you."

"No," I said, beginning to feel a little sick. "No, he didn't tell
me."

"As you may have seen, a ship came in during the night. I'm
afraid it was bearing some alarming news. Jehanne left with the
courier on the tide, feeling her place was with the king. You and
the prince are to leave in the morning on the next ship out of the
harbor."

"Thank you, my lord. What alarming news, my lord?"

"A matter of state. It's not my place to discuss it with you, but
if the prince has not, I'll ask him to do so."

I curtsied and made my way slowly back to my room. I closed
the door and sank down on the bed, my thoughts racing. On an
impulse, I sprang up and barred my door. But no one beat at the
door to be let in. Evening came on. I heard the busy noises that
meant dinner was prepared. Part of me wanted to stay barri-
caded until the morning. But another part of me realized I
shouldn't draw attention to my alarm. I should pretend everything was normal. I should come out and eat at board with the
rest.

After all, I had no idea what urgent matter had drawn Jehanne
away, and certainly no idea I was in any danger. The viceroy

hadn't acted as if he thought I was. He was just surprised to find I didn't know what was going on.

Why hadn't Ansgar told me? Maybe, I reasoned, it's because, before he could tell me, I left him in the garden. Nothing sinister.

If only, I thought desperately, *if only I had my powers*. Then I'd know. Even if I didn't know for certain, they'd tell me if there was any cause for alarm. Now I was moving blind. I was as blind as my father. Blinder, because he knew how to get around without his eyes. I still hadn't learned how to judge the world without my powers.

I had only my ordinary wits to guide me.

Oh, very well, Companion. You've made your point. Yes, my wits are fine, and they've served me well. Yes, yes, yes. You're right, and I know by now you give me good advice, much as you might annoy me from time to time. Beyond good advice. You have behaved heroically.

I made my way into the great hall. My way took me out of one building and downhill to the hall, and as I made my way around the outer wall of the hill fort, I could look out over the harbor. There at anchor rode a big knarr, its sail bearing the insignia of Haakon. I felt a crushing load lifting from my breast. There it was, the ship that would take me away from here. It wouldn't matter that I'd be sailing with Ansgar. The trip would be short. Already, the weather looked to be fine. Soon we'd be in Haakon's courts. Ansgar could continue to press his suit, but my parents were Haakon's allies. I knew I'd be treated with every courtesy. Jehanne would be there. Wherever her true allegiances lay, she was still a friend.

And I'd see Fiona again!

Anyway, I had made myself clear to Ansgar. I would not be his bride.

Underneath all my anxious thoughts lay a deeper anxiety. My heart ached for Gwyl. By now, my parents should have heard from him how his project in Lunds-fort was going. Perhaps I'd receive word once I reached Haakon's court.

I slipped into the hall and took up my usual place at the left hand of the viceroy. He nodded and smiled to me. I settled onto the long bench. I was a bit pleased to see Ansgar was not there. Maybe he wouldn't be, and I wouldn't have to face him until we sailed.

As I was thinking these comforting thoughts there came, from behind us, a flurry, a man rushing through the hall, stopping breathless before the viceroy, bending the knee to him. The viceroy scraping back the bench and stepping over it to receive the man's message. His sharp intake of breath.

Something has happened, I thought.

Ansgar strode into the hall then. His face was set. His eyes glittered with a strange light. He stopped just inside the doorway and stood proudly erect, looking over at the viceroy.

"Please, attention," said the viceroy in a loud voice to the assembling diners. His tone stopped us all. The diners entering the hall stopped dead. The diners about to settle themselves on the benches stopped in mid-stoop. "Please, everyone. Please rise," said the viceroy.

I stumbled to my feet. Everyone did. We all stared at the viceroy.

"King Haakon is dead," he said in a strangled voice. Then throwing his arm out toward Ansgar and dropping to one knee, he cried out, "Long live King Ansgar."

And we all dropped to our knees before Ansgar, the new king of the Ice-realm. "Long live King Ansgar," all of us chorused.

CHAPTER SIXTEEN

Unkindness

The next day, the viceroy ushered men to my room to get my bags and boxes and take them down to the wharf. I stood aside as they carried the things out. The viceroy and one man were left.

"Olaf, here, will see you down to the wharf, my princess," said the viceroy. Something in the way he said it made me uneasy. Or perhaps it was you, Companion. You were flitting about the rafters as if you were a bat.

But I followed this fellow down to the wharf, and he handed me aboard ship, where two mariners took me in charge and led me to the bottom of the ship. There were actual small rooms cleverly set into the sides. It was a large ship, Haakon's royal knarr, sent over to bring his son and heir back to the Ice-realm. Although now, I realized, it was actually Ansgar's royal knarr.

I could see my boxes had been stowed around various places in the bottom of the ship, but the two mariners ushered me into one of the little rooms, and closed the door. There was a long narrow shelf that could serve as a bed. It was a compact and fascinating little chamber. I'd never seen anything like it, so at first I enjoyed myself, sitting on the shelf amongst comfortable cushions.

Soon I was aware we had headed out to sea. Without being able to see the horizon, I worried I'd be sick. The seas weren't rough, but the rocking and jouncing in such an enclosed space made my stomach feel uncertain.

A breath of air, and the sight of the horizon, would surely set me to rights. I had found myself to be a pretty good sailor, especially when I wasn't stuffed into a barrel for the voyage.

I could tell you were feeling confined, too, Companion. I was sure you'd prefer your favorite spot on the stretcher beam of the sail. So I clambered out of the cushions and put my hand against the little door.

That's when I realized. When I pushed on the door, it did not give. It was barred from the outside. I was a prisoner.

I felt a rush of panic as strong as any lightning bolt. What could it mean? I rattled the door. No one came. I beat at the door with my arms and then kicked at it with my foot. I shouted. No one came, although I heard noises outside. People were just outside. They must be hearing the pounding at the door and the shouting. And they were ignoring it. *At least*, I thought to myself, crawling into the cushions of the bed shelf, my throat raw from shouting and my hands and arms sore and bruised, *I haven't been stuffed into a barrel.*

I spent the rest of the short voyage, only a day, a night, and a part of the next day, dozing among the cushions. After that first attempt to get out, to call attention to myself, I just lay in a stupor. I roused only when one of the mariners opened my door to hand me a mug of ale and an earthenware bowl of stew late on the first day. I didn't even try to barge my way out. I questioned him about why my door was barred, and when he couldn't or wouldn't answer me, I thanked him, took the food, and ate it. I couldn't even summon any kind of outrage into my voice. It had become pretty clear to me what had happened. I was Ansgar's prisoner. At first I tortured myself with all the reasons this could be. Then I just tried not to think at all, although that, of course, proved to be impossible.

You, I see, had filtered through the chinks of the door and up to your perch, Companion. At least that's where I assume you went.

When the second day drew on to noon, I heard shouts and the rattle of metal against wood, the sounds mariners make when they haul on ropes, the high whinging sounds of the ropes being winched and tightened. As I soon learned, the mariners were steering the knarr against a pier in one of the coves of the Ice-realm's main port and mercantile center, Tradetown. Two of the mariners opened my door and escorted me off the ship. They kept a tight grip on me. I didn't try to wrench myself away from them. Where would I go?

From far down the pier, I could see Ansgar's party. Retainers surrounded him. I could see someone bringing him a horse, and Ansgar swinging into the saddle. He and his retinue, banners flying, trotted away from the harbor up a winding road that led inland.

I and my two custodians stood on the dock alone. Gulls shrieked and swooped. The lines of the knarr slapped idly against its sides, and rivulets of waves kept rolling in with a hiss. As I watched, a cart turned down the road to the harbor. It came to a stop beside me. The mariners helped me in. I sat between two other stout fellows who, I presume, were sent to guard me. Then the ox driver clucked to his animal, and we followed the same road Ansgar and his party had taken.

I bestirred myself to address a few words to my companions or guards, or whoever they were, but they answered me in some unknown language, so I stopped trying. Ahead of us, I could see the swirls of dust stirred up by Ansgar's party settling now, only to be stirred up again by our own passage. Ansgar's party. *The king's party*, I reminded myself. Ansgar was king.

After several hours of lurching up the road, which became ever steeper, we entered the outskirts of a big town, and then the city walls.

One of the men beside me gestured around him and said something in his strange Ice-realm language. He was telling me the town's name. I rolled the unfamiliar syllables around in my mouth. Later I discovered the name of this town, in our own language, was Old Town. It was the Ice-realm's capital.

An imposing fortress frowned down over the town. The same man gestured to it and said more unfamiliar words. Among them, along with the town's name, I distinguished *Haakon* and *Ansgar*, as well as the Ice-realm's word for *king*, which I already knew from talking with Jehanne and Ansgar on the Northmost Isle. I was pretty sure, then, that the fortress must be the royal seat. I could see a cluster of pennants up there near its gates. I surmised it was Ansgar's party, entering his new royal residence.

That's not where the wagon brought me, though. We wound through the narrow streets of the town below the fortress until we came to a neat longhouse built of logs. The men deposited me there, and a woman came out to take me by the hand and lead me inside.

Everyone was kind to me. They settled me in a kind of cottage behind the longhouse, and left me there with my things. It was comfortable but simple. The door wasn't locked. I was free to go, but where would I go if I had a mind to flee? I set my mind to learning my surroundings anyhow. *It may come to that*, I told myself. Flight. I'd need to be prepared.

I spent several days settling myself there, wondering when I'd have a chance to talk to Ansgar. After all, I was at least nominally a diplomat traveling to the king from a foreign power, however small. Why would Ansgar insult my parents the way he had, by taking me prisoner and then leaving me here to wait in simple surroundings? But that appeared to be what he was doing.

I knew his actions couldn't mean anything good. Although I was relieved he no longer seemed to consider me a possible bride, I couldn't figure out why he'd treat me as an enemy, if that was what he was doing. It was confusing. Here in this compound full of women, I was not treated as an enemy, not really. But not quite a visitor either.

In fact, I was treated as something between a guest and a servant. Yes, actually a servant. The insult to my parents was profound. I found myself getting angrier and angrier. In case I could find a way to get word to Fiona and Pierrick, I tried not to let my anger show. I needed to be canny. I needed to appear, on the surface, cooperative.

On the third day, the same woman who had greeted me at the door of the longhouse arrived in my small cottage with flax for me to spin. And a spinning wheel!

I was bored, so I did it. Badly, yes. You don't need to tell me, Companion. I know I'm no good at it.

When the woman returned, she regarded me with exasperation. She'd brought me more flax, but now she took it away with her.

We couldn't speak each other's language, so I didn't know how to question her about my puzzling status.

A servant brought me food each day, so I wasn't even eating with the others I saw moving in and out of the longhouse. If I had, maybe I would have picked up a few words and found out some things.

Toward the end of a series of long days in my cottage, the same woman returned, speaking to me in a loud and maybe angry voice, a flood of words. I think maybe *frustrated* would be the word for it, not really *angry*.

I had been dressing simply. She strode to my things and began pawing through them. I rose from the bedstead, the only seating, to protest, but then I sat back down. *Let her*, I told myself. *Maybe you'll find out what you're doing here.*

Now she turned to me and thrust my richest clothing at me. A stream of language poured out of her. She gestured in the direction of the fortress. I could pick the word for *king* from her frenzied speaking, and *Ansgar*. She put the clothing in my arms and gestured at it, talking all the time.

"Put it on?" I asked her. Then I mimed doing so. She nodded vigorously. While she waited, I did. Then she took me by the arm and led me into the longhouse, through the length of it, and back out onto the road, where a horseman waited, holding a horse for me.

Now I knew real dread. I was a terrible rider.

He motioned me forward and helped me mount, boosting me up into the saddle. He handed me the reins. When I just looked at them, he shook his head and muttered a few choice words to himself. I could guess what they meant. Finally he mounted himself, took my reins, and led me beside him plodding away from the longhouse, through the streets of Old Town, and up the long winding road that led to the fortress.

We rode into the keep. Another retainer helped me down. I stumbled down into his arms, and he steadied me, trying not to smile, I saw. That made the anger start to rise in me, but I stuffed it down. These poor men had been ordered to mind me. It wasn't their fault I had no idea what to do around a horse.

I saw these men wore the royal insignia. This second man led me into the great hall of the fortress and left me standing there, blinking in the smoky light. After my eyes got used to the dimness, I saw, far down the hall, Ansgar seated in an imposing carved chair on a high platform. Retainers clustered about him. Others, more richly dressed, looked to be councilors conferring with him.

I had no idea what to do, so I sat down on a low bench by the door and waited. I wanted to rush down the length of the hall and shout at him, but I forced myself to stay calm.

In a while, Ansgar looked down the hall and saw me there. He turned to a man beside him, spoke to him, then turned back to the others. Nothing in his eyes signaled he had any special connection to me at all. The man he'd spoken to made his way down the long hall toward me.

When he reached me, he said to me, in my own language, but with no ceremony, "His Highness King Ansgar asks me to tell you, I'll be able to answer any questions you may have."

I got to my feet and felt my color rising. "Why was I brought here a prisoner? How will I explain this discourtesy to my mother, Mirin the First, Her Highness, Queen of the Fire Isle and Elector of the People? How will I explain this to my father, His Sacred Majesty Walter the First of the Sceptered Isle, Prince Consort of the Queen of the Fire Isle?" When the man stood looking at me, speechless, I rounded on him, my voice raised in a fury, "No, I misspoke. Not a discourtesy. A crime!"

The man actually winced. "His Highness is busy with many cares at the moment. He has asked me to speak to you."

"I'll speak to Ansgar, or to the Lady Jehanne. To none other," I told him, deliberately leaving off Ansgar's titles.

He regarded me soberly. Then he said, dropping his voice to almost a whisper, "The Lady Jehanne is dead."

"Dead." I looked at him blankly.

"She followed her lord where he feasts in the halls of the heroes."

That, I knew, was how they referred to the afterlife. Jehanne had told me. I felt a jolt of panic. Of grief. I couldn't think. How could Jehanne be dead? The man's words made no sense to me.

"Then I'll speak only to Ansgar himself," I said to him, trying to still my fear. My lips felt numb.

After a moment, the man turned on his heel and left me standing there.

I was beginning to feel faint, so I sat down. Jehanne was dead. My friend. I didn't see whether the official returned to talk to Ansgar or not. My head was swimming. Green and black spots were popping into my field of vision.

When I looked up again, Ansgar was frowning down at me, the other man at his elbow. He motioned the man away.

"Are you sick, lady?"

I nodded.

"You've had a shock." He sat down beside me.

"Jehanne is dead?" I looked up at him miserably.

"Yes," he said.

"How?"

"They say she didn't wish to live when she found my father dying."

"She took her own life?" I couldn't keep the incredulity out of my voice.

"They say she did. Now listen to me, because I don't have time for nonsense."

At his tone, I put aside my grief and looked up at him. His eyes were hard. "I'll explain this once, but that's all. You should have listened to me, in the garden, Keera. You should have accepted my offer. That was the only chance you had, and you threw it away."

"I don't understand," I said.

"Once I became king without a betrothal to you, it was too late. Now, as a matter of policy, I've become your custodian."

"I don't understand. You knew you'd become king? But we only received word of your father's death afterward. After our meeting in the garden. So—" I said, thinking hard. "When we talked in the garden, you must have already known it."

"Yes," he said.

"But why—"

"That's none of your concern. The important thing to know is that the moment in the garden was the only moment you had to accept my suit. Once you rejected it, once it was known I was king, our relationship, yours and mine, changed irrevocably."

"I don't understand," I said again. I felt stupid.

"Once I became king, I accepted certain conditions of policy. One—" His voice grew sharp. "Are you listening? This is the only time I'll explain."

I nodded, trying to pay attention to the way my life had turned upside down, it seemed, in an instant.

"One, your parents and I are at war."

"And I am thus your prisoner," I said slowly.

"And two—" he was ticking these terrible things off on his fingers.

But I was far ahead of him. "That can only mean one thing, Your Highness," I said, my voice dripping with venom. "You've made alliance with Caedon."

He bowed and rose from the bench, ignoring my tone. "And, of course, you're Caedon's property. If you had been my affianced bride, Caedon would have had to choose between reappropriating his property or offending me and upending our alliance. Of course he wouldn't have done that. But now, because you're not my affianced bride, I'm only keeping you safe until Caedon claims you from me. So you see where you stand, mistress." He turned his back on me without ceremony and strode up the hall, motioning to his retainer to attend me.

The retainer stood silently by me as I rose to my feet.

"I'd like to get word to my friend, the Lady Fiona of the Northmost Isle, that I am here in the Ice-realm and wish to see her," I told him.

"Our king has told me you might ask this. Our king regretfully refuses your request."

"Please take me back to that house where they're keeping me," I told him. I felt a new finger of fear now. Suppose my presence and friendship endangered Fiona. Now that Ansgar was allied with Caedon, suppose Fiona was in danger already. Pierrick certainly must be, if anyone realized his connection with my father.

After my return to that low place of my not-quite-imprisonment, I removed my fine clothes and got into my bed. I turned my face to the wall. But it was a long time, assailed by fears and doubts, before I could sleep.

I spent a dreary season in Ansgar's custody. A few times, I thought about trying to get some message to Fiona, but I realized how precarious her position probably was now. I feared to make it worse.

No one menaced me, but after that first misbegotten attempt, the woman of the longhouse, my keeper, stopped giving me work to do, so I was horribly bored. My anxiety rose, too, about my parents. They were probably worried sick about me and re-gretting their decision to send me off as an ambassador. Most of all, though, I worried about what might be happening to them. Now they were the Ice-realm's enemies, and Ansgar had joined forces with Caedon. How could the tiny Fire Isle fight off such a powerful combined enemy? I had no further communication from Ansgar, or from any of his officials, only my imagination working overtime.

One thing changed about my condition. I was no longer treated as a sort of guest. I ate with the others in the longhouse, even though I wasn't given any work to do. As I gradually picked up some of the language of the women around me, I found that the longhouse was a house of bondswomen who were kept busy weaving and sewing and embroidering for the royal household. I myself was little more than a bondswoman. Or, rather, I was a bondswoman, but Caedon's, not Ansgar's.

One day I got the message I'd been dreading. *Make ready. You'll be traveling to Lunds-fort to be handed over to your owner.*

That's the first I realized. Caedon was in Lunds-fort. Now my anxieties soared almost past bearing. I would be in his power.

And Caedon had either taken Lunds-fort from the eastern barons or had formed an alliance with them. That meant Gwyl was
in jeopardy, too.

I'd thought a bit about trying to escape the Ice-realm, but I
quickly saw how useless those thoughts were. I didn't know the
language, and I had no friends here beyond Fiona and Pierrick,
whose hands were certainly tied.

My thoughts strayed to Jehanne from time to time, in the
midst of my other worries. I wondered how her death had really
happened. Whenever I thought of her fate, I felt ill, a mixture of
sorrow and fear. I wondered over the timing of it all. I'd figured
one thing out. Ansgar had known of his father's death well before
the ship came to announce it. He'd known when he had proposed
marriage to me, and probably earlier than that. But he had been
smooth and cheerful with me, and with Jehanne, too. Meanwhile
his own father lay dead. I didn't think Jehanne could have kept
such a terrible thing from me, if she had known.

Ansgar deceived us both.

As soon as he had realized I wouldn't become an easy pathway
for him to acquire the Fire Isle, he'd given that thought up and
had settled for the next-best option, using me as a counter in his
negotiations with Cacdon. Just a game piece he was moving
around on his tafl board.

As for Jehanne. She'd clearly rushed to Haakon's side when
she heard he was dying. But when she arrived here in the Ice-
realm to find him dead, or to stay by his side as he died, what
motivated her to kill herself? Grief? She seemed too level-headed
for that. I knew she loved Haakon, but her desire for me to betray
Gwyl and marry Ansgar had revealed a practical side I didn't

know she had. Why would such a practical woman commit suicide when her protector died?

I could think of only one reason. She felt threatened in such a terrible way that death was the preferable option. Or it might be. . .

I didn't want to go there. And you, gibbering up on the rafters, Companion, you're not helping.

Yes. I'm going to say it out loud, at least in my own mind.

It might be Ansgar had her killed.

Why would he do something like that? I knew now he was ruthless. Was he also bloody-minded?

Gibbering, gibbering, gibbering. My Companion. Settle yourself. I know this is distressing. I'm distressed too. But I need to think.

By the time my last few days in the longhouse ended, I'd learned enough of the Ice-realm's language to follow some of the gossip. A confined group of women, sewing and spinning all day, were going to talk, even though the mistress walked up and down among them, shushing them and scolding.

That's the way I learned the most chilling piece of information of all. It was only gossip, if you will. But I thought these women knew what they were talking about.

"Did you hear?" whispered one to her nearest neighbor at the spinning wheels. "They say the Lady Jehanne was carrying the King's child when she died."

Now that I heard these whispers, I connected them with some things I'd observed about Jehanne—how glowing her skin was, how radiant she appeared. How she seemed to be rounding out. Nothing I'd consciously marked on. But now, I thought about it.

If Jehanne were pregnant with Haakon's child, what kind of complication would that present the childless Ansgar? I was sure he wouldn't stay childless long. I wouldn't be his bride, but some other woman would leap at the chance of such advancement, married to one of the most powerful monarchs in the Twelve Realms. Yet even if he'd had a child to inherit after him, the presence of this other child would be a constant threat.

I was sure of it now. Ansgar had had Jehanne murdered, probably the second she set foot on the wharf of Tradetown. Or maybe before. Maybe on the ship. It would be a simple thing to toss her overboard. I knew that from bitter experience. The vision rose before me of my poor old husband's uncomprehending, terrified face as his clothing dragged him under the waves.

Stop it. I'm trying to think here. Stop it stop it stop it

Please, Companion. Please stop your screeching. I can't hear myself think, and I need to do that. I need to think.

Try to breathe, I told myself. *Try to take some deep breaths.*

Listening to the women talk, I started believing that Haakon had died a week or more before that longship had brought Jehanne the news.

And I wondered about something else. I saw the way the women talked about Ansgar. Or rather, how they didn't talk about him. They were afraid.

How did Haakon die, anyway? To hear Jehanne speak of him, Haakon was a vigorous man. True, he was old enough to have an adult son. Still. . .

My mind raced.

I thought back to Caedon's role in the poisoning of Ranulf. In the outright killing of Artur, rightful king of the Sceptered Isle, the murder that began the Rising, the rebellion of the Six Proud Walkers: my father Wat, his brother John (both of them Artur's bastard half-brothers), my true grandfather Drustan, Gwyl's father Rafe, Artur's youngest brother Avery, and Avery's best-beloved, Conal.

Caedon had engineered the crown prince's murder at the behest of Artur's second brother Audemar, so everyone said. I had come to believe Caedon had manipulated Audemar into it. I had come to believe Caedon was the true murderer, even if Audemar were the real one. True, real. Do you see?

You agree with me. You know a lot, Companion. I wonder how you do? I wonder how much.

Now Caedon and Ansgar were allied.

I realized it now. If I had agreed to be Ansgar's bride, he would have snapped up the Fire Isle and still allied himself with Caedon.

My parents had believed they were dealing with an honorable man, Haakon, and had sent me to him. They didn't understand. Haakon's son Ansgar was not an honorable man. Perhaps he was even a murderer, the worst type of murderer, the type who kills his own father.

I thought of Old Dee then, how he'd explained something to me once. He'd explained how the words *kin* and *kind* are related. "They're the same word, Keera. If you're kind to someone, it's because you are treating that someone as kin, someone connected to you by nature."

Ansgar was unnatural. He was unkind.

The nights were worst. In my bed, I sobbed for my parents, for Jehanne, for Fiona, for Old Dee, even. And I sobbed for Gwyl. I cried out of longing for him, and out of fright that he might have been hurt or even killed.

On the day I was sent away, a chill rain was falling.

"Make ready, mistress," my keeper said from my doorway, that morning. By now, I knew enough of her language to understand her.

My small chest was already packed. I nodded to it.

"I'll send one of the men to get it," she said. She was not really unfeeling. She just had a job to do and was doing it. "Go to eat a bit of breakfast before your voyage," she said to me.

I made my way into the hall of the longhouse and sat down at the board. I had become friendly with a few of the bondswomen, and now they smiled shyly and sympathetically at me. By now, they knew my story and pitied me.

I tried to eat but could force down little. Soon I stood up. I'd have to present myself to my escort. I figured I might as well get it over with.

But as I stepped out of the door of the longhouse, one of the bondswomen followed me into the dooryard. She took me in her arms and hugged me tight.

"A good journey," she whispered to me.

She shoved something into my hand. A parchment.

I turned to her in surprise, but she had already moved hastily away from me and back into the longhouse. The men of my escort surrounded me then, and marched me away.

The mariners on the knarr taking me to Lunds-fort along with Ansgar's other rich gifts for Caedon didn't even bother locking me up. No barrel, no locked cell. I sat on the little shelf in a tiny room of the knarr, as before. This one had no comfortable cushions, though. Now that I was alone, I pulled the small piece of parchment out of my sleeve where I had secreted it after the bondswoman had thrust it into my hand.

I unrolled it and read it. It was from Fiona. My eyes filled with tears.

Keera, I have tried everything to find out where they were keeping you and how I might get to you, but in these last weeks it has become too dangerous. Pierrick and I are in hiding. Sorcha's husband is protecting her, but I don't know how long he'll be able to do that, and it fills me with fear. As you know, I'm Caedon's enemy. As you've probably heard, he had Father killed, and my mother died soon after. But don't fear on my account. Pierrick and I have a plan to head west, with our son Alan. Yes, we have a son! How terrible that you must hear our happy news like this. Meanwhile, I fear for you, my dearest friend. I hope you have heard from Gwyl. Pierrick is trying to get word to him about your plight, and he has sent word to your parents. Don't despair, my dearest, dearest friend. Your Fiona.

I rolled the parchment up again and put it into my belt pouch. I didn't feel so alone now. Fiona was thinking of me, even while she herself was in terrible danger. Pierrick was by her side to help and protect her, and he was getting word to Gwyl and my parents. When I thought of their child, a place inside me glowed. *One day*, I thought, *Gwyl and I will have a child together*. And I have you, dear Companion.

Still, as I stepped up on deck to watch the grim coastline of the Ice-realm recede into the distance, my mood was as bleak as the gray, cold weather. At least Pierrick was getting Fiona and their child out of danger. Perhaps her little sister, Sorcha, was safe as well, protected by her well-connected husband. I shivered. She might think she was safe. But I, knowing Caedon as I did, doubted she really was.

During the voyage to Lunds-fort, you rode your customary perch on the stretching beam of the sail, Companion, your high sad keening mingling with the wind. The mariners paid you no mind, but I heard you up there.

I thought of telling you to stop it, but I didn't. You were only giving voice to my own forebodings.

Get Out of Jail Free

Jouncing in a wagon over the rough cobbles of the Lunds-fort streets, I knew my eyes must be getting bigger and bigger. I'd never seen such a large town. This, I knew, was where my own father's people had come from. His mother had been born here, or close by, and then she'd come across the border to the Sceptered Isle to live as King Ranulf the Fourth's mistress. His concubine. That's why my father and his brother John had such foreign-sounding names. And Old Dee, who had that same foreign name, John. I'd thought about it before, and what it could mean about Old Dee's origins. Now I thought about it again. No wonder his queen had wanted to see him in Lunds-fort. He had connections there, maybe deep and profound.

Now I found myself worrying not just about Gwyl but about Old Dee, too. Both of them in Lunds-fort, but when each of them had left to go there, it was a neutral town and the Baronies were not insinuating themselves into the conflicts of the other realms. Now they were. Now it was a much more dangerous place. I sent up a prayer to the Children that Gwyl and Old Dee were both safe. Perhaps Old Dee's queen would keep him safe. *Elizabeth*, I whispered to myself. Perhaps she was powerful enough that no one in the Baronies would think of offending her or offering any manner of discourtesy toward her or her emissaries and minions. *Unlike my own sad, disgraceful case in the Ice-realm, emissary or no emissary*, I thought bitterly.

Lunds-fort was almost its own separate realm. It was a rich city, teeming with people. The Eastern Baronies owned it. They had owned it time out of mind. The main stretch of their lands was across the Narrows from Lunds-fort. But Lunds-fort and the surrounding countryside, that slender strip of countryside, served as the Baronies' foothold on the coast between the border of the Sceptered Isle and the sea. Many's the king—from the Sceptered Isle and from the kingdoms to the north, before they'd been absorbed into the Sceptered Isle—who had tried to take Lunds-fort by force. It was a strategically important port city, but it was too well fortified to be seized easily. It was surrounded by thick walls built, they say, by the Old Ones before they'd abandoned the isle ages and ages ago and left for their realm in the south.

The Twelve Realms of the known world. The number used to be higher, but now there were twelve, as I knew from my studies long ago on the Northmost Isle, when I was a girl sneaking into the Lady Goddess's school and reading Her books. The Sceptered Isle was one, the realm which had grown to include the Western Isle where I was born and the lands to the north, including the Northmost Isle where I had lived out my girlhood.

There were eleven others, including The Eastern Baronies, The Ice-Realm, and my mother's realm, the smallest and weakest of the Twelve, the tiny Fire Isle. I wasn't counting the unknown reaches to the west, beyond the Great Sea. If any realm was ripe to fall, though, I knew it was the Fire Isle, too small, too defenseless, coveted most by the Ice-realm. Sooner or later, I feared, it would be absorbed into the Ice-realm just as the Western Isle had been absorbed into the Sceptered Isle.

Among all the near-by realms, the town of Lunds-fort was in perpetual contention. After the Old Ones of the Southern Primacy had left it, the Eastern Baronies took possession. But the Ice-Realm wanted it, and the Sceptered Isle, too. If Ice-Realm and Sceptered Isle joined forces, they might be able to take it. Or if the Sceptered Isle allied itself with the Baronies, the Sceptered Isle might eventually possess it through shrewd diplomacy. If not for the accidents of history, the Sceptered Isle would have it already. The Eastern Baronies were hard-put to defend it, since they had to move armies and material across the Narrows to do so. And so, as the poor ill-fated Lady Jehanne had told my parents, Haakon thought Lunds-fort was ready to fall.

For now, though, it was still part of the Baronies. I'd found out that much. Caedon didn't own it yet. As self-styled monarch of the Sceptered Isle, he wanted it. But so did Ansgar. I thought about that. I had my doubts their alliance would last long. I thought I saw what Caedon was doing. Ally with Ansgar to fend off the threat of the Baronies, then turn on Ansgar and take everything for himself.

I saw why these powerful contending men would want Lunds-fort, all of them. It was magnificent, a rich river town fortified by its walls and its proximity to the sea. The city was full of timbered buildings jostled together, some butting up against the thick stone walls of the Old Ones. Its streets were crooked and narrow. It was dirty, but it held a fascination that made me look past the dirt.

I could have looked forever as we rode through the town.

All too soon, we reached our destination, a big forbidding fortress reached by a wide bridge across the mighty river that snaked through the town on its progress to the sea and the harbors just beyond the city. I was handed out of the wagon and brought inside.

Soon I found myself alone in a small whitewashed chamber. A single window, high-set into the thick walls. For furniture, there were only a bed, a table, a bench, and a chamber pot, nothing more. The pot was just a battered thing, not even a close-stool. As I settled myself on the bench to see what my fate might be, I wondered at how my life had become just this: waiting, endless waiting, in some small barren room while others decided what would become of me.

I felt like a caged bird who longs for a little bit of sky.

I felt so lonely.

I know. I do have you, my Companion. If only you were real.

Oh, pardon, dear friend! I didn't mean to wound you! I know you're real. The farwydd gave you to me. Perhaps she did because she knew how lonely I'd be. And you have done mighty deeds. Don't think I've forgotten those. It's just that—well, even though you have, you maybe don't belong to this plane I live on. That's how Old Dee described what you are. So you are real in your own plane. Just not in mine. But you are powerful enough to reach across the planes, when the Children will it so, and this I have seen with my own eyes.

Do you know, I've just about forgotten my quest with its two tasks? Life in all its messiness and meanness has intervened between me and those fantasies I used to have. I've forgotten all about the farwydd's riddle. I think I've lost hope of ever finding out what it is trying to tell me.

Let me try to explain myself better. I would never want to wound you, dear Companion. I do know you're real, at least in the sense that you're some type of spirit she has given me to ease my way. But maybe I'm disenchanted and older now, not that foolish young child I used to be.

I just sometimes wish you were a girl like me. I miss my friend Fiona. Maybe that's all my lonely mood is about. I can only hope Gwyl's brother got her safely west.

Don't cry. Don't cry, dear Companion.

But as I was thinking these thoughts, and about how I was too old and had seen too much to think I'd ever fulfill my quest, the two tasks rose up in my mind to accuse me. The first of them, restoring my father's eyesight, I had truly despaired of and set aside.

But the second: kill Caedon.

There was a time when I wanted Caedon to take me so I'd be close enough to him to carry out that task. There was a time when he did take me, and I regretted it because it put Gwyl in such danger.

But now I was in his grasp again. And now.

I sat up straighter.

Now I'd be in a position to carry out that task.

All of my jaded thoughts from only moments before fell away from me.

I'd find a way. I'd wait, and I'd find a way.

After the last time, though, I bore no illusions about how easy such a task was going to be. If Caedon had me killed immediately, as it appeared he was about to do last time, I doubted I'd be able to stop him. I doubted Gwyl and his brother would leap to the rescue, this time.

If he wanted to keep me and do—

Please no screeching, dear Companion.

—do whatever he wanted with me, well, then, I might have time to figure out how to kill him before he killed me. I started thinking about that, how I'd do it. I doubted a knife would work very well. Surely he'd have me searched, when he got me in his power, and he'd find that knife. And then—I knew this as well as I knew my own name, and it burned me to the core—then he'd laugh at me.

But suppose I could make a potion. A poison. I knew about potions. I knew which herbs to use. I'd have to find out how I could get out into the countryside to find those herbs. Or get them some other way.

After that, I felt I had a sense of purpose again. Yet the days crawled by endlessly, and still Caedon didn't come to claim me.

After a few days, I realized that although I was kept in the fortress, I was free to move about it. No one looked at me twice; I was just one of the many who lived here. Some were awaiting sentencing for some crime or act of treason they'd committed. Some were hangers-on of officials residing in the fortress. Some were servants.

I realized no one knew where I fit among all those residents, and no one cared.

The few times I'd gone to the big gates that let people in and out over the great river, though, I realized I'd have quite a challenge trying to get out into the town, much less into the countryside beyond.

Yes, go ahead and say it, Companion. If I could get into the countryside, why wouldn't I try to get away? I had come to this same grudging conclusion myself—that rather than wait around for Caedon to seize upon me, I should be thinking about how to get away. I thought about my parents, and about Gwyl, and how horrified they'd be to learn I was once more in Caedon's power. How much they'd want me to get away if I could. And here, to do it would be much easier than in the Ice-realm. While they spoke a language of their own here in the lands owned by the Baronies, they spoke my own tongue, too, close as they were to the border. As for their language, I knew a little of it already, and I was picking up the rest of it fast. So I knew that if I could only get out of the fortress, it would be fairly easy to penetrate into the

Sceptered Isle mainland, and maybe, from there, to find passage to the Western Isle and beyond.

Once I got out of the fortress. There was the rub.

I made it my job to learn the fortress, top to bottom, and to befriend its residents, even the guards. I was energized. I'd be responsible and mature. I'd get out of the fortress, and then I'd get out of Lunds-fort. Or, as Old Dee might put it, I would get out of Dodge.

But then. Then I'd think about my task. I'd think about Caedon, getting closer. In the kitchen, in spite of my sensible thoughts about knives and how they could simply be plucked away from me, I found myself a knife. In the mews, I found myself a whetstone.

I realized I'd still have to get away, if the Children willed I could carry out my task and kill Caedon, so I continued my efforts to learn the fortress. After all, I reasoned. My farwydd hadn't forbidden me to do it. She'd just made my task impossibly hard.

Not impossibly, I told myself. But hard. Very hard.

And besides, I told myself, look how the farwydd had sent you, Companion, to rout the forces of Caedon back on the Fire Isle. True, he did escape, but he was sent away in defeat. Surely that meant the Children were on my side and against Caedon.

I made friends with the women in the kitchen shed. They had the implements I needed to use if I found the right herbs to make my poison, and they had the knives.

I made friends with any number of others, even ones who couldn't directly help me in either escaping or accomplishing my task. The man who kept the hawks in the mews was one of them.

Now that, dear Companion, near broke my heart. I haven't mentioned this, because it's too painful. When I was taken in Ansgar's ship a prisoner to the Ice-realm, I lost Hildr. She had been left behind. Someone else probably owned her now.

So I was both attracted to the mews and saddened to go there. Quickly, though, this old cadger in the mews, one of the assistants to the fort's chief falconer, learned how good I was with the birds. Soon I was helping him with them. I became a fixture at the mews. The cadger was a crusty older man, but underneath his calloused exterior was a kind heart. I got into the habit of bringing him a bun from the kitchen shed each morning, and then helping to train the younger birds, or soothe the restless ones, or even assist with the sick and hurt ones.

Every morning, he'd sit before an upended barrel with his bun, his mug of ale, and his two friends. One of these men was an hostler. The other was a guard in the fortress dungeons. As the weeks went by, the three of them near-adopted me as a surrogate daughter. For my part, I was fascinated by all the news of the city that they brought with them to enliven their morning chat. I kept my ears open for any tidbit of information that would help me walk out of the fortress to my freedom.

The three men were full of stories. The hostler regaled his friends with gossip about the high-born lords and ladies that he horsed in his stables. How someone as high-falutin as one fancy lord was actually a terrible horseman. (Here I felt a pang, being a terrible horsewoman myself.). How one pompous lady fell off her horse and onto her broad rump while the hostler and his assistants stifled their laughter. I didn't have a broad rump, but I felt a secret sympathy with her humiliation. I remembered the men in the Ice-realm, and how they'd had to hide their laughter at my awkward attempt to climb aboard the horse they'd held for me. But for all that, the ostler was good-hearted, and his gossip gave me valuable information.

The other two men would tell stories in return. My cadger friend was full of stories about his birds. I thrilled to these stories, although my heart ached for Hildr.

The guard was full of interesting accounts of his prisoners. The bravery of a high-born lord accused of treason who went to his death without betraying his companions. "Not even torture could loosen his lips. We all loved him. We all cried to see him hanged," said the guard. And there was a whole family being kept in one of his cells—father, mother, and two tiny boys. The guard didn't know why they were being kept there—"Enemies of some higher-up," he speculated—but the little boys reminded him of his grandchildren, so he carved them animals out of wood and brought them to their cell so they'd have playthings.

There was one other thing I set myself to do, especially as I had the run of the fort, and especially as I soon discovered the fort was the place where all the important business of Lunds-fort was carried out. I'm sure you can guess what it is, Companion.

I realized that Gwyl might be in this very fort with me, or if he were out in the town, he'd very probably have to come into the fort to conduct his diplomacy. (And spy, I reminded myself.) So I set myself to find him. Finding Gwyl would change everything. Just as his brother Pierrick had helped Fiona escape from the Ice-realm, so Gwyl and I would escape Lunds-fort. Maybe we'd find Fiona and his brother. Maybe we'd head west with them.

As you can see, I had many conflicting plans rolling around the inside of my head, up and down those folds Old Dee once described to me and pointed out to me in the most interesting of all his grimoires, the Saunders Medical Atlas of the Brain and Book of Power.

It was hard to ask around, though. I didn't want to put Gwyl in any kind of danger with suspicious questions, and I didn't want anyone to realize I had a connection with him. Especially not anyone who might report back to Caedon.

My search was not going well. The people in the kitchen were a gossipy lot. I got them talking about all of the interesting foreign travelers and diplomats they had served at the Lord Mayor's many banquets. The Lord Mayor of Lunds-fort is the most powerful man in the city, you see. Did you know that, Companion? Oh. I see you do. Well, then, you know he lives in richly-appointed rooms with the best view from the fort. He conducts all the business of the city from these rooms. His maidservants have described every luxurious feature of these rooms to me, so I feel I know them well.

Oh. You've been in them. Well, la-di-da.

No, Companion, don't get angry. I didn't mean to be rude. You can help me. You'll be a powerful resource for me, when Caedon finally takes me.

Now see what I've done. I've made you go twittering up to the ceiling to thrash about up there. Come back down, please. I promise not to talk about it any more.

Where was I? So the kitchen gossip. Yes, I heard many interesting stories about many important people. None of them were Gwyl.

After a while, I spent less time gossiping with these servants and more time with my friends the cadger, the ostler, and the prison guard. I didn't think anything they'd tell me would be directly helpful, but you know? I liked those nice men.

One day, though, as the prison guard was talking about this and that, I felt the hair on my neck actually stand up during one of his tales, just as if a wave of that electricity Old Dee had described were coursing through me.

The other two were urging the guard to describe his most interesting prisoner.

"You wouldn't believe this old fellow I'm keeping in one of my cells," he began. "This old man is old as the stones at the bottom of the fortress well. I don't know how old he is. He has a long white beard. But to hear him talk! He uses the strangest words. He says the strangest things."

A sudden impulse led me to ask, carefully, "What strange words? What kind of strange things?"

"I think the old man is in for witchcraft," said the guard. "Some of the words he says. . ." Here the guard dropped his voice and we others leaned in. I saw the cadger and the hostler shiver. "They are words of power."

"Like what?" I asked.

The guard shook his head. "I don't like to say, mistress," he whispered.

"Like murmur? Like pursan? Like arex, remex, morax?"

The guard jumped to his feet and made a particular sign against evil I'd seen followers of the Lady Goddess make. "Nine Spheres, mistress. Where did you hear those words?" he said.

"You're not a witch too, are you, mistress? If you are, I'd keep it to myself, I would, else you'll be taken up and hanged."

"They're not going to hang Old Dee, are they?" I burst out.

"How do you know his name?" said the guard, backing away from me and making that sign again.

"Oh, sir," I cried. "I don't mean to alarm you. The man just sounds so much like someone my family knew, when I was a child. A harmless old man who'd go around saying such things, but we knew he wasn't a witch. It's just that he wasn't right in the head. And he traveled to Lunds-fort, and then no one saw him any more."

"Oh, then, mistress, that's all right," said the guard, sitting down, relieved. But he still had a spooked expression on his face.

"I hope your prisoner isn't Old Dee. Such a nice old man, though addled. I'd hate to think he was a prisoner, or that some ill fate might have come to him."

"No harm in taking you to see him," said the guard. "He's locked up tight, he is. You can get word to his people, maybe, if it's the same old man. And indeed, you've the right of it. He is a nice old man. Hasn't given me a bit of trouble."

I could scarcely contain myself, but I made myself look calm and sound off-hand. "Oh, that would be a kindness," I told the guard. "His daughter has worried about him these last three years and more."

The guard offered to take me to the cell that very afternoon.

My heart was fluttered. I knew the guards at the fortress had a thriving side business, taking people in and out of the prison's cells to visit their relatives. They made a nice bit of coin doing it, and their superiors looked the other way. Probably their superiors got a cut. My nice friend the guard said he wouldn't think of charging me.

I carefully watched the sundial in the fort's kitchen garden and presented myself at the iron-bound doors leading to the dungeon at the time the guard had appointed. He lit a rush torch and led me down a crabbed spiral set of stone stairs. "Mind yourself, mistress. The damp can make these stairs slippery," he called back to me.

The stench increased the further down into the dungeon we went. At one point, we passed a cell where some unknown prisoner was making a hideous groaning sound. The guard acted as though it were all perfectly normal, so I tried not to gag from the smell or startle at the cries of torment.

"Here's the cell, mistress," said the guard, stopping at a stout door and sliding a covering away from a little grating.

I stood on tiptoe to look in.

Sitting slumped over in the straw was an old man dressed in rags. He had a long white beard, but really, he could have been anyone. I stared in.

Then I called softly, "Old Dee, could that be you?"

The man sat up and turned his face my way. Even in the dim rushlight, I saw his bright blue inquisitive eyes, and I knew him.

Tears started from my own eyes. "Old Dee, it's Keera."

"Keera? Keera, my darling girl," he said. He managed to haul himself to his feet and brace himself against the wall and come painfully to the door. "Keera, it's you!" he exclaimed.

"Old Dee, we've all been so worried about you. Did you bring the queen her horn?"

"Yes, I did, Keera, but then—" he stopped and scratched. I could see vermin crawling on him. "But then something went wrong when I tried to come back. And I'm stuck here." He murmured something under his breath that made my flesh creep. "That dratted Gilles," I thought I heard him say.

"But Old Dee," I said, trying to ignore the part about Gilles and keep my voice low. The guard was picking at his fingernails with his knife. I wasn't sure if he were listening or not. "I thought, when you left so long ago, you might have opened a magic portal to do it. Can't you do that now?"

"No, Keera, I'm afraid I can't. They've stuck me in this small space, like Merlin in his rock. Holy moly, god knows I've tried to cast my portal spell, but I just don't have enough scope for it. I need a lot of space for that one," he said, spreading his arms out wide.

"Holy guacamole," I murmured sympathetically. "This kind guard has allowed me to speak to you," I told him then, because the guard was giving me a strange look now. I raised my voice. "I'd like to get word to your people. They don't know where you are."

"My people?" said Old Dee blankly.

"You know. Gudrun and . . . and Grimalkin, and the folks back home."

"Oh, yes, my people," said Old Dee, catching on.

"Maybe they can go to the authorities and explain how you're not right in the head. Maybe they can get you out," I said, again in a louder-than-necessary voice, giving Old Dee a meaning look.

"Oh. Oh, yes, I hope you can do that, Keera," he said.

"Well, mistress," the guard interjected. "That's all the time I can give you with this prisoner."

"Kind mister guard," Old Dee called through the grating. "May I have one word more with my visitor? It has been so long since I heard a voice from home."

"Very well," said the guard. To me he said, "Pray be quick about it, mistress. I'm going to check down the corridor. . ."

I saw he was getting anxious that his superiors might find out about my visit. It wasn't really allowed, although I knew he and the other guards were lax about the rule when the prisoner wasn't dangerous and his relatives had means or influence. I had neither, except of course the best currency of all, friendship. The guard made his way a little bit down the corridor, taking the rushlight with him, leaving me and Old Dee in darkness.

"Keera," Old Dee said quickly, realizing his opportunity. "See what you can do about getting me out of this cell. I think if I had just a bit more space, I could call up the portal and get out of here."

"I'll try my utmost, Old Dee," I whispered back.

"But Keera—quickly—I have some news for you. Now brace yourself, and don't cry out. There's another prisoner here. It's your dearest man, your Gwyl."

"Gwyl is here?" I did have to stifle a cry.

"He's here. He's near. I worked out a way to communicate with him."

"Tell him I love him," I said in a panic. The rushlight was coming back down the corridor. "Tell him I'll try to get him out. I don't know how," I said, practically moaning.

"Get me out first. Then we'll find a way," said Old Dee.

"Mistress, it's time," said the guard, at my elbow now.

"Thank you," I told him, managing a smile as he forced the rusted cover back over the grate with a terrible scrawing sound that made me want to scream out. I forced my voice to sound normal. "I'm going to let Old Dee's people know what has happened to him." As the guard walked me back up out of the dungeons, I kept up a constant bright chatter, trying to allay any suspicions he had of me, desperately trying to control my rising sense of panic. *They have Gwyl here in this dark, filthy place.* My thoughts were quickly spiraling into a frightening set of conclusions, and I couldn't let the guard see that. I had to control myself. "Do you think they can go to the prison officials and explain? And maybe take Old Dee back home with them?" I asked in a reasonable tone of voice.

"I doubt that, mistress," said the guard, shaking his head. "That'd be hard, that one would. Once the prisoner is charged and put into his cell, it's a hard one ever to get him out. Only one way for that." He pointed with his finger to the sky, and I shuddered. I knew he meant only death could release these prisoners. Old Dee. And Gwyl.

"Do you have any prisoners sentenced to be hanged?" I asked, as if it were a matter of simple if grisly curiosity.

"Many," said the guard.

"Not Old Dee, surely," I said.

"No, not he, mistress. Not unless his witchcraft harmed anyone."

"Oh, he's no witch."

"The law says he is, mistress."

"But he hasn't harmed anyone?"

"The law says he hasn't, mistress."

"Oh, that's all right, then. He won't be hanged. His people will be relieved," I said. "I'll go to the scrivener and have him write to them today." No sense letting the guard know I could read and write.

I didn't dare ask the horrible question weighing on me now. Was Gwyl sentenced to be hanged? But I knew now, the only way I could help Gwyl was to help Old Dee.

A few days later, I brought the subject of Old Dee up to the guard again. "I've heard from Old Dee's people," I told him.

"So soon?" The guard's eyes opened wide.

"His niece was traveling to Lunds-fort. She brought me a basket of berries from the countryside," I told him. "It was good to hear about how they're doing, all the people back home. And I could tell Katherine what I'd learned about her poor old uncle."

"Ahh. I'm glad you could, mistress," said the guard, who really was a very kind man.

"I'm wondering," I said. "I suppose it would be too much to ask, to allow them to see Old Dee in the common room of the dungeon. They could bring him fresh clothes. I saw how he was crawling with vermin."

"You know," said the guard, scratching his chin and thinking. "The prison warden does allow such, sometimes. Especially in cases like this, where the prisoner is no threat and has done nothing much."

"Could Old Dee's people go to see the warden? Or write him a letter?"

"As for trying to see the warden." The guard looked dubious. "He's a busy man with no time for visits from simple people. But as for a letter. You might try, mistress. You might indeed," said the guard.

Then I spent a few days getting writing materials together and composing a letter from Old Dee's fictitious niece. I brought it to the guard, who promised to get it to the prison warden.

A week went by. A week during which I could neither sleep nor eat. I was worried that the guard and his friends would be able to take one look at me and see I was in a dreadful state.

One morning, after I'd helped the cadger with the hawks and falcons in the mews and we'd sat down at his barrel with buns and mugs of ale, and I was keeping myself deliberately calm by clamping down on the edge of his barrel so hard that red ridges were rising on my palms, the guard happened by to join us. And to bring me news.

"Mistress, the warden says Old Dee's family can visit him. He'll give me the day and time, and you can get word to them."

"That's wonderful!" I said. I thanked him profusely, hoping I was striking just the right note—gratitude on behalf of the people from home with no edge of hysteria showing. The edge of hysteria that was like to push me right over it.

And may I say this, Companion? Without you to talk me down maybe once an hour, if not more often, I think I might have gone over that edge. Gone over and exploded. So I thank you for that.

After another exchange of letters with the fictitious niece, the day and time were fixed.

The morning before the supposed visit, the guard came by the mews to let me know how things with Old Dee were going. "Mistress, the visit is arranged. They'll bring Old Dee to the Common

Room when the fortress bell tolls noontide, and then they'll admit his family."

"What a kind office you've done them," I told him.

I tried not to think too much about Old Dee for the rest of the day. As you may imagine, that was an exercise in futility. I stayed in my room and worried.

My room, as it turned out, was directly above the dungeons, although many floors higher.

Noontide came, the noontide of the visit. I didn't know what to expect or think.

Oh, stop it. You didn't either, Companion. Don't pretend you knew.

I tried to lie quietly on my bed. I fretted and stewed instead. The bell tolled. Was it happening now? Was Old Dee being brought into a room with enough space to call up his portal? What if the prison officials grew suspicious when no family appeared beforehand, to wait to be admitted? What if they didn't let Old Dee out of his cell after all?

And of course I didn't know what it would take for Old Dee to call up his portal. Did it involve a lot of conjuring motions and spell-casting? Suppose the officials grew suspicious then and whisked him back to his cell before he had a chance to call it up?

I was in the middle of these worries when, far below me, I heard a deep hollow boom. The very walls of the fortress shook.

Those closer said afterward there was a light so bright they shielded their faces with their hands.

Old Dee disappeared.

To my distress, so did the guard. Not through Old Dee's portal. Into a cell, for aiding Old Dee's escape.

I hadn't thought I'd put the kindly guard in jeopardy.

The cadger and hostler discussed their friend's fate anxiously. They told me he'd been imprisoned, because he'd come under suspicion. After all, he'd arranged for Old Dee to be brought up to the Common Room. And then, they whispered, through his witchery, the prisoner had conjured up a spell and disappeared.

"Oh, no," I said, covered with guilt. "It was because of me. He would never have gotten in trouble if I hadn't asked him to arrange the visit. I should go to the prison warden and explain."

The cadger and hostler hastened to discourage me.

"Don't do it, Keera," said the cadger, while the hostler earnestly nodded his agreement. "You'll only be taken yourself. It's bad enough our friend's been taken."

"I'm already a kind of prisoner," I told them.

"But soon your owner will come for you," the cadger told me kindly. "And you'll leave this place and live a happier life."

I kept my doubts about that to myself. But still, the guilt gnawed at me.

I felt a welter of emotions. A storm of them. Guilt, yes. At the same time, I felt elated. So elated I wanted to run and jump and shout out freedom to the heavens. Then, a mere instant later, I'd turn disconsolate. Old Dee was free. But I didn't really see how Old Dee would be able to help Gwyl. For one thing, Old Dee could hardly just stroll back into the fortress once he'd busted out the way he had.

For another, where had he gone? Maybe back to his queen. Somewhere else, at any rate. I'd figured that much out. Somewhere other than here.

So I was surprised and—I admit—a bit apprehensive when, a bare two days after Old Dee's miraculous deliverance from prison, one of the maids in the kitchen shed told me a fruit seller was looking for me. She gestured to the back of the shed. Sitting beside the fire in the shed was a man, not so old, erect, clean-shaven.

I wondered what he could want. I wondered if he was maybe from the authorities. If maybe they'd had their suspicions that I was involved in the prison escape. Supposing this man was here to entrap me into admitting my role? Then they'd stick me in one of those dark, stinking cells.

I sidled over to the man in a great deal of trepidation. When he turned his piercing blue eyes on me, though, I knew. He didn't look like Old Dee, but he was Old Dee just the same.

"Old Dee," I said. "You are indeed a powerful neurologist." I threw myself into his arms, sobbing with relief. Then I got a grip on myself, because I didn't want the kitchen people to wonder at me. I stepped back and composed myself.

"Thank you, Keera," Old Dee replied.

I felt a sense of relief when I heard his voice. These were Old Dee's eyes, and that was Old Dee's voice, even if the rest of him didn't much look like himself.

"Now we have some work to do," he continued. "We must give young Gwyl his get out of jail free card."

I didn't quite know what he meant by that, but I understood the gist of it. I nodded, sitting forward on the edge of the three-legged stool I'd pulled up to him.

"He'll not pass Go, he'll not collect two hundred dollars, but we'll get him out."

"Old Dee," I began. My lip quivered.

"Oh, forgive me, Keera. I always forget how upset you get when I use the language of my—of my art. What I mean to say is, we have work to do, we're going to get him out, it may not be pretty, but what we want is, we want it to work. Am I right?"

"Okay," I said to him, letting him know I loved and respected him anyway, in spite of his frightening words of power.

"And Keera," said Old Dee. "Before we can do that, I need to understand your own circumstances a little better."

"But Old Dee, I've been so worried about you. How did you get imprisoned here?"

"I had visited my queen, and cast my portal to get back to you. But then—" He looked at me hard. "This part is difficult to explain. I have an enemy who is constantly lying in wait to thwart me. His name is Gilles."

When he said that, Companion, a chill shot up both of my arms. They broke out in actual goosebumps. I remembered what he had muttered in his cell. I recalled the dream I had had so long ago. *Gilles. I adjure thee.* And I thought of the woman's face in the pool. Your face, Companion. Gilles is your enemy, too. I see that now, although not what it means. I recalled my father's voice, its tone of revulsion, as he spoke the name of Gilles, and I recalled that somehow Gilles had something to do with the death of Gwyl's father. And something to do with Caedon and his success.

"This Gilles had you imprisoned?" I asked Old Dee, trying to still my trembling.

"He engineered it, I believe."

"I don't understand," I whispered.

Old Dee patted my knee. "Better that way," he said. "Gilles is a dangerous man."

"At least tell me how you escaped when they took you out of your cell," I said.

"I cast my portal. Thanks to you, I got enough space to cast it, and so I did cast it, and I walked through it."

"I thought that's what had happened, when I heard the boom."

"Yes, often I can manage not to create such a display, draw so much attention, but I didn't have time for the niceties."

"Old Dee, the poor guard who helped you was imprisoned. It makes me sad. It's my fault for involving him."

"Oh, then, we must get him out as well," said Old Dee. "He's a very nice man. He was always as good to me as his profession would allow."

"Thank you!" I flung my arms around him again and began to cry.

He patted me on the back until I stopped. "Holy moly, Keera. You've grown up, you know that? You were a skinny little thing, and now you're this blooming young woman." He smiled at me. "But still just as intense."

"Where did you go, Old Dee? When you cast your portal?"

"That's hard to explain, Keera. I went back to the place I came from, and I had a long hot shower."

"A shower?"

"A wonderful type of bath where water comes pouring down on your head from a pipe in the ceiling."

"That sounds good," I said, although secretly I thought it sounded a bit frightening. "And you got rid of all the vermin," I said. He smelled incredibly clean. I don't think I've ever smelled anyone who smelled so clean.

"That was the easy part, the vermin," he said. "They didn't survive the trip back through the portal. Jesus, Mary, and Joseph, I was glad to get rid of them," he said.

"You look very different, Old Dee."

"Yes," he said. "I thought that was wise." He gestured vaguely to his surroundings.

"I agree," I told him.

"But I still want to know what you're doing here," he said. "You didn't know I was in the prison, did you? How did you find it out?"

"By the grace of the Children," I said. Then I thought of my mother. "Or luck."

"Lucky. I'll say it was lucky. I can't quite believe it was pure luck."

I had a sudden suspicion and looked around. There you were, Companion, preening yourself just as if you were a big satisfied bird, up on the rafters.

"Maybe she did it," I said.

Old Dee looked around at you too, now. "Maybe she did. By George, maybe she did."

I knew by this time not to ask it, who this George might be.

"Well, however you did it, I'm glad you did," Old Dee said.

"But how did Gwyl get in there too?" I asked. My anxiety about Gwyl came roaring back, after my first excesses of joy at seeing Old Dee. "That seems like luck, too. Bad luck."

"Not so hard to explain. No magic involved with that one. Gwyl had come here on some kind of mission, am I right?"

"Yes."

"And he was caught in a bad situation. The political conditions changed rapidly here. The Eastern barons were keeping out of the conflict between Caedon and the Ice-realm, and suddenly the barons were Caedon's allies. Caedon, your old enemy. He seems to have a talent for the political."

"Holy guacamole, yes," I said.

"I'd like to know how he brought that off," said Old Dee. "It was a brilliant stroke of diplomacy. Why, the man is practically Machiavellian."

"Machia-what?"

"That's a reference to a brilliant political mind from the—let me see. From the Southern Primacy," he told me.

"Oh," I said.

"Just not yet," he added. "Never mind. Okay, Gwyl got caught here, and Caedon knew who he was, so Caedon had him thrown in prison until he could get around to—"

"—to killing him?" I finished, my voice quiet.

"Yes, I believe that's Caedon's plan," said Old Dee.

"When?" I felt my fists clench into tense balls. I felt the panic start to rise again.

"That I don't know. So the sooner we get him out, the better. Anyhow, this is Lunds-fort's main prison, the one where they keep the dangerous prisoners. Of course this is where Caedon stashed Gwyl." Old Dee spoke to me in a calming voice, and he put his hand over mine. "Easy, now, Keera. We're going to get him out."

My eyes filled with tears. "Are you sure, Old Dee?" I whispered.

"Quite sure. Now Gwyl. He's a handsome lad. Do I understand Gwyl to be your intended?"

"Yes," I said, blushing.

"And you love him?"

"Yes," I said, blushing harder.

"That's lovely, Keera. I think a lot of Gwyl."

"How were you able to talk to him? You were stuck in that cell," I said. "You couldn't get out. How do you know what he looks like?"

"I could communicate with many of the prisoners around me."

"How in the Nine Spheres could you do that?" I felt I was getting over-excited. I didn't want to draw any extra attention from the kitchen wenches, and I knew they were already casting curious glances in our direction, but I had to know.

"I couldn't cast my big portal spell, but I could cast some of the smaller ones," he told me. "For instance, I can send a projection of myself a short way out and away from me."

"A projection?"

"Sort of like her," said Old John, pointing to the ceiling where you were hovering now, Companion. "So then," he continued, "when I knew I was trapped, I decided at least I could probe as far as possible and find out who was around me. Maybe some of them had a way to help me. I didn't know. But I had to try anything I could. I was in that cell a long time, Keera."

"And when you probed, you found Gwyl."

"Yes, he was being kept only a few cells away from me."

"So while I was talking to you, he was really close? And I didn't know it?" I felt like the tears were about to spill over again.

"I'm sorry, Keera, There was no time to explain any of that, not if I were to get out. And if I didn't get out, I wouldn't have been able to help Gwyl. Or any of them."

"There are others you want to help?"

"Many. I think I'll be able to help a lot of them. Let's start with Gwyl, though, shall we?"

"Oh, yes!"

"But let me tell you about Gwyl. I quickly learned how he was connected to you. In almost our first conversation, he told me that he served a valiant king. When he described that king, his missing arm, his eyes, I knew right away it was your father. From there, it only took a few questions before I found out how much he loves that king's valiant daughter."

I couldn't help it. I began to blush again.

As for you. You are really behaving kind of disgracefully, Companion. I see what you are doing, all those backflips and pirouettes up by the ceiling. Quite distracting.

But Companion. I wish I were up there doing them with you.

Old Dee was saying something to me. I turned my attention back to him. "Keera. You keep evading my question. Why are you here?"

"Caedon caught me," I said, keeping it simple.

"Your enemy."

"Yes. But just as he hasn't gotten around to Gwyl, he hasn't gotten around to me, yet, either. When he does, I suppose he'll take me off with him to his royal seat in the Sceptered Isle, wherever that is now."

"Tambourne," said Old John. "King Ranulf's seat of power, I believe."

"Oh," I said.

"Now tell me this. Were you trying to get out of the fortress? Or were you waiting for Caedon to take you off with him to Tambourne?"

"I was waiting—" I began hesitantly.

"—to go off with Caedon to carry out your second task," Old Dee finished. "Keera, Keera, Keera. Didn't we talk about this?"

"Yes," I said miserably, not meeting his eye.

"Leaving Gwyl here to rot," said Old Dee. He was merciless. "Leaving your parents on their island to grieve. Leaving your father with his eyesight unhealed."

I hung my head.

"Let's say no more about it," said Old Dee, giving me a brisk pat. "We're all getting out of here. Me. Gwyl. You. And then we're heading back to your parents to regroup."

Regrouping. I tried that word out silently. To *regroup.* I liked it. It was a fine word, one of the best Old Dee had given me.

CHAPTER EIGHTEEN

Run Softly

Old Dee and I were standing against the top strake of Gwyl's big skeid as it stood in to port at Mist Cove, my mother's capital. Gwyl came to join us, folding his arms around me. I looked up into his face and smiled, masking my concern at how thin and pale he still appeared.

"Caedon hasn't taken the Fire Isle. Not yet. But he will soon. There's nothing we can do to stop him, not with Ansgar's troops and Caedon's together," said Gwyl, releasing me and flipping his sun-stone over and over in one hand as he always did.

I loved him for that.

I loved him for each familiar gesture he made, because I'd come to believe I'd never see him making them again, not until we met in the Land of the Dead.

Getting him out of the Lunds-fort prison had been a near thing, in spite of all Old Dee's powers.

"Where are they now, do you think? Caedon's troops?" Old Dee asked Gwyl. We were all looking out over the harbor and the approaching pier. Old Dee had reverted to his elderly wisp-bearded appearance by now. "Can't scare Gudrun when I meet her again, now can I?" he'd said to me.

"I hear they're massing in Tradetown, getting a flotilla ready for an invasion," Gwyl answered Old Dee.

"Tradetown. That's the big port town in the Ice-realm," said Old Dee.

Gwyl and I nodded.

"That's not very far away," said Old Dee.

"In good sailing weather, only a few days," said Gwyl. He scanned the horizon, his gray eyes narrowing against the sudden rays of sun pouring down on us from the clouds. "The weather looks to be pretty good," he said finally, in a flat voice.

I stole my hand into his, and he gripped it as if he'd never let it go.

Old Dee gave us a kind look and walked away a little bit down the expanse of the ship.

Gwyl bent down to me and kissed me. "I wasn't thinking this earlier, as we sailed here," he said. "But now that we're here, I'm actually a bit afraid. That's strange, isn't it. I never thought I'd see you again."

"I had the same bad thought," I whispered back. "But here we are."

"Tell me," he said, and I stiffened. Here was the question I'd been dreading, the same one Old Dee had put to me. Over the past weeks of our flight from Lunds-fort, Gwyl had never asked me. The question had just hung between us, mostly a distant thing I could brush aside, especially since he hadn't asked it. But now I could feel it coming. Maybe, even though I've lost my powers, I still have some of that second sense my mother has described to me. "Why were you in Lunds-fort?" he asked me.

"A long story."

"Try me." His voice was grim.

"Don't be angry with me. I can't stand it," I said, bursting into tears.

He folded me against him and stroked my hair until I stopped crying with a hiccup. "The only thing keeping me alive in there was knowing you were safe," he said. "But you weren't."

"We don't live in a safe world, Gwyl," I said.

He sighed then. "I want the world to be safe for you."

"I want the world to be safe for you," I countered.

"Let's not argue," he said. "Just tell me."

So, after all that time, I did. I told him about my mission, and how my parents were misled and betrayed. How the Lady Je-hanne was betrayed and probably murdered. How Haakon may have been murdered. How Ansgar was surely a traitor and maybe even a parricide. That's a father-killer, Companion. And

finally—the hard part—how Ansgar had handed me over to Caedon.

"But Caedon hadn't come for me when I discovered Old Dee,"
I concluded. "And he hadn't come for you."

"He was going to have me executed," said Gwyl. "I had only a
few days left to me."

"I know," I said. "Old Dee told me."

"Old Dee," said Gwyl. "That's the part I really don't understand. I thought I was dreaming him. I didn't think he was real.
Time stopped for me, inside that prison. Nothing seemed real.
Everything seemed to be a dream, especially when the fever began. But I was glad I had someone to talk to, in there."

"He's real," I said.

"I see that now. But—"

"He's a powerful neurologist."

"A what?"

"A sorcerer."

"Oh."

"You don't believe in such things, do you, son of the Child of
Sea," I teased him. "Yet you took Old Dee's magic needle and
sailed the world with it."

"I never believed in such things before," said Gwyl. Now he
drew the magic needle from his belt pouch and stared at it in his
palm. "But this thing may have changed my mind. It's better
than fleas," he added.

Fleas, I thought blankly. But I rushed on. "And you didn't
know me, when I had my powers."

"You had powers? Like Old Dee's?"

"Not exactly like his," I told Gwyl. "I had my own powers."

"What powers? I don't think I like that idea, that you have some kind of witchy powers."

"Do you know, when I was a child, the neighbors wanted to stone me for a witch. But Mother got me away from them."

"You're scaring me, Keera."

"It's true, though. You should know that, before you marry me. It might make you want to marry someone else."

"Never!" said Gwyl, smiling at last now and pulling me closer to him.

"Lucky for you I don't have my powers any longer. I'd know exactly what you were thinking. Every thought. You'd have no privacy from me. How would you like that, me inside your mind all the time? The farwydd sucked my powers away from me, may the Dark Ones take her."

"That's blasphemy," said Gwyl to me.

"Now you're teasing me. And what about her?"

"Her? Who?"

"Her." I pointed to the stretcher beam where you, dear Companion, were basking in the sun above the sail.

"I'm going to promise you something, Keera. I promise to love you and marry you and make babies with you in spite of your spooky qualities."

"Anyway," I said, taking a reasonable tone. "You may not believe in her or even see her—" here I pointed you out to him again, and he just shook his head—"but how do you explain Old Dee? He wasn't a dream, was he?"

"No," Gwyl said. "I have to admit to you, no, he wasn't."

As I thought over the journey Gwyl had made from prisoner near dead of jail fever to free man, I marveled at it. I marveled at how Old Dee had rescued all of us.

Once he could use the full extent of his powers again, he had cast a projection of himself, a pretty gory-looking one, according to him, although he didn't give me the details. He'd walked into the prison; frightened a guard, who ran screaming down the corridor; took the guard's keys; and began opening up as many of the cells as he could before he figured the guard had gotten over his hysteria long enough to summon help. He'd led the prisoners to an obscure part of the fortress and hidden them there.

Then, painstakingly (because, he said, doing so drained his powers so fast), he'd cloaked himself and each prisoner in an impenetrable cloud and had walked them, one by one, out of the fortress. From there, he'd had to let them take to their heels—reluctantly, because he didn't know how they'd fare.

He'd made sure to rescue my own kind guard, the poor man I'd duped into getting Old Dee free. I only hope that man is well and happy now.

And of course Old Dee had rescued Gwyl. But Gwyl was so weak and ill that he wasn't even able to walk without help, much less get out of the city without detection. If he hadn't been executed, he would soon have been dead in there, headsman or no headsman, noose or no noose.

As for Old Dee, after undoing his projection, renting an inn-room, and hiding Gwyl there, he had had to spend many weeks nursing Gwyl back to health and hoping no one would find him and re-imprison him. No one bothered trying to hunt down many of the other escapees, poor forgotten souls as they were.

But Gwyl was an important political prisoner under sentence of death. Caedon's spies and the Lunds-fort authorities scoured the city looking for him.

At the same time, Old Dee wasn't very much help to Gwyl, or so he said. Old Dee's strength was so depleted by his tour-de-force of neurological magic that he was almost as weak as Gwyl. "I thought I'd catch the jail fever too," he told me later. "I'm amazed I didn't catch it when I was imprisoned for so long. Lice are the vectors, you know. I think I was dealing with the louse-borne variant. If I'd caught it then, I'd be dead for sure. I'm amazed I didn't catch it from Gwyl, later on. I suppose I had a false sense of security. I suppose I thought, if I caught it, that I could just cast my portal and dose myself up with doxycycline. But I was so weak that I doubt I could have cast it. Then where would we be?"

I didn't know what he meant, "vector," "doxycycline," all his usual confusing words of power, but I knew from the days when my mother and I worked out the reason for the terrible dis-ease on Northmost Isle that bad conditions can lead people on a direct march to the Land of the Dead.

"Were the prison's wells too close to the jakes?" I asked him.

He gave me a shrewd look. "The dis-ease you fought and defeated in your youth, dear Keera, is caused by different unsanitary conditions, but I see you understand the principle." He stopped to think about it. "To tell you truly, there are no jakes in that prison. The prisoners are left to fend for themselves. That certainly doesn't help sanitation overall, but at least there's no connection with the water supply."

I shuddered and looked away.

As for me. I was the first person Old Dee had gotten out of the fortress, even before he went into the prison. He'd made me promise to get into the countryside and stay there. Otherwise, he said, I'd jeopardize his work.

It near killed me to leave. You gave me a good talking-to, Companion. I know at the time I was rude to you, but I'm thanking you now.

Keera. For once in your life, pay attention. You can help best by not interfering.

That's what you said to me, remember?

How hard that advice was to take.

I was busy, though. Gwyl was one prisoner Caedon wanted back, and I was another.

And where could I possibly go? It was easy to slip across the border from Lunds-fort into the Sceptered Isle, but that simply meant leaving a realm where Caedon had an alliance and into a realm Caedon actually controlled. I had never thought of that, back in my days at the fort when I schemed to escape it.

Old Dee and I figured my best chance was to stay in the territory of the Baronies where Caedon couldn't outright commandeer any troops to look for me. But Caedon had plenty of other resources, and he looked.

Old Dee thought about magically disguising me as he had disguised himself when he found me in the kitchen shed, but he said the disguise would just wear off, and his powers were so depleted that he wouldn't be able to keep refurbishing the disguise.

He also thought about sending me through his portal to his own plane. That, too, would take too much of his power to accomplish, not if he also wanted to protect Gwyl.

The thought of it gave me a shivery feeling, though.

But you know, Companion, I had spent my entire childhood on the run living rough. I knew how to do it. And that's what I did. I dressed myself in rags. I rubbed dirt on my face, as Aevarr and I had done a few years earlier to escape being detected by Caedon's men. I lived as a beggar off field greens and berries and the occasional fish. I wasn't the hunter and fisher my mother was, but I had learned a few things from her.

Old Dee and I agreed I'd stay near the coast, close to the small town of Oldford, on a smaller river that fed into the vast river flowing through Lunds-fort to the sea. The river through Oldford flowed under a bow-shaped, three-arched bridge at an ancient fording place, built by some old king, I forget which one.

The river was called the River Bright. That was an apt name for it, and the town was a beautiful place, too. It was said to have been settled by the Old Ones long ago.

I stayed just outside this town. Old Dee and I agreed we'd be able to leave by sea from there, navigating around the southern capes of the Sceptered Isle to the west, and from there to the Fire Isle.

"Leave the details to me, Keera. Just stay safe there until I can get word to you," Old Dee told me, and I promised I would.

It was an anxious time. I won't deny it. I think I would have run mad, except that every so often Old Dee got a message up-river to me assuring me Gwyl was getting well and regaining his strength.

And there was another thing. That was the loveliness of the meadow where I camped above the little river.

You loved it too, Companion.

I'll never forget the day you came into your own. I know you've had your own fears and anxieties. But there in that meadow, you regained some sort of peace. I was glad of it.

I was walking pensive along the riverside when I spotted an amazing sight: two swans, floating down the river, silvery-white. Sisters, I thought, in my fancy.

You and I are sisters, aren't we, Companion? Sisters of a sort? In my fancy, I felt you and I were those swans.

It was a calm, bright day with a sweet breeze blowing out of the west. All my cares lifted from me, all the anxieties I had felt in the courts of princes. The meadow was studded with flowers. When you saw the swans, Companion, you ran across the meadow toward them, exclaiming. You turned yourself, I swear you did, into kind of a mist and floated along the river in their wake, singing, toward Lunds-fort.

I thought for a while I must be dreaming. Maybe I was. The sun was hot, and I had lain down lazily in the meadow grass. Perhaps I drifted off. Perhaps that's all it was, a beautiful dream during a summer nap in the grass. When I roused myself to look down the river after the swans, they were gone. You were back by my side. But on that day we both knew a kind of peace we'd never known, either of us.

After that day, I found I could wait patiently.

Word finally came. A traveling peddler found us and handed me a parchment strip. He pulled his forelock and went away with his cart and his wares. *Meet at the riverside at midday, two days after the Summer Festival of the Lady Goddess,* the parchment read. I kissed that parchment. I knew who had penned the words. Gwyl had.

It was easy to remember the day. From the meadow, remember how we saw all the banners of the Lady Goddess waving above the roofs of Oldford, Companion? And how we heard the pipe and tabor of Her procession, drifting to us across the meadow? We were ready.

Old Dee and Gwyl pulled to a sandy spot along the river bank in a small skiff, Gwyl at the tiller. I let out a glad cry and ran to wade through the shallows and clamber in. It was cramped with the three of us. I was worried it would overset, especially since I kept reaching over for Gwyl and hugging him to me. And we had a tense time as our tributary fed into the big river through Lunds-fort. The river served as a highway for the citizens of Lunds-fort, and many boats crowded the river there, ferrying people from one bank to the other. But in the crowd, we were inconspicuous, just one more small vessel crammed with boatsmen's fares, as far as anyone around us knew. We made our way past Lunds-fort to the sea, and from there we set out on our voyage.

Gwyl knew of a small island to the south of the Sceptered Isle. It was out in the Narrows, a choppy and treacherous body of water. At least the island belonged to the barons and not to Caedon. That reassured us. Gwyl knew that isle well. As a mariner, he'd stopped there before. He knew a man there who'd sell us a larger ship.

"I doubt we can row ourselves to the Fire Isle without swamping," he told us with a wry smile. "I can't, at least. I'm as weak as a girl."

I frowned at that statement, but he kissed my sour expression away while Old Dee tactfully looked off in another direction.

The ship we bought was an awkward wooden thing with no sail and only a keel plank, no real keel like Gwyl's own skeid. Or so he explained to me. When I looked blank, he just said the boat was designed for hugging the coast, not for sailing, and that it couldn't even carry a sail. But we could hire rowers on the island, Gwyl knew, and we would able to make our way to the Western Isle in it. From there, Gwyl could get a message to his people, who'd be able to get to us quickly in his skeid and then away from the territory of the Sceptered Isle entirely.

Old Dee provided us with all the coin we needed for these enterprises. "I'm an alchemist as well as a neurologist," he told us calmly. "We alchemists turn regular stuff into gold." And so he did. I brought him rusty nails I found along the docks of the island, and he did something with them, who knows what, and gave me a bag of gold in exchange. Then we could buy our splintered awkward hulk of a ship.

Gwyl, of course, was skeptical. "Suppose he already had that gold, and just did some kind of quick-change act to impress you. Suppose you just think he changed nails into bags of gold."

"But then how did he get so much gold?" I asked him. "Explain that one." Gwyl had no answer.

We all had plenty of time together, and during that time, Gwyl began to lose his skeptical turn of mind. One evening, drifting in a calm under the stars, the only sounds the rhythmic clack and plash of the rowers, I made Old Dee explain his portal spell to Gwyl.

"I needed space," Old John explained to Gwyl. "And I didn't have enough."

Gwyl looked at him, puzzled.

Old Dee said something then that he had said to me, some-thing I hadn't understood at the time but was too busy thinking of other things to question. "It's like how that sorceress could contain Merlin in his rock," he told us.

"Merlin?" I asked. I wondered who this Merlin could be, and why he was in a rock.

"The Merlin of song and story," said Old Dee. "Merlin the Ma-gician. Surely you've heard of him."

"Oh. You must mean Myrddin Wyllt, the mage who went mad when he saw the horrors of war," I said. "But I never knew any sorceress put him in a rock."

"Surely you know about Merlin, Keera. I mean, look, wasn't your own assassinated crown prince named for King Arthur?"

"Huh?" I said. "Which king was he?"

"Don't tell me you live practically in the days of Arthur and you know nothing of him."

"He was," said Gwyl now. "You're right, Old Dee. We know about Arthur, over where I come from. And they know about Ar-thur in the Sceptered Isle, too, Keera. Ranulf named his oldest son for Arthur. Old Dee is right about that."

I looked at Gwyl in surprise. Until now, he had stayed quiet. He thought Old Dee was just telling tales, or was maybe a little out of his head. Against all the evidence of his own rescue, I might add. So I was surprised when Gwyl spoke up.

"Our prince," he said to me. "The one murdered before you were born. The one our fathers fought to avenge. This Arthur, the King Arthur of the tales, was a great war leader in the time of the Old Ones. My mother told me that. She said Ranulf had named his oldest son after this great man in hopes that crown prince

Artur would prove just as great a king. But it didn't happen that way."

"See, Keera. Arthur. . .Artur. The same name," said Old Dee to me, nodding approvingly at Gwyl. "And I suppose you're right, Gwyl. The historical Arthur lived quite a bit earlier than this."

"But what does that have to do with Myrddin Wyllt?" I asked. I was confused.

"Merlin, not Myrddin," said Gwyl.

I faced him down stubbornly. "Myrddin," I said.

"Keera, my dear one, I know all about Merlin. Isn't his tomb in my own country? On my own coast, in the forest of Brec'Helean. And yes, Old Dee. You're right. Everyone where I come from says an enchantress imprisoned him. We all think she put him in an oak tree, not a rock." Then he said, after a few minutes, "But that's just a story."

"Oh? Could have fooled me," said Old Dee. "Whether it's a story or not, I'm here to tell you that's the way she did it. If she could contain him in a small enough space, a rock, say." Old Dee paused and thought about it. "Could easily have been a tree. In either case, he wouldn't have been able to use his portal spell to get out, because he wouldn't have had enough scope to cast it," said Old Dee. He gave us a stubborn look. "Doubt me if you will. I know the man well. Trucker based out of Asheville. He's no friend of Gilles, either, I can tell you that, Keera."

Gwyl turned away. In the moonlight, I could see he looked troubled. I stole my hand into his and we sat there gazing out over the waves while Old Dee harrumphed, muttering about imprisoning rocks and someone else he might have known, named Sylvester.

"Never mind," he said. "The two of you can just pretend I never said that." Then he tactfully busied himself getting ready to transform a pile of nails into gold.

And then we forgot all about Merlin or Myrdinn or whoever he was or might have been, or what might have imprisoned him, or how, and we forgot entirely about the nails. Gwyl and I inched closer and closer to each other until we were entwined in each other's arms.

From the moment I climbed into the skiff with Gwyl at Oldford, we had clutched to each other fiercely, like drowning people. Ever since, I haven't been able to stop touching him. At last I understood my parents.

During our meandering voyage back to the Fire Isle, especially from Oldford to the island in the Narrows to the Western Isle, we were able to get out onto shore from time to time and wander. We found secluded coves and little wooded copses. We found time to be alone.

Although you've discreetly never mentioned it, you must have seen, Companion.

But then, I've noticed, you've chosen some of those private moments between me and Gwyl to skim over the ocean, doing backflips. Or to hover around Old Dee, peering at anything he happened to be working on. Or to playfully mess the hair of our rowers, who looked over their shoulders nervously as you wafted past them down the sea chests they sat upon to pull their oars. Thank you, Companion, for occupying yourself elsewhere when Gwyl and I found time to be alone. I'd feel shivery if I knew you were watching.

And I did feel shivery, at first.

The first time Gwyl and I wandered away by ourselves, neither of us meant to. It just happened. I should say, I didn't mean
to. I can't speak for Gwyl.

We found ourselves alone on the wide beach of a tiny inlet. I
was tired, so I sat down in the sand, wiggled my feet out of my
turn-shoes, and put my toes into the water. The cool water felt
delicious. Gwyl slung himself easily down beside me and slipped
his shoes off too. The sun was hot that day. Gwyl took off his tunic and flung it away into the reeds. I felt a pang of jealousy. I
wanted to do the same, but of course, a modest maid, I couldn't.

We both lay back in the warm sand, and then as if we'd
planned it, we turned to face each other. Gwyl reached out and
began to toy with a lock of my hair and smile at me.

Gwyl never tousled.

He ran his fingers through the lock of hair. With his other
hand, he reached out to pull me closer, and then he leaned in for
a kiss. I closed my eyes; the sun poured blissfully down on us
both. Through my closed eyelids it poured into me, red and inviting.

Gwyl's lips were warm on mine.

He ran his finger down my cheek. Down my neck. His other
arm tightened about my waist and pulled me even closer, and as
he did that, the tunic I was wearing hitched up. I had been wearing men's things since Gwyl and Old Dee came for me that day
in the little skiff to row us toward the sea. Under the circumstances, it was a more practical kind of clothing than a long
kirtle. My mother had taught me that, from our years on the run.

The sand against the skin of my back was gritty but somehow the scratchy feeling was good. I squirmed against the sand. Gwyl reached to pull my tunic down for me, and then. And then.

His hands just found their way under my tunic. They did it by themselves. My eyes opened wide and I could see Gwyl's wide eyes were as surprised as mine.

"You feel so good to me, Keera," he said. His voice was hoarse.

If I were a modest maid, I would have pulled away.

I must not be a modest maid. I didn't pull away. I moved closer. Every part of me was tingling. I wanted to press my bare breasts against his warm sandy gritty chest, so I did.

I wanted it. I did it.

And then we began to touch each other. I felt like those explorers who sail west to find an unknown land. They're afraid at first, but they bravely go ashore. I felt like the ones who map the unknown worlds they find.

This is you, Gwyl, I said to him, although I don't think I said those words out loud. *You are my new-found land. And here I am.*

True, we were betrothed. We'd be married soon.

Just then, though, we weren't thinking about ceremonies and decorous words. We only thought about drinking each other in. With our mouths. With our hands. And then with all the rest of us. We were awkward with each other, but we didn't care. We were together now, and we couldn't be parted, in spirit or in body.

When it was time to leave our cove, we got up and brushed the sand from each other's bodies. We ran splashing into the water and ducked under. We came up out of the water like two seasgs—the good sea creatures, not the naiads and murdúchann and Blue Men—and we laughed at each other and pressed our clean glistening slippery bodies to each other.

To wade back to the beach and shake out our sandy clothes and put them back on felt like a desecration.

After that, we found other moments to be alone. We lay in warm sand or grasses, and we learned each other's selves in every place, way, and sense so completely that we'd never forget. We made sure of it. We'd nearly lost the chance, and we weren't going to let another go by.

And you, my dear Companion. You've been happier and more serene than I've ever known you to be. I credit the swans, and the sweet flow of the river, and its song.

CHAPTER NINETEEN

Learning the Sword

My parents were there at the docks to welcome us. My mother and then my father hugged me so tightly I worried I might not be able to breathe. He can do a lot with that one arm of his.

"We were so worried about you," my mother said, wiping tears from her eyes.

"We blamed ourselves, letting you go," said my father. His voice broke.

"And you, Gwyl. We worried about you," said my mother, raising him from his position kneeling at her feet. She led him to my father.

"Gwyl," he said, clapping Gwyl on the shoulder. Then hugging him too.

"Things changed quickly," I said. "You couldn't have known. Lady Jehanne didn't know. I think she paid for that with her life."

"Then it's true," said my father. "She was killed."

"We believe so, yes, my Prince," said Gwyl.

"A sad thing. I mourn for her," said my mother. "Even more now. We couldn't know whether she had betrayed you, Keera."

"I don't believe she did, Mother. She had some . . . some different ideas about what I should do with my life, but I think she acted in good faith."

"What different ideas?" said Gwyl. He looked grim.

"She didn't realize, Gwyl. You mustn't hate her. She was as deceived by Ansgar as any."

"They tried to force Keera into marriage with Ansgar," he told my parents. "When she refused him, he sold her to Caedon as soon as he became king."

"So that's how it happened Keera fell into his hands. We weren't sure," said my mother. "And Jehanne was a part of this?" She sounded shocked.

"I think of the Lady Jehanne kindly," I said. "I don't think she realized what she was advising. Her death shows she didn't, especially if Ansgar had her murdered."

My mother was guiding us all from the docks to the horses we'd ride to the palace. Gwyl helped me up on mine with a grin, his black mood set aside. He knew how uncertain I was around horses, and he couldn't help teasing me about them. "You, who are usually so brave," he whispered to me, grinning wider at my scowl.

Mother looked from one of us to the other and smiled, too. "Don't feel bad, daughter," she told me. "I'm not a good rider myself. These men grew up on horseback. We two didn't."

"I'll teach you," Gwyl promised me.

"Caedon had a man teach me," my mother murmured, ignoring my look of astonishment.

As I sat in the saddle, grabbing the reins so hard my fingers were turning numb, I remembered learning how to hawk, and I felt a pang for Hildr.

Gwyl rode close to me and reached out his hand to touch me. "I know you're thinking of Hildr," he said.

"Am I that transparent?"

"I'm getting to know you well. Good thing you don't have those powers of yours any longer, or you'd know me too well." He gave me a wink. When he got that roguish look of his in his eye, I wanted us both to tumble off our horses and into the nearest grassy patch, but we had work to do that day, and my parents were right there, so instead we all rode off for the palace.

Once there, we settled in, all but Gwyl and Old Dee, whom my parents had sent ahead of us to the palace in a comfortable cart. Old Dee had graciously allowed this, but I knew better. Old Dee only looked like a frail elderly sort. What he really was—well, that, I really couldn't tell you. I thought I knew. Now I'm not so sure.

Old Dee made his bows to my parents and accepted their profuse thanks for saving me and Gwyl. Then he headed out to his old cottage, and to Gudrun.

Before he left, he bent over to give me a kiss on the cheek, and he whispered to me, "I'm going to find the magic hat."

I looked up at him, startled. The magic hat. I'd forgotten it.

"It will work? You think it will?"

"Let's try it and see. You can check one of those tasks of yours off your list, if it does," he whispered. And then he was off, swinging his walking staff as he went.

"What an amazing old fellow," said my mother.

"You don't know the half of it," I told her.

But Gwyl had to go, too. That gave my heart a sad wrench.

"I need to see about my little island house, check on my fleet, the sailors. And Aevarr and his mother, too."

I nodded, but I was disconsolate.

"I'll be back within the week."

Where had I heard that before? I was chilled. Now I understood why my mother had trouble letting my father out of her sight.

I would have gone with Gwyl, but I had duties at the palace. I was still my parents' diplomat and courier. I needed to tell them everything I'd discovered during my misbegotten mission to the Ice-realm. I knew Gwyl and my father had spent a few hours together, assessing the risk of a coming invasion. Both of them had emerged from my father's study with dark looks on their faces.

Preparations for war were all around us. My mother had named my father her chancellor for war and general of her army.

"I'm trained in hand-to-hand combat, although the Children know my skills are rusty. I'm trained for guerilla actions, not for war. Your father is," she'd told me. "He's the best support any ruler could have in war-time."

Before Gwyl went, though, my mother arranged for us to have a simple wedding. "It's a matter of state, but under the circumstances, everyone will understand. We are preparing for an invasion. We can't spend time and resources on a large state wedding. Are you disappointed?" She looked at us both, a crease of worry between her eyes.

We reassured her that no, we were not disappointed. Anything but.

And so, with my parents as witness and a few others, we were married before priestesses of the Child of Sea and the Child of Fire in the great hall of the palace.

"And now," my mother told me, "the two of you can go ahead and move into the same bed, so you don't have to sneak around the palace any longer."

I blushed.

She just smiled at me and kissed me. "You can't keep your hands off each other," she observed. Then she hugged me close. "And I know how that feels," she whispered.

Gwyl and I had a few blissful days together before he had to leave for his little isle. One of those nights, as we lay together in the rushlight, sleepy but reluctant to sleep because we wanted to savor every minute with each other, we began talking to one another about our childhoods. Gwyl was lying on his stomach with his arms around me, his head in my lap "so I can breathe in the delicious scent of you," he told me. I was stroking his shoulders.

"Gwyl," I said, hesitant. I had been tracing a faint scar on his back with my fingertip.

"Go ahead and ask it," he said.

"What are these scars about?" For weeks I had wondered. Now I asked. Across his back spread a network of scars, many of them faint and fading but a few still angry raised welts of puckered skin.

"I told you I had a difficult childhood. Not the same kind of difficult as yours, but pretty difficult. My step-father beat me."

What he told me made a quick anger rise in me. I kept my voice steady. "Whyever would he do such a thing?"

"I never pleased him. I can't remember a time I ever did. And when I angered him, he beat me with a stick and with a whip he owned."

"And did he do that to Pierrick, too?"

Gwyl flipped over now so he was face up. I stroked his hair off his forehead. "No," he said.

"Yet the two of you are very close, or seem so."

"Pierrick is his actual son. Maro calls Pierrick his golden princeling. Me, I was just this misbegotten thing he'd taken in as a favor to his wife. He'd married her to, you know, make an honest woman of her."

"Maro is your step-father?"

"Yes."

"That must have been terrible. To live with a man who didn't love you, but did love your brother."

"Pierrick and I were as close as we could be. Close in age. Close friends. The closest. And still are."

"That's remarkable."

"I suppose. I remember this shed Maro would take me to, to beat me, and then he'd leave me there. My mother never came to see about me, after. But Pierrick did. He'd bathe the wounds. He'd bring me food. He'd sit with me in the dark until I was better."

"So did he hate your step-father for what he did? His own father?"

"I'm not sure. I'm not sure I hated him either."

"I don't understand," I said. "I hate him, and I don't even know him."

Gwyl smiled up at me in the golden light. His fine gray eyes of the Sea Child were fringed with the blackest, thickest lashes I'd ever seen. I had to kiss him or die, so I did.

"When children grow up like that, it's just the way things are," he said after a while. "I think I believed I must be the bad son and Pierrick must be the good son. But there came a day when I didn't believe it any longer. That's when I started to learn how to fight."

"Learning the sword? I thought you said you did that to defeat Caedon."

"I did. Maro was a strange man. Is. He's still there, in our little village over in the Baronies, last I heard. I don't know much about how they're doing, him or my mother, but Pierrick makes a point of finding out. So, Maro. Maro hated Caedon with everything he had. I grew up knowing that about him, above all.

How much he hated Caedon. I never wondered why he hated him so much. It was a fact of life."

"Like the beatings."

"Yes, like that." Gwyl got a faraway look in his eye. "But it was strange. He hated Artur and the other sons of Ranulf, too. Well, most of them. I don't think he hated Audemar, which was maybe even stranger. How did he even know these people well enough to hate them that much? He was just a humble man in a little village. As I got older, I started to wonder.

One day, I heard a rumor in our village, that my mother Bertrys had been servingwoman to the Princess Diera, during the Rising to bring her to her throne. I rushed right home to ask her. When I got to our cottage and opened the door, there stood a young man berating my mother, calling her a betrayer. He rushed past me out the door.

""Were you the Princess Diera's serving woman?' I shouted at her. 'Did you betray her?' At first she denied it. But as I pressed her, she admitted it. That's when she told me how she had had to flee for her life when Caedon went after Diera."

"And she was pregnant with you."

"'One of those dirty rebels got me with child,' she screamed at me," said Gwyl. He drew a ragged breath. "Apparently Maro was the man who arranged her flight. Apparently Maro rescued her from death, and then he wed her. So both of them were connected with those people and those events. Maybe Maro was some kind of retainer for the people in the castle where my mother lived. I don't know. I only know they went to our village on the coast of the Baronies for refuge. My mother gave birth to me there, and then a year later to Pierrick."

"And so you found out one of the members of the Rising was your father."

"Yes, although none of the details. So, anyway," he said, after a pause. "You see how strange it was that Maro should hate Caedon and also hate anyone who had anything to do with Ranulf's children. My father, for example."

I thought about that. "Sounds like maybe he was a supporter of this Audemar, the man who usurped the throne."

"Yes, it does."

"That must have hard for him, then. To care for the son of a man who was his enemy," I said.

"I suppose it must have enraged him."

"But to take it out on a little boy—"

"Anyhow, that's when my mother told me Caedon had had my father killed. She wasn't sorry. She'd come to hate my father. He'd put her in danger, she said. She called my father a dirty rebel. Maro was her protector, she told me." He stopped, and his eyes looked haunted. "Then she told me I should be glad Maro beat me. Glad that he wanted to beat my father out of me."

"What a terrible thing to hear." I wanted to tell Gwyl about true mothers and real mothers, but I stopped myself. I realized that while he'd had a real mother, he'd never had a truc one. And he'd never known his true father. His true father hadn't even known he existed. That made me sad enough to cry out in grief. I didn't do that either, though. I just held him. I thought maybe my parents were almost like his parents, too, the parents he yearned for and never had.

"I told Maro then I wanted to learn to fight, when I found out about my father," said Gwyl after a while. "I told him I wanted to go to the wars to fight against Caedon. I had the idea I'd kill Caedon. Revenge my father."

A shiver ran up my spine. That's what I'd been thinking, too. But Gwyl had trained carefully to do it, and I had just planned to use my powers.

"When I told Maro that," Gwyl went on, "That's maybe the first and only time I got any kind of approval out of him. He agreed I should learn. I'm guessing he wanted to kill Caedon himself but knew he never could. I'm guessing that had been eating at him for a long time. So he paid for me to train with the best arms master the nearby market town had, and he sent Pierrick with me. We both learned.

"Pierrick is a good swordsman. But I was driven. I don't even know where Maro found the money, or why he thought it was a good idea to spend it this way. As far as I know, he didn't do anything to help us at home. He didn't farm. He didn't work, just sat around all day looking out the window and brooding. My mother worked. She worked helping with the animals for a rich farmer down the road from us. But when we needed it, Maro always had money for us. I don't know where he got it."

Gwyl smiled up at me. "We got good, Pierrick and I. By the time we were near-grown boys, he and I would rise every day at dawn and walk to the even bigger town down the coast, to an even better arms master. That's where, one day, I learned who the real fighters against Caedon were. I learned about your father. Maro had stopped beating me by then. I think he knew that if he continued, I'd try to kill him. I think he realized the lessons he paid for had come back to bite him. I think he saw I'd be able to kill him, if I tried. And I saw something else, too. Saw what he was, a coward and a bully."

The day he learned about my own father and the remnants of the Rising, Gwyl told me, was the day he left home. He went to his mother and told her he was leaving. At first, she'd said nothing. But she had gotten down a box where she kept her most precious things, and she had taken out a golden brooch.

Then she spoke. The last time he'd heard her voice, Gwyl told me. "This was your father's," she had said to Gwyl. "Take it with you. I don't want it. I don't want anything of that man's. Not this. Not you."

Gwyl walked away from his home that day. As he walked down the path out of his village, he heard a shout behind him, and a pelting of feet. It was Pierrick, his brother. They left together, and they've never been back.

The rushlight had burned low now, and I gently moved Gwyl off me onto the furs of our bed. I got out of bed and snuffed the rushlight out. In the dark, I got back in under the furs with Gwyl, and we held each other fiercely.

That was the day I too learned about the sharpness of a sword. His words buried themselves in my heart and cut me there so deeply I think I'll feel the hurt for him until I die.

I Just Want to Go Home

I saw Gwyl's skeid off and felt the familiar tightening in my throat as the dragon-prow stood out to sea. Then I went disconsolately back to the palace.

A sense of foreboding rose in me. How could it not? Every time Gwyl and I had been parted, something bad had happened.

In the pleached garden of the palace, the days were beginning to grow cooler. The moon, which had been full when Gwyl left, had waned, and then it had waxed again. Now it was full once more. My mother and I were seated on a bench picking through a basket of fruit. I suppose most highborn ladies would have had their embroidery near. By mutual agreement, my mother and I left that to others who enjoyed it and were good at it. We'd lived a strange life together, she and I.

"Keera, it's true, then—your powers have left you, and they've never come back?"

"Yes, it's true, Mother." I felt glum. If I'd had them, I would have known—maybe not fully but somehow—whether Gwyl fared well or ill. Now I was blinded.

"Don't grieve, my daughter. You have powers inside yourself, you know."

"Like your second sense, I suppose."

"Don't underestimate it. We all have that sense. Some of us just cultivate it more than others do. Cultivate yours, Keera."

I promised I would. Then I told her about my riddle. "If I could solve it, I'd get my powers back. I've figured out so many parts. But not all of it, and not the whole."

I quoted it to her.

> *The ravenous wurm of the mountain*
> *devours the great streets of men.*
> *Battle storm of Hildr, life-harm of the hall,*
> *the hound of the forest with its hot mouth*
> *swallows every house; fell dog*
> *of willow, ash, yew, oak*
> *casts its baleful eye on the yard-gate.*
> *Woe, that red-gaping hound of the wood.*

Firebird the True, carry her on your back
to the isle of the thousand suns.

I used to have the parchment. I didn't any longer. But by now, I knew the riddle by heart.

"The ravenous wurm of the mountain devours the great streets of men," I said. "That's the earthquake, shaking our silly structures to pieces—houses, roads even. Even the strong roads of the Old Ones."

My mother nodded.

"Battle storm of Hildr. I know what that means. Hildr, my merlin, was named for one of the Fire Isle's old gods, the battle maiden, the thunder. And her storm is the storm of the arrows she shoots down on us, the lightning. So that's how she can be life-harm of the hall. And the earthquake and Hildr's storms both can cause the mountains to spout fire, as they did when Caedon's forces were overwhelmed before Grandfather's estate. Hildr's storms, the fire from the mountain—they can swallow every hall. The fell dog of fire casts its fiery eye on the gates of houses, on the trees surrounding us, and destroys everything. So I understand all of that. It's the main part of the riddle. What I don't understand, still don't, are the last two lines."

Firebird the True, carry her on your back
to the isle of the thousand suns.

"I don't know what that means. I know Firebird the True must be my firebird. I keep waiting to see her again, but I never have."

"This is the firebird you think you saw when you were little."

"I did see her."

"You saw her," my mother corrected herself with a smile. I saw then that even my mother didn't really believe I'd seen my firebird at the moment I had been born. She didn't quite believe I could remember that moment. But I did.

I did, Companion.

Oh. Oh my.

I see something I hadn't realized.

Oh, Companion.

You believe me.

You believe I saw my firebird. Thank the Child for you, Companion.

"And I saw her in the garden," I told my mother, continuing our conversation about my firebird. "That time."

There's something my mother did believe. She knew the time I was talking about. My vision, which had been her vision, and my father's vision too. We had all shared that moment, even if I was the only one who had seen the pear tree burst into flames and tower up into my firebird.

"The last time I saw her, I was in that barrel. On that ship that carried us to Father."

"You saw her then?"

"Yes, I did. I thought I might be dying. I thought she had come to take me across the border to the Land of the Dead."

My mother put her hand to her mouth. I've never seen her look so afraid.

I comforted her. "I didn't die, Mother."

"It was a near thing." She could barely get the words out.

"You needed your rebec."

"Oh, daughter," she said.

We sat in silence then, and she stroked my hair as I leaned my head on her shoulder.

Then I sat up and smiled at her. "Do you remember who pulled me out of that barrel?"

She looked at me in confusion. Then she saw. She laughed out loud. "The young seaman. That was Gwyl!"

I nodded. We smiled at each other.

"I put all of that past me," she said. "Once I saw your father, I don't think I gave those experiences another thought. Although I've thought about you in that barrel, many times since, and shuddered at it."

"And I didn't think about that young man at all. Not until I met Gwyl at Grandfather Fylkir's board, and he told me."

"Neither of us remembered him," said my mother. "But he remembered you. Your father told me he'd sent a man to you, when you were in your grandfather's hands, but I didn't know it was Gwyl, and neither of us knew why Gwyl was so eager to go. It's pretty clear now." She grinned at me.

The twilight settled itself around us, and the low moon hung in the eastern sky. As we watched, a brilliant star shone out, hanging like a rich jewel just below the moon.

"Do you see that star?" I said to my mother, pointing it out. "That's really a planet." Old Dee had showed me once, and explained what it meant, that this type of star is really a planet, and that all the other stars are really stars, and how they move, and how there are times when one planet or other nears the earth and looks brighter than usual, and how this particular planet is our near neighbor and almost a twin to—

Well. This is hard to understand, Companion. Old Dee seems to think we are a planet too and not the center of the nine crystalline spheres hanging by a golden chain from the lands above, pendant from the abode of the Gods.

Arm in arm, my mother and I gazed at the planet together. Old Dee called this brilliant planet *Venus*. He said that was a name the Old Ones used for the goddess of love and beauty, and I know that much is true, because I read of Her in one of the Old Ones' books. So when the orbit of Venus brings it closer to our own planet's orbit, Old Dee told me, Venus shines more brightly in our sky.

Old Dee called this brilliant planet in the sky our twin. That means he thinks we are equally beautiful, so that's nice, even if he's wrong. He said that from space, our planet looks blue and not shiny. He said Venus looks so shiny because greenhouse gases over the ages have turned Venus into a ball of mist that reflects the sun's light, and that if we are not careful, we'll turn the earth into even more of a twin than we already are, and no one will be able to live here.

Space? Orbit? I don't know what he meant by those words either, Companion. I'm just telling you what he said.

I'm glad he told me this planet's name, though. Venus. She is indeed the most beautiful planet in the sky, isn't She? So She is well-named.

But there's a perfectly reasonable explanation for the beauty of this planet, and for the reason we see Her so clearly, and it's much more believable than Old Dee's, so that's what I described to my mother. "This star, which is really a planet, is fixed to one of the nine spheres, and the moon is fixed to another. They just look like they are near each other," I told my mother. "They're actually on different planes altogether, but the spheres are clear, and from our place here at the center, we can see right through one plane to the next."

"I know that to be true," said my mother, nodding. "As the spheres revolve around, bearing the heavenly bodies upon them, they sing. If you have ears pure enough, you can hear them."

We both raised our eyes to the planet Venus, hanging like a teardrop from the horn of the moon, or appearing to, and we waited. We listened.

"I can't hear anything," I said after a moment.

"Me neither," said my mother. We both sighed.

A servant came out with cloaks for us, but still we sat together in the garden, watching the other stars wink on. "All those stars," said my mother, marveling. "They are all set into yet another one of the spheres, another plane, like jewels set into some rich ornament. We can see through the crystal sphere that bears the moon, and the sphere that bears the planets, to that sphere, the one that bears the stars. They fill me with wonder, Keera." After a while, she said, "There are marvels all around us. The spheres are marvels. Your firebird is a marvel, and so is your riddle."

"I've never seen my firebird again," I said. "Not after those three times. And I don't know what it means, in my riddle, to be carried on the back of my firebird to the land of a thousand suns."

"Nor I, Keera. I have no idea," said my mother. "Maybe that's one of those things that stays a marvel. Maybe you'll never understand it. And maybe that's just fine. I've known many mysteries in my life. The mystery of Diera and Gwyl's father Rafe. That's one I'll never know the answer to."

"Gwyl's father loved the queen."

"Yes, and something happened there. I'm not sure what. When Diera was crowned, she read a proclamation from Avery her poor butchered uncle—your father's own brother, Keera. This proclamation filled us all with joy. King Avery declared that Diera was his successor. He established the legality of her rule. I didn't realize it at the time, but I was there when he wrote that proclamation, the night before he was killed. Keera, I remember this so clearly. Avery wrote a long time that night. He wrote more. And then he rode out to die. Gwyl's father Rafe rode out to die." My mother sat quietly. I could see she was tormented by these old memories.

"I watched Diera unroll the scroll of his proclamation, I listened while she read it," she went on, "but I saw another scroll by her, too. I watched while she looked at it. I saw her expression. I don't know what it said, this other scroll the queen read." My mother sighed. "I only know that the sadness in her eyes will haunt me to my dying day. Do you know what I think?"

I shook my head no.

"I think this other scroll may have said something about Rafe. Something about Rafe and Caedon. And I'll never know what." She looked over at me and smiled. "There have been a few times where I've wished for powers like your lost ones, Keera. That was one of those times. Then I'd know for certain, because I'm sure what I saw was important. As it is, my own second sense tells me tantalizing things, too often not enough."

My hand stole into hers, and we sat together, thinking about the riddles both of us despaired of solving, until it got so late we knew we should get ready for sleep. And so we went in.

My riddle remained an enigma, but the next day, Gwyl's whereabouts did not. My parents and I were in the garden again. It was their favorite place, and it had become mine. A cry from far below at the ports alerted us.

"A ship," my mother breathed.

I rushed to the wall overlooking the harbor and climbed up on a bench so I could see better. The sailors were disembarking at the port. "Gwyl!" I cried.

I knew he couldn't hear me, at this distance, so I waved my arms.

He looked up and saw me. He spurred his horse up the hill toward the palace, and I leaped down off the bench and rushed to the portal gate to welcome him. He galloped through, slung himself off his horse and into my arms. He crushed me to him. I inhaled the delicious male Gwyl scent of him. I was crying and laughing at the same time.

"My Keera. My wife," he murmured into my ear, over and over.

I looked over now and saw my parents gazing at us fondly. They'd come down to greet him, too. Well, my mother was gazing. My father stood beside her, a broad smile on his face.

And you, Companion. You were welcoming Gwyl home in your own way, by bursting into thousands of dazzling, glittering pieces and reassembling yourself.

Gwyl blinked, as if he were looking into sunlight too strong for his eyes.

"She's happy for us," I whispered to him.

"She is, is she," said Gwyl. He stared down at me for a moment. Then he kissed me deep. "What did she make of that?" he whispered back to me.

You had composed yourself by now. You were still glad. You could have been the jealous type, but you aren't. You're my true friend, Companion.

"I brought you something. A present," he said. "One of the crew is bringing it up from the ship."

He and I, and my parents, went in to the great hall now and sat around the hearth fire while my father and Gwyl discussed the growing threat and what Gwyl had observed during his brief voyage around our big island to his own small one off shore.

"Nothing around south to the western edge, my Prince," said Gwyl. "I'm thinking Caedon will attack from the north and west. He'll probably sail with his troops to the sheltered northern coves where his ships can ride at anchor and off-load."

"So we march our men north," said my father.

"Suppose, though," interjected my mother. "Suppose Caedon sends a second party to the west. As he did on the Western Isle when he defeated Audemar. You were only a baby then," she said to me. "We had to flee for our lives."

"I remember," I said.

She gave me an indulgent smile.

So did Gwyl.

"No, I do," I protested to him, and almost simultaneously my mother was assuring him, "Yes, she did."

He just shook his head, hard, as if he were a waterdog shaking off droplets from a dip in the sea. "But you can't do spooky things like that now, right?" he said to me in a low voice, aside.

"No. Not now." It made me sad. But I remembered my mother's words. I needed to cultivate my second sense. I needed to rely on softer, quieter powers now. And I needed to appreciate the marvels around me, even if I didn't understand them. Maybe especially if I didn't.

Gwyl looked up then and a smile spread over his face. From the door to the hall, one of his crew members was motioning to him. The seaman had a large covered object in both hands.

I jumped to my feet, my hands clapped to my mouth. I saw right away. It was a large covered cage.

Gwyl brought it over to me and gently uncovered it.

"Hildr!" I screeched.

My father turned his head in bewilderment toward my mother.

"Her merlin," said my mother to my father.

"Ahh," he said.

I was already pulling on the gauntlet Gwyl handed to me. I was already holding out a finger.

"Hildr knows her way home," Gwyl whispered to me. "She knows who loves her."

Hildr hopped daintily onto my finger. She emitted a satisfied *chip chip*.

My father was cocking his head and smiling. We all were. Even Hildr.

But things rapidly grew serious. Gwyl and my parents, and my parents' other counselors, drew aside in a small group to discuss the coming situation. I sat in for part of it, but then I stepped aside to pay more attention to Hildr. I had missed her so.

That's when I saw Old Dee at the door to the great hall, thanking a servant. I ran to him.

"Look, Old Dee!"

"Hildr, welcome home," he told her.

"How was Gudrun?"

"Fine, as always," said Old Dee.

"And Grimalkin?" I worried as I said this. Grimalkin had been an old cat, even back when I knew her.

"She's fine, too," said Old Dee.

He looked at me hard, and his face was troubled.

I knew. We were not going to complete my first task.

"It's not going to work, is it?"

"I suppose we were over-optimistic, thinking we could make a device for transcranial magnetic stimulation in the tenth century," he said. His eyes looked tired.

"The tenth century? Old Dee, you must worship the Lady Goddess," I told him. "That's the way those people think."

"The La—no, Keera, it's just habit in me to talk about time like that."

"We who worship the Children don't think of it in the same way." But I was stalling. I didn't want to face what I thought he'd just told me, in spite of the odd words of power he insisted on using.

"I did some further research, while I was—uh—away, through my portal," he told me. "It seems that in cases like your father's, where the injury is quite a bit in the past, alternating

current would be better than direct, and—well, and look at this,"
he said. He reached into his bag and pulled out the magic cap. It
had been sadly chewed by mice. "And this." He pulled out the box
I had made, with the nails and the copper wires. It had somehow
gotten smashed. "We'd have to start all over, and I'm not sure it
would work. In fact, I'm pretty sure it wouldn't," he admitted. "At
least we can salvage the lode-stones." He pried them out of the
ruins of the box and stuck them into the sack he carried. "They're
pretty rare around here."

I felt tears sting my eyes. My hopes had revived when he went
away off to his cottage. I had started believing again, after so
long, that we'd be able to accomplish my first task. *Check it off my
list*, as Old Dee put it.

But now, it seemed, we couldn't.

Old Dee silently shoved the ruined objects back into his sack
with the lode-stones. He took my hand and squeezed it.

I led him to my parents, then, and they greeted him with all
civility. They called servants to take him off to a warm bed and a
bowl of stew so his energy would be up to it when the evening
meal was announced.

Old Dee was moving like an elderly man. A frail, very elderly
man leaning on his gnarled staff. I watched him go, worrying
about him.

During the evening meal, as the servants set up the trestles in
the great hall and began bringing in the bowls of food and the
platters with our trenchers on them, and as we began taking our
places down the long benches, Old Dee reappeared, leaning on
his staff. One of the servants ushered him to a place. I was glad

to see he was looking a bit more energetic now. In fact, I noted with interest, there was a positive glint to his piercing blue eyes.

I felt relieved. We began eating, but the talk was subdued. Just before the meal, a messenger had come. We were all pretty sure what it meant, although my mother had only taken it, with her thanks, whispered a few words to my father, and motioned us all to our places around the board.

As the dishes and bowls were being cleared away, my mother stood. "It's a fine evening. Let's all go up into the pleached garden where we can look out over the sea," she said.

We all did. We trooped up to the high terrace and stood talking quietly among ourselves. Old Dee moved to me as Gwyl and I stood somberly gazing out over the sea.

"This is a good spot," he said to me. "Lots of room for operations and procedures."

I glanced at him, puzzled.

Before he could continue, my mother addressed us in a commanding voice. "Good friends, you've probably guessed. The message I received before our meal confirmed what we've all been thinking. Caedon's ships have been sighted rounding our northernmost cape."

We'd all known it was coming, but still, there was a collective intake of breath.

"My Prince Consort and I, with Lord Gwyl, will be leaving for the north in the morning. Our troops are already mustered to begin their march north," she went on. "May the Children guide us."

"Your Highness," one of her lords called out from the crowd of us. "It's too risky for you there. Stay behind here in the palace, we pray you."

There was a general murmur of assent.

"There may be traitors abroad, Your Highness," called out another.

"My loving friends," said my mother, smiling around at all of them. "You're careful of my safety, I see. I assure you, I wouldn't want to live if I couldn't trust my people. Tyrants like Caedon—let them fear, but I will not. I'm resolved, in the heat of the coming battle, to live and die amongst you all, to lay down—for the Children and for my people–my honor and blood, if need be, in the dust. I know when you look at me, you see a woman, and some of you think a woman is a weak and feeble thing. But I have the heart of a king, and a king of the Fire Isle too. I scorn foul Caedon. Let him do his worst."

"By George," Old Dee whispered to me. "That's a fine speech, that speech of your mother's. My own queen is about to face the same kind of emergency, a small valiant force of patriots against overwhelming odds. Do you think your mother would mind if I took her noble words back to the queen I serve?"

"Of course not, Old Dee. By all means, do," I whispered back, as proud of my mother then as I'd ever been. "I hope she can use them."

One by one, the lords and ladies of the Fire Isle came to my mother to kneel before her and kiss her hand and wish her well. One by one, they filtered away back into the city to their own houses.

Soon only the few of us were left. My mother and father. Gwyl. Me. Old Dee. And you, too, my Companion.

We gathered together in a knot, looking out over the sea. Only Old Dee stood apart, alone on the wide stone terrace. My mother leaned against my father. He lifted his face to the breeze blowing in from the ocean and inhaled the spicy odors of early autumn.

"This is a beautiful place," my father said.

If only you could see how beautiful, I thought with a pang of grief.

Out of the corner of my eye, I caught a flicker of movement.

Old Dee was slowly raising his staff. Now he was holding it above his head with both hands.

I gasped. The others turned around and gasped, too.

"Gilles," Old Dee called out in a voice that echoed over the hills. A huge voice. "I adjure you. Stay back."

A strange odor filled the air, the crackling odor that precedes a thunderstorm. Somehow, blue lines of force were gathering around Old Dee's staff, standing out vivid in the twilight.

"Manifest!" Old Dee called out in his uncanny voice. "Manifest!"

What could he mean by that, *manifest*? I thought, but then I noticed something else almost as strange as Old Dee's behavior. It was yours, Companion.

You had been floating peacefully above our heads. Now I saw you stand up on the air, up on your toes, your legs spread wide, your arms flung out. Sparks outlined you.

The others exclaimed. They could see you too.

"I see her, Keera," Gwyl called to me.

Stranger still was what my mother cried out. "Jillie," she sobbed.

Slowly Old Dee lowered his staff, now held in his right hand, while he still held his left arm aloft, his index finger pointed sternly at you, my Companion. My mother's lost sister Jillian.

He raised the staff in his right hand and pointed it now at my father. My father leaned hard against the force of Old Dee's summoning, but he was powerless to break it or resist. Old Dee stepped back, motioning with his staff, and my father's body dragged forward, following.

I tried to rush to Old Dee, to stop what he was doing, but I was rooted to the spot. None of us could move, only my father, who hitched across the stones of the terrace as if he were a dead thing brought to life.

Now my father dangled helpless before Old Dee.

Keeping the staff pointed toward him, Old Dee raised his gaze to you, my Companion. In a low, vibrating, carrying voice, he chanted to you. "Arex," he chanted. "Remex. Strange." With a terrible look on his face, he called out in a bellow. "Charmed."

You, Jillie. The sparks outlining you flowed from red, to orange to yellow. To blue. To a blue-white that made us all flinch away. With a tremendous crack, the blue-white sparks gathered and arced up. They blitzed down upon my father, as if Hildr the God of the Thunder had unleashed her fury on him. The crack was followed by a majestic boom that echoed off the surrounding mountains.

Boom. Boom. Boom.

My father had fallen face down on the stones of the terrace. We were released; we rushed to his side, screaming in horror.

My mother sank down on the stones beside him and reached for him tenderly. She lifted him up into her arms. Gwyl and I helped her. She cradled him against her.

Before anyone could say anything, my father stirred. He pushed against my mother and rolled over, looking up at the sky. He blinked.

He looked around himself with his one eye.

"I see you, Mirin," he said in a quiet voice.

He looked at me. "And this is my daughter," he said, holding out his hand to me. I took it, weeping.

He looked around for Gwyl. "And this. This must be Gwyl, my friend. The son of my friend."

"Old Dee!" I screamed out then, realizing. I jumped to my feet and ran to him. He lay crumpled up on the stones, his staff beside him.

Above us, an unearthly shrieking began. We looked up.

Jillie, if that is you—you're not outlined in sparks any longer. A dull flame surrounds you, and it is flickering out.

"Dr. John Dee," you shrieked at Old Dee. "Why don't you leave me alone? Why don't you let me go home? I just want to go home."

Then you blazed up into a mighty flame, and we couldn't see your features any longer. Your flame dwindled away and away until it was very small, only a glowing cinder. A strong wind blew up out of the sea and carried you off, over the terrace wall, and into the air.

I looked back at Old Dee now. Old Dee wasn't there any longer. Just a pile of his clothing, and his gnarled old staff. I went to him, or what was left. I prodded his staff with my toe. It was just an old stick.

Then I went back to my father. He was sitting on the stones of the terrace, leaning on his right arm, and we gathered around him. He looked and looked into our faces as if he would never finish looking.

How we laughed and cried then. Eventually, my mother and father went off to their room to be quiet and alone. "I don't know if I'll still see in the morning," he said to us. "But to see you all now, it's the Children's own gracious gift. And the gift of that old man," he added, looking soberly at the pile of clothes that used to be Old Dee.

My mother looked over at it too. "Yes, and Jillie's gift. She's gone now," said my mother, and wiped her eyes. "She came back to make things right, and she did." It was the bittersweet edge to our happiness.

At last I understood why the farwydd had sent you to me, Companion. In my mind, which can no longer exercise this power, I call out to you anyway. I call you *Sister*. I call you *Aunt*. I call you *Kindred*.

Gwyl took my arm, and we headed toward our own soft bed. As we were about to leave the terrace, though, I gave him a smile and a hug, and I ran back to where Old Dee's clothes lay in a forlorn little puddle. Gwyl watched me for a minute, and then he understood. He headed in without me, so that I could have a last moment with my old teacher, the man who had done so much for us all.

I folded up his clothes neatly, meaning to take them to Gudrun at the cottage later. But I felt something tucked into one of the long turned-up sleeves of his robe, and I drew it out. A small parchment. *Break my staff*, it instructed. *Throw the pieces out to sea.*

I sent out a message into the universe, wherever Old Dee might have gone. *I will.*

There was something else. This was a parchment, too. Or not exactly. It sort of looked like a parchment, but it was too squared off. It was small. The letters on it reminded me of that magic book I'd seen in Old Dee's cottage long ago. They were much more regular than any letters anyone I knew could have penned, and they were very—I don't know how to put this—very stark and unadorned. This is what they said:

> John D'Nofrio, M.D.
>
> Practice limited to Neurology
>
> Clayton Medical Building Suite 400
>
> 5001 Wydown Avenue
>
> St Louis, MO 63105

I put the two parchments in the pouch at my belt and gathered up the clothing. Later the next day, Gwyl and I went down to the shore. Gwyl broke Old Dee's staff over his knee. Together we threw the pieces far out into the waves. I shaded my eyes and watched as they floated up and over a wave and then were lost to my sight.

Gwyl squeezed my hand hard.

Goodbye, Old Dee, I said to him. Not out loud.

It felt lonely—no Old Dee, no Companion.

I shook myself hard, feeling how ungrateful I must appear to my Child. I had Gwyl. I had my parents.

Just the same, an icy hand squeezed my heart when I thought about the trial that lay ahead of us.

Firebird the True

In only a matter of hours, my mother's small and ill-equipped army was assembling under the brow of the palace hill, making ready to march to face the enemy. My mother and father rode out, clad in leather armor, swords at their sides, and Gwyl with them. I had wanted to cling to each one of them, to drag them back into the safety of our fortified stronghold, but I knew that was a childish impulse.

We all knew that every one of that host, including my mother and father, and including my young husband, could very possibly be riding into death.

As I scanned the faces of the brave young men and women pulled up before my parents, I picked out Aevarr's freckled face, still the face of a boy.

Hildr was on my arm. I raised her high to salute him. I'm not sure he saw.

Gwyl circled around to me and leapt lightly off his horse. He drew me to him and gave me a last kiss. "If anything happens to me, Keera, you must leave. You must get out. You know what he's like, Caedon." His voice was tense, his face drawn. He swallowed. "But if I live," he said, "I'll be back for you. If we have to flee this place, we will." He pointed down to the harbor. "One of the snake-ships is there. If the worst comes, get down to the ship and get on it. I've left a few of my men there, the older ones who shouldn't be fighting. They'll know what to do. They'll know where to take you."

I didn't argue. I didn't say, *I'll never leave this land before I find you, whether you're dead or whether you're alive.* I nodded and kissed him.

He gave me a searching look. "Tell me you won't do anything foolish."

"I promise," I said. *I'm just not telling you what, exactly, I'm promising,* I said in my mind.

"Don't try to look for me, if I don't come back. Don't. Caedon sends his men out to kill the wounded. I won't be alive."

"I can't stand this," I told him. I was close to breaking. "Go, and the Children go with you."

He kissed me again and vaulted back onto his horse.

My mother looked back at me, and my father did too. Love was in their eyes. "The Children be with you, Keera," they called back to me.

And then the host headed out.

I rushed into the great hall and up to the terrace to watch them on their way.

I felt frustrated enough to throw myself off and smash myself onto the stones below.

Why couldn't I have learned the fighting skills of my mother? Why couldn't I go with them?

But I knew I could not.

I'd have to wait. Once more, I had to wait.

The bitterness of it made me scream.

And once I started screaming, I found to my terror I couldn't stop. Several retainers came running. I gestured to them to keep away from me.

I screamed and screamed.

They stood in consternation, watching and shaking their heads.

That's when I saw real fear take them. They looked up and trembled, some of them falling to the stones of the terrace on their knees.

I screamed again, a raw sound ripped from my throat.

The heat of all the suns enveloped me. Now I too looked up.

A vast creature of fire rippled above me.

In front of me, the servants were falling to the ground and shielding their faces.

But I began to laugh. I lifted my arms to the creature as it swooped down to me, the creature I knew would come for me.

Firebird the True, carry me on your back!

My firebird enveloped me, and flew with me straight up, an arrow into the heavens. As we flew, the heavily muscled great wings beating the air and heating it to burning, I sent up a prayer of thanks to my farwydd. She had kept faith with me after all.

Below me, I saw the palace dwindle, and the city. The sea was a flat pewter expanse stretching to the horizon.

I gripped my firebird with my knees, feeling my clothes burn away from me, and the fiery fragments drop from me into the sea.

I sent up a prayer of praise to the Child of Fire.

Some say what they saw that day was a comet of fire with a blazing tail. Some say they saw their Child. Some say they saw Hildr God of Thunder riding to battle with Her mighty bow.

We rounded the headland to the west and soared up even higher. Below, the army of my parents crawled like ants across the land. Ahead of me I glimpsed the vast host of Caedon, where his ships rode at anchor in the north.

I remembered now the Fire Child and how she had swept down upon my grandfather Fylkir. And upon Caedon.

Why had I not remembered? The Fire Child had Her justice then. She'd have it now.

The firebird banked and swooped down, skimming the tops of the waves. Underneath us, the sea boiled. As we passed over, the boiling intensified, and a tall column of smoke and ash exploded underneath us. The blast wave bucked us straight up into the sky as if we rode it.

I held on to my firebird's neck, hugging my body to her as we flipped over and soared back down. Chunks of rock and debris spewed past us. We felt as though we were in the center of a fountain of rock.

My firebird looked back at me with her liquid flaming eye.

"There," I pointed.

We arrowed down to the camps of the enemy where we saw they had all thrown themselves flat to the ground with terror.

"There," I screamed.

On the summit of the hill, a black tent flew Caedon's insignia, the golden wolf standing out on its staff, blown back from the hot wind of our coming.

A puny figure stepped from it, raising its fists to the sky.

"There."

There was some mighty force around him, pushing back at us. We swooped down on him, blazing, but the force around him held steady. We came in for another run at him. And when we did, I saw a figure standing beside him, towering. This figure, malevolent and powerful, held his arms wide. And then I saw him look down at his creature, Caedon. I saw him drop his arms, step back, dwindle away.

The flame that was my firebird burned down to the figure that was Caedon, cringing and powerless. We screamed down upon him, flamed down upon him.

My firebird opened her beak to scream, and flung from herself blazing tongues of flame.

As we sizzled past, I saw this man for who he was, a burnt soul, charred to the cinders of the Dark Ones who made him. My firebird bleched out great gouts of flame, enveloping him, dispersing the particles of him to the hot wind in our wake.

We strafed his armies. Aflame, they ran and fell.

Our destruction complete, we soared up to the heavens and back to the boiling place in the sea. A mass of rock had heaved itself up beneath us, and a cone of fire rose in its center.

My firebird skidded down to the sea and onto the new land she had made.

Beneath us, the angry sea rose and jarred us as we lay at full length on the land. The land—this new island—rucked and juddered upon the surface of the sea. Clawing my hands into its soil, I rode its howling surface.

My firebird dwindled away beneath me, until at last I lay prone on the ground, alone. Above me the cone of fire rose up too bright to look at, and rivers of fire roared down from its top.

> *Firebird the True, carry me on your back*
> *to the isle of the thousand suns.*

I don't know how long I lay there on this new island that the Fire Child had made.

Days, maybe.

When I came to myself at last, I was alone on a wide beach, the mountain's cone smoking over me.

The ground was hot to the touch, almost too hot to endure.

I moved to the edge of the sea and rolled in. I didn't think my legs would bear me up.

From there I half swam, half staggered the short distance to the Fire Isle's land.

My clothes were gone. My hair was burned away. I held my arms out and looked at them, scorched blackened things. I knew the rest of me must look the same. Was fulfilling my mission worth this?

Yes. It was.

Everything inside me felt scoured away.

But my firebird had come back. She towered over me. I looked to her as she bent close. It seemed for a moment I melted inside her, to her heart.

Then we were separate.

With a majestic leap, she lunged to the sky. She circled me, swooping low, and then she shot upward. I watched her go. I lost her in the bright fastness of the sun, and I knew somehow I wouldn't see her again.

I looked around me now and realized I recognized the place. I was at the foot of my farwydd's mountain.

It took me all day to toil up her slope, charred halting thing that I was, to the portal leading to the inside of the mountain's cone.

I reached it. I knocked at her door. It opened, and I half-staggered, half-crawled inside.

As before, she was a mighty presence too bright for my eyes to make out. With a finger of fire, she motioned me close. Slowly, painfully, I came to her.

"My riddle," she commanded.

And so I told her what it meant, my voice such a wisp that I wasn't sure how she heard me.

"You've done well, my child," she told me. "And your companion?"

"She did a good thing, a mighty deed, and now she's gone," I whispered.

"Indeed. She implored the Fire Child to bring her home, and She did."

"I came here to accomplish two tasks."

"Did you accomplish them, my child?"

"I did," I said, forcing myself to stand upright, forcing my voice stronger. "But when I came to you, I asked the wrong questions. You took away my powers, so I needed a lot of help. In spite of my weakness, many helped me. Among us, we accomplished my tasks."

"That's all as it should be. All unknowing, you've fought a mighty enemy."

I looked at her, puzzled. Caedon had been a mighty enemy, and I and mine had known him too well. But I thought she might be speaking of someone else.

"But you have had a mighty ally, and you have gained his respect and love. Well done," she told me again. "And now you have earned your reward. You may choose."

"Choose?"

The farwydd held out to me her two hands, fists closed.

"One of these hands, the left, encloses your powers. Choose my left hand, and you will have them back," she said.

I looked up at her and waited.

"The other hand, the right, encloses love. Choose my right hand, and you will have the gifts of love—love of parent. Love of kin. Love of friend. Love between flesh and flesh, heart and heart, soul and soul. In time, love of child. Which do you choose?"

I did not hesitate. I reached out and touched her right hand. She opened it.

Now she put this hand, her right, on my head and pronounced a blessing. "In the name of the Fire Child, well chosen, my child." She moved her hand to my naked shoulder, and touched my mark, the mark of the firebird, with her burning finger.

As she did this, my body shuddered. And healed. I felt the hair curl out from my scalp and trail in tendrils about my shoulders. I felt my limbs straighten, my skin grow whole again.

"Now, go back to those who love you, and whom you love."

I woke in my own bed, with Gwyl hovering over me. My mother and father stood beside him.

When they saw I was awake, they exclaimed with joy and relief.

"Caedon is dead," I said.

"Yes," my mother said.

"But I choose love."

Gwyl embraced me then, and my mother and father smiled at each other and leaned into each other's arms.

I called for a mirror. Gwyl brought me one. Looking into the mirror, I saw I was myself again. I angled it so I could see my shoulder.

There was my mark, transformed, the flame transfixed by love's burning dart.

There was only one more task to complete, one more message to send.

Old Dee, I told him, in words only he and I could hear. *The tectonic plates have shifted. A new land has risen up. Of our bones are coral made. These are pearls, that were our eyes. My father sees. Love has won. And Jillie has gone home.*

ABOUT THE AUTHOR

I hope you have enjoyed *Firebird*, Book Three of the Harbingers series. Please leave a review of my novel on amazon.com and other sites. I care about what my readers think! Please visit my author page on amazon.com, and my author web site, www.janemwiseman.com. Follow my blog about speculative fiction, www.fantastes.com, or follow me on Twitter, @jane_wiseman. See my Pinterest board about this novel, Medieval Life—Firebird .

I also hope you will stick around for Book Four of the Harbingers series, *Ghost Bird*. I've added an excerpt at the end of this book. You can find the full novel soon on amazon.com. Have fun! Jane

Jane Wiseman splits her time between Minneapolis and the Sandia Mountains of New Mexico, trying not to take the dreaded wrong turn at Albuquerque. She loves fantasy in all its forms, enjoys her family, reads all the time, tries to write the kind of stuff she'd like to read, and paints.

A note of acknowledgment

Thanks first of all to my wonderful editor and daughter, Margaret Govoni. You steered me away from many mishaps and missteps. All the rest are mine alone.

Thanks to Bob, beta reader extraordinaire.

Thanks for all the helpful suggestions I've gathered from a number of great online Litreactor workshops,

www.litreactor.com,

and from the writing workshops at the Tinker Mountain Writers' Workshop

www.hollins.edu/academics/workshops-online-writing-courses/tinker-mountain-writers-workshop-residential/

and the (sadly now defunct) Taos Summer Writers' Conference. The instructors' comments and suggestions were of course incredibly helpful, but I have valued beyond measure the comments and suggestions of my fellow workshop attendees. Thanks to all of you! You may not have been able to save me from all my writing sins, but you saved me from many.

Thanks too to the Anam Cara Writer's and Artist's Retreat www.anamcararetreat.com, on the Beara Peninsula of southwestern Ireland. What a beautiful, peaceful place to write. Thanks, Sue!

And thanks to all you Norrathians out there, especially a few special battle buddies of mine. You know who you are. You are my fantasy friends in the purest sense of all.

NOTES ON FIREBIRD

from the author

This novel is a work of fantasy, not historical fiction . Just the same, it is indebted to history. Please go to my web site, janemwiseman.com, to learn more, and visit my Pinterest board, Medieval Life—Firebird and to the sister boards Medieval Life—10 th Century, Medieval Life—Halcyon , Medieval Life—Ghostbird, Medieval Life—Gyrfalcon , Medieval Life—Shrike , Medieval Life—Stormbird , Medieval Life—Martlet , Medieval Life— Nightingale , Medieval Life—Dark Ones , each connected to a different book of the Stormclouds/Harbingers fantasy novels.

The time-period is roughly early medieval, in a geopolitical environment resembling several of the Celtic, Anglo-Saxon, and Scandinavian kingdoms vying for power in the 10th and early 11th century. The landscapes of the novel vaguely resemble medieval Iceland, as well as the western and northern isles that stretch between Ireland, Scotland, and Scandinavia.

Twelve Realms:

> The Sceptered Isle stands in for the united Heptarchy (seven main kingdoms) of mainland Anglo-Saxon England, but also includes the northern part of the realm (Scotland), the Western Isle (Ireland) and the northern isles (islands off the coast of Scotland— Inner and Outer Hebrides, Orkney, and Shetland Islands). It does not include the area around Lunds-fort (London), however.
>
> The Eastern Baronies stands in for a loose confederation of powerful feudal lords spreading across medieval France and parts of Germany. In my tale, the Eastern Baronies also own territory on the mainland of the Sceptered Isle—the land around Lunds-fort (London) and along the eastern edge of the mainland—in addition to their strongholds across the Narrows (the English Channel).

THE SOUTHERN PRIMACY stands in for medieval territories in Italy (as well as Portugal and Spain), the homeland to which the Old Ones (ancient Romans) pulled back as their empire dwindled.

THE LYRE-LANDS stands in for the vestiges of ancient Greece and the lands rimming the Aegean in the medieval era, including that vast metropolis the Vikings knew as "the Great City," Constantinople (Istanbul).

THE REALM OF THE ASP stands in for the ancient Near and Middle East.

THE BURNT LANDS is a vague concept to people of the Sceptered Isle and similar northern realms. It stands in for North Africa and below, through Sub-Saharan Africa, but people in the northern realms know little of these lands.

THE ICE-REALM stands in for medieval Norway and, in a loose sense, the other parts of Scandinavia.

THE FIRE ISLE stands in for medieval Iceland.

THE MOUNTAIN FASTNESSES stands in for the Alpine regions of Europe.

THE TRADE ROAD FORTIFICATIONS stands in for the old Silk Road of the late ancient world through the Renaissance, stretching along the Eurasian steppes.

THE SILK LANDS stands in for China and southeast Asia.

THE FORGOTTEN KINGDOM stands in for the Indian subcontinent. No one in Mirin's world knows much about this place.

ALSO:

UNKNOWN LANDS (the Americas) across the Great Sea stretching to the west. Travelers have come back with tales of these lands but no one knows whether they really exist.

THE CONCEPT OF TWO COMPETING RELIGIOUS GROUPS , worshippers of the Lady Goddess vs. worshippers of an elemental universe controlled by earth, sea, fire, and sky, is fantasy but based on some actual bits of information about belief systems in the post-Roman British Isles and medieval beliefs in general, especially medieval ideas about the body and healing. (Present-day astrologers have their own settled ideas about these matters. I know nothing about their ideas and don't pretend to.) There is a sense that older gods once ruled the lands, but no one remembers much about them.

THE OVERALL CONCEPT OF THE UNIVERSE IS PYTHAGOREAN: nine revolving crystalline spheres carry the heavenly bodies (sun, moon, stars, planets) around the earth at their center. This idea from the ancient classical Near East was widespread in the medieval period, obviously long before anyone knew anything about the way the physical universe really works.

THE RIDDLE the farwydd tells Keera is inspired (pretty loosely) by "kennings," or brief poetic descriptions, found in medieval Scandinavian poetry. You can find more about them and their medieval sources on the web site Skaldic Project: Skaldic Poetry of the Middle Ages, http://skaldic.abdn.ac.uk/m.php?p=kenning&i=58. Some of the "kennings" making up my riddle are authentic; some are not.

THE ELF CHILD SONG Keera remembers from her mother is very loosely based on Child Ballad 40. See the play list at www.janemwiseman.com to listen to it.

THE FIREBIRD in this novel bears some resemblance to the firebird of Slavic legend. It has more in common with the mythical phoenix.

THE LANGUAGE OF TRADE Keera uses in the marketplace is inspired by William Caxton's little book for travelers, *Dialogues in French and English*. Although Caxton's book was published much later than the time period of my novel (maybe mid-15th century), I'm thinking the give and take he described is pretty timeless, so I have used it. You can find it here: https://archive.org/details/dialoguesinfren00caxtgoog

THE TRISKELION is an ancient symbol common in many parts of the world, especially Brittany in northern France. It is a triple interconnected spiral, sometimes represented as three running legs. Sometimes the ends of the spirals resemble the heads of birds of prey. Black and white is a good traditional color for a Breton flag or pennant. Gwyl comes from that part of the world.

SHIP-BUILDING IN ANGLO SAXON AND VIKING CULTURES is a complex topic. Apologies for any technical details I've gotten wrong. Likewise, navigation in the 10th and 11th centuries has attracted a great deal of archaeological and scientific research. The compass and magnetism were unknown, and even the astrolabe, but many authorities on Viking navigation think Viking mariners might have used so-called sunstones and similar devices to tell the position of the sun even in overcast conditions: https://www.livescience.com/44366-vikings-sun-compass-after-sunset.html A great deal of evidence shows that Vikings navigated using natural aids, as well. A finely-honed sense of smell, for example, alerted mariners to the proximity of land. Sight was important, too--well-known landmarks were much easier to see from far away in the unpolluted environment of the era. Even animals played a part, such as birds that, when released, would fly toward land. There's even some evidence Vikings may have navigated by flea, which apparently (unlikely as it sounds) flock to the north side of a container. No one in the 10th and 11th centuries had a shortage of fleas. (See Graeme Davis, *Vikings In America*, ch. 2, "Stepping Stones to America," in the section titled "Vikings to the Faroe Islands.")

TRAUMATIC BRAIN INJURY and resulting damage to the optic nerve--I'm indebted to web sites about traumatic brain injury as it may indirectly affect the optic nerve, and to sites explaining experimentally treating the resulting blindness through various forms of electromagnetic brain stimulation, such as transcranial magnetic stimulation. But I employ this information in the service of fantasy, not fact. As far as I know, there's no experimental program or clinic located in St. Louis that uses these techniques, no actual medical facility is implied, and there's no Clayton Medical Building Suite 400, on Wydown Avenue. (63105 is Clayton's real zip code, though.) I just wanted to put St. Louis in my book. It may be these techniques will become widespread, if they really do work (but probably not the way I'm imagining them). Bottom line, I'm not well-educated medically, and I don't know. There's a real SLUH and a real Mary I. I have no connection with either high school, and of course the fictional Dr. John D'Nofrio's fictional children don't actually attend them.

NO REAL HAWKS OR FALCONS CARRY MESSAGES or have homing instincts like carrier pigeons. Only fantasy hawks and falcons do. I have incorporated real details from the kind of merlin, the smyrill, that is common in Iceland (a falcon, not a hawk); from the bird lore of puffins; and from the sport and pastime of falconry. The birds in my novel are all fantasy birds, however.

THE "JAIL FEVER" GWYL CONTRACTS IS TYPHUS, one of the many feared diseases of poor sanitation and crowded conditions that were capable of decimating whole populations in the Middle Ages, and did. Unlike the typhoid fever epidemic in *Halcyon* (Book II of the *Harbingers* series), typhus is carried by lice (or, in a different form, by fleas). Untreated by antibiotics and other modern means, typhus has a death rate of 10-60%.

SURTSEY ISLAND--I'm indebted to web sites detailing the fiery, explosive creation of Surtsey Island, an Icelandic landmass that emerged in 1963 as the result of an undersea volcanic eruption. A number of islands worldwide, just in recent memory, have been created by such eruptions. These undersea explosions are some of the most powerful and destructive acts of nature known. Some of the online resources I consulted are:

http://www.surtsey.is/pp_ens/gen_3.htm;

http://earthsky.org/earth/surtsey-and-the-birth-of-new-islands;

https://www.youtube.com/watch?v=e73uesIwOLc;

http://volcano.oregonstate.edu/submarine;

http://ocean.si.edu/ocean-videos/submarine-volcanoes-erupting.

APOLOGIES FOR MY PETTY AND NOT-SO-PETTY THEFTS! (Lawyer alert. . . lawyer alert. . . when I say "steal," I am joking. The literary device I am using is known as "allusion," and I am using it in the creation of a kind of literary mash-up.) In this book, I stole from Scandinavian medieval skaldic poetry; from *Beowulf*; from Norse mythology; from the Child Ballads (traditional ballads from Scotland and England first collected by 19th century folklorist Francis James Child); from the words of news columnist Molly Ivins, from the Parker Bros./Hasbro game Monopoly; from Edmund Spenser's 16th century poem *Prothalamion* (and a smidge from *The Faerie Queene*); and I stole shamefully, frivolously from W. B. Yeats's great poem "The Second Coming." I badly mangled a line from a hymn written by William Cowper. I also pilfered a variety of sources on Arthurian texts and lore, especially the lore surrounding Merlin and his connection with Brittany; a little bit from 17th century English poets John Donne and John Milton; and quite a lot from William Shakespeare (especially *Hamlet*, *The Tempest*, *Midsummer Night's Dream*, *The Merchant of Venice*, *Richard II*, and *King Lear*). I outright plagiarized the speech of England's Elizabeth I at Tilbury on the eve of the ill-fated invasion of the Spanish Armada in 1588 (even more shameful that I made Elizabeth out to be the plagiarist); and stomped and romped over the life of Dr. John Dee, a real mathematician, astrologer, proto-scientist, believer in all manner of crazy mystic theories, and advisor to Queen Elizabeth I during the English Renaissance. Many scholars have argued that the character of Prospero, in Shakespeare's *Tempest*, is based on or at least inspired by John Dee. No one actually thinks John Dee was a time-traveling mage and neurologist. (His "black stone" is actually an Aztec mirror, and I'm not sure anyone knows how he got it.) I have also hinted at the life of real 15th century French baron Gilles de Rais, a supporter of Joan of Arc who later turned to the occult and became one of the most prolific serial killers (mostly children) history has known. More about Gilles appears in *Ghost Owl*, Book IV of the Harbingers series, and especially in the prequel series, Stormclouds. Book II of that prequel series, *The Call of the Shrike*, has a lot about Gilles, and Book III, *Stormbird*, as well. Gilles also appears in the companion **Betwixt and Between** novels, *The Martlet is a Wanderer* and *The Nightingale Holds Up the Sky*, and in *Dark Ones Take It*, the origin story of Caedon and his brother Maeldoi, the Dark Rider.

excerpt from

Ghost Bird:
Harbingers, Book IV: Child of Sky

*One for sorrow
Two for mirth,
Three for death,
Four for birth,
Five for silver,
Six for gold,
Seven for secrets never told.
Eight for Ghost Bird, eight for Owl
underneath the Nine Spheres' bowl.*

From Chapter One:

Keera watched as Gwyl scanned the horizon, the stiff ocean wind blowing his dark hair back off his face, his gray Sea-Child eyes keen. He called out a command to his men. Gwyl served as his own kendtman, and Keera knew she should trust him. She did trust him. He knew what he was doing. Still, she was afraid.

A snatch of one of her mother's songs came to her. "One for sorrow, two for mirth," she hummed to herself. It was a song about the owls. Ghost birds, some called them. She'd always loved the owls, but the song seemed somehow ominous to her. There was mirth, but there was also sorrow. The two were paired. *You can't have one without the other*, she whispered to herself.

"We'll outrun that ship, whoever she is, never fear," Gwyl murmured into Keera's ear, pulling her to him. He seemed to know when she was troubled. He always seemed to know. "We're fast," he reassured her.

"Is it the same one?" Keera stared back at the vessel. It had been following them for days.

"Looks like it."

"That ship has kept up with us."

"Yes. They're fast, too." He began flipping his sun-stone over and over in his left hand, a habit she knew he had when he was worried about something. "Her master knows what he's about." The respect in his voice was grudging.

"So we didn't lose them, back there."

"No." He bent down and kissed her.

"What does that mean? If they're just pirates . . ."

"Well," he said, and she looked up into his face as he thought it over. "Whoever they turn out to be, it might mean they know who we are and where we're going. Not many come out here, this far to the westward."

Keera shivered, pulling her cloak tighter about herself. Pirates wouldn't, she thought. They'd stay close to a harbor where they could run their loot quickly to land and exchange it for good solid coin. She'd never considered before actually hoping for pirates. The mysterious ship that seemed to be following them might be worse than pirates. Her imagination kept harrowing her. What would be worse than pirates? She recalled the time Caedon's ships intercepted hers, and the danger it meant. But Caedon was dead. Thank the Children, he was gone to the Dark Ones who surely must have taken his twisted spirit, one of Their own, to Themselves. Who, then?

Ansgar, she decided. The unscrupulous king who had stepped into the power vacuum Caedon left behind him. Acting as her parents' diplomat had taught her a lot about the more unsavory corners of the politics of the Twelve Realms. But she didn't want to share this uncomfortable insight of hers with Gwyl.

She was feeling a little sick again, and finally that's what stopped her dwelling on these possible enemies. She kept her hands clamped hard on the topmost strake of Gwyl's skeid, trying to keep her eyes on the horizon. That way she hoped to steady her stomach and not lose her breakfast. The fresh breeze kept her feeling a bit better than she had five days before, when they headed out from her parents' rocky outpost for this long voyage.

By now they were well past the boundary where, sailors claimed, the Northern Sea gave way to the unknowns of the Great Sea stretching far off to westward.

Keera felt a bit foolish, getting sick like this. She was the Fire Child's own, not the Sea Child's, as Gwyl was, but she was familiar with water, since her mother also reverenced the Sea Child. Keera had spent her entire childhood in and around water. So she couldn't easily account for the queasy feeling she felt as the big skeid cut through the waves.

Giving her a quick embrace, Gwyl left her side to stride the deck, calling out to his mariners as they managed the billowing black sail with his insignia woven in white wool: a triple spiral, each spiraling stripe ending in the fierce head of a bird of prey. His skeid was called Dragon Wind, and he was hugely proud of the painted dragon's-head prow. He'd hired a master woodworker for the fine carving of it, and he had clambered all over it and around it, helping to paint it himself: golds, blues, reds.

The skeid's hull was riven oak, clinker built, a ship to make a man of the Ice-realm proud. Gwyl was not from there. He was the Sea Child's for sure, as many of the Ice-men were, but he had grown up eastward on the promontory of the Baronies that extended its rocky topmost corner into the choppy waters of the Narrows dividing the Eastern Baronies from its rival kingdom, the Sceptered Isle.

During his young manhood, the misfortunes of war and family had driven Gwyl from his home to roam the islands sprinkled between the northern reaches of the Sceptered Isle and the Ice-realm. There he'd apprenticed himself to a master mariner and ship-builder of the Ice-realm. There he had encountered Keera's father, Walter I, exiled monarch of the Sceptered Isle, the last of Ranulf's line (if you didn't count the usurper Audemar). And there, kendtman on one of Wat's ships, Gwyl had met Keera. She remembered half-fondly, half with a shudder the time he had pulled her out of a barrel and released her from a bad fate to the terrified arms of her mother, Mirin, Wat's beloved wife, a queen in her own right.

None of them would have believed, in that moment, that Keera and Gwyl would one day wed. None but Gwyl, that is.

"I knew the moment I saw you," he whispered to her once. "I knew I needed you more than life itself."

Keera had laughed at him. "I was thirteen! I was half-dead. I must have looked dreadful."

"You did," he assured her. "Dreadful. Filthy. Skinny. Your red hair all in a mop of tangles. I knew it right away. It was you I had to have."

"Did you know you'd find me when Father sent you off to the Fire Isle?"

"Of course. We figured out that's where you must have gone. I volunteered right away. I wouldn't let anyone else take on the task. Here's my chance with the king's beautiful daughter, I told myself."

"I don't know if I believe that," said Keera. "You and your sugared words." But she hadn't had time to say anything more about it, because then Gwyl had dragged her down under the furs with him, and then the music their bodies made was so delicious she forgot what they'd been talking about.

shrike
publications